To Michael & Jackie

With much love

Nisha.
x

GW00541677

About the Author

Patricia Halliday was born in post-war Germany, has travelled extensively and now lives in Devon. *The Harvest of Betrayal* is her debut novel drawing on her experiences of living in France and Africa. Her interests are fly fishing, riding and rifle shooting with her husband.

FOR MY HUSBAND,
MY PARTNER IN EVERYTHING, ALWAYS.

Patricia Halliday

THE HARVEST
OF BETRAYAL

AUSTIN MACAULEY™
PUBLISHERS LTD.

A CIP catalogue record for this title is available from the British Library.

ISBN 9781786293015 (Paperback)
ISBN 9781786293022 (Hardback)
ISBN 9781786293039 (E-Book)

www.austinmacauley.com

First Published (2017)
Austin Macauley Publishers Ltd.™
25 Canada Square
Canary Wharf
London
E14 5LQ

Acknowledgements

Austin Macauley is a publishing house which encourages debut novelists; this gave me the initiative to present the manuscript of this book. I am so grateful for their invaluable help and support. Special thanks go to Lynne Teasdale for her editorial work.

My husband Pentti Kalervo, without whose patience and belief the story would not have been written has my eternal gratitude.

The car pulled over onto the grass verge just beyond the open gates of the property. Gregoire Dupont laid a hand on his son's arm to indicate that he should remain in the car. He would do this alone. It was difficult to guess his age: he had thick, white hair and walked with a straight back unaided by a stick. In fact, he was well into his eighties.

As he left the car, he started to move forward and then stopped, as if undecided to take the last few steps to the gates. He breathed hard once or twice and then covered the remaining distance. He stood in the opening, feeling his heartbeat thumping in his throat and chest. The last time Gregoire had stood here, the gates had been open then too; he had been just a boy in his teens watching the enemy preparing to leave.

Gregoire had always called them 'the enemy', somehow giving them a nationality bestowed a certain dignity and humanity on them. He had watched as trucks were being prepared, soldiers were barking orders at each other while others were making a hurried attempt to burn the huts and tents lining the driveway. His nostrils had felt the tang of acrid smoke as huge bonfires were being fuelled with papers; all those words describing enemy deeds floating up into the air on blackened embers like clouds of malevolent butterflies.

Not many of the villagers had been at the gates, no doubt fearful of the power the enemy had to alter their lives in the flash of a rifle shot. Gregoire and a couple of his friends had heard the rumour that the end was in sight for the hated occupiers and the bravado of youth had overcome their better judgment. Where does a retreating army go? He would have liked to ask, but the usual sentries at the gate were absent. Entering the property, even with harmless curiosity, was out of the question.

Now, as an old man standing in that spot, he could almost still smell that smoke.

That day, back then, a smart black car had swept out of the gate, the driver dressed in civilian clothes, the commandant himself. He had no escort, no accompanying fellow officers, just the man alone. They later learned that he had been found near Bayeux, shot through the head. The man had been judged by patriots to be guilty of war crimes and executed on the spot, left beside his car on the side of the road for all to see. His every move had been followed from the gates to his place of execution. The escape lines and Resistance workers he had been sent to eliminate were the very tools of his own destruction.

Gregoire stood still for a moment, breathing more calmly now. He signalled to his son that he would be a while longer; memories were not to be denied now. He walked through the gates and looked about.

The property had once belonged to a family of French nobility, the last of whom had died during the war. For decades the place had been left empty whilst claims on the property had been investigated and in turn dismissed, until the final claimant had donated the property to the Catholic Church.

The sale by the church to a property developer was the latest incarnation, and now the new houses in the grounds of the estate were in the process of being finished. Although the main house was certainly not on the grand scale normally associated with the word 'chateau', it had always been accorded the respect of that title. It had been a delightful building, well-proportioned and elegant but not in the same league as famous chateaux. In the tradition of large country houses, the building had been constructed at the far end of an impressive drive. A prior, somewhat eccentric, owner with a dislike of formal gardens and majestic entrances had taken the middle of the drive and had made an island with oaks, maples and apple trees. A few pine trees interspersed ensured some colour in the winter, but it rendered the house almost invisible from the gate. The drive was thus now divided into two, the house was now accessed by either side of the island which later generations had retained.

Gregoire remembered the day the enemy had arrived. Word in the village was that the then owner, Philippe de Lusignac, and his daughter had been moved from the chateau to the small hunting lodge. The house was to be the quarters and offices of the occupying enemy: that is, their commandant and senior officers. The soldiers were to be billeted in tents along the long lawns in front of the stables and other outbuildings until the huts were completed. The trucks had driven slowly through the village, on their way to the chateau some two kilometres away. The slow speed was not so much a mark of care and attention as a show of power – enough time for everyone to understand the might of the enemy now living in their midst.

Now, of course, all sign of enemy occupation was long gone. In place of the outbuildings and tents there were now lovely new stone houses, three on each side of the drive.

Seeing no-one, Gregoire started a slow walk down the left side, admiring the design of the new properties. He reached the end of the drive and the chateau was in front of him. In truth it was lovely. The lack of grandeur and formality made it look inviting and comfortable.

But the orders which had emanated from this very house had shackled the village to grief, fear and shock. Gregoire's own family had been directly affected. The passing years tend to leach away the immediate pain, so Gregoire was taken aback at the suddenness of the strength of emotion he now felt. He remembered the touch of his father's hand ruffling his hair as he left home on that fatal night. Gregoire closed his eyes at the vision of his father, lined up with the others in the village square, hands tied behind his back, then his familiar voice raised in *"Vive La France"* before the shots rang out and twenty men lay dead.

Gregoire sat on the steps of the curved stone steps which lead up to the terrace – the same terrace from which the hated flag had flown. He saw one new balustrade, replacing the original which had been broken when that same symbol of oppression had been torn down.

The new buildings were nearly complete now. There were a couple of gardeners finishing flower beds and planting bushes, but they paid him no attention. The last phase of this redevelopment was almost finalised.

Gregoire looked up and saw his son's concerned face as he came down the drive to find his father. How wonderful that his son had none of the awful memories of the connections with this house. He had never experienced anything akin to those terrible years, and for that Gregoire never stopped giving thanks.

Earlier in the day, Gregoire had been able to lay another memory to rest. It was a promise he had made on the day his mother was buried, a promise made to himself and to his dead parents. After his father had been executed, his mother had never recovered from the shock and grief. She became distracted and confused, a shadow of the much-loved woman who was Gregoire's mother.

On the day the enemy had finally left the village, there was a service of thanksgiving in the church. Gregoire had been serving on the altar, assuming his mother was in the pews. In fact, she had climbed up to the bell-tower and in an act of total despair, had thrown herself to the ground.

She could only understand that all that pain and suffering was for nothing. The enemy had gone, it was true, but why all the celebration? Her husband was dead, nothing would ever be the same again. The pain would be eternal. How did it all happen? Old men in suits and uniforms covered in gold braid in grand cities, who signed pieces of paper on antique tables, condemned so many men to the firing line and families to a life of grief. Did any of them understand what thousands of families now had to endure? Did the sight of bullet-holes in stone walls ever greet them as they left their houses to go about the business of trying to piece back their lives? The pointlessness of it all was unendurable.

When the congregation had left the church that morning, Gregoire's mother was lying dead on the steps, her blood and grief seeping away into the stones. The priest would never countenance her burial in the church graveyard, despite pleas by the villagers that her suicide was the act of a sick woman suffering from unbearable sorrow. He would probably have forgiven her mortal sin of suicide, but in his view, her sin was her loss of faith in God.

So she was buried outside the church walls, but Gregoire had noted the very spot by the shape of the stones in the wall surrounding the cemetery. He vowed one day he would have her reburied in consecrated ground.

And today, he had.

Back then, he had left the village almost immediately after his mother was buried, to live with two uncles in Brittany, one a builder and the other a carpenter; both had joined together in a construction enterprise. Gregoire had spent his life in Brittany, learning the building trade and inheriting the firm from his uncles, now long dead. He had married and had three sons who were now running the business. He had never stopped trying to obtain permission from the church to rebury his mother. A few months ago, the letter he had longed for arrived and he started the tedious process for a disinterment and reburial; bureaucracy ever the stumbling block of many a good intention.

The service had been a great healing point for him. He felt his mother was finally at peace and he could leave the area now without regrets. He hadn't actually planned to stop at the chateau, but the road back to the motorway took them within a short distance. On an inexplicable impulse, he had asked his son to come this way. His son now sat beside him on the steps, his arm resting lightly on Gregoire's shoulders.

The wartime history of the area – and many others like it in France – was well-documented, but in reality, people who hadn't been there could not possibly understand the daily fear of living with an enemy. Not one aspect of life remained unchanged; neighbours informed on neighbours, imagined slights were dealt with severely and brutally, infringement of rules could result in death, even children's war games could be seen as seditious.

And now, with the houses finished, there was to be another invasion, another occupation, more foreigners – expatriates – however, these occupiers were coming with their Earl Grey tea and their Marmite, not with rifles and jackboots.

****

Diana sat patiently in the car, watching Simon pacing at the gate; he was trying to see past the trees to the house itself but it wasn't clearly visible – only the slate roof, the corner of a stone staircase and an upper window gave a hint of what lay beyond the trees.

"He's late," he said over his shoulder, not really expecting her to answer.

They were waiting for the agent to show them over the development and although Diana didn't believe that they would really move to this corner of South West France, she had agreed to this visit because Simon was in the first flush of enthusiasm for a new idea; she always supported him until his own excitement diminished and the prospect of carrying the project through would pale into insignificance until forgotten altogether. This latest idea of a second home in France would, she was sure, wane as soon as possibility was on the verge of becoming reality.

On this occasion, Simon had picked up *Country Life* in the dentist's waiting room and seen the glossy page with the usual estate agent's verbose and colourful description of 'This Exceptional Opportunity To Acquire Part Of This Superb Estate' and so on. They had arranged a meeting with the developers in London and Diana had gone in the relaxed certainty that it would result in the usual flash of vigorous enthusiasm only to end in indecision and finally, inaction. A second home in France did, she admitted to herself, have some appeal, but her comfortable and secure life in London suited her very well.

The developer was a man called Angus Moreton, a man in his late forties who had come with his French business partner, who was also the handling agent in France. Both men seemed professional and were expansive and attentive.

The brochure and photographs were stunning. The estate had been the subject of some sort of inheritance problems lasting many years after the war and had fallen into a state of complete disrepair. The main house was in the classic style of a small French manor house – three stories and attics – and was for the most part renovated to its original state, allowing for updating and modern appliances. The original kitchen entrance was in front on the ground floor, a curved double staircase ran from both the right and the left of the kitchen entrance to the terrace on the first floor.

Moreton explained that originally, deliveries and servants would enter by the lower door and the residents would mount the staircase to the reception areas.

When the house was originally constructed, there were also two long two-storey buildings, one either side of the driveway and at right angles to the house. One was the stables and accommodation for the stable hands, and the other would be the laundry, dairy and other utility purposes.

By the time Moreton had gained title to the property, these outbuildings had all but collapsed under the weight of ivy and many years of neglect; rotten beams had given way, bringing down the roof; rain and wind had completed the job of decay.

These buildings had been cleared and three new houses had been constructed on each site, making six newly built properties.

Moreton was very enthusiastic about the development. "The new houses have all been constructed to a very high specification but regardless of the price, all six properties have been sold for some time now – I think that speaks for the quality of the houses."

"Who are the owners of those houses? I'm just curious." Diana had been wondering why the houses had sold so readily, but not the chateau.

"No, that's fine. Actually, our first advertisement drew a lot of interest here in the UK, and most of the sales emanated from that." Moreton smiled as he spoke.

"And why has *this* house been on the market for some time? I assume it has been, since the advertisement in the magazine was over a year old and the house is still available."

"Good question." Moreton smiled again. "Frankly, it's gorgeous and although it sounds enormous, it really isn't. We've called it *La Maison Neuve*, which actually means 'The New House', perhaps not the most imaginative of names, but we liked it. It has four bedrooms on the second floor each en-suite and each leading off the lovely large landing. The original servants' entrance is now a wonderful open space through to the kitchen, which leads out to the garden beyond. Don't forget, the drawing room and the dining room are actually on the first floor. We did think we'd sold it once, but the prospective buyer pulled out at the last minute – problems with raising a mortgage, I think."

Simon had been rather silent, but spent most of the time looking though the portfolio of photographs and reading the specifications.

The French partner had introduced himself as Jean Claude Laurier and was somewhat younger than Moreton. He had also left most of the talking to Moreton and Diana but now spoke. "Madame, if you will allow, we would like to offer you a trip to Saint-Sulpice to view the property at our expense. The village is a delight and the surrounding countryside is beautiful."

Without thinking, Diana answered him in fluent French but before her thanks were finished, Simon interrupted rudely. "Here's what we'll do. We don't need you to pay for our trip. We'll go over and take a look, then we'll get in touch when we've seen the area and we're ready to see the house. After all, if we don't like the area, there's no point in seeing the house, is there?"

To ameliorate the awkward silence Simon's outburst had produced, Diana continued to speak to Laurier softly. "May I ask a couple of questions?"

"Of course, Madame. With pleasure."

"An estate such as this must have certain rules, you know – dos and don'ts. I mean, for example, how are the common areas maintained and financed?"

"Actually, once we've sold this house, the entire estate will be the property of the residents who, together, will make up their own rules, I assume. There are *some* rules, of course, which exist so far: for example, no caravans or trailers may be kept in the driveways, dogs must be kept under control – mostly for insurance purposes. There are always *Departement* rules, for example, no bonfires are permitted in June, July and August – the reasons are obvious, there can be long periods with no rain in the summer. The rules are not onerous and generally, people behave as they wish others to, *n'est-ce pas?*"

Simon gave the man a look of total dislike.

"I own the agency in Périgueux and Bergerac which is handling the property," he continued. "I would be delighted to show you around if you just let me know when you'd like to visit. If you wish, I can make a reservation at the hotel in the village. There are two, in fact, one is better for the rooms, the other for the cuisine."

Laurier and Moreton rose as Simon got to his feet, indicating that the meeting was at an end.

"May I just say, Mrs. Lewis, your French is excellent. Clearly you have studied the language from more than just a conversational level." Laurier bowed over Diana's hand.

"Oh, thank you, how kind of you to say so," Diana smiled and replied. "Actually, I took a degree in French, specializing in French literature and I've spent some years working for a small company which translates documents, manuscripts, manuals – that sort of thing. I love it, the company, I mean. It's small but I find the work very fulfilling. I'm actually very lucky. I have a job I love and I can work from home any time I wish."

The conversation in French had left Simon at a disadvantage, which made him feel patronized. His French was passable to order in a restaurant in France but he was by no means fluent. But his dislike of Laurier was obvious, a reaction he always exhibited when feeling that he was being sidelined in a conversation.

Within two weeks of this meeting, the visit to the estate had been arranged. Simon and Diana had taken three days to drive down to Saint-Sulpice-sur-Lauzac, stopping wherever they decided on the spur of the moment. Diana still had no belief that Simon would actually want to go through with the purchase of this house, regardless of how appealing it might be. So it was with quiet amusement that she now watched his anxious and impatient pacing at the gate of the estate; a handsome tall gate with a small gold plaque on the gate pier to the left: *La Chênaie* and *Chemin Privé*. Diana had thought the name rather fanciful – The Oakwood – but looking through the bars of the gate beyond the property to the wooded hills beyond and around, she could see that it was, indeed, a perfect name.

Jean Claude Laurier arrived twenty minutes late and shook hands with Simon, offering his apologies as she did so. Diana got out of the car and also shook hands as Laurier exchanged a few words with her in French. He was asking if they found the hotel comfortable and how their journey had been but Simon, already out of temper with having to wait at the gate said, "Can we get in here now, please and could we keep questions and comments to English?"

"Of course, I do apologise, it was rude of me. I just assumed ..." He wisely left the rest of the sentence unsaid and his apology seemed sincere but he quickly turned and walked to the gate where he pressed several numbers into the keypad under the brass plaque.

"Please follow me in your car."

Once through the gate, the drive divided into two. Laurier explained there was no 'right way round', but obviously numbers one, two and three would use the left drive and four, five and six would use the right. Nevertheless, the main house would use either side and there was more than enough room for two cars to pass each other.

The trees in the oval island were the reason than the house could not be seen from the gate. Driving slowly past the three houses on the left, Diana could see that they were indeed built to a very high standard. They were actually stunning in their simplicity of lines; the colour of the stone looked warm and rich in the early September sun. The properties seemed happily settled into their own landscape with large but simple gardens consisting mainly of lawn, bushes and trees. Diana noticed that there were none of the typical flower beds and attempts at English gardens here.

Their first view of the house itself actually surprised her. She had seen many small chateaux and country manor houses in her years in France, but this house was breathtaking.

As Angus Moreton had described, it wasn't huge, but obviously much bigger than the new houses. The two stone curved staircases leading up from the drive to the first floor terrace were the originals but had been restored and cleaned. The big oak double doors on the ground floor underneath the terrace leading to the kitchen were also restored, but happily not painted.

As they had been driving down towards the house, Diana had experienced a sharp, inexplicable and sudden wish to belong to this place. It left her feeling anxious to get into the house and unsettled by such an emotion.

"Can we go in through the kitchen?" Diana asked. "I just love those doors; did they belong to this house or were they retrieved from some other building?"

"We found them outside, covered in ivy and ferns. We think someone had taken them off and was intent on coming back to take them, but either forgot or found them too big and heavy to transport. So yes, they belong here."

Somehow Diana seemed to forget that this visit was just to indulge Simon's latest supposed project. She was filled with excitement and interest. She was breathless with anticipation for what lay behind the big, oak doors. As if sensing her feelings, Laurier handed her the key "Please," he said, "open the door." As she did so, she thought of her front door in London, also a big, heavy door which had always meant a welcome home, a wonderful mother and a contented childhood. She had that same secure feeling now.

The key turned surprisingly easily, given its size. The doors opened outwards and Diana pulled them back to their full extent. Slightly inset was another door – plate glass set into a plate glass wall. Laurier produced another key and unlocked the door.

"This was done to allow maximum light into this hallway but at the same time, give the security of a locked door. So, during the day the big oak doors can be opened without leaving the hall as open access."

If Diana had had any reservations at all before arriving at the house, these were dispelled instantly as the entered the hall. On the left was a staircase leading up to the hall outside the drawing room and the cloakroom was on the right.

But her interest was captivated by the second set of plate glass doors leading into the kitchen. Sunshine was flooding in through the huge windows lighting up a room in which she felt she could happily live forever. The colour scheme was kept to a soft oatmeal which gave warmth to the room, even without the sun.

Diana would always count this first step inside as the very moment when her total and absolute commitment to this house began. The kitchen was obviously fitted out to a very high and sophisticated specification with the usual amenities, but her attention was completely engrossed by the view from the windows running the length of the rear wall.

The sudden possibility that this could be what she would see every single day, changing with the seasons, overwhelmed her.

Laurier was trying to involve Simon in some conversation in an effort to dissolve the cool barrier which appeared to have developed between them. There did appear to be a slight warming on Simon's part, and Diana hoped that this was due to the atmosphere of the house.

The rear wall with the windows overlooking the garden and the lake beyond was divided in the middle with two doors which led out to the terrace into which was set the swimming pool. Beyond that spread lawns fringed by oak and chestnut trees. The lawn sloped down to the lake, a body of water of about thirty acres. On the right of the kitchen was another staircase, this one leading up to the hall just outside the dining room.

Diana was impatient to see the rest of the house, and without waiting for Simon and Laurier, she went up the staircase to the first floor hallway outside the drawing room. The hallway was bright and light without the attempt to recreate 18th century colours of blue and rust, the walls had been kept to neutral shades of oatmeal and cream. The tiled floor was highly polished. But what drew Diana across the hallway was the view through the open doors of the drawing room and dining room – the vista enhanced by the benefit of being one floor higher. She stood trying to control her pounding heart, unable to turn her eyes from the sparkling water of the lake and the colours of the trees.

The terrace design and curved stone steps of the front of the house was repeated here at the rear, accessed by the huge doors. Diana was finding it impossible not to envision herself and Simon sitting on this terrace, watching the sunset over the lake. Reluctantly she left the window and its wonderful view and wandered back into the front hall.

She took the staircase up to the second floor to investigate the bedrooms. The four bedrooms were of similar size and what had originally been en-suite dressing-rooms were now bathrooms. The two bedrooms in the front of the house looked out over the drive and the central island. The gardens of the two nearest houses were also visible but were pleasantly colourful with trees and bushes.

Knowing exactly how she would feel and what she would see, she pushed open the door of one of the two bedrooms facing the back. She wasn't disappointed. She leaned up against the tall window, watching the light playing back and forth on the lake, imprinting this moment on her memory. What had begun as one of Simon's soon-to-be-abandoned projects was now becoming her driving passion. She didn't want to join Simon and Laurier just yet: their apparent dislike of each other would cast a pall over her feeling of contentment and her overwhelming desire to make this house her home. She loved this house. She wanted this house.

When she felt she could no longer justify her lone wanderings, she went to find Simon and Laurier. Simon was already exhibiting impatience to be gone, which filled her with panic and sadness. She smiled encouragingly at him and turned to Laurier. "Tell me a little of the other people who live here," she said.

"Well, the first to arrive were Mr. and Mrs. Lawson in No. 3. Unfortunately, Mrs. Lawson died a while ago but Mr. Lawson stayed on. The lady in number six is French by origin, but she and her daughter are both British. There are two sisters in number two, and a retired surgeon and his wife in number one. They are all British."

"All British?" Simon frowned and gave Diana a questioning look.

"Yes, well the first advertisement was in a prestigious magazine in the UK, and before we needed to re-think our advertising strategy, we had enough interest from that one launch. It was really quite amazing, the interest in the new houses was far above our expectations."

"Monsieur Laurier, would you give us a few minutes to wander around on our own?" Diana was anxious to be alone with Simon to gauge his feelings. "I'd love to walk down to the lake, may we?"

"Of course. Please do." Laurier smiled, but the fact that this visit had been a waste of time was most prominent in his mind. Simon had exhibited very little interest outside of the obvious questions, and years of experience had taught Laurier to read facial expressions and body language for positive signs. It was strange though. Before, he had had the distinct feeling that it was the woman who was just going through the motions and that the husband was the keen one. Now, there seemed to have been a complete reversal of attitudes. If his experience had shown him anything, it was that this woman was completely absorbed by this house, more than that – she was almost obsessed. Perhaps the sale might go through after all, although he felt she now had the huge hurdle of that husband of hers to convince.

Laurier watched the two of them walking down to the lake. He saw Diana take Simon's arm and lean towards him with a smile. He put his hand over hers and they made their way over the lawns.

"Well, darling, what do you think? I can't explain it, but I love this house, I really do. I really hope you feel the same, do you?" She sounded almost panicky.

Simon looked at her. Where had this intensity come from?

"Oh God, Diana. It's fabulous, anyone would think so, but this is far and away bigger than anything we had in mind. It's just altogether too much, and it's probably way out of the price range we'd planned." Simon sounded strident as he always did when he knew he was about to give up on something. "Look, this all started because I thought we might buy a house in France to spend a few months of every year and for me to do some research for my book. This place is like taking on a part of history. It's a responsibility. It's not what I'd imagined at all." His voice had risen slightly and he was on the verge of becoming irritable.

It hadn't escaped Diana's notice that his concerns and plans were always in the first person singular.

"Is this why you're being so odd with Jean Claude? Because this is such a departure from the original plan, you don't want to go through with it and you don't know how to tell him? Is that it?" She turned to face him and pulled his arm around so that he was facing her. Her expression surprised him. She looked disappointed and hostile.

"Simon, listen to me. I can't explain, I really can't." She took a deep breath and looked away to the lake. "I admit I went along with this idea of a house in France in case it was something you really wanted to do, something you might enjoy and there was the possibility that you'd find it helpful with the book. I will also admit that I honestly didn't think anything would come of it. But something's happened, that's what I can't explain. From the moment we drove down the drive, I felt that we belong here. I can see us here; don't you feel it too?" She was breathless in her enthusiasm, and close to tears now. She was anxious and sounding sharp – so determined to make him feel what she was feeling.

"Diana, listen. If we bought this place, what about the house in London? You said you'd never sell it but we'd never be able to manage *this* place *and* keep the London house. This place isn't just a lock-up-and-leave, you know. We'd never -"

Diana interrupted him sharply. "For heaven's sake, Simon, the advertisement was plain enough, you could see what the place looked like and just what made it worth the visit. NOW you decide that it's not what you're looking for at all!"

"I admit I was a bit carried away with the whole thing, but I think it's time we took a sensible path and looked at smaller houses. I can't see how, on the strength of one visit, all your ideas have changed."

"Can't you? Am I so compliant and predictable that my own dreams can't be accommodated? Are all my wishes just too big?" Her throat was throbbing with the effort of holding back the tears. Simon was near to panic. In truth, he would have told the agents at the London meeting that it wasn't what he was looking for, but something about the Frenchman's attitude had irritated him – almost a patronizing assumption that this house was really out of his league. And now? His wife was behaving with a determination he had rarely seen and certainly didn't welcome. What a bloody mess.

Simon and Diana turned back towards the house. Laurier watched them approach and he also felt a sense of disappointment. If he had read the signs correctly, the sale was not about to go through and he was trying to think of something – anything – to put the deal back on the table. He decided against a lunch invitation and on the spur of the moment came up with another idea.

"Well, it's a lot to think about, isn't it?" He spoke before Simon had an opportunity to come out with a decision to leave. "So, here's what I propose: I shall give you the code to the gate and the keys to the house. That way, you can come and go as you wish whilst you're still here, you might like to have a chat with some of the other residents. Then you can leave the keys with Henri at the hotel. How does that sound?" The next moment would decide whether or not the sale had any chance at all.

It was Diana who stepped forward to take the keys. "Thank you. That would be lovely. We'll probably be leaving on Monday or Tuesday, but we'll call you if we have any questions." Diana was relieved that Simon hadn't come out with a straightforward refusal. They were silent as they drove back to the village, Diana was framing her arguments in her head and Simon was doing likewise.

They took a table at the café in the square and ordered *pastis.* The village of Saint-Sulpice-sur-Lauzac was centred around the small covered market – a raised stone platform with the roof supported by open arches. On three sides of the square were the shops usually found in any French village: the bakery – in this case two – a pharmacy, a café and a general store. There was also a pâtisserie whose window was wonderfully arranged with delightful boxes of chocolates; a butcher and a small bank. On the fourth side of the square ran the main road to Bordeaux and Bergerac in one direction, and in the other the road ran to the towns along the river. The Church of Saint-Sulpice was on the bank of the river on the edge of the village on the way out to Bergerac. It wasn't the prettiest of churches, but quite impressive in magnitude considering the size of the population of the village, and it did boast a very lovely stained glass window which was locally made to replace the one damaged in the war.

Neither Diana nor Simon seemed willing to start the conversation they knew they must now have. Diana was reluctant to give Simon the opportunity to raise a blank refusal, and Simon was unsure how to manage the mood Diana seemed to be in, one of surprising determination. He felt uneasy and not a little guilty.

"Okay," he said. "Let me go first. We obviously need to talk about all of this, and I think we need to try not to be emotional."

"Simon, stop. Just stop. I admit I'm emotional, this whole place has had an effect on me I didn't expect. But leaving that aside, I will also admit that I didn't think you'd go through with the plan for a house in France. I did go along with it though, because I had other reasons for hoping it would work. I'd hoped that the prospect of another book might -"

"Oh, for Christ's sake, Diana! Don't you think I know what these last few years have been like? Of course I want to write again! But this isn't -"

"Listen for a minute! We've been amazingly lucky. Your first book did well and Mummy was incredibly lucky selling the business. She's left us a beautiful home and we've always been very comfortable. We're happy with our lives – "

"And what's so wrong with all of that?" Simon was now feeling panic surge into his stomach, tightening the muscles and making him pant slightly.

"Darling, absolutely nothing. That's the point."

"What point, for Christ's sake?"

"The point is, we've never done anything like this. We've never taken risks; we've never done anything which might take us away from our comfort zone. I know the house is more than we thought we'd pay for a second home but we *can* do it. We can. Look around you. It's not just the house, it's the village, the hills, the woods – all of it. I can see us here!" Her enthusiasm was bordering on madness, he thought.

He sipped his drink and fell silent, looking at his wife who seemed to have developed a different personality in the last few hours. She was a woman of certain passions but not what one would call generally passionate. Her personality was one of a fairly self-assured woman but not one of great hopes, demands or aspirations. When they met, their affair was one of mutual attraction, a recognition of a happy life-partner with no great emotional upheavals behind her, nor expecting any in the future.

Physically, she was an attractive but not beautiful forty-three-year-old woman who enjoyed the life they had made together. She was slim but not thin, fairly tall with light brown hair, showing flecks of grey which she refused to colour. She had good dress sense, was rarely scruffy but liked casual clothes. Her clothes for other occasions were well-cut, of good quality but not fussy; elegant would describe her appearance when she was dressed to go out. Her collection of jewellery wasn't large, most of it inherited from her mother and, like her personality, nothing was ever too loud, too much or too exuberant.

Which was why Simon was so completely perplexed at her present determination to go against his own wishes in this matter of the house. He'd been married to her for twenty years, and he thought he knew all her moods and her level of acquiescence to his own wishes. She enjoyed sex but was undemanding; she was generous without being profligate; she was popular but equally happy to be with him alone. Their circle of friends, he realized, consisted mostly of *his* friends: those same friends envied him her easy-going nature, her willingness to fall in with his plans and her apparent inability to cause him any anxiety or disturbance.

Children had never been any part of *his* plans and she had never raised any objections, and he now realised that he didn't have a clue as to whether she minded or not.

But he loved her, he counted on her levelheadedness and whilst waiting for his first (and only) book to be published, she had supported him in every way, including financially.

Her family had come from generations of master stonemasons until her grandfather had branched the business into a property company and later, a chain of builders' merchants. The post-war building boom had ensured the prosperity of the business and her father had taken no risks with the investment of the family money. They were, in fact, very wealthy.

When Diana's father died, her mother Emily inherited the business, together with her brother-in-law, Diana's Uncle Gerald. Gerald and Emily sold the business in the 1970s following Gerald's heart attack.

The house in Holland Park Avenue was the only home Diana had ever known. It was light and bright and had become home to Simon also, immediately after their marriage. With Diana's father now dead, Emily had offered the newly-weds space in her house. Diana had continued her work as a translator and Simon had written his book. When her mother died, Diana was the sole inheritor of her estate.

Simon's book was a novel set in the American Hospital in Paris during the Second World War and it was in Paris that Simon and Diana had met; he was doing research for his book and Diana was taking a holiday, having just finished her degree in French at university.

Simon's book was published but wasn't critically acclaimed, despite which it sold fairly well. There followed some articles for magazines and talks about making a mini-series of the book for television, but these talks did not convert to reality. He was invited to do a television documentary about Paris, a programme of four episodes concentrating on 'the hidden gems of the city', after which there had been no further offers.

It was the idea of a sequel to his book which had started him thinking of a second home in France.

"Darling, let's do this." Diana was more placatory now as she spoke, but still had a look of determination on her face. "Let's go back to the house tomorrow. We'll be entirely on our own. I've had another idea too." She looked at him for a long second. "We could actually rent out the London house. No Simon, listen." He had tried to interrupt. "We could. Remember Alison James and that oil-man husband of hers? They rented their house out when they were posted to Saudi, they rented to an American company for one of their top executives through this agency which specialised in high-end rentals. The contract is a yearly thing. It wouldn't do any harm to just find out about it, would it? That way we'd keep the London house and we'd have this place too – it would be perfect." She was again breathless with anxiety that he should at least not refuse outright.

Money wasn't actually the problem Simon was concerned about; they would be fine financially, even though this house would take a big chunk of their bank account. He was more concerned about the permanence this property would require of him. What he'd said was true – there would be a certain responsibility about living here. The estate itself seemed to be the sort of place which would encourage closer connections with one's neighbours, and – God forbid – a certain reliance on each other. He wasn't ready for that. He really did think a house in France was a great idea, a sort of writer's hideaway. He fully admitted this visit to Saint-Sulpice was entirely his fault, but it really wasn't what he wanted and was now going to have to find a way to step back from it. He'd imagined a small, cosy French farmhouse in the *Auvergne* or somewhere, a place where the views would encourage peaceful writing but where he could pack up and leave if the mood took him.

Diana seemed to think of this place as a complete move from London, and he was totally at a loss for the moment. He also realised with a shock that he really was just thinking about himself and his own plans. His imaginary hideaway had the advantage of being for him alone, and he'd have had

Diana and the London home to come back to whenever the mood took him or if the writing wasn't going well.

He was tired, the whole day had taken on a surreal quality. He felt unsettled by Diana's attitude and just wanted an end to it for the time being. He looked at his wife and smiled.

"Alright, darling," he said. "Let's have dinner and an early night. We'll go back to the house after breakfast and have a really good look around, but let's not argue any more tonight." He squeezed her hand and she responded with a warm smile.

The following morning they drove back to the house. It had rained during the night and the gardens glistened in the sun as the captured raindrops on the trees and bushes shimmered. Diana saw that although the houses had open plan gardens in the front, they had fenced-in gardens at the rear.

They pulled up in front of the two big, oak kitchen doors but Simon said, "I want to go in through the front door, I'd like to go up this staircase just once!"

Diana had brought a flask of coffee from the hotel and had stopped at the pâtisserie to buy croissants, just warm from the oven. Simon's mood seemed lighter and she was overwhelmed by a feeling of optimism.

At the top of the staircase, whilst Simon was unlocking the door, Diana looked up the drive, trying to imagine what this property must have looked like before the new houses had been built. The sense of the house's history had yet to find a place in her feeling of belonging.

They walked through the hallway to the drawing room and stood at the large windows, looking out onto the early morning shadows across the shining grass. The woods on the right and left of the house extended in a horseshoe shape around the lawns down to the lake. On the far left and far right of the lake, the woods came almost to the water's edge, just a width of shoreline enough to stroll around. From the

31

terrace, they could just see what appeared to be quite a large clearing in the woods.

They sat on the steps of the right-hand staircase and Diana poured the coffee. As Simon was tearing his croissant, he said, "Diana, look. I need to say what's on my mind, I've been thinking about it all night." They'd had a pleasant dinner the previous evening and he'd made love to her as if it was all for her, both of them finding his tenderness unexpectedly erotic. "I've never really been openly appreciative of everything you've ever done. You've supported me when I needed help the most and you've never once thrown it back at me. You've never thwarted my hopes and you've always encouraged me in everything. No, let me go on -" Diana had tried to say something. "I've been trying to think when you last wanted something badly, or wanted something from me. I can't honestly remember a time when something seemed to matter to you as much as this house. I'll be frank here, I think it's going to be fraught with problems, but if you seriously think we can manage two houses without it being detrimental to one or the other, then let's think about this as a possibility." The sentiments sounded sincere, but if the whole thing proved too problematic, he felt sure he could extricate himself without too much effort. He was good at that.

Surprise and shock showed on her face. "Simon, I don't know what to say. You have no idea how I feel about this house. Even sitting here on the steps leaving crumbs for the birds feels just perfect. I'm overwhelmed, thrilled, really absolutely thrilled." She experienced a wave of such happiness, she knew she would remember this moment for ever.

"Don't get carried away, Diana. We still have a few hurdles in front. Let's take an honest tour of the place, eyes wide open to flaws and drawbacks because there are bound to be some. The things we *can* live with are self-evident. What we need to look for are things we *can't* live with and what to do about them." Simon stood up and reached for her

32

hand to pull her to her feet. "The place is probably haunted for a start!" Diana felt so light-hearted and laughed delightedly.

The four bedrooms were all of a similar size but obviously the two facing the rear gardens and the lake were the most appealing.

"This would be ours, presumably," said Simon as the opened the door to one of them.

"Simon, I've been thinking. There's no obvious study or office downstairs, you'd have to use one end of either the drawing room or the dining room. But you could have one of these bedrooms to use as your study, so why not pick the one you want? After all, bedrooms are just for sleeping. You'd need somewhere you'd be comfortable, so you choose."

"I hadn't noticed; how could I have missed that?" he replied. "Actually, a room upstairs isn't such a bad idea, so maybe one of these two rooms facing the lake, then that would leave the other two bedrooms on the other side of the landing for guests if we want anyone to stay. Which I don't! If I'm going to write, I've got to be firm about peace and quiet."

They spent three hours inspecting the house and exploring the woods. The clearing in the woods which they had spotted proved to have been a fairly large dwelling of some kind, now long gone except for a few posts and some piles of tiles, mostly covered in moss and brambles. The lake sparkled in the sun as they turned to go back to the house for a final tour before locking up.

"Do you want to talk to any of the neighbours?" Simon called as he reached the front door.

"Not just now, darling, we've so much to talk about. I just want to go and have a coffee and let it all sink in."

"Um, too late, I think" he called as a woman was climbing the curved steps to the front door.

The woman now reaching the top of the steps appeared to be in her early sixties, plump but not fat and wearing rather colourful layers of clothes; a green tee-shirt was matched with orange trousers, she wore a pink cardigan and a multi-coloured scarf was wound around her neck. The whole effect was completed with large pink sandals, showing toenails painted a very dark maroon.

"Hello." She was out of breath and the word became elongated. "Um - are you - um - going to be the new - um - owners? Are you? It's such a beautiful house - um - it would be wonderful to see it lived in. We've been here a while and - um - so if there's anything -"

Simon smiled and put out his hand, anxious that the woman should take a moment to get her breath back. "Hello, I'm Simon Lewis. And …?"

"Oh yes, sorry. How silly - of course - yes - I'm Hilary Findlay at number one, although we'd like to give it a different name but - um - never got around to it. Is this your wife? Hello, I'm Hilary Findlay. I was just telling your - um - husband, is it your husband? Yes? Oh good, got that right anyway, one never knows these days - um - yes, well, here we are then."

Diana found the right moment to interrupt the woman's breathless sentences. "Hello. I'm Diana Lewis. How kind of you to come over, but actually we're just locking up, we have a meeting in Bergerac. We'll be in and out for a few days whilst we try to make some decisions, but I'm sure we'll meet again."

"Oh, sorry - yes - well - um, there we are then. Do call in if there's anything we can help with - um - yes - well, goodbye then."

Diana watched her walking away. Simon laughed and said, "Well, Dee, does that take the gloss off?"

"No, not really, but I have a feeling that some ground rules will have to be established fairly early. At least she was well-intentioned."

Back at the hotel, Simon telephoned Laurier to tell him that they were seriously interested in the property but had many questions, not least of which was negotiating the price and finding a *notaire* to handle the purchase; a local man for preference with a good knowledge of the area and of the necessary paperwork for foreigners to purchase a house. A meeting at the house was arranged for that afternoon.

Diana and Simon sat over lunch discussing the immediate plans for the future. They decided that once the legal procedure of purchase had been undertaken, they would return to London to put their house into the hands of a letting agent for executives as Diana had suggested. Diana had already agreed that it was neither a sensible nor practical proposition to keep both houses going, but nevertheless, letting the Holland Park Avenue house was a difficult prospect for Diana.

The lingered over their coffee until the hotel proprietor came over to their table. "Thank you, Monsieur LeClerc," said Diana. "That was a really enjoyable meal. We have some things to do here, so if the room is available, we'd like to stay on for a few days."

"As you wish, Madame, with pleasure." Henri LeClerc was plump, jovial and welcoming. Diana and Simon loved this hotel with the terrace overlooking the Lauzac River.

Henri was still hovering at Diana's elbow. "Is there something you'd like to say, Monsieur?" she asked

"Well, it is common knowledge in the village that you have been to look at the chateau and – forgive me for being impertinent – but we are hoping that this might mean the house will now have a new owner."

Diana looked at Simon, who gave her a small nod.

"Well, you're right. We *are* looking at the chateau but we are just in the early stages. We love the house and the village is delightful, but please understand there are many questions to be answered yet and many plans to make. But I promise,

Monsieur LeClerc, if everything works out you will be the first to know!"

The sunlight pouring into the kitchen gave enough warmth for the doors to the garden to be open. They perched on the island worktop in the kitchen and dealt with the important issues of house purchase in France. Laurier was well-informed and helpful, willing to give them all the time they needed to come to the final decision.

Three hours later, the majority of the details had been settled: a price agreed; dates to be included in the *compromis de vente* (an exchange of contracts); rights to prevent hunting on the land; the taxes payable to the *Departement;* the necessity to obtain a *carte de séjour* (an identity card for foreigners); registering the car with the *Departement* number plates – all the details which make up a move to become an expatriate in France. Bank accounts were to be set up, registering the electricity and water accounts, insurance cover – all these and many more incidental questions were dealt with in turn. The residents had the responsibility to maintain the communal areas.

Contrary to blighting her enthusiasm, Diana experienced overwhelming joy that all this administrative work was for *their* house, *this* house that she wanted so badly. In a matter of two or three weeks, they would become owners of this wonderful place.

The *compromis de vente* would be ready for signature in a couple of days, after which Diana and Simon would return to London. Ten percent of the purchase price was due on exchange of contracts which Diana arranged with her bank. The development company belonged to Angus Moreton and Jean Claude Laurier, so there were no delays with the transfer of proprietorship. The completion date was to be three weeks hence, October 1st.

Henri greeted them on their return to the hotel and in response to his questioning look, Diana gave him a broad smile. "*Felicitations! Felicitations*! I am so happy for you, the village will be so happy for you," he broke into English for Simon's benefit. "I am sure you will find your heart's home here," he said.

"Oh yes, I think so," said Diana, "I really think so."

The contracts were signed on Thursday. Simon and Diana left on Friday morning, leaving her car in Saint-Sulpice. Diana would stay in London just for a week or so, leaving Simon to deal with packers, talk to his agent and have his car serviced ready to drive back. Diana would return to start furnishing arrangements for *La Maison Neuve*. The week in London passed in hours of packing, telephone calls, sorting essentials to leave for the tenants, and for Diana, a few moments of grief at leaving her beloved house in the hands of strangers.

"We can take it back any time we want within reason," said Simon, "but letting this house was always going to be a worry once we'd decided to live in France. Don't worry darling, it's all going to be wonderful, you'll see."

Diana waved to Simon from the taxi on Sunday morning as she left for the airport to return to Saint-Sulpice. Despite her misgivings about letting the house, she felt such tremors of excitement. As she came out of the arrivals hall of Bergerac airport, she was thrilled and surprised to see Henri waiting for her.

"Welcome to your new home!" He kissed her on both cheeks. As they were getting into Henri's car, he said, "There is an invitation for you from Madame Findlay for tomorrow evening, to welcome you and to meet your new neighbours."

"How kind," said Diana, but she felt dismayed. She wanted a few days wandering around the house, exploring the woods and getting to know it all. This was home now.

The hotel restaurant did not open on Sunday evenings, so Henri had prepared a tray for her with pâté, cheese, salad and crusty bread. He had also left a half-bottle of champagne on ice in her room. He had moved her room to one on the corner, facing the river on one side with a small balcony, and facing a small side street on the other. Although it was late September, the evenings were only just beginning to give a hint of autumn. People were walking along the river bank in short sleeves, T-shirts and lightweight trousers. She sipped champagne, watching the sun disappear behind the wooded hills on the other side of the river and felt a strong sense of contentment.

The telephone woke her the following morning; Simon was dealing with packers and removals people and, despite her having left lists and marked items as to what to leave behind and what to send to France, he still had queries and problems. Diana resolved most of his problems, and was still smiling when she hung up.

She had slept well and felt an immense happiness as she sipped her coffee, overlooking the river from her balcony. She had planned to spend the day at the house, just picking up some bread and cheese from the village for lunch. The prospect of meeting the neighbours in the evening wasn't as onerous as it had appeared yesterday, and in fact, she was quite looking forward to it now.

Her feeling of euphoria was intense as she put the key in the lock of the large oak doors to the hallway. As she went through the hall to the kitchen, the September sun was lighting up the room, showing the dew glistening on a magnificent cobweb across one of the windows. She spent a few happy hours re-visiting rooms and making plans, envisioning finished rooms full of comfortable furniture and the items collected in their twenty years together.

In mid-afternoon, she took her sweater and set off to walk a little in the woods. The clearing on the right-hand side was not as close to the house as she remembered and she spotted a small boat-house further along the shore that she hadn't noticed before. She tried to imagine what the clearing had contained, obviously a building of some sort but clearly a fire had destroyed whatever had been there and the forest had stretched its fingers to try to reclaim the space.

The little boat-house was no more than a shed really, with a small jetty. Diana wondered why the redevelopment of the estate had overlooked this little hut, but it was so far from the house and in no way detrimental to the overall venue. She would have a new boat-house built at some stage; maybe there were trout in the lake and they'd need a small boat. She had wonderful plans in her mind.

It was time to return to the hotel to shower and change before her evening at the Findlay's house. She had been invited for 6pm for 'drinks', so had planned to return to the hotel at about 8pm for dinner. 'Drinks' usually indicated that guests were given small things to nibble but were expected to dine elsewhere.

Hilary Findlay met her at the door, and despite her earlier, rather eccentric appearance, actually looked very nice. She wore a navy skirt with a navy top shot through with silver thread and the maroon toenails were now encased in silver ballerina shoes. Diana herself was wearing a cream skirt with a matching cream jacket bordered with intertwined black and cream silk. She was relieved not to feel overdressed.

"Hello, hello. Come in. This is my husband, Bob, and um - this is Francine Cooke and her mother, Véronique."

Diana shook hands with Bob, a very pleasant, slightly plump man seemingly much more reserved than his wife. Francine Cooke was a woman in her fifties, fairly plain looking and very overweight. By contrast, her mother Véronique was a slight French woman, and slim. In her eighties, Diana guessed.

"Unfortunately, the Grey sisters can't be here," said Hilary. "They're off at some horse show or other. Um - Bobby - drinks, please. Um - now, Véronique has been - um - Diana, what would you like? Bobby do the - um - what was I - oh, excuse me, the doorbell." With that, she disappeared off to the hallway.

Diana wasn't sure how much of this stilted chatter she could stand. She felt a hand on her arm and looked down into the warm, brown eyes of Véronique.

"You speak French, I hear." A statement, not a question. "How lovely. We can gossip! Actually my daughter speaks French but not well, much to my disappointment, and some of the others barely bother. I think the rule is to speak loud and slowly so that the natives can understand!" She let out a delightful peal of laughter.

Francine, the daughter, had wandered off, seemingly oblivious of her slightly rude behavior. Hilary was coming back with another couple, also it appeared, British. "Diana, this is James Wilson and Amanda - um - drinks - Bobby - please - yes - introduce yourselves - good, excuse me." And she was off again in the direction of the hallway.

Diana found the conversation friendly and warm, generally there were questions to her about *La Maison Neuve*: was she going to keep the name? Did she plan to live there full-time? Did she have children? All the usual niceties of welcoming someone to a new neighbourhood. James Wilson was a friend and business partner of Angus Moreton, the developer of *La Chênaie* and the two had several properties in the UK in their portfolio. Amanda was the architect who had designed the new houses on the estate. Diana guessed that they were in their thirties, quite young she thought to be so involved in the property market, clearly more adventurous than Diana had ever been.

When Diana has first arrived, she had noticed a tall, slim man of about sixty standing against the wall, looking out into the room. His face was angular and he seemed a little remote from the others in the room. Another man, rather grey-looking and slightly unkempt came an introduced himself as John Porton-Watts. He apologized for his wife's non-appearance and wished Diana every happiness in her new home. He wandered off to find a drink, leaving her for a couple of moments alone.

A voice from behind said, "How do you do? I'm Julian Lawson." He had a pleasant voice which accompanied a disturbing level of intimacy with his direct eye contact. It seemed to Diana to be girlish, if not childish, to react to this man in this way. Physical attraction was not something she experienced very often: she never understood their friends' dalliances with other people, and one or two of her closest friends enjoyed affairs regularly. She was not so naïve that she didn't recognized this feeling for what it was, and it took her by surprise.

"How do you do? I'm Diana Lewis." She offered her hand.

"Yes, you must be," he said taking her hand firmly, still keeping the eye contact which was making her feel uncomfortable now. "I'm sure you've answered all the questions there are to be answered about your house, your plans, and your husband. And I'm sure Hilary has already offered to do your family history – it's her passion. And since you speak French, you won't need Véronique to hold your hand at the doctor's surgery or the dentist." Diana thought him to be rather supercilious at this point, but the physical draw was still there.

"And how do *you* manage at the doctor's surgery and the dentist?" she retorted, feeling his remarks to be patronizing of his neighbours.

"Actually, I do speak French, albeit not as a native but well enough. Edwina and I took French lessons when we decided to come here, we went to the *Alliance Française* and already spoke quite well when we came here. It seemed the sensible thing to do. It's improved since we arrived,

41

obviously become more idiomatic. And I'm sorry, that was rather barbed and you're right to be annoyed with me." He touched her arm in apology, his intimacy confused her and left her feeling out of her depth with this man.

"Edwina? Is she here?" Diana asked, looking around the room.

"Only in spirit. She died three years ago."

"Oh God. I'm sorry. Actually Laurier did tell me, but it had slipped my mind. I'm not usually crass. I know nothing about anyone except Hilary appeared on the doorstep on our first visit, but we were in a hurry and didn't have time to chat."

"Well, Diana," he said, still engaging the eye contact, "you've only just arrived and we don't want buyer's remorse setting in so soon, so let's start again." His smile gave a hint of the humour he would be capable of, at the same time keeping her drawn to him.

Trying to keep her equilibrium, she said, "Family history? Really? I mean, digging into people's family closets?"

"Yes, really. So beware – if you have nobles or highwaymen tucked away, she'll find them. Although with a name like Lewis, she'll have to spend quite a bit of time, there must be whole tribes of you."

"Actually, my family history is quite well known to us, so she'd be very disappointed. My parents' side is quite well documented and Simon has no interest in his forebears." In fact, she knew that Simon was slightly ashamed of his family roots, his father having achieved a middle rank in the army where any budding ambition rested and expired. His grandparents were pretty humble working folk and his great-great grandparents had both died in a workhouse.

Diana enjoyed Julian's company. He was intelligent, quietly spoken but still managed to convey an intimacy which disconcerted her. She felt unwilling to leave him but aware that the party was given for her to meet other people, she felt obliged to circulate a little before deciding it was time to leave. Hilary saw her to the door and hugged her. "I can't tell you how pleased we are that you're coming to live here. Finally that lovely house will be cherished, it so deserves it after its dreadful past. Please don't let all the stories of the place put a pall on it for you, it's all so long in the past."

Since Hilary had managed this piece of information without her usual stammering and thought-confusion, Diana didn't ask her about those remarks. She had all the time in the world to find out about the house and its history and she had no intention of letting anything take the gloss off her present joy. But she was curious all the same.

****

Laurier and Angus Moreton had been happy to give her free access to the house, even though completion of the contract was still a few weeks away. She was able to spend time taking measurements and meeting the curtain maker. The company came who would fit one bedroom as a dressing room, leaving just the one bedroom as a guest room. The other important room would be Simon's study, and apart from ordering bookshelves for one wall, she would leave the choice of furnishing until Simon joined her.

Returning to the hotel early one afternoon, Henri was just clearing the restaurant after the last of the lunchtime diners had left. "Oh, Madame! Have you eaten? Non? Let me see what I can do."

"Henri, please, just a sandwich would be fine. Can you join me for coffee or a *digestif*, I would love to talk to you about something. And please, do you think you could call me Diana? I'd really like it if you would."

"Thank you, that's very nice of you. I will try to remember."

The windows out to the terrace were closed, since the day had become overcast and slightly windy. Diana sat at a table by the window looking out to the river and waited for Henri. He returned with a baguette sandwich of home-cooked ham, a pot of coffee and two glasses of Armagnac.

"Henri, this looks wonderful, thank you." She took a bite of her sandwich and they exchanged small talk until she had finished. She picked up her glass and sniffed the Armagnac appreciatively. "Henri, I need to ask you something. I've been doing some research about the history of this place on the internet. There's quite a lot written about SaintSulpice, the saint, the village, the *Departement,* and so on, but I can't find much about the estate and the family who owned it. I know it's been many years since there was any family involvement with this estate, but even so."

Henri took a slow sip from his glass, put the glass on the table and leaned forward. "Diana." He sounded unsure as to how to continue. "Your war was very different to ours, but no less terrible, I know. But since the Romans, you have never had to live as a conquered people."

"Aren't you forgetting something? The Norman Conquest? We nearly lost the English language altogether for three hundred years. And to the French!" They both laughed but Henri soon lapsed back into a thoughtful silence.

Diana put a hand on his arm and he smiled. He continued after a moment's hesitation. "People cope with fear and humiliation in different ways. Some people can be brave who are least expected to be and others cave in at the first obstacle. This town was no different from a thousand others in France, it had its heroes and its cowards and even today, families are split over events that took place then." His voice and his countenance took on an air of sadness.

"For quite a long time," he continued, "there were no Germans in this area, we were in the *zone non occupée.* We carried on as normal and although there were rumours of resistance groups setting up around and about, especially in the woods and the hills, many people remained convinced that the war would pass them by in this corner of the country. All that changed at the end of 1942. It was dreadful." He sipped his Armagnac and looked out over the river. He fell silent again.

"Henri?"

"Yes. The estate – your estate – is now called *La Chênaie* but in those days it was known as the *Chateau de Lusignac*. It was a big estate, many hectares. The house itself is large but modest by comparison to other estates, much like the modesty shown by the de Lusignac family. The house had been in the family for many generations and some say its survival in the Revolution was due to the esteem in which Charles de Lusignac was held by his tenants and the local people. He was generous and helpful, he educated the peasants' children. Can you imagine, Diana, a peasant's child in those days who could read and write? *C'est incroyable.* He provided well-paid work, maintained the workers' houses on his estate and in return, no-one went hungry, cold or ill if he could help."

Diana had intended to return to the house in the late afternoon but she felt drawn to the story Henri was unfolding, so she settled in her chair and sipped her Armagnac.

"It is said that Robespierre's men down here couldn't find anyone at all to speak against this member of the aristocracy. He was never brought to trial although he faced several inquisitions. The de Lusignacs have always been well-regarded for generations: they have died in the service of France, they have paid their taxes, they have provided good employment and have borne their tragedies with grace. They honour their flag and their country. The last de Lusignac, Philippe, was in residence with his sixteen-year-old daughter, Sophie, when the Germans finally arrived in this part of the world. De Lusignac's wife had died when the child was seven years old, of blood poisoning following a dog bite." Henri again paused but Diana didn't prompt him this time.

"In December 1942, the Chateau was taken over by the Germans under the command of one Colonel Gunter von Trosch and his officers. Philippe and his daughter were moved out to the hunting lodge. The lodge had been built about a hundred years before, one of the de Lusignacs was keen on hunting with horses. The *chasse à courre* – it could house six guests, with kennels at the back and two single storey buildings for grooms and servants."

Diana immediately thought of the large clearing in the woods, but chose to wait until the end of Henri's story before asking about it.

"Once the Germans arrived, everyone felt fear. Stories had already reached here of retributions against villages for acts of sabotage and of punishments for running escape lines for allied soldiers and pilots. At first, the colonel was not as bad as people had feared but in his search for underground activities he was ruthless. His principal task in being sent here was to uncover escape lines and resistance cells, and other partisan groups. He also, in his favour, did take a firm stand against any bad behavior of his own troops. The troops were banned from wandering freely on the estate and in the woods. He permitted Philippe and his daughter to continue to use the grounds and to keep their lodge private. Like most of the German occupiers, he did not regard resistance work as patriotic, but rather an act of betrayal by the vanquished. A conquered people had no rights other than those bestowed on them by the Reich."

A picture began to take shape in Diana's mind of a very different village to the gentle and friendly place of today.

Henri sipped his drink and continued, "Honestly, Diana, what is the good of resistance anyway against such force? Every minor act of sabotage was repaid ten-fold with horrible consequences. Most people just wanted to find a way of getting through."

"Were members of your family here then, Henri? Were they involved in any way? Is this very painful for you?" Diana was now concerned that she was asking Henri to relive unhappy memories, bringing hurt to this lovely man.

"Diana, most of us haven't spoken of these things for many years. When I finish, you will understand that there wasn't a family in this village who wasn't touched by events which took place then. People lived in outlying areas, very rural and without telephones; people just trying to get on with their lives."

Again, he paused as if determined to get everything in the right order before finishing his story.

"Philippe de Lusignac was actually a member of a group which formed part of an escape line, the *Cloche* – 'The Bell' - because the next time the church bell would ring would be the day of liberation. The *Cloche* had been formed long before the Germans arrived in the *zone non occupée*, and they ran several routes down to Spain. Philippe never did go on trips with escapees, he was too well-known and too closely watched – any prolonged absence would be noticed. But he had channels of finance through the Resistance to London, to his friends and business contacts. He arranged funds in some sort of deal with his banks, whereby he would obtain funds in local money and the equivalent amounts were paid to him outside France. I'm not sure how it all worked, but he did successfully find money for these activities."

Diana nodded, trying to curb her impatience at Henri's slow telling of the history. She found herself drawn into this family, into this story, she so desperately wanted to know more.

"They didn't just help allied airmen, they helped some Jewish families also. This line had been operating since early 1940 and no-one knew exactly how far it stretched, but it was thought that it started on the north coast and went down as far as the Pyrenees. They helped many people to get to Spain. Once the Germans took over his house, his movements were obviously more restricted, but he cultivated a relationship with the colonel which he hoped would help the village and deflect attention away from the Resistance. Also, of course, from him and his daughter. The daughter had always been educated at home and was a rather shy, reserved girl, unfortunately rather plain and naïve. Her governess was a *Parisienne* who was friendly enough in the village, but mostly kept very much to herself. She left when the family moved into the lodge, presumably went back to Paris."

The picture of the burned-out clearing kept coming to the fore of Diana's thoughts. She felt now that this was going to be an important part of the story.

"One neighbouring escape line had recently collapsed, betrayed by one of their number so several airmen and other servicemen were left stranded. Together with a number of airmen already en route, it was becoming a very dangerous situation. It was decided that three groups would leave on three successive nights, to continue on the stages set up along the route. Easter that year fell in April. April 25th, 1943" Henri paused, clearly now moved with emotion. He was lost in some ghastly memory.

"Henri, take a minute. I'm so sorry, this is obviously full of grief for you, please don't distress yourself any further. I'm so sorry I asked you."

Henri looked at her, his eyes now moist and his face sagged with pain. What could he be about to tell her that grieved him so?

"Diana, so many things happened, not a village or town is left without scars, even today. We cannot imagine those times; we just have to remember those people with honour. Another Armagnac, I think."

Henri collected their glasses and went off to fetch refills. Diana was very aware that the rest of the story was going to be almost more than Henri could bear, but she couldn't help herself. She had to know now.

"You must understand that escape groups and resistance groups were being betrayed all the time. The stranded group was now dangerously large and they had to be moved before any more arrived. They finally therefore decided to leave in one group, not three, with more escorts. That terrible, terrible night, the Germans had information of the plans and all of them were captured. A firefight had broken out when they were surrounded and several soldiers were killed, together with three of the group. The rest were rounded up and brought to the village square. The whole village was roused by the soldiers and brought to watch as the members of the group were lined up against the walls of the village covered market. They were kept waiting for death for an hour before the firing squad was called to attention and the shots were fired. The leader of the group was made to watch the others being shot and then he was hanged from the flagpole in the square."

"And the escapees?"

"They were captured and sent to prisoner of war camps."

****

The tears were flowing freely down Henri's cheeks now as the memories became vivid images in his mind. Diana put her hand over Henri's and squeezed. "There's more?" she asked.

"*Oui*. The following morning de Lusignac was found outside the gates to the estate. His tongue had been cut out and was nailed to his chest with a knife and a note which read, '*COLLABORATEUR*'.

"WHAT?" Diana's shock could not have been more intense. "WHAT?" She repeated her shout in disbelief at what she'd just been told. "He was a collaborator? How? What had he done? How did …?"

Her understanding simply refused to take in this intelligence. This story, this horrible, dreadful story belonged to her beloved house. Her home.

"Was it true?" Diana asked, hoping that there was still something to mitigate the horror of what she'd just been told.

"It was said that -"

"It was said? It was said? By whom? What …?" Diana still struggled to find something to cling to that this story would not be true.

"It was said that he confessed. Had it just been the circumstantial events, he might have had the benefit of the doubt. We were people then who took minor situations and made serious judgements from them. We were a nation of *corbeaux* – crows – informers. The smallest action could be misunderstood and worse, then reported. There was a kitchen maid, Juliette Lamy; her husband had been taken to a labour camp in Germany and she was living with her two children with her mother-in-law. There was a door from the kitchen up to the main quarters which was used by the gardeners, the household deliveries, cleaners and so on. It was much the same as it is now except there is no hallway: it was a place where estate workers could leave their boots and coats when they came into the kitchen for lunch. There was a staircase leading up to the family quarters for the staff to take up food and suchlike." Henri paused again, sipping slowly from the glass. His face bore the look of someone determined to continue with a sad story, regardless of the pain he might feel.

"On this night, April 24th, de Lusignac appeared at this back door, very agitated and told the German guard he needed to see the colonel urgently. Juliette was surprised to see him at this entrance, it was never done for the baron to enter the house by this route, something very important must have brought him here. She was very curious. She prepared a tray of coffee and told the guard she was taking it up to the officers' drawing room. She arrived at the top of the stairs as the colonel and the baron were coming into the hallway. The colonel had his arm around the baron's shoulders and then they shook hands. She overheard the colonel say that he was very grateful for the information and he would, 'put matters in hand immediately.' He also said that this kind of matter should be brought to him at once in order that action might be taken rapidly."

"Is that all? Was there no further evidence than an overheard conversation? Please tell me it wasn't enough to condemn a man to death?" Diana's voice rose slightly as she became more distressed.

"You cannot imagine those times, Diana. No-one trusted anyone and snippets of gossip were misconstrued all the time. More than one man went to his death on the strength of innuendo and malicious chatter. Juliette reported to her mother-in-law what she had heard, and the mother-in-law told her friend's husband, a member of the Resistance."

Diana sensed that the final thrust of the story was coming and kept silent.

"Two nights later," Henri continued, "that terrible night of 26th, the group was captured and the rest you know. It was clear that the conversation Juliette had overheard concerned the whereabouts of the group and even more obvious that Baron de Lusignac had reported it to the colonel."

"Was there no doubt at all? Was there nothing in mitigation? It just seems to go against everything you told me about the man. Why would he do such a thing? It's unthinkable."

"There was no doubt. Word got around that he confessed. Diana, there are still people alive in the village who were there at the time, do you understand what I'm saying?"

Diana nodded but without any real understanding.

"So, after the night of the shootings in the square, Philippe de Lusignac, our loyal baron and patron, asked permission to leave to chateau in order to visit the bereaved families. He hadn't been a prisoner on the estate, but he needed permission to leave. The baron left the estate, was seen briefly in the village and was never seen alive again."

Diana realized the muscles in her back were aching with sheer tension. "Does everyone on the estate know the story?" She was thinking back to Hilary Findlay's parting remark.

"Oh, I imagine so, at least some version or other. You must understand, Diana, every village and town in France has its scars written on wall plaques, war memorials and gravestones. Roadside markers where people were shot for helping the Resistance. Whole villages were destroyed in retaliation for acts of sabotage. Some houses in the village have still not repaired bullet holes in the walls and you must have noticed the scars on the arches of the covered market." Henri got up and walked to the window, the river looked grey on this overcast day.

"Tourists now eat platters of seafood beside commemorative plaques of people who were shot, they drive past the road markers where brave French patriots lost their lives, some betrayed by their own countrymen."

"What happened to the daughter?" asked Diana.

"Pardon?"

"The daughter, Sophie. What happened to her?"

"They sent Juliette to tell the poor girl that her father had been killed. Sophie became hysterical and she wouldn't be calmed, she screamed and cried and banged her head – she frightened poor Juliette, who asked if one the guards could fetch a doctor. He came and gave her something to calm her. She was handed over to the care of the *cure*, Père Martin, who would decide what to do with her. The governess had already gone back to Paris by this time, so the poor child was without anyone really, except an old maid. Père Martin's housekeeper looked after her and it was decided to send her to the care of the *religieuses* in Bordeaux. She was moved from there to another convent after a while, I'm not sure where. Word has it that she stayed and took vows to become a nun. Poor girl, she was never going to be pretty but it seemed to me that she had no life at all, very little education and almost no contact with other young people."

"Where is Philippe de Lusignac buried?" asked Diana.

"Ah." Henri paused again and turned from the window. "When his body was found outside the gates, the Germans put it in a coffin and took it to the church of Saint-Sulpice at the request of some of the local people. Even this very small act of humanity by the Germans seemed to condemn de Lusignac as being 'one of theirs'. His coffin was placed in the church to await burial but the body was stolen in the night. It is believed that it was taken back to the lodge where he had been living."

"The fire!" exclaimed Diana. "They put him in the lodge and set fire to it!"

"Well, that's the story everyone believes and no-one had ever doubted it."

****

The first of October came and with it the completion of the Lewises' purchase of *La Maison Neuve*. There was some more documentation to sign but the whole process was remarkably uncomplicated as long as the required number of all copies was provided. The transfer of the funds completed the transaction and suddenly Diana was the actual owner of the keys which she had held since first setting eyes on the property.

Diana had returned to the house the day after Henri's recounting of the tragic family's history of the house, expecting somehow for things to have changed; she almost expected an atmosphere, a malevolence, a ghostly ring of jackboot on tile, but there was not. Not even a hint. Not a moment's unease came to her. All she felt was the same overwhelming love for this house. She stood at the window of the drawing room looking out to the right where the clearing in the woods was virtually all that was left of the lodge.

Henri had told her that Père Martin had been allowed to go to the site, to perform a blessing, a last benediction to the dead. There was no proof, of course, that de Lusignac had indeed perished there, but everyone firmly believed it to be so.

Colonel von Trosch had no objection to the daughter, Sophie, being brought to say her farewells, and to Père Martin's knowledge, the girl had not spoken a single word since being told of her father's death. She was taken the following day to Bordeaux and then, Henri believed to a convent in Tours, well away from the area.

"So much sadness in so beautiful a place," Diana had said to Henri the day before. "Perhaps this is a healing point, a new start, new memories. No-one has lived here since those terrible times, have they?"

"No, no-one has. Perhaps you're right, a new beginning. A restoration of goodness and happiness in this place. We are all in the village so delighted that you have come to live here, we will do everything we can to help and to make you happy."

Laurier had told her that there had been numerous problems in getting clear title to the place when he and Angus first decided to buy it. No family could be found except spurious claimants, whose attempts to gain ownership were legally rebuffed. But they must have found someone who *was* legally entitled because they had managed to clear the title in the end. Laurier, though, had made no mention of the history of the house in the brochure and accompanying paperwork.

On a whim, Diana decided to call him. "Hello, Jean Claude. Yes, fine thank you. Yes, the shipment arrives today, I'm just waiting for the containers. Yes, of course, I'll tell him. Jean Claude, when you and Angus finally bought this house, was there anything here in the way of family stuff, you know, papers, photos - anything at all?

"Well, there wasn't much. The house had been empty for so many years and there were mountains of rubbish. Mostly it had been ransacked and frankly, vandalized. We found a couple of German document boxes in very bad condition that contained some stuff which probably did belong to the family, but they were mostly old household bills, a couple of damp photos, some blank pieces of paper, a couple of little notebooks with information about estate wages, that sort of thing. Why are you asking?"

"Jean Claude, are you aware of the fate of the family who owned this house?"

The long pause made her wonder if Jean Claude was still on the end of the line. Finally, he spoke. "Diana, there are no areas of my country which were not humiliated and scarred by the war. Many of our beautiful country houses were requisitioned for use by our conquerors, many families found themselves in an impossible position where any other action than submission or apparent collaboration was impossible. Survival became the currency of the era. If I didn't tell you, it's not that I was trying to hide anything – anyone in the village could have told you the story – but believe me, most people want the past to stay there."

"Yes, I see, of course I do," said Diana, "but I love this place and quite honestly, the family intrigues me. If I promise that it's just my curiosity and nothing more, would you let me see what you've found?"

"Well, I'm not even sure what we did with them, but I suppose you are probably the nearest thing to the rightful owner now. When the Catholic Church was gifted the property, they never even sent anyone to see it, they just wanted to offload it as soon as possible. Let me see if I can find them and I'll bring them down. You can show me then what you've done with that lovely place."

"Just one more thing, Jean Claude. You mentioned it took a long time to get clear title. I assume the daughter inherited, didn't see?"

"Well, after the war, all confiscated and requisitioned property matters were handled carefully, as you can imagine. Families who had died suddenly had cousins and relatives coming from everywhere making claims, documents had to be investigated and it all took years. French bureaucracy does not believe in speed. This family was no exception, two people came forward but in the end, the daughter was declared as the sole inheritor. By this time, she had joined an order of nuns and had taken her final vows. The property was gifted to the order, who in turn gifted it to the diocese. The church lawyers took years to go over much of the work which had already been done. Then it was finally put up for sale and it had been on the market for years before we bought it."

"And in all that time, the house was abandoned and falling into ruin," mused Diana, more to herself than to Laurier.

"Then there were boundary problems. Apparently the original property line only went as far as the far side of the lake. The woods on the hill on the other side belonged to another family but were given to de Lusignac in payment of some debt or other, but it had never been formally recorded. It was a mess and a nightmare at times, but finally we succeeded."

"So, it's not haunted, then?" Diana laughed.

"Diana, there are ghosts everywhere in France, but none that will harm you, but rather thank you for loving this house."

****

The shipping containers arrived in mid-morning and it was after 3pm when the last box was delivered into the house and the men had left. Diana decided to leave any unpacking until the following day and to go for a walk before finishing for the day and going back to the hotel.

She hadn't planned it, but she knew where her feet were taking her; she was drawn to the clearing where the lodge had been. She tried to imagine what pressure de Lusignac had been under to betray his own people and to expose his daughter to such danger. For a family who held such noble ideals for so many generations, she found it hard to comprehend that he had taken such an irreversible step. "Perhaps he was threatened in some way," she thought, and realized she was desperate to give him the benefit of the doubt. Somehow, this thought, rather like a sort of vow at this place, made her happy.

She sat on a pile of logs and breathed deeply, feeling a great sense of peace. It came as a shock to her to realise that she had not told Simon anything of Henri's story. She had never held anything back from Simon. She regarded this house as *their* home, but in fact she had come to understand that it did, and always would, mean more to her than to Simon. She had never wanted anything of her own, from first meeting Simon she had always wanted to share everything with him. Perhaps it was because she had wanted this house so much when Simon clearly didn't.

"It'll be different when he gets here," she thought.

When Diana had met Simon in Paris, she thought he was perfect. He was good-looking and interesting to talk to. He didn't seem to want wild night-life but he did have a lot of friends. He'd take her to the Louvre one day and then to a flea market the next. He seemed to have an enthusiasm for life's experiences which she found exhilarating, being naturally more reserved herself.

Diana knew her life had been easy: enough money, a loving home, good education and no pressure to become something else. Simon's background was very different. His father, David, had joined the army very young and had risen through the ranks to the point of major. Any ambition or chances of furthering his career ceased without any apparent reason. His wife had struggled and failed to put their humble background behind her and to rise with him. Major Lewis had never been one of the popular officers with his comrades in the officers' mess and he had retired without leaving much of distinction behind him, save for the obvious achievement of having risen through the ranks in the first place. They had bought a house in Weybridge in Surrey before the property boom and Mrs. Lewis always had the air of someone who couldn't quite understand how they had arrived there.

Diana remembered the night she and Simon had got engaged. Emily had invited the Lewises to dinner at the house in Holland Park Avenue. Mrs. Lewis had hidden her discomfort in several glasses of gin and tonic and the evening had taken on a rather strained atmosphere. Although Diana had made an effort with the Lewises over the years, there was never a degree of comfortable relationship between them.

Diana's determination to have this house was the first time in many years that she had surprised Simon. She had seemed energised and very motivated, she had even initiated love-making several times during the week in London. Sex between them had always been good, but usually he was the one to make the first move.

Diana let out a sigh and gathered up her coat to start to walk back to the house as the light was beginning to fade. She stopped to watch the ducks on the water which was rippling now on the chill evening breeze. She was surprised and a little annoyed to see a man coming towards her, still some distance away. As the man drew near, she recognised Julian Lawson.

"Hello," he said. "You've caught me, I'm afraid. I got rather used to walking in these woods when the house was empty. I thought you'd be in the house, I saw all the vehicles arriving with your stuff, so I thought I'd risk a little stroll. I adore the woods at this time of year."

"Hello," she replied but without warmth. "That's alright for today, but I'm rather afraid it's going to have to stop. We're quite private people and I think Simon wants the peace to work."

"Please. I really am sorry. I quite understand and I promise it won't happen again. Honestly." He seemed sincere and she felt herself warming to him again. "How are things going?"

"Actually, I've done nothing today except hang around and make coffee for the removal men." She smiled and relented. "I'm really quite pleased to see you, come in and have a drink, I do know where the wine is but it will have to be cups."

They went in through the glass doors from the garden into the kitchen, the floor was piled high with boxes and the table and chairs were still in their wrapping.

"We might have a problem after all," said Diana. "I haven't a clue which box I put the corkscrew in, so it'll have to be coffee after all."

Julian could have offered to go home and bring one, but he thought she might then use the opportunity to end the encounter.

"Coffee's fine, thank you. Just black, no sugar."

"Tell me," she said, looking at him across the kitchen waiting for the kettle to boil. "I met a chap that night at Hilary's drinks party called John something?"

"John Porton-Watts," he replied. "He's married to Eleanor."

"Yes, that's him. Tell me something about him, he didn't stay long enough to speak to and his wife didn't come that night."

"No, she wouldn't. She doesn't often leave the house. It's a very sad story, actually." He watched Diana as she ladled coffee into cups, thinking how natural she looked: she wore little make-up, her hair was tied in a loose pony-tail and her pink jeans and T-shirt were neither tight nor too young. Fresh-looking, he thought.

"Sad?" asked Diana as she handed him a cup. "Sorry, no saucer!"

"Yes, sad. Until five years ago they lived very differently. The Porton estate had been going downhill for years and five years ago they were obliged to sell up. The house is now a country hotel with all the usual amenities, you know – swimming pool and the rest." He sipped his coffee and found it surprisingly good for an instant product.

"Actually," he continued, "Angus and Jean Claude were interested in it but they'd not long bought this place and couldn't arrange funding. John has accepted their change of circumstances with what I would call quiet resignation. Eleanor can't, poor woman. Hilary has tried to get her to go out once or twice but one of Eleanor's problems is that the world is made up of inferior beings. At least, *her* world."

Diana said, "Well, I'm not the most judgmental person in the world, but isn't five years long enough to make a new life and deal with the past? As for thinking the rest of us to be inferior, I will admit Hilary is hard work, but she is extraordinarily kind and everyone else seems delightful."

"Well, I can tell you one thing, Diana. Eleanor is not going to be a friend of yours." Julian looked at Diana directly.

"Why ever not?" Diana was surprised at the bluntness of his statement.

"Oh, Diana, don't be obtuse! It's because you live here in this house and she doesn't."

A small frown passed over Diana's forehead, then she got up from where she'd been sitting on a packing box and threw the rest of her coffee into the sink. "If I drink any more coffee today, I won't sleep for a week." Clearly, she intended him to leave now. "Well, it's time I got back to the hotel. Simon will want to chat and I need to get started early in the morning."

Sensing a change in her demeanour, Julian said, "Don't let me take the gloss off your day. I'm afraid I'm rather blunt – one of the advantages of approaching old age." Diana imagined him to be in his late fifties or early sixties. He leaned down and brushed her cheek with his lips, and gave her shoulder a slight squeeze.

"If you need any help in the next few days, let me know. I'm off to Paris on Saturday for a couple of days but here are my numbers, both here and there."

He handed her a card on which was printed his name and several phone numbers – no addresses either here or in Paris.

He left her to lock up the doors on the upper terrace and waited for her on the drive. When she descended the steps and came up to him he asked, "When will your husband be coming down?"

"Well, he has a meeting in London with his literary agent on Friday, then he's driving down over the weekend. He'll probably be here for a week and then go back to Paris to find a small apartment for a few months while he does his research. When the research is finished, he'll come down permanently to write. But he'll probably come home for most weekends."

"I might be able to help with the apartment," said Julian. "I have a small apartment in Neuilly, it's empty most of the time."

She looked at him quizzically. "Why on earth would you want to do that? You haven't even met Simon yet. It's extraordinarily generous, but we can't accept. Do you offer your apartment to every struggling writer who needs one? Honestly, it's very kind but I'm sure he'll find something."

"Come, Diana. It's just a two-bedroomed apartment, quite small but very central. Think no more about it, Simon can have it for as long as he needs it."

They had reached her car, and she turned to face him. She felt that same seismic shift in her emotions as he gave her that same intimate look, his face inches from hers. He kissed her cheek again, lingering very slightly.

In the car on the way back to the hotel, she tried to rationalise this intense longing he engendered in her.

****

Diana had intended to have a quick dinner at the little Italian restaurant and pizzeria in the village, but Henri seemed to be waiting for her and had her table ready for her. Before dinner, she had phoned Simon to let him know that the shipment had arrived safely and she'd begin work the following day. "How did your meeting go with Edwards?" she asked.

"Well, they're interested in a sequel but I've only the vaguest outline at the moment. I think I'll go from here straight to Paris, and then come down after I've found a place to stay."

"Simon, you can't!" she exclaimed. "That wasn't what we agreed at all." Again she surprised him by not falling in with his plans as she would normally have done. "At least come down for a week, after all you'll have the car and all your stuff, you can't leave a car loaded with bags in Paris, you'll never find anywhere to park, for a start."

"Diana, it's just that I would rather -"

"Simon, just listen. I might be able to save you the trouble of looking for somewhere if you'd just come down for a week. One of the residents here has an apartment in Paris and he's prepared to let you rent it."

Simon was silent on the end of the phone line, Diana was anxious at her end, he could tell. "Oh well, alright, you're probably right. And who's this chap anyway, who has ready apartments at his fingertips to lend to all and sundry?" he lightened his tone.

"Tell you when you get here, you can meet him."

Diana slept badly, her mind refusing to rest from the tasks she had set herself for the following day. But mostly, she knew, it was the effect Julian had had on her. At the time it had seemed wild, wonderful, dangerous even. Now it felt like a problem. It was a problem because she knew that Julian would be in her every thought and hoped that Simon's arrival would bring her back to reality.

Diana spent the next two days unpacking and arranging furniture. She and Simon had decided that, after all, they would prefer to take all their furniture with them to France. Her mother's Knowle sofas had been part of her home for as long as she could remember, and had been reupholstered many times; she really couldn't think of leaving them for strangers. In the end, the decision had not been hard and a couple of frantic days of internet shopping had enabled them to furnish the London house with good but not exceptional family furniture.

As busy as she was, Diana found she was half hoping Julian would appear. "Is this a form of infidelity?" she wondered. Simon and Diana had spent some time apart during their marriage but not for long periods at a time. He adored her, of that she was sure, so any flirtations or momentary blurring of the fidelity outlines seemed unimportant to the point of non-existence. Forgiveness was her second nature. Diana herself had never crossed the line, she hadn't needed to. She loved Simon intensely and completely.

Towards mid-afternoon of the second day, she was unpacking in the dining room. She had already finished the kitchen, since they would then have somewhere comfortable to eat and sit whilst trying to make order out of chaos in the upper floors. She jumped at the sound of a loud ring and realised she'd never heard the doorbell before. Before she could cross the hall, the door opened and a woman in her late forties or early fifties stepped in, coming towards Diana with her hand outstretched. "Hello," she said, "I'm Margaret Grey. Sorry we haven't popped round before, we've been rather tied up and you're not yet here in the evenings. My sister Jennifer is still over at the stables."

"Hello, I'm Diana Lewis. Do come down to the kitchen, everywhere else is a bit of a mess but there is a clear space down there, and I do have the makings for coffee."

"Well, if it has to be coffee, so be it."

Diana laughed at the easy introduction and thought she would like this woman.

They went down to the kitchen which now looked more or less as Diana wanted it. With the units and appliances already fitted when she moved in, her only real task was to find a home for everything. The table would seat six people but there would normally be only the two of them for breakfast or informal dining. The chairs were solid wicker with arms and the seats had thick, comfortable cushions. Diana felt Margaret's scrutiny as she made the coffee and searched for the biscuit tin.

"We have a stable yard in the next village," Margaret said. "Do you ride?"

"I used to, I used to enjoy it very much but I haven't ridden for ages. I believe you keep horses in livery. Is there much call for that here?"

"Saint-Jerome-sur-Lauzac is just a few kilometres away and is positively bursting with expatriates," Margaret laughed easily. "They even have a cricket team, for heaven's sake! We do riding holidays in a sort of co-operative venture with the hotel there, and we have a camp-site too. Then there's the little expatriate darlings who want to go in for competitions, so yes, there's more business than we can actually handle at the moment, we're looking for someone to come in as a partner. Interested?"

"No, not in the least!" Diana found herself warming to this rather forthright woman, but having a glimpse of a sense of fun behind the rather ebullient, down-to-earth character.

"Well, it's nice that you're here, anyway. We were all rather fed up with seeing the old house empty. Any more coffee?"

The two woman chatted amiably for half an hour, Diana really enjoyed the other's amusing anecdotes of ambitious mothers pushing their children to ride beautifully and tales of horse-riding disasters. When Margaret stood up to leave, she said, "Have you met everyone now, except us that is?"

"I've actually met everyone but mostly just to say good morning in passing when I'm coming and going. I've met Julian a couple of times and of course, Hilary. I'm actually having tea with Véronique tomorrow afternoon."

Margaret looked quickly at Diana and then looked away through the window. "What do you think of Julian?" she asked.

"Hard to say, actually," said Diana. "I hardly know him but he seems fairly self-contained, self-satisfied, I suppose I mean." Even talking about him seemed to disturb her. "Why?" she smiled "Is he special to you, are you involved?" But asking the question, she realised she didn't really want the answer to be in the positive.

"Oh, he's not interested in me," said Margaret, saying it lightly though it was evidently painful to say. "Love unrequited, that's me. Had a dreadful marriage, had a disastrous affair and now firmly single and likely to remain so. That's not to say I don't sometimes try to interest him, but I've drawn blanks so far. There. Now you know. Jennifer thinks I've wasted most of my life on the wrong men, and she includes Julian in that. But she's not really one to talk, she's more the pot but I'm less of a black kettle. But I do care very much for him. Simple really."

After Margaret had left, Diana sat on in the kitchen, thinking about her feelings for Julian. It was true that she hardly knew him but that didn't stop him from invading her thoughts whenever her mind relaxed from her tasks in hand.

She resolved to work hard to straighten the house by the weekend, when Simon would arrive and they would spend the first night in the new home together. Julian would be away and once Simon was with her, these feelings for Julian would become insignificant.

Henri had found a chap called André from the village to come and help Diana bringing in logs for the fires, taking away packing boxes and generally helping with lifting and moving furniture. It was still warm during the day, but the evenings had a distinct chill in the large rooms and Diana was determined that fires would be lit and everything in its place and welcoming for when Simon walked through the door.

She worked hard again the following day and made huge progress. She left André working when she went for tea with Véronique. Véronique's daughter, Francine, opened the door and seemed a lot more friendly than when they had met at Hilary's drinks party. Véronique was delighted to see her and took her through to their drawing room. It was the first time Diana had been in one of the other houses on the estate and remarked on how beautifully it had been finished, every attention to high-specification detail had been observed, and doors opened and closed almost silently

The front door opened into a generous hallway, with a cloakroom on the right and just past the cloakroom was the door into the kitchen. The staircase went up on the left hand side to the bedrooms. Straight ahead was the large drawing room with an open-plan dining area to the right. The kitchen was reached either through the door in the hallway or through the dining area. The drawing room had a glass wall with a door leading out into the garden.

Although Diana had at first been disappointed to see the rear gardens fenced in, she realised that each house had a swimming pool of about eight metres by five, in a shape that was a cross between an oval and a bean shape. Clearly, people needed privacy in the pool areas and the fencing had actually been quite artistic. The Cookes' pool had a small amount of terracing around it and a very pretty rock garden had been made around one side: the big rocks had apparently been found in the ground when the pools were being dug out. Like the front gardens, no attempt had been made to make an English-type garden but there were fruit trees and bushes with plenty of colour. The entire garden area covered about an acre and a half and just ran off into the woods at the bottom of the garden. The patio outside the drawing room door was covered by a blue and white striped awning.

"It's just lovely," said Diana enthusiastically. "Really lovely. The garden is a complete sun-trap, it's beautifully warm out here, even at this time."

"Yes, the season is just coming to an end, we've been lucky this summer, we've had plenty of rain at night with the thunder storms but it's been gorgeous during the day. It's not always like that. In some years, it doesn't rain for three months and the grass doesn't go brown, it goes white." Francine had joined them and was clearly intending to be more friendly.

Diana found an hour had passed pleasantly, Francine had made very good scones and the tea was Earl Grey. The conversation had mostly been one of questions to her of their plans, how Francine and Véronique could be of help, and Diana left feeling that her initial sense of affection for

Véronique had not been misplaced. Francine had shown herself to be a rather clever woman but not one who felt the need to assert her cleverness over other people. Her weight had obviously affected her self-esteem.

Diana returned to the house to find the hallway full of smoke. André was in the process of putting out the fire in the hall fireplace. "It's blocked," he said. "Those wretched birds have built a nest on top of the chimney, I'll get up there tomorrow but I'll have to go and hire a roof ladder first, if that's alright."

"Of course, let me get you some money." Diana went down to the kitchen where she realised she had left her bag. "How easily we slip into trusting country ways." she thought. "How lovely."

When Diana arrived at the house on Saturday morning, she had brought most of her things from the hotel, anticipating spending Sunday night in the house with Simon for the first time. The house was now furnished, the rugs were all in place and the curtain maker had worked wonders to produce curtains for the drawing room, dining room and their bedroom in the time. The rest would follow later. She was planning a trip to the supermarket in the afternoon and making her shopping list, she realised she hadn't thought about Julian for a couple of days. She was happy, she was fully immersed in her new life and was really excited at the prospect of seeing Simon later the following day.

Like most French houses, *La Maison Neuve* had shutters at all the doors and windows, except the kitchen door and the kitchen windows. Diana had never used the shutters but thought the house would look odd without them. Security was not something to which she had given a lot of thought, the house was in a gated community from the road, but there was no way to protect the entire estate from the rear, the woods which belonged to the estate ran off into woods owned by others or the *Commune de Saint-Sulpice*. The villages around were relatively crime-free and the whole ambiance was one of ease and safety. When Diana went for her daily walks in the woods and around the lake, she never thought to lock up, and André had the run of the house.

However, Diana decided that she ought at least to lock the doors when she was going shopping, since André was not working on Saturday. She was just turning the key in the glass door of the kitchen hallway when she heard the gravel crunch behind her. She knew without turning that Julian would be standing there, and his reflection in the glass just confirmed her sense of his being there.

"Hello," he said. "I'm just off to Paris, do you need anything before I go?"

"No, thank you. I've actually managed quite well." She thought she sounded tart.

He smiled and leaned forward to kiss her on the cheek. "Goodbye then, we'll see each other next week."

"Simon is arriving tomorrow." She had no idea why she had said it except that she was feeling gauche, confused and flushed.

Still smiling he said, "Yes, I know. Perhaps you'll come to dinner, I'm a fair cook and then he can decide if he wants the flat. I've photos and stuff on the computer I'll email to you – let me have your email address." He produced a small notebook and waited for her to spell it out. He wrote it down and put the notebook away; he looked at her. "Good. I'll do it this evening. See you very soon."

Her previous feeling of well-being and settled emotions dissipated in an instant, to be replaced yet again by such a moment of fierce longing that it left her breathless and bewildered.

She drove to the large supermarket on the outskirts of Bergerac and spent a couple of hours filling a trolley with everything she thought she needed. Taking her shopping back to the car, she realised that she hadn't looked at her list at all and made a second trip to fill up with those things she had missed.

When she left the house that night to return to the hotel, her settled feeling returned as she locked up and found she could really look forward to the following day.

Henri was there to see her off after breakfast on Sunday and bade her an effusive farewell, giving her a bottle of champagne to share with Simon when he arrived that evening. The church bells were ringing in the two villages as the faithful made their way to services. She found herself thinking of Philippe de Lusignac as she drove through the gate, making her way down the drive to her new home, and thought it strange that she couldn't find it in her to find him as guilty as the rest of the world had judged him.

The rain had started early that morning with a strong, cool breeze and she was grateful that she had finally mastered the central heating system, with André's help. The boiler seemed rather large and complicated, housed in a room of its own just off the utility room. The oil tank was hidden in the trees to the right and some complicated system of pipes and valves ensured that it was delivered to the boiler. The house was warm, the fires drawing well now that the debris had been removed from the chimneys, and as evening drew in, Diana began to prepare their first dinner in their new home.

Simon arrived at about eight in the evening, tired and thirsty. He'd forgotten the code to the gate and had texted her when he was about half an hour away. As she texted the number she realised that she was actually thrilled at his imminent arrival and her feelings for Julian now seemed juvenile and pointless. As the lights of his car came down the driveway, she ran down the steps in the rain and joyously hugged him as he stepped out of the car. They walked in through the kitchen hallway doors, she pulled the heavy oak towards her and turned the beautiful, huge key. They were home.

****

Despite Simon's long journey, they stayed up late, talking and sipping wine in front of the fire. The meal had been simple, Diana's dislike of prepared foods was tested when faced with wonderful local pâté, and the beautiful desserts available in the local *pâtisseries*. She had settled for making a beef casserole with red wine but buying the pâté to go with crusty bread; the dessert came from Madame Bernaud's shop, showing an amazing array of cakes and desserts and home-made chocolates. Diana was forever surprised at the variety of shops and goods available in even the small villages. She bought a glazed *tarte Tatin* and ice cream.

They had talked several times a day whilst Simon had been in London, but it seemed they had so much to tell each other. The familiarity of the furnishing made Simon feel immediately at home; the warmth and soft colours of the house gave them both a sense of well-being and even excitement at being able to start this life now.

Neither of them were late risers so Diana was surprised to see it was eight o'clock when she awoke. Simon was still sleeping and she watched him for a few minutes. She felt such a strong wave of love for him and was thrilled to feel it after her emotional turmoil over Julian. She leaned across and lightly kissed his cheek. His eyes opened and he reached to cuddle her. Because Diana had had a regular job in London, sex in the morning was not something she really enjoyed. There were times she felt slightly resentful, particularly if she had already showered and was in the process of dressing, but these were the times that seemed to excite Simon. Knowing that she rarely, if ever, put him off, he would lead her back to the bed and take off her underwear. She felt sometimes that he played out some little fantasy in his mind when he was doing this, but she never asked and never refused.

This morning, though, it was Diana who wanted to make love and Simon enjoyed her taking control. They touched, teased, kissed and moved with each other's bodies. They showered together, which they hadn't done for some time. When they had dressed, Simon went down to start coffee while Diana made the bed; she straightened the curtains and looked out over the lake and the woods. Her eyes went naturally to the clearing, which although quite a long way from the house, was clearly visible now that some of the trees were losing their leaves. During their talk the previous evening, Diana had not mentioned the de Lusignac story and was not sure why.

"I love what you've done with this corner," said Simon. "Your little desk looks perfect there."

She had taken a corner of the kitchen at the foot of the staircase to the dining room as her office corner. Her small desk fitted under the window and gave her an uninterrupted view across the lawn to the lake and the woods on the hill beyond.

"Yes, I thought I'd keep all the boring stuff down here, you know, bills and household stuff, no point in taking it all upstairs to your study just to bring it all down again when it's been done."

"It's perfect," he said again. "That window seems slightly bigger than the rest."

"Yes, it's where the original back door used to be," immediately imagining de Lusignac that night, in an agitated state, coming in through that door.

"How on earth do you know that?"

"Oh, I don't know. I suppose Laurier must have told me." She was still reluctant to share the story with him but realised she would very soon have to. All the residents on the estate would be aware of some version or other of it and she wanted to be the one to tell him what she considered to be the true story. She also realised that she wanted him not to think too badly of de Lusignac, but she couldn't for one moment imagine why.

She decided quickly. "After breakfast I want you to take a walk with me, there's something I want to show you."

They were in no rush to go out, the weather was dry but blustery so there was no reason to postpone the walk. Diana was quiet on the way down the lawn, she slipped her hand through Simon's arm. "I love you," she said. He smiled at her and kissed her forehead.

André had told her that during the winter, he and the other two fellows who cut the communal grass, weeded the driveways and did other general gardening, spent time in the woods, chopping up felled trees for firewood. Any trees which had fallen over were piled into long logs awaiting being sawn into fireplace-sized logs. Some had been there for some time, she noticed, since ivy was starting to climb over the piles. "Forest fingers," she smiled to herself.

They reached the clearing, which was brighter now that some of the leaves were starting to fall. Diana had previously found a pile of stones and rubble with a flattish top on which she had sat several times, making it her own place. She beckoned Simon to sit beside her and slowly, she told Simon of the family, of the bravery, the treachery and the murder. She told him of the family history and the fire in which the grand old honour of de Lusignac had perished. She told him of the blessing of the site to ensure that de Lusignac did not meet his maker completely without grace. Finally, she told him of the legal problems faced by Angus and Laurier to obtain clear title.

Simon sat silently looking out over the water. She had no idea as to his thoughts or feelings at that point and waited for him to speak. He surprised her with his answer. "It's just history, Dee. Think of all the places at home where modern houses are built on old bloody battle scenes, not necessarily famous ones but soldiers fighting and dying one way or another. People munching hamburgers at the site of

73

numerous hangings, bankers' offices in enormous blocks, making fortunes with the bones of how many victims of some crime or other historical event underneath."

Diana was surprised at his apparent disregard for the fact that they were the first people to live in the house since the Germans left. The first since de Lusignac had been murdered, for that's how she thought of his death. Of the two of them, Simon was the more imaginative and passionate and yet he felt nothing of the drama which had unfolded in this house. She turned back to face the water, tears forming in her eyes as she thought of de Lusignac's appalling death and the fact that she appeared to be the only one who cared.

Now that she had told Simon the whole story, she did what she had always done; she took her cue from him. She looked at him and realised he had already put the whole subject aside and was making plans; she walked over to him and put her arms around his neck. "Come on," she said. "Coffee first and then I'll give you the grand tour. You're going to need a bit more furniture in your study and we have the television man coming this week, so you'll have to decide what you want where. French television will do wonders for your fluency level! The telephone engineer put all the connections where I thought they should go but you may want to make a few changes."

When they got back to the kitchen, Diana went over to her desk and logged on to her computer. "There's an email from Julian, you know, the chap who's offering you his Paris apartment. Gosh, it looks lovely. He's inviting us to dinner on Saturday to talk about it."

They looked at the photos together. From the front, the large street door had evidently once been used to drive coaches through. Now there was a much smaller door let into it. "Good start, looks like a prison door," said Simon. He moved to another photo, the interior behind the large door looked like an L-shaped hallway with a concierge's office immediately in front. "So far so very traditional, but very old fashioned, I bet it smells of onions, too!" The next photo showed the full floor-to-ceiling glass door leading out into a courtyard and the main apartment building was to the rear through to the courtyard.

The photos went through a slide show of a lovely old elevator, mahogany with an elegant wrought iron gate. Then the pictures emerged of the apartment, clearly decorated by a professional: the total effect was stunning. The photos progressed through the two bedrooms, the beautifully appointed bathroom and the kitchen and living areas.

"He's very generous to offer it to us," said Simon, "and it's perfectly placed in Neuilly. Have you talked to him about rent or such?"

"No, I haven't even said we're interested, he just sort of offered it and then was gone. In fact, I'm not sure myself why he'd want to be so helpful."

"Well, actually, it would work out quite well. I found a researcher - well, a student I suppose, who'd be very happy to spend three months in Paris helping me with the research, and with two bedrooms I wouldn't have to worry about finding accommodation. Actually it was my agent, who has a friend of a friend who would like a research job for a while, you know how it goes."

"Well, then shall we accept his dinner offer?"

Diana emailed Julian to accept his invitation and thanked him for the photos, suggesting but not confirming that Simon would like to take the apartment for a period of three to four months. She also said that there would have to be a proper business basis to the arrangement, so perhaps when they arrived for dinner on Saturday, he might have a plan worked out.

The week was one of the happiest Diana could remember. They each made parts of the house their own without having to lay down boundaries. Simon had ordered a few more pieces of furniture for his study, some filing cabinets and other pieces of office equipment. They saw the other residents from time to time, although the Wilsons had closed their house for the winter and returned to the UK.

Margaret Grey was becoming a friend to both of them, spending the odd evening with a glass of wine in the kitchen whilst Diana prepared the evening meal. Diana had met Margaret's sister, Jennifer, in the driveway once. Jennifer was younger than Margaret and much prettier, but she had the sort of attractiveness which one found lovely whilst actually looking at the face, but the instant the face was no longer there, its details were hard to recall. "Just like all those blonde so-called celebrities," Simon had said. "They all look the same to me." Next to Margaret, Jennifer seemed bland and only seemed at all animated when talking about their horses and the equestrian events they were involved with.

Of Julian they had seen nothing, even though Diana had ended her email with an invitation to drop round at any time. Véronique and Francine had been for coffee one morning and Simon was enchanted with the little French lady. He enjoyed her quick wit and easy repartee, and even Francine seemed to be more relaxed with Diana.

Diana had invited the Findlays at the same time as Francine and her mother, thinking that Hilary's ebullience would be diluted a little in company. They learned that 'Bobby', as she called him, was a retired vascular surgeon. He had retired quite early due to rapidly developing arthritis. Apparently he had been very good in his field in his day and had published several papers. He adored Hilary and seemed oblivious to her annoyingly disjointed conversation. Diana put it down to nerves because on a one-to-one basis, she seemed calmer and more intelligent.

Neither did they see anything at all of John and Eleanor Porton-Watts, although Diana saw their car disappearing out of the drive on the odd occasion. She had told Simon what she knew of their situation. "It must be so hard for them to have been born and raised into such status and then lose it all."

"Hardly *all*, Dee, you couldn't buy one of these houses on this estate if you were completely on your uppers," said Simon.

"No, but *comparatively* speaking, they *are* on their uppers. This is nothing like what they're used to, it would be like our losing Holland Park Avenue and moving into a two-bedroomed high-rise. Don't you feel guilty sometimes that we've had everything so easy? This house is the biggest risk we've ever taken and even that has worked out beautifully."

"No, I don't feel guilty in the least. Thankful, happy, privileged, but never guilty."

On the day they were invited to Julian's house for dinner, Diana and Simon decided to drive to Périgueux in the morning to do some supermarket shopping and to look around the beautiful old town. Diana had wanted to go walking in the little narrow streets and explore some of the shops tucked away down in the side streets. The weather was fine but threatened rain; nevertheless, some of the cafés had their little tables and umbrellas outside. The shops were a delight; they found a wine shop next to a delicatessen whose aromas of salamis and cheeses drew them in. They bought a bottle of Billecart-Salmon champagne to take to Julian in the evening, and a bottle of an exceptional vintage which they planned to keep and use to celebrate the publication of Simon's new book.

They chose one of the cafés in a little square to have a light lunch before heading back to *La Chênaie*. "I'd love to change the name of the house," said Simon. "My French isn't brilliant but *La Maison Neuve* seems just a bit parochial, don't you think?" Simon had chosen the soup of the day, a heavy vegetable soup it turned out, with bread and cheese. Diana had opted for an *omelette aux fines herbes* and salad. She had finished her meal and was idly watching

Simon finish his when his comment came out of nowhere, it seemed.

She laughed, "Actually, I didn't like it at all at first, but quite honestly, I can't imagine it being called anything else, particularly now that I know its history. It seems sort of fitting now – after all, it is a new beginning for the place. The New House. Yes. I like it, I do."

As she looked around her while they finished their coffee in a companionable silence, she saw John Porton-Watts walking into the square, arm in arm with another man: a little younger, it seemed, and talking animatedly to John. He hadn't noticed Diana and he hadn't yet met Simon, but some instinct made her turn her head and reach down into her bag as John walked past with his companion.

She didn't see the need to mention this sighting to Simon, it felt inconsequential and she actually had no idea of the relationship between the two men, but they did seem very comfortable with one another.

It started to rain heavily on the way home, a drive of about an hour. By the time they drove up outside *La Maison Neuve* it was quite dark, even though it was only four in the afternoon. Diana noticed that the Porton-Watts house was in darkness and wondered where Eleanor might be, but in the comfort of her warm kitchen she thought no more about it. The lake looked dark purple in the evening light and she realised that she missed having her afternoon walk. Simon had found her fascination with the clearing slightly macabre and was now accompanying her on walks sometimes to change direction, and they even walked all around the lake to explore the woods on the far side.

While she was showering before going out to dinner, she realised happily that Julian had not invaded her thoughts at all since Simon had arrived. She had been happy, busy and productive. She was thrilled that Simon had said no more about leaving very soon, but no doubt this was something they would talk about once it was decided whether or not he would take Julian's apartment.

It had been an unwritten, unspoken rule between them that neither checked the other's telephone for messages, nor each other's email. It had developed at the beginning of their marriage when Simon had wanted a pen from her handbag and had brought it to her for her to reach inside. It was an element of trust lacking in many of their friends' marriages and partnerships. By the same token, Diana would never open Simon's briefcase, nor riffle through the papers on his desk. It was lovely, Diana thought. Margaret had told her that it wasn't trust, it was complacency, but nevertheless, it was a vestige of privacy in their marriage which they both cherished. It would never have occurred to Diana that Simon had anything to hide, and vice versa.

During the week that Simon had been at *La Maison Neuve*, he had received many phone calls on his mobile but none on the land-line. He made no explanation and Diana asked for none. He had his own banking arrangements to organise and their UK accountant handled their affairs separately. Simon's tax affairs had been quite complicated at one time, he set up his own company to do the television programmes and the proceeds from his book still trickled in. They now had an income from the Holland Park Avenue House too. Diana was thinking of talking to Francine Cooke to see if she was able to advise on French tax matters, but for the time being they had used the services of a French *advocat* to draw up French wills and community property documents.

Simon was just finishing a phone call when he wandered into the dressing room. It was basically her room, although with fitted wardrobes on both sides, Simon's clothes were stored in there also. Both sides of the room had mirrored doors which reflected light from the two large windows. She had put her dressing table under one of the windows; in front of the other window there were two small upholstered armchairs with a table, lit by a porcelain lamp. Diana used the en-suite bathroom of this room as her own, leaving their bedroom en-suite for Simon. She was sitting at her dressing table, putting her hair up into a chignon, taking pins one at a time from her mouth, she looked at Simon and said, "What is it?"

"Oh, just Edwards, he wants to know when I can make a start; he loves my ideas for a sequel. Listen, Dee, if this chap is serious about letting me have this apartment, I think I'll leave next week. The researcher can join me a week later and we'll make a start."

Although she had known that this had always been the plan, she nevertheless felt a sharp shard of disappointment that it would come to pass so soon. Her lifetime habit of fitting in with Simon's plans and schemes rose to stop her from protesting too much. "Oh darling! We've had such a lovely week. Yes, I know, you really do need to get started but I'm sorry it's come so soon."

"I'll try to come down every weekend, Dee, but I'll probably come and go by train. The train service is superb and where on earth would I park a car in Paris?"

She slipped on a black jersey dress with a cross-over bodice, and reached for her gold pebble necklace. As she fastened her gold and pearl earrings she said, "Well, hadn't we better wait and see what conditions Julian will want to put on the deal first? Are you ready? We've time for a quiet drink together before we go, if you like."

"By the way, you look stunning," said Simon, meaning it.

****

It was still raining hard when they walked over to Julian's house. They wore raincoats and Diana wore wellingtons, carrying her shoes in her raincoat pocket. As Julian opened the door to them, he smiled at her footwear. She had bought the only wellingtons she could find in the general store in her size, a vibrant pattern in many colours. She had brought a pair of gold ballerina shoes with her; she occasionally wore heels when she went to restaurants but had a dislike of stabbing carpets and parquet with stilettos. As Julian took her coat, he pushed a hairpin back into place which had come loose at the back of her neck. The touch of his hand gave her such a jolt; she looked at Simon to see if he had noticed her flushed face.

She had hoped that the emotions Julian had raised in her before were a thing of the past, but she knew with absolute certainty that he had found something in her which Simon had never touched, much as she had loved him and loved him still. In one moment, the knowledge came to her that Julian was now a threat. He had the power to jeopardise everything she held dear; she knew that he would be an ever-present danger to her resolve.

She excused herself and went into the cloakroom to compose herself.

The hallway was identical to the Cooke's house except in reverse; the staircase was on the right instead of the left, as was the kitchen. But the interior couldn't be more different. She had expected comfortable chintz-covered furniture and a lifetime's collection of china ornaments, photographs of family and even perhaps a piano. In reality, the floors were a sea of very pale blue carpet, two pictures hung on the hall wall with picture lights accentuating the subjects; one was a garden full of colour with the closest dahlias dripping with dew, but the garden went off to the horizon in a blaze of reds, yellows, oranges and green foliage. The clever positioning of this large picture against an off-white wall, with not a single other thing on the wall stunned her. The almost 3D effect was arresting.

The other picture was a landscape, a river to which the artist had given sparkle and movement, the river came towards the viewer and left him standing in the middle. The river was banked by fields and just going out of the picture on the right was a stone-built house. But the clever part of this picture was that it reflected a glittering frosty morning with a watery sun, which must be almost impossible for an artist to achieve, she thought. This picture was also placed alone on a wall and lit from above, making the frost seem tangible.

After the initial awkward moments, of introductions and foot-wiping, coat-handing and umbrella-stacking, they went into the drawing room. The simplicity of the interior might have looked cold but was relieved by clever, warm lighting. The pale blue carpet went all through the house and all the interior doors were made of bevelled glass panes, so the impression was one of unbroken luxury. Where Véronique's drawing room had a door leading out to the patio, Julian had removed the glass wall and built on a beautiful conservatory without a dividing door, and since the conservatory then just became part of the drawing room, the carpet continued out into this extension. The whole effect was very elegant but comfortable at the same time.

The table sparkled with candle-light, which picked up the crystal edges of the bevelling and was reflected in all the glass of the windows. Despite the elegance and comfort, Diana felt ill at ease. Never in her entire marriage had she ever been so attracted physically to another man; there had been friends and acquaintances who flirted with her and she enjoyed the company of men, but this was entirely different. It wasn't just physical longing, she wanted to know everything about him. This was so new to her she didn't know how to describe it, but in any case, she didn't welcome it.

She watched the two men becoming acquainted and exchanging first-meeting small-talk, Julian was about fourteen or fifteen years older than Simon, but she really wasn't sure. They were of similar height, but Simon was of a larger build, though not fat, whereas Julian was really slim.

"Darling, I was just saying how lovely the apartment in Paris is, and it's really so very kind of Julian to offer it. He's got a whole file of stuff he'll let me have, you know, where everything is, local shops etc. I told him we know Neuilly quite well; in fact, I was living there when we met." Simon had opened his arm to beckon her in. She joined him and he dropped his arm onto her shoulder.

"Well, it's yours if you want it. Please don't embarrass me by offering money for rent, I was just telling Simon that it's empty most of the time."

"But you go up there from time to time, surely. You've just got back, haven't you?" Diana was feeling more at ease in talking to him directly now, having taken control of her feelings.

"Actually, I haven't stayed there for some time, I have been staying elsewhere."

The shock of the stab of jealousy took her breath away and she felt sick.

Julian looked at her as if he understood everything about her. He smiled but had no intention of elucidating further and said, "Let's go in for dinner. By the way, Diana, Laurier has left two boxes here, he came this morning but realised you were out. He said he should have called first but he was coming here anyway, the Wilsons wanted him to arrange something to do with their swimming pool."

"Boxes?" asked Simon.

"Oh, I just asked if they found anything from the house's history when they developed the place, anything that anyone had found. It was just curiosity, but he said there were a couple of boxes in the attics or somewhere – they're probably just old household bills and things of no interest, but Jean Claude said I could have them."

As they sat down, Julian placed medium-sized vol-au-vents in front of them, stuffed with seafood in a very light sauce which, she discovered, was sorrel. There followed a venison casserole with cranberries, baked potatoes and green beans. Instead of the French tradition of serving salad, then cheese, and then dessert, he served a grapefruit sorbet. "Cleans the palate after venison," he said, and put out a platter of fresh fruit and a cheese board with four local cheeses laid out on top of fern leaves.

Simon's telephone rang and Diana gave him a look of annoyance. As he took the phone out of his pocket to silence it, he looked at the caller and refused the call. Julian was serving coffee when Simon excused himself to go to the bathroom. Diana got up and went over to the bookshelf to peer at the titles. She felt Julian very close behind her and said, "Don't. Please don't, Julian. Please, please don't."

"I promise I'll do nothing to hurt you. But if the day ever comes when you need me, I'll always be here for you. And you know why."

"You think you feel that way now but you can't ... I have to ... I love Simon. I can't do what you want, you're making me unhappy." She was fighting tears, strong emotion became a fight for her marriage and now that the words had been spoken, she knew of the depth of his feelings for her.

They heard the cloakroom door close and Julian went out into the hall, spoke a few words to Simon and went upstairs.

"He's gone to get your boxes. Are you OK, you look a bit odd? God, that was an amazing meal. Did you know he was the Lawson of the Lawson Garden Centres? You know, there was one near my parents' house in Surrey? I suppose these must be his children," pointing to a framed photo of a woman with two teenage children.

Julian had never mentioned children, but when she thought about it, they had never spoken much about anything. Everything to do with their relationship up until now, she realised, had been on a recognition of mutual strong attraction.

Recognition. She understood now that Julian had read her completely. Just as she had known that he had wanted to touch her when he had been standing behind her.

"Are these your children?" Simon asked as Julian came back into the room with two boxes slightly larger than shoe boxes.

"My step-children" he replied "Edwina had been married before and her husband died just after Josh was born, in fact he never saw Josh – he was killed in a car crash on his way down to the hospital. I adopted them when Edwina and I got married four years later. Phoebe is two years older than Josh and I suppose I'm the only father either of them have ever known – and of course, with that comes the problems that other fathers have too." He smiled sadly but said, "Josh is married and works for the company that bought my company. He's done very well and comes to see me from time to time. Phoebe has not been happy, I'm ashamed to say."

"Ashamed? Why ashamed?" said Diana.

"Because when a child is unhappy, and remains unhappy, the parents always feel guilty. When Edwina died, I thought the news would drive Phoebe to do something rash. I tried to bring her here but she wouldn't come. Josh tried to help her but she set herself on a course of self-destruction that neither of us could control. I managed to persuade her to see a doctor who was a friend of a friend; he diagnosed bi-polar disease. It's made an enormous difference. She lives in a sort of halfway house, looked after but not managed, freedom but not free, medicated but not drugged. She's happier now than I have ever seen her. She's a brilliant artist – the picture in the front hall of the dahlias is one of hers."

"It's absolutely stunning," exclaimed Diana, meaning it. "I think it's brilliant, I couldn't take my eyes off it when we came in."

"Then it will surprise you to know that the one opposite is also one of hers. Totally different in style, colour, emphasis and emotion. It's calm, peaceful and happy, the other is riotous, confused and blatant. But lovely just the same, I think."

Simon collected the boxes and they started the leaving process, putting on coats and boots and Julian leaned over to kiss Diana lightly on both cheeks. He moved from one cheek to the other, slowly pausing in front of her mouth just for a second. Simon was patting his pockets and leaning down to collect the umbrella from the stand, so had seen nothing, but Diana felt guilty just the same.

****

Simon spent most of Sunday organising his things to leave for Paris the next day. The researcher would be arriving later in the evening and they would start the serious research for Simon's new book. Chris, it appeared, was a student of French history from the post-Revolution period and was well acquainted with the records offices, archives and other depositories and would make an excellent researcher.

Simon had planned to return every weekend, but as he pointed out to Diana, the sooner the research was collected and annotated, the sooner he could return to *La Maison Neuve* to actually do the writing. He therefore now decided that he would probably stay a month in Paris to really break the back of the initial research. He would then come down for at least a week to work on a whiteboard to plot his characters and sequence of events. He would then return to Paris and stay for a further few weeks to see if he could progress with the research to the point where he was ready to write.

Diana had been uncharacteristically snappy and irritable with Simon, which although he noticed, he decided to ignore it, putting it down to the fact that she really wasn't happy at his leaving so soon. Diana, contrite and guilty, was trying to bring back the easy atmosphere between them.

"Have you got everything? You'd better take that other bag if you're not coming home for a month. Do you remember the group of shops just off Avenue Victor Hugo? It was just like a village, I loved it. Anyway, there used to be a laundry and dry cleaners there, you two men won't want to be doing washing and ironing and you can't leave Julian's linen in a state," she laughed, feeling everything had gone back to an amiable state between them.

They shared a bottle of wine over lunch in the kitchen of roast chicken and salad. They had lit the fire in the drawing room and took their coffee up there. Simon poured an Armagnac for both of them and they settled to read and talk comfortably. Diana was sure now that Julian presented no challenge to her peace of mind, being here alone for a month. Her feelings for Julian were definitely wrong. Simon mattered, and as they made love on that last evening together, she tried to show him how much she loved and cared for him. He left just after breakfast the following morning, she waved him off and went back into her wonderful and now familiar kitchen.

The weather had turned fine again, a beautiful autumn promised and the fresh morning air was flavoured with the smell of wood smoke. The gardeners were beginning to burn leaves and most people had started lighting fires in the previous week when the cold, wet snap had passed through. Geese and ducks were landing on the lake in large numbers for a day or two and then were gone, seeking protection from the oncoming winter by flying who knows where, Diana thought as she held her coffee, watching the awkward landings and loud take-offs.

The boxes that Laurier had given her contained, as he had predicted, little of interest. The boxes themselves were very tattered, cloth-covered box files with the faded German army symbols on the front, barely visible. The papers were mostly receipts and payment slips for work done on the estate but there was one thing which caught her interest; a small notebook with notations in good script followed by dates and figures. The title page of the notebook had the initials, 'P.H.B. London.'

Diana thought that the initials must refer to a person, a company or a place. She sat at her desk and doodled the initials on the pad. London was obviously London in England. The amounts of money could be deposits or payments, but on the third page she found that the sums had been added up, which coincided with the end of a month. Suddenly, the doodling of the last initial became 'Bank' and she realised it was the Pelling Hancock Bank, a private merchant bank in London, still operating today.

Diana was stunned to realise that this was probably de Lusignac's personal account book for the amount being deposited to his account in London for the loans he arranged for the Resistance. How on earth had this book survived? It's true it was fairly nondescript but if it had been found in the house, wouldn't the Germans have known he was working for the Resistance? She turned the little book over and over in her hand, no sensible answer would come to her. Although, apart from the initials, there was little to indicate that this book was anything other than a personal ledger of some kind.

There were a dozen or so photographs, one of a lumpish sort of girl with her hair in pigtails, an older couple, a group photo taken by the lake which was obviously a hunting party, and one of the couple with the then much younger girl, taken on a different day. Although there was nothing to justify her hope of something which would somehow exonerate de Lusignac, she held the little notebook to her as if the man himself had handed it to her.

She suddenly sat up straight "Good God, what happened to the money?" If de Lusignac was killed during the war, and the property in France was left to decay, did anyone ever know about the money, and if they did, did anyone ever find it? She doubted if the bank would even tell her, but she sat down to write nevertheless, explaining the circumstances.

She realised that the letter had gone over six pages. She emailed the letter and put the original in an envelope to post the following morning.

André's friend's sister had started work at the house on Wednesday, she would clean and do some ironing and would come in three mornings a week. Her name was Celeste Lamy and Diana wondered if there was a connection with the Juliette Lamy, who had reported de Lusignac to the Resistance. In this part of France, there were still extended families living close to each other, so in all probability there was a relationship but Diana was reluctant to ask. Celeste was in her forties, with a large bust and large hips but Diana was amazed at her agility and speed when climbing the stairs. She seemed to glide but at a speed many people of fewer years would envy. She was divorced, with a son of twenty who was studying medicine at Bordeaux University, a fact of which she was immensely proud and for which she had had to make huge financial sacrifices.

Celeste had quickly become the mistress of the house-cleaning routine. She was an assertive woman without being disrespectful and would never have *'tutoyer'* Diana, the familiar form of address. At the same time, she was friendly and, to Diana's shamed-faced enjoyment, a gossip. Celeste also worked for the Porton-Watts, but was not permitted in the house in the mornings. Coffee was taken in the kitchen and although Diana joined her, Celeste would never permit Madame to make the coffee. Diana enjoyed these breaks and over a short period of time she learned more about her neighbours than perhaps they would have been comfortable with.

The Porton-Watts, she learned, had separate bedrooms. Madame Watts would spend many days in her room and never went shopping. To Celeste this was tantamount to sin, allowing her husband to shop, cook and generally run the house when clearly, she wasn't ill. John Porton-Watts went to Périgueux twice a week, since he preferred the market there. Diana recalled having seen him with another man and wondered if shopping was the true reason for his trips but she kept silent on that point. They had a son from whom they were estranged.

Diana never understood a child being distanced from a parent. Her own beloved mother, Emily, had been, until she met Simon, the most cherished person in her life.

Celeste told her that Julian had a woman in Paris, that the Findlays enjoyed nude sunbathing and that Francine Cooke wanted to change sex. She didn't like the Wilsons and was glad that they had gone for the winter. "He never used to speak as he passed," as if this was possibly the worst crime she could accuse him of. She tried hard to imagine the Findlays nude sunbathing and enjoyed the image it conjured. As for Francine, how on earth would Celeste know a thing like that? "Because my cousin's girl is a receptionist at the surgery and she swears she heard it being discussed!" So Diana felt she could fairly safely discount any such notion. And of course, the Grey sisters weren't really sisters, they were − you know − women who liked women. She discounted this also.

"I wonder what she says about me?" Diana muttered under her breath as Celeste picked up her bucket of cleaning items and left the kitchen. And did Julian have a woman in Paris? And did she care? Yes, she did. She minded and she didn't like minding.

Diana did once broach the subject of de Lusignac. Celeste gave a sigh and said, "Madame, there are still families who are split because of the war. There were some people who used the Germans to settled old scores and grievances. People were taken away because of words dropped in the ears of one or another German soldier on nothing more than information given by someone with an axe to grind. It really hurt to listen to people afterwards saying that the French were a nation of *corbeaux.*"

"*Corbeaux*?" said Diana "Crows? Strange, how did that name come about?"

"I'm not sure Madame. But that's what informers were called, and it's what we became known for."

"And de Lusignac? Was he considered a traitor just because he lived here with the Germans?"

"No, Madame. Before the war, the family had a very good name, and they were well liked and respected but they had never lived as everyone else. They found it very hard to give up this big house and move to the lodge with just Aimée to look after them. But they still lived better than most."

"And that was enough to condemn him?"

Celeste bristled and Diana thought she had gone too far. "No, Madame, of course not! People don't talk much about what happened, but as far as I know, something terrible took place and he was taken by the Resistance for questioning. They say he admitted it. That's all I know." Celeste had picked up the coffee cups and put an end to the conversation.

Diana's relationship with Margaret had developed into an easy, undemanding friendship of genuine affection. She told Diana that Jennifer, Margaret's sister, had taken up with the French stable hand, a man fifteen years younger than herself and which was why she was rarely seen at *La Chênaie*. They were living in a small cottage at the stables and Margaret had decided that the wisest course of action was to let the relationship run its course, as it surely would. Margaret had control of the finances and whatever picture this chap had of a financially comfortable future with an older woman, Margaret was intent on painting a different one. But for the moment, Jennifer could have her man. "She's hopeless," Margaret said. "But then, what do I know? My judgement of men has left me, before now, bruised, battered, heartbroken and almost flat broke. No, whilst she's getting whatever it is she wants from him, good for her, I'm always around when her heart is broken and the pieces need mending! And I keep the cheque book!"

****

91

The first two weeks of Simon's absence went surprisingly quickly. Diana had always been afraid of the dark, but night lights in the bedroom, hallways and stairs gave a comforting light and she found she could sleep peacefully. Before closing the curtains in her dressing room each evening, she looked at the houses up the drive. The Porton-Watts house always seemed to be in near-darkness, just the flickering of a television or computer screen in the upper room. The Wilsons' house was completely dark since they had left for the UK. The two houses at the top of the drive were almost out of sight, but the brightness on the driveway indicated people still up and having conversations. She felt lonely. And then there was the nearest house. Julian's house. Every night when she went to bed, his lights were on. Occasionally she could see him moving across a window and once, he stopped at the upstairs window and she imagined him looking out at her in her window.

She talked to Simon several times a day and his research was going wonderfully well. He'd planned a trip to Aix-en-Provence and on to Nice, but his plans were still rather fluid, so he'd let her know. She had stopped herself from asking if she could join him. It would seem like defeat; this house had not been her idea at the outset, but it became her obsession in the end. Asking to join him now would be admitting that it didn't fulfil her, and it really did. Simon was imagining her busy all day, shopping in the village, cooking for the freezer, walking in her treasured woods and having supper with neighbours from time to time.

And he'd be right, she was doing all those things and the time was passing quickly, it was true. But she missed him.

Since hunting was now banned in the woods, animals had started to reappear. She had seen deer and judging from the state of the turf on the lawn, there were probably wild boar in the woods also. She had started a plan in her mind for the boat-house. She could see a small lodge with a jetty, just enough to keep some easy chairs, a fridge for some cold drinks and a small rowing boat – no motors on this lake. She walked all around the lake to find the water inlets and discovered that there were two, plus a fairly large outlet which at some time, someone had covered with a grille, leaving her to wonder if there were fish in the lake. A small duck island was attached by a rope to the old jetty, all of which was in need of repair.

Behind the boathouse was a stand of very tall pine trees, the stand itself must have been quite extensive at one time, but there were many fallen trees in between. She was childishly excited to discover the size of the pine cones which had fallen either from the standing trees or the toppled ones.

She picked up four or five and decided to come back with several bags. She was thinking that they would make a magnificent garland at Christmas for the big fireplace in the drawing room. She held one close to her nose and sat down on the nearest pile of logs. The sun was warming the ground now and the autumn smells of mushrooms, composted leaves and wood smoke were all around. She spent half an hour collecting the beautiful big pine cones and put them on the floor of the old boat shed. Half of the roof was missing but there was one corner, which gave enough protection until she could return with bags.

She laughed at her actions. "They've been outside for years," she thought. "They're not going to come to any harm for the next few days." But she wanted to protect them in any case. She collected a few more and put them on top.

The floorboards were all loose and many were rotten; her foot caught the edge of one, which crumbled. She was wearing her multi-coloured wellies but it had hurt just the same. She kicked off her boot and bent to rub her foot. The corner of an old tin stood up through the gap and she picked it up. It was about eight inches by eight inches and about five inches deep, much bigger than it had looked sticking out of the hole.

Diana had no idea how long she stood, one boot on and one off with the tin in her hand. Her heart was pounding and she could feel the pressure of it in her ears. The box was rusty but remnants of paint remained and she could see it was the box of a child's jigsaw puzzle. The box had not arrived there by accident; it had been placed beneath the floorboards. This much Diana understood in a second. She went back outside; the afternoon sun was losing its warmth and evening would be soon upon her. She found the pile of logs and slowly opened the box.

The first thing Diana saw was a bundle made of some sort of oilcloth with a pattern, an old kitchen table cover perhaps. As she opened the bundle, she saw a letter on top, underneath which was a silver-backed comb, a paper envelope with a dried butterfly which had long since crumbled, a German uniform insignia – she wasn't sure which - a small pocket book of German poetry and another group of letters.

Diana carefully opened the letter which had been on top. It was written in Germanic handwriting but in French: although the French was not good, the gist was clear. Diana sat, trying to take in the implication contained in the letter. "Oh my God! My God!" Her eyes filled with tears. "They murdered the wrong man."

****

Diana had no recollection of how long she had been sitting on the logs. She had left for her walk in early afternoon, but already dusk had fallen and even now was pulling the dark after it. She heard her name being called from across the water and saw two torch beams. Her immediate reaction was to hide the tin, but she couldn't bear to leave it behind. She was wearing her Schoffel jacket, the pockets weren't big enough to take the tin but she slid it under her arm beneath the jacket, hoping that she would be able to return to the house without having to show it to anyone. She had absolutely no idea as to why this was her reaction.

"DIANA!" she heard again.

"I'm here! Stay put and I'll come to you." She kept to the lake's edge as she made her way over to the two searchers: Margaret and behind her came Julian.

"Oh God, Diana, we thought something had happened to you. What on earth are you doing out here in the dark? You look frozen. Simon has been calling and calling you and when he couldn't get an answer, he rang me to see if you were with me. I said I'd go over to the house, but it was all in darkness, your car was outside and I was so worried." Margaret's concern was now giving way to relief, which in its turn was turning to annoyance. "I banged on Julian's door to get him to come with me in case we had to carry you or something, you daft bat."

Julian had been silent through Margaret's remonstrance but now said, "I think you ought to call Simon right away, where's your phone?"

"I don't bring the phone when I come out in the woods, it disturbs the wildlife and frankly, disturbs me too. Nothing can be so urgent that it can't wait an hour or two, can it?"

Julian insistently handed her his own phone and she dialled Simon's number as they were walking back to the house, keeping the tin box wedged under her arm inside her jacket. She really didn't want to have this conversation in front of Margaret and Julian, feeling like a recalcitrant child about to be upbraided by a stern parent.

"Hello, darling, I'm fine, I was just out and about and didn't have my phone, but all's well, don't worry. I'm just going to give Margaret and Julian a drink then I'll call you later. No, really. Yes, of course. Sorry for the flap. 'Bye, darling."

She handed the phone back to Julian and said, "You two have been awfully good, and I'm so sorry to worry everyone. It's just that I found - um - the most amazing pine cones and sort of lost myself collecting them. Wait till you see them, they are just like Christmas trees with little droopy points. I've plans to do something with them for Christmas."

Diana realised she was waffling. She wanted to be alone but her manners simply wouldn't permit her to leave the other two and walk off home. As they passed the edge of the woods and came to the lawn, Diana gasped. "God, I've never seen the house from this angle, at this time of night, all lit up. Isn't it just lovely?" she stood still and thought just how perfect it was. "Thank you for putting on the lights, it looks so marvellous."

"Well, we had to light up every room to make sure you weren't lying dead on the floor somewhere," said Margaret putting her arm through Diana's. "Silly cow, you worried us half to death, poor Julian was sure he was looking for a corpse." Diana had the box tucked under her right arm, Margaret had grasped her left. It was only later Diana realised that she was actually hiding this find from her friend and the man who seemed to be part of her life.

They went in by the lawn, through the patio to the back kitchen door. As she passed her desk, Diana slid out of her coat, keeping the tin out of sight and excusing herself, went to the cloakroom, saying over her shoulder as she went, "Margaret, get some glasses out and I'll pour us a drink in a second." She stowed the box in the console in the hall and returned to be grateful. "I really do thank you both, you've been so good and I'm sorry to scare you like that. Now shall we stay here in the kitchen, it's warm since we lit the range and there's no fire upstairs?"

"I prefer kitchens in any case," said Margaret. "I'm usually in these togs anyway," pointing to her riding boots and breeches.

Julian had been very quiet during the walk back whilst Diana and Margaret chattered in the easy manner of two friends, of whom neither put on an act for the other. Diana was aware that he watched her from time to time, but not in a predatory way and he certainly hadn't become a stalker. She had barely seen him for the past three weeks and when she had, he had been very proper, but casually friendly. The three talked for about an hour, then Julian stood up and said he would leave. Diana didn't try to stop him and Margaret hadn't finished her drink.

"Don't come to the door," he said, taking his coat from the back of the chair. "You two stay put." He leaned over and kissed Margaret on each cheek and then prepared to do the same to Diana, but after the second cheek, his arm slid around her shoulders and gave her a squeeze, then he looked at her intently and said, "I agree with Margaret, you *are* a daft bat!"

After Julian had gone, Margaret said, "Well, any thought I might have had of having any chance at all with Julian has just gone out of the window."

"What?"

"God, Diana. Don't tell me you haven't noticed. You really can't be that dim. He was absolutely distraught when I came to his door to come with me to look for you. He's a man in love. More than that. He's a man in love and devoted. To you." Margaret had said this without the slightest edge of malice.

"Alright. Perhaps you're right, I did notice. Here's the thing. My life with Simon is all I want, it's all I have ever wanted and I'm terrified of anything that might threaten it. And you're right, of course. The first time I met Julian, he was watching me across the room. We were at Hilary's, you weren't there. I was staying in the hotel and Hilary had asked a few people to come and met us, although Simon wasn't there either. We didn't hit it off very well at the start, but we got over that. There was a moment or two when I was in danger of forgetting the important things in my life, there really was." Diana took another drink from her glass of wine. "I had all those awful feelings you got when a boy kissed you for the first time, or held your hand for the first time."

"It's been so long, I can't remember," laughed Margaret. "Actually, that's not strictly true, and in Jennifer's case, I suspect she's overdone the sensation. So, duty and honour called you back into line and Julian is left with unresolved - um - what's it called? Oh yes, unresolved sexual tension!"

Talking to Margaret was like being sixteen again, with a 'best friend' with whom one shared everything. But not everything in this case. Diana hadn't mentioned the tin box.

After Margaret had left, Diana locked up and took the box upstairs. As she went round closing curtains upstairs, she stood at the window of her dressing room and saw the outline of Julian in his upstairs window. "He's watching for me," she thought. She didn't find the thought creepy or unsettling, she actually found it reassuring and almost raised her hand, but didn't.

She closed the curtains and sat in the armchair. As she opened the box again, she spread out the piece of oilcloth. It was dry and cracked but had done a reasonable job of protecting its contents. She reread the contents and then knew what she must do.

****

"Jean Claude? Thank you for calling me back." Diana had phoned the Périgueux office to ask for Laurier promptly at 9am. He was out showing a client a property but called her back within the hour. "There's something I need you to do, can I buy you lunch?"

They met at a rather smart little restaurant where Jean Claude was known not far from his office. She declined wine since she was driving.

They both ordered goat's cheese salad to start and *sole meunière* to follow.

"There's something I want to ask you before the main reason for wanting to see you today."

"OK, now I'm curious," he laughed.

"Where were the two boxes found, you know the two you gave me?"

"Actually, the two boxes were apparently German document boxes, or so it seemed, so I imagine they got left behind when the Germans left the house. They'd had a good effort at burning everything, including their desks and chairs. Perhaps no-one bothered much with them because there were only photos and receipts from the estate. They had much more pressing disposal matters to attend to. Don't know for sure, but they weren't hidden really, just stuffed up there with piles of old German first aid manuals, piles of requisition forms, boxes and boxes of torn up sheets most of which were rotten, some bird cages and all kinds of absolute junk. So, I can't really answer you for sure. Now, what did you want to ask me?"

He sat speechless when she had finished telling him what she had found in the boat shed and why she needed his help.

He shook his head. "Diana, this is a mistake. Think about what you are doing."

"I've thought about nothing else all night. I know it's the right thing to do. Will you help?"

Jean Claude was clearly unhappy at her request but she argued gently with him until he said, "I don't promise anything, but let me make a few phone calls."

Having made a decision, she drove home feeling happy and excited. As she picked up her mail, she noticed there was a letter from Pelling Hancock. It was a very nice letter but firmly refused to divulge any information whatsoever about whether or not there was an account held in the name of de

Lusignac. However, if she had any information she could share with them, they would be grateful.

"So, I was right, it *was* his bank account," she thought. Now she knew that her decision to ask Jean Claude for help was the right one.

She was greatly surprised and very happy to receive his phone call the following morning, giving her the information she had been seeking.

It would take four to five hours to drive to Lourdes, but the problem she had was trying to come up with a reason why she wanted to be away overnight. She wasn't worried about Margaret or Julian, she would simply say she was visiting a friend, but Simon was a different matter. His own research was going well, although he gave little detail: but it was quite intense, he had told her. It would probably take another two months or so. In the end, she told him that she was going to a manufacturer that specialised in glass chandeliers to find a different one for their bedroom, which she didn't care for, and another for the dining room.

Simon seemed perfectly happy with this explanation, in fact he didn't enquire as to where exactly she was going.

Diana had called in on Margaret to say she was leaving in the morning to visit a friend. Margaret seemed to think it a brilliant idea since Diana had been alone for nearly a month now. A change of scene and a chat with an old chum was just what she required.

****

The drive was just lovely. The sun was out but slightly overcast and her first sight of the Pyrenees was breath-taking. As she got closer, she was filled with a feeling of well-being which she took as a good sign. She missed the road she was looking for and ended up in the middle of Lourdes. "If this town was known for nothing else it would be the number of shops selling religious items," she said out loud, but everyone knew this town was famous for miracles. Another sign: she smiled. She doubled back and found the right road, leading to a leafy suburb, which petered out into open country. She found the address without any further trouble and drove through the open gate.

A lady in what she took to be a matron's uniform, listened as Diana asked for the person she had come to see. She waited whilst Matron went along a corridor and knocked on a door. Diana couldn't hear what was said, but a minute later, Matron stood in the doorway of the room and beckoned her forward. She stood back as Diana went in.

A frail old woman, who must be in her eighties, sat in an armchair by a large window. Over the top of her brown cardigan she wore a large crucifix. A plaid blanket covered her legs and her head was covered in thin, wispy grey hair, cut short.

"I knew someone would come one day." She held out her hand to Diana. "I'm Sister Marie Agnes."

"Sophie," said Diana, taking the hand carefully, aware of the painful arthritis crippling it. "Sophie de Lusignac. I'm so pleased to have found you."

Diana had brought the tin box and its contents in her holdall, and not sure how to continue, to reached into the bag and brought it out. She placed it in the woman's lap, who put both hands over the top and let the tears fall down her cheeks.

"Sister, you know why I've come?" The old woman nodded slowly. "Your father was innocent, wasn't he? It was you who told the Germans about the escape that night."

"Yes, it was me. My father confessed because *he* thought it was me. He couldn't ever have been absolutely sure, but he was sure enough that he gave his life for me."

"Will you tell me? Will you tell me how it all came about? Somehow, since I heard the story, I have always known that he wasn't a traitor. My husband thinks I'm haunted by it, but now I see there was a reason. Would you say it's God's purpose for me, sister?" Diana smiled kindly.

"Everything is ordained by God, child. Everything. The story is not a fairy tale, you know. It's haunted me all my life. I have never known if I did the right thing by concealing it, but I did and my reasons you may find valid or not. I have prayed and it seems that God now wants me to tell you. I shall. Please try not to judge me, God will do that."

"Sister, I haven't come to judge or accuse. I have followed the signs laid out for me and they have led me to you. If you believe that was ordained by God, then it probably was." Diana laid a hand on the old woman's arm.

"I had been in a state of excitement all day," Sophie de Lusignac began her story.

****

Sophie had been in a state of excitement all day. She was going to meet Klaus that evening, his note had said he could get away. Klaus was on the colonel's personal staff, he had suffered a shoulder wound in an air raid and had been returned to lighter duties. The colonel himself walked with a limp due to a wound received in the same air raid, but with a different unit.

Klaus Koenig was a quiet, bookish lad who loved wildlife: his main interest was butterflies. Whenever the colonel had no need of him, he would wander the woods, looking at all kinds of plants and insects. He knew he'd be in trouble for walking around the estate, but he was careful and always went alone. He was thin, gauche and had a kind nature, not at all like some of the German thugs Sophie had heard stories about from old Aimée. The woods footpaths and animal trails all the way through, it was possible to walk through the woodland paths for miles to this estate from at least two of the nearby villages. Sophie knew the woods intimately; she had played in them all of her life.

She knew she wasn't terribly clever. Jeannette, her governess, had tried hard and was very kind but Sophie simply wasn't interested in books. Jeannette had tried to interest her in her appearance, nice clothes and a good haircut, but Sophie knew when she looked in the mirror that she was just a lumpish sort of girl. Skirt waists were always riding up, stockings never stayed up and blouses were always too tight around the neck. For the very short period when she had attended the local school years ago, she never made any friends and was much happier in the chateau with the servants and the cook.

Moving to the lodge had been difficult. They had no servants now except Aimée, who could cook fairly well but was no real company. Papa was always here and there, she never knew when he would be in, and he dined with the Germans a couple of times a week. Jeannette had left to go back to Paris: Sophie believed that she had family there. In any case, there wasn't really anyone to talk to and who would want to talk to her anyway. She was fifteen, sixteen in four weeks' time.

And then she met Klaus.

The colonel had been called to Paris for a few days and went by train instead of taking the car. He found car journeys of any distance hurt his leg and took too long. Klaus had some administrative duties but was left alone by the other staff, mostly because he wasn't a hard-drinking, womanising soldier. The other staff, with the exception of the officers and the colonel's personal staff, were billeted with the other main body of soldiers in the huts in the front of the chateau and at the police barracks in Bergerac.

Walking in the woods was, to him, perfect peace. He missed his family very much, but if he had to be in this war, this period at the chateau was wonderful.

Sophie had a favourite place up behind the boat house. She would sit and listen to the wind in the trees and know that absolutely no-one knew she was there. The path was quite well-trodden, flattened by animals she supposed, as well as herself. She had seen Klaus once before, walking the bottom path: he sat on a pile of logs and just listened and watched. The next time she saw him, he saw her also.

His French was reasonable if he took a little time to think, but he still made some fundamental mistakes. He apologised for disturbing her and turned to leave.

"I'm so sorry, I know the staff are not supposed to use the woods, but I just love it so. I do beg your pardon, please, forgive me."

"What were you looking at?"

"Probably nothing at all - and everything. If you watch for long enough you see all kinds of things." He started to relax as he talked of things he knew about. "Do you see this spider? Have you ever seen anything more beautiful than his web?"

They wandered off slowly, he pointing out things she had never seen and she was fascinated by every word he uttered. The path would soon be coming into view of the lodge and by an unspoken decision, they took another path which led them higher into the trees and thick bushes, out of sight.

They met by arrangement, several times, and on the fourth day he took her hand for the first time. They were sitting on a pile of logs which had been there a long time, since there were no regular gardeners now to keep the woods cleared and the logs chopped. His hand rested on top of hers and she turned her hand upwards to fit into his. They had found an ease in each other's company which they never had with others. Neither knew quite how to go on but both knew they wanted to. He looked at her and they both tentatively leaned towards each other, a bumping of noses and then their lips met, just lightly, but the thrill she felt was a shock.

Neither were experienced enough to continue with what they had started and although they kept their hands joined, they sat close together, neither talking nor kissing any more.

"I have written you a note," he said finally.

"A note? What kind of note?" Sophie asked

"It's really saying things I can't say aloud. You mean so much to me, I have never had a friend like you, I am afraid because I can't say things I think girls like, you might not like me anymore." Klaus was so intense she wanted to laugh.

"Of course I like you, I like you very much." Her teenage voice was so earnest.

He handed her a folded sheet of paper: she wasn't sure if she was supposed to read it now or later. "Read it later," he said, as if understanding her uncertainty, "but perhaps it is better if no-one else sees it." Both of them understood what it would mean for them should her father find out about their meetings, and the colonel would be furious and confine him to the chateau – or worse.

As they walked a little higher above the boat shed, they sat once more and held hands. "Do you see that tree?" asked Klaus.

"This big one there? Yes, I see it."

"I will leave notes for you there when I can or if we can't meet. My colonel is back tonight and I will never know when I am free or not, but I want you to know that I am thinking of you. There is a small ledge where the branch bends over, do you see it?"

Sophie was thrilled. This feeling of constant butterflies was what she imagined true love would be like. Jeannette had been given the task of explaining the facts of life to her once her periods started. She had emphasised that making love was really between two married people, it was the ultimate declaration of love and was precious. Actually, Sophie thought it sounded horrible and couldn't imagine anyone would enjoy it. But since she had met Klaus she wondered if it would be that terrible after all. She experienced strange feelings when she was with him. When he kissed her she felt that if he touched her anywhere else, she wouldn't mind.

Sophie found a reason to go to the tree every day. Her appetite had caused some comment at home; she had always been a hearty eater, but now she had no desire to eat meals of Aimée's cooking. Her father always brought treats from the chateau after he had dined with the Germans, but now they held no delight for her.

Her skirts were now a little looser and her skin looked fresh and bright. Her father thought it was all the exercise she was taking, but first love had given her a bloom. She wondered if other people thought about it all day, the being with someone else, kissing, touching and how on earth did anyone get around the business of taking clothes off?

Even this far south it was cold in February. Sophie had managed to smuggle out a blanket and a couple of sweaters, which she hid in an old haversack she had found in the kennels so that she and Klaus would have something to sit on and cuddle up into. On nights when they were due to meet, she would go to her room just after Aimée had said goodnight, and leave her father reading, or leave a light on for him if he was out with the Germans. She would then go silently along the corridor to a back bedroom which was only four feet off the ground, since the lodge was built into a slight incline.

They had touched each other through their clothing but neither were really sure how things got done. When Klaus put his hand on her thigh, she wanted to let him go further but was really afraid. He was kind and never tried to force her into anything she wasn't ready for and in any case, he was just finding his way himself.

They met in this way through the month of March, and when the weather was bad, they risked the boat house, quite sure that no-one would ever go there.

One evening, Klaus was particularly excited, his hand on her thigh, he asked her if he could just touch her further up. "Just once, I won't hurt, I'll stop if you say so."

She had said nothing but relaxed her legs enough to allow him to move his hand further up. She had never felt anything like it, it was like an electric shock.

Sophie knew then that she would love him forever, that she would allow him to do anything. She was going to work out a time when they would come together completely, since they were going to be together for their whole lives. She had never loved nor been loved like this. Klaus would live with her at the chateau after this ghastly war and they would never be parted. No-one had ever known a love like this. This was special, this was totally theirs and would last forever.

On the night of April 23rd, it was raining slightly. The evenings had been getting lighter so their meetings had to be later and later, and she couldn't imagine how they were going to manage in the height of summer, but they would find a way, he loved her and she adored him. In any case, tonight it was quite dark because it was cloudy and the clouds were heavy and black, promising heavy rain for later.

Her father had been out all evening so getting out of the house had been easy. She was absolutely beside herself with excitement. She had decided that this was the night she was going to let Klaus do what he'd been wanting to do for some time. He fired her excitement with his touches. It couldn't be wrong when you loved someone so absolutely. He'd promised her a hundred times that he'd be careful, he'd talked to someone about how not to - not to - have a baby.

She thought they'd probably use the boat house, the drizzly rain wasn't that nice to lie in. But she'd wait up in the woods for him to arrive, she'd be able to see him coming and give each other their secret call. When she heard someone approaching, she almost ran out from behind the tree but stopped at the last minute, because she thought the shape was of two men, not one. With a shock, she realised one was her father, and the other the young butcher's lad, Georges, was it? They were obviously waiting for someone else. The path was just below her and she was well-concealed. She was deathly afraid that Klaus would come along and had no idea what to do.

Where the third man came from she couldn't say, he wasn't there one minute and then he was there the next. She was afraid she would wet her pants with fear. The men shook hands and her father said, "Well, the day after tomorrow it is. Mon Dieu, I hope there aren't any problems, it's a lot of people to move right under the noses of the Germans. Make sure no-one, absolutely no-one shows themselves outside Fournier's barn during the day and for God's sake, no lights of any kind tonight nor when they leave the day after tomorrow night. Tell them to wait for a cigarette until they're over the Pyrenees." he laughed lightly. "Here's the most money I could get, it should go quite a long way but take great care anyway. My prayers will be with you all, my brave, brave friends."

The other man said, "It is going to be difficult. We've never moved a group like this. Fournier isn't happy about all those people in his barn and there's an English pilot who's in a bad way. He's alright physically but he's been through a hard time and he's not coping at all well. His co-pilot was horribly injured and he can't get the sight of it out of his mind. Apparently they were very good friends and he was almost hysterical at leaving the body behind without burial."

Georges said, "Luc wants to leave him behind, he thinks he's going to be a danger to the whole group."

"We're not leaving anyone behind," said the other man. "At least, not alive."

There was a little more conversation, most of the rest of it Sophie couldn't hear because the men had started to move off.

The men dispersed. Sophie couldn't believe what she had heard. Her father in the Resistance? What was he thinking? The Germans were living in their house, for heaven's sake. They were right under the noses of the Germans. And the boat house? Their special meeting place? After tonight they had better move further up the hill, and well away from the paths.

But they had tonight. Tonight she was going to become a woman. She was going to give the man she loved everything. He was late, very late. She had almost given up when she heard him whistle softly, their signal. He'd tried to teach her to whistle but without any success: she would answer him with a cat-like noise. But she recognised his step as well. She was in his arms the moment she was near him.

He felt a change in her as they settled down on the blanket in the boat house. It was raining quite hard now but she knew she'd never think of rain again in the same way, this rain was special. He realised she was putting up no resistance at all and that tonight they would both experience the wonders that the soldiers talked about all the time. He could hardly contain himself as he drew off her underwear. It really was going to happen. He wasn't sure if he was supposed to keep touching her or undo his own clothes. In the end, he unbuttoned his own clothes and lowered himself on top of her. It was awkward and he wasn't sure if he was in the right place but two seconds later, he experienced such bliss he groaned aloud. Sophie cried out twice but then seemed to relax a little and let out little moans.

"WHAT THE HELL IS GOING ON HERE? GET OFF HER, YOU FILTHY BASTARD, GET OFF." Her father had appeared in the doorway and was incandescent with rage. He pulled the back of Klaus's collar and kicked him as he sat on the floor. He was screaming at her to get back to the house. She had never been so afraid. She thought he was going to hit her and she fled back to the lodge. She was deathly afraid for Klaus, and didn't know what to do. She had no idea how much time passed before her father came slamming back into the house.

"Get up to your room. I'll speak to you in the morning. Right now I don't want your face in front of me, you disgust me."

Never in her whole life had she ever been spoken to like that. Never. The shock of it sent her into gulping fits of crying and coughing until she was sick. He made no effort to help her up the stairs as she vomited, and not a glance in her direction to see if she was alright. Aimée had woken up with the noise and although she hadn't understood what had caused it, she recognised the girl's distress and helped her to her room. She bathed Sophie's face and stroked her hair as the girl wept and coughed.

Sophie heard the door slam as her father left the house again. She was so afraid for Klaus. She had no idea why her father had come back to the boat house, and if it hadn't been raining, they wouldn't have been in there and would have been safe. Oh God, why did it have to rain? Where was Klaus, where was her father, had he gone to kill Klaus? Oh God, the Germans would kill her father. Oh God, Oh God.

Sophie had finally cried herself to sleep. Aimée had managed to understand most of the story: the girl was in love, her father had found them together experiencing bodily joy for the first time and had become wild. The fact that it was a German probably made matters worse, but Aimée thought the whole thing would blow over. Of course, why not? It was only what young lovers had been doing for generations, wasn't it? After all, she should know. Young people always found ways to be together. Her father would calm down, watch her more carefully for a while and all would be well. He was such a good man, he couldn't stay angry for long, could he? Didn't he remember what it was like to be young? And if she couldn't see the young man any longer, well, there were many others weren't there? Yes, of course she was in love, otherwise she wouldn't have let the boy touch her like that, would she?

Sophie decided to brave her father early the next morning. There was no sign of him, his bedroom door was closed which it never was during the day, so she assumed he'd been really upset and gone to bed very late. He didn't make an appearance until lunchtime and he looked dreadful. She was very remorseful and longed to have his good opinion again. She had no idea how to behave in this instance. Should she try to embrace him? Tell him she was sorry? What?

In the end, he asked her to come and sit beside her. "I don't want to know how long this has been going on, nor how many times you have been with him. You are barely sixteen and you will ruin your life if this becomes public. Who will want you if they know you've been with a German? Do you know what's happening to women who are going with Germans?"

Much as she wanted to get back into her father's favour, she found it hard to listen to him talking about Klaus as if he was just anyone. "But Papa, I love him very much."

"I'm sure you think you do. But it is out of the question. Out of the question. You have a position in this community and do you know what will happen to women who have German boyfriends? Have you any idea what you've done?"

She couldn't look at him, she wanted to be out of this house, out of his sight and be with Klaus, but young as she was, she was just beginning to realise that everyone was going to make that impossible.

"I'm going to contact Jeannette and ask her to take you to the coast for a while. I'm at a loss to know how to behave with you. In the meantime, you may not go further than we can see you from the house."

After tea, she asked if she could go for a walk. "Only half an hour," she said. "I have a terrible headache. I promise I'm not meeting anyone. Please, Papa, I'm so unhappy." It was still light so he relented.

Once out of sight, she ran for the tree to see if by any wonderful chance he had left her a note. He had. She was so happy. She unfolded it quickly and instantly shock hit her; she could feel her heart breaking.

Her father had stormed over to the chateau the night before, demanding to see the colonel and demanded that he remove Klaus from the place immediately. The colonel had been horrified and had been very placatory with her father. He promised to attend to it and thanked him for the information. "As a result, my darling, my only love," Klaus wrote, "I am being transferred out first thing in the morning. I will have gone by six in the morning and by the time you read this I will be on a train or transport. I'm not even sure where they're sending me."

Sophie fell to the ground. He father had done this. He had connived with the Germans to separate her from the only person she had ever loved. She hated her father. Hated him. Hated him. How could he have done this? She was his daughter and he didn't care about her. She would never love again, never, never and she hated him. She hated him so much she wanted to hurt and wound him the way he had done to her. She would show him.

She kissed the letter which she then held to her heart. She had kept all of Klaus's notes and little gifts in a jigsaw tin she'd brought from the chateau when they moved to the lodge, with some other books and jigsaws. The ground at the side of the boat house had subsided a little leaving a gap. She had been keeping the box in this gap, pushing it well under the floor of the boathouse, and covering the gap with a few stones. Inside was a small book of German poetry Klaus had read to her. Even though she didn't understand, she adored just listening to him saying rhyming words of love in his own language. She picked up the little pile of letters and hugged them to her, with a small insignia off his uniform. Her tears fell onto the back of her hands as they clutched this evidence of his love, sure that her heart would never heal. And her father was to blame.

Hate for her father came over her in a hot flush. She would not let him see her breaking her heart in this way, she had to convince him that she had made a stupid mistake and needed to be forgiven, only in this was would be able to think of something to have her revenge without arousing his suspicions.

Then she had it. It came to her in a blinding moment of fury against him. She knew what she would do.

Sophie came back to the house as she had promised, behaved like a contrite daughter and kissed her father when he went out. Her father had special permission from the colonel to go out in the evenings. He had been such a pillar of the community, there wasn't much that happened of a public nature without his presence. But on this occasion, he had permission to go to the meeting of the local council, a privilege the Germans had granted, giving at least the idea that the village was still in French hands. None of the rules they passed nor any of the suggestions they made could, of course, be enacted without German approval. It was just a token.

Aimée was exhausted from the events of the night before and went to bed after an early supper.

Sophie went upstairs and put on her nightgown. She then went downstairs and took a sheet of paper from her father's desk and printed: TOMORROW NIGHT. FOURNIER BARN. RESISTANCE MEETING. ESCAPE LINE. She wrapped the piece of paper around a stone and secured it with a piece of string she had found in the kitchen. She put on Aimée's black coat and hat and put on a pair of her father's socks, which were inside his boots. It was dark now and she approached the chateau unseen. There was a light in the kitchen but she couldn't see anyone in there. She launched the stone as hard as she could and heard the window crash as she ran away. She knew her way in the woods very well, and reached the lodge as the soldiers were just coming out into the garden to look for the culprit.

Sophie crept back into the lodge without putting on any lights, tore off her father's socks: none of the boots would therefore look wet. She hung Aimée's coat and hat back up on the hook and ran to her room, diving into bed in her nightgown. She put her father's wet socks under her bed.

Nothing happened for a while. After a time she heard shouting from outside but no-one came to the lodge. Her father came back just after midnight and all was quiet.

After she had been in bed for a while, she began to worry about what she had done. But after all, they didn't know her father was involved, because he wouldn't be there, would he? But it would spite him anyway. All they would do would be to send them to prison camp, and that's not so bad is it? And her father wouldn't be among them. And the British airmen would be treated quite well, wouldn't they?

The following day, her father had tried to see the colonel to discuss allowing the gardens of the chateau to be used for a fête which the villagers wanted to hold to mark the feast day of Saint-Sulpice. He was told that the colonel had gone to Périgueux for an emergency meeting and wouldn't be back until later, it would be better to leave it until the following day.

Little did her father know what the following day would hold.

****

All day Sophie fluctuated between rage at her father, abject misery for Klaus and guilt over what she had done with the denunciation. As the day wore on, the guilt became almost more than she could bear. What had she been thinking? Even if she wanted to tell her father now, he'd gone over to see the commandant first, and since the man had gone out, de Lusignac had come back to the lodge to say he was going out. He told Sophie she was to stay in the house and they would discuss his plans for her when he returned.

Aimée produced a light lunch, but Sophie had no appetite at all, her guilt was making her restless, nervous and sick. Could she stop it somehow? But then everyone would know she'd been involved. And for sure her father would never, never forgive her, he might even kill her himself. And then of course, the Germans would know her father was involved with the Resistance. What could she do now? She couldn't even think straight for guilt weighing her down.

As evening fell, Sophie thought she would scream with the burden of what she was carrying. Aimée thought the girl was still brooding about her lost love and thought it best to let her get over it on her own. Her father came back finally, and looked so worried, she couldn't have told him now. He was obviously concerned that the escape was going to take place any time now and there was absolutely nothing now Sophie could do. She was terrified to do nothing, and she was terrified to do something.

She said goodnight and went to her room. She begged God to help her, she cried into her pillow and promised God anything if he would just make it come out alright. She would be good for ever, be a dutiful daughter, never cross her father again if only God would make it turn out alright. Please, God. Please.

They were woken in the middle of the night by the noise of loud banging on the door. When she first woke, she had just momentarily forgotten the nightmare she suffered all the previous day, but it came back to her with frightful alarm. Her father told her to stay in her room as she came out to see what was happening.

"Get back in there and stay there," he said. She noticed that his clothes were crumpled, he had obviously been to bed fully clothed. He spoke to the soldiers, collected his coat and left with them. Sophie slept no more that night, waiting for her father's return. He came back just after dawn, looking ill.

Sophie wanted to go to him and put her arms around him. She was devastated at the hatred she had felt for him, and the guilt of her actions had softened her rage. He looked at her, as if he wanted to say something, but said nothing. He went to the bathroom to wash and clean up. He went to his room and changed his clothes.

When he came out he said, "Come here and sit down." He indicated the chair beside the desk. He looked completely beaten and demoralised. Sophie realised that she had left the drawer of his desk slightly open when she removed the piece of notepaper. He very deliberately and very slowly closed the drawer and looked at her. "The Colonel - he - he has shown me …" Then he opened the drawer again and fingered the notepaper. His face went white and he again slowly closed the drawer. He didn't speak for a moment and then said, "I'm going to the village. A tragedy of terrible proportions happened last night and I have asked the colonel if I might visit the families." His voice was choked with pain.

Sophie sat, not speaking. In that moment she knew – she knew – beyond any shadow of a doubt, that the colonel had shown her father the incriminating note and that he suddenly knew where it had come from. She'd been so stupid, how many other people even owned notepaper, let alone notepaper of quality?

God had deserted her. Whatever tragedy had taken place was her fault and her father knew it.

As he left to go to the village, he turned and said, "Never doubt that I love you, my Sophie. All will be well."

Sophie spent most of the day in her room. Aimée had told her that she had heard from Juliette that the Germans had rounded up a large group of Resistance partisans and some foreign airmen. They had roused the entire village and made them watch whilst these poor men were lined up and shot. The leader was made to watch also and then hanged.

Sophie wanted to die.

116

Her father didn't come home at all that night. The following morning Juliette came to the door, her face hard and unsympathetic. She broke the news that her father had been found at the gates, he was a traitor and had died a traitor's death. Sophie could take no more. Her days of guilt, pain, loss and heartbreak poured into the screams she let out. She fell to the floor and banged her head again and again, trying to make the world safe again, trying to let out all the infamy and betrayal, hoping that physical pain would wipe everything away.

Juliette, hating this family but nevertheless fearful for the girl's state of mind, sent Aimée to ask the colonel for a doctor to come. After all, the father was the worst kind of traitor but the daughter couldn't be held responsible, could she?

After she had been sedated with a drink of some kind, Sophie sat drugged and grief-stricken in a chair whilst the Germans came and emptied everything out of the house – papers of every description, photos, books, everything emptied into boxes and stacked at the door awaiting removal. Sophie was led out of the lodge to the Colonel's car. The doctor had asked if he could remove her from this place and take her to the priest's care. The housekeeper could look after her whilst they decided what to do with her. The colonel's pity on the girl had extended to exhibiting humanity after the inhumanity of the night before. While Aimée was packing a few of her things, Sophie watched through drugged eyes, the drawers with the infamous notepaper being turned out, everything of their lives being put in piles, waiting to be taken over to the chateau for other people to pick through.

Sophie had very little recollection of the following few days. She remembered being told that her father was in the church in a coffin, but she couldn't bring herself to go and see him. She vaguely remembered Père Martin's housekeeper telling her that his body had been taken and she didn't know where. But it didn't matter to Sophie. She retreated into her world of silence and pain. She vaguely recollected being taken back to the lodge by Père Martin, but where was it? Did she live here at all? Was it gone, burnt to ashes? He was praying, was he? Some sort of blessing? She no longer knew, nor could she remember anything but sorrow. She was taken to Bordeaux, to a convent which was a nursing order of nuns. She still hadn't spoken up to this point.

She thought it was about two weeks later when she was taken to Tours, to another convent. She spent months without speaking and the nuns were content to lead her to prayer, feed her, keep her clean and clothed.

One night, Sophie suddenly asked to see a priest and spent a couple of hours telling him everything. Of course, she was absolved from her sins, but it brought her little comfort. She did however, become an active part of the convent and had a talent for growing things. Over the next few years, she became a postulant and then took her final vows. Perhaps God had forgiven her, but she had not forgiven herself. Her talent for gardening was her sanctuary. The huge vegetable garden was her domain, she was in charge and it was profitable. After the convent's requirements were accounted for, several trucks a week would take boxes of fresh vegetables to market.

Until she was overtaken by crippling arthritis, Sophie had worked the gardens until her late seventies. The nursing home in Lourdes provided care for elderly nuns who were unable to look after themselves and could not stay in busy convents, nuns who had earned their rest after a lifetime of work.

****

Diana sat back in her chair. She had known half of the story, and since finding Klaus's letters had worked out most of it –

but not all. However, Sophie's revelation was still a shock, that her father had willingly given his life to save her.

The two women sat in silence, tears rolling down the cheeks of the old woman. Diana squeezed her hand. "He knew it was you."

"Yes. He knew it was me. I don't know how he handed himself over. He must have known that they would get to me eventually. It was the notepaper. He recognised it immediately, obviously. The colonel must have shown it to him when my father was summoned in the night. There were a hundred ways an informer could have told the Germans about the escape group, I was really not very sensible to send it through the window. The Germans knew there were paths all through the woods but no-one would have been idiotic enough to come through that way to send a message through the window. It would have been suicide for anyone else other than someone living on the estate." The old nun was rubbing her sore hands and ignoring the tears running down to her chin. Diana took a tissue from her pocket and dabbed at the cheeks and chin of this troubled woman.

"The other way my father knew it was me was finding me – me and Klaus – together in -"

"The boat house." Diana finished the sentence of the old lady's train of thought.

"Yes. He knew then that I'd been in the area when he met the other men. He might have suspected Klaus if it hadn't been for the paper. If it had been Klaus, the Germans would have come for my father straight away and kept him until the raid was over. No, for my father, he drew the only conclusion that made any sense. And of course, he was right."

"You have suffered a lot over the years. Can you not find peace, even now?" asked Diana.

"Peace? No, never peace. I have found times when the whole episode seems to be like a dream, but it's always a bad dream. And then there was poor Klaus too. All he ever did was to fall in love. I often think of him and wonder what happened to him. Did he survive the war? I have no idea. I like to think of him going home at the end of the war, marrying some lovely girl and having a family, but we'll never know."

For all the enormity of what Sophie had done, Diana couldn't equate this tormented woman with the spiteful sixteen-year-old taking revenge for an act of parental discipline. Of course, it was all true, but Diana's nature didn't permit total condemnation of anyone, which is why, perhaps, she had always had a doubt about de Lusignac himself.

Sophie closed her eyes as if picturing everything anew, but Diana realised she was actually drifting off to sleep. She softly removed the tin box from her lap and crept out of the room. She went out into the garden, a pretty area with an orchard off to the right. There were some benches under the trees, so Diana put on her jacket and took her bag over to one of them and sat down.

She had been sitting for about half an hour when the matron came over with a steaming cup of coffee. "You must be cold, sitting here. I've brought you some coffee, it's just black, without sugar."

"How lovely. You are kind. What a beautiful setting here, it's so peaceful and serene."

"Yes. This place was built in the 'fifties but was recently refurbished. All the bathrooms have been done out with specialised equipment for handling disabled people. And it is peaceful, except I fear for your poor Sister Marie Agnes there will never be any peace."

"Do you know her story?" asked Diana, puzzled.

"No, not at all. I know her family died tragically during the war, but something else seems to haunt her. I hope you haven't come to bring out her ghosts, whatever they are." It was said kindly, but with a deal of concern for her charge.

"No, but perhaps to help her lay those ghosts to rest. Time passes and even ghosts grow old. I promise I'm not here to cause her any pain."

"Good. She's a sick woman, I'd not like her to spend her last few months grieving or suffering."

"Last few months? I thought she was just retired. I know she has arthritis but she -"

"Has cancer. Quite advanced. And this is a hospice."

Diana looked around her. Of course. How could she have missed it?

Beautiful gardens, every level of comfort, wonderful atmosphere. Of course it was a hospice.

"Where are you staying tonight?"

"Actually, I'm booked into a hotel in town but I haven't been to check in yet, I came straight here. I'd like to spend a bit more time with Sister Marie Agnes when she wakes, if that's alright."

"Would you like to stay here? We have rooms for relatives. Those who can afford it make a donation, but those who can't are just as welcome."

"Thank you so much, I'd love to stay."

The matron led her back to her car and waited for her to pick up her bag. They went up to the first floor and she opened the door to a bright room, furnished in modern comfort with an en-suite toilet and shower. There was a tray on a table by the window with a kettle, and some packets of tea, coffee, sugar and powdered milk. The quilted bed cover looked so inviting, Diana had an urge to just lie on the bed and wrap the cover around her. The Matron said dinner was at six thirty and if she wished, she could take it in Sister Marie Agnes's room. Sister Marie Agnes would probably sleep for a couple of hours; she did most afternoons.

Diana watched the door close and went to sit by the window. She checked her phone and saw three messages from Simon and one from Jean Claude. She phoned Simon first. He answered just before the ring went to the answering service. "Hello darling, I'm so pleased you called," and he sounded pleased. "How are you? God, I miss you."

She smiled. "I miss you, too. How are things going with your research?"

"As a matter of fact, I've done quite well. I thought I'd bring my notes home and start my whiteboard. I'll catch a morning train on Saturday, if you can meet me at the station."

"That's absolutely wonderful! I'm so thrilled, I can't wait to see you. What about Chris? Will he stay there or do you want to bring him with you?"

"No. I'll come alone, I've stuff to do that only I can do and there's a bit more research to do here. So, how are things with you? With the house? Have you managed to find something to replace that hideous chandelier in our bedroom? God, I hate looking at that thing."

"No, I haven't." She felt terrible: lying was not a language they spoke between them. "Perhaps we ought to do away with the chandeliers upstairs and do some other kind of lighting. Anyway, we'll see. I'm so pleased I'll see you in a few days."

"So, you'll be home tomorrow then? Where are you anyway? Did you actually tell me where you'd be? Darling, I'll call you tonight, got to go. I love you. 'Bye." And he was gone.

She dialled Jean Claude's number. She liked Jean Claude, he was bright, witty and made her feel feminine. He was a bit of a flirt, but nothing she couldn't handle. And he knew where the boundaries were.

"Bonjour, Jean Claude."

"Oh, Diana," he pronounced it Dee-anna, "I've been wondering how you were getting on. Did you find her?"

"Jean Claude, I need you to promise me something."

"I will, if I can and it's not illegal."

"No," she laughed. "But I do ask for your word."

"OK."

"Yes, I did find her and yes, most of what I told you is true. But there's more, and it's a dilemma. I'd rather see you to tell you, it's rather difficult for me to just sit here and recount it. I'm leaving tomorrow, is there any way you can come to the house tomorrow late afternoon? I know it's cheeky to ask, but it would be an extra hour on my journey to come to you and then another hour to get home afterwards. I don't want to rush what I'll tell you. You haven't told anyone about finding her details for me?"

"Actually, it was all on file here. The lawyers, of course, had to deal with her directly at some stage over the sale of the place. Even though she'd gifted it to the church there were still some outstanding legal issues. We French are good at those. But when I tracked it down, the convent didn't have any problem giving me the address of the nursing home."

"Then will you give me your word that you'll say nothing to anyone, and I'll tell you why when I see you?"

"Of course. I give you my word."

"So you'll come?"

"Yes, I'll come. Do you want to go for dinner somewhere?"

"No, that's kind but I'd rather stay at home to talk – I'll dig something out of the freezer. So, I'll expect you about seven?"

"Fine, see you then. Drive carefully."

****

Diana rested on the bed for an hour, but when she felt herself slipping off to sleep, she got up and had a long, warm shower. She had no hair dryer with her and found none in the bathroom, so she just left her hair loose to dry until she would go back down to Sister Marie Agnes.

She found herself wondering how someone could live all those years with the enormity of what they had done. All those deaths, and then the ultimate sacrifice of her father to save his daughter from any suspicion of treachery. Diana's nature was not judgmental, but when she thought of all those men who had died, she found it hard to equate those deaths with the frail, dying old woman in the chair downstairs. Thirteen men had been shot that night, and the leader then hanged. Three German soldiers had died and one of the British airmen in the attack and round-up.

Diana brushed her hair back into a barrette, she didn't bother with lipstick, she picked up her handbag and went downstairs.

Sister Marie Agnes was awake and waiting for her. It was still half an hour before dinner would be served, but a maid came in to see if they would like something to drink, they could have wine if they wished or one of a selection of cold drinks. Diana chose sparkling water and Sister Marie Agnes joined her.

Diana found it difficult not to watch the old lady. She realised at times she was staring and tried to understand why she was doing it. She was still trying to see the heartbroken sixteen-year-old behind the wrinkles and pain.

"Bring your chair round this side," said Sister Marie Agnes. "I'm a little deaf on that side. I need to explain something to you. We will wait until the meal has been cleared away and then we can talk uninterrupted. In the meantime, tell me something about yourself. You told Matron that you had bought our old family home."

"Yes. And I love it. Of course, apart from the room sizes, you know, the original walls forming the rooms, I imagine very little remains the same. The dressing rooms are now bathrooms, the bedrooms now have built-in wardrobes and we love it, it's just a beautiful, wonderful place. Our

124

bedroom faces the lake, and Simon's study is in the other bedroom. Of the two front rooms, one is a guest room and the other, a dressing room."

Diana spent the next half an hour recounting the development of the estate, describing the neighbours and for obvious reasons, completely avoided any mention of the clearing in the woods. Dinner came on two trays, nicely set out. Diana had been sent an individual casserole dish of *cassoulet*, and a small plate of cheese, some salad, two bread rolls and a dish of grapes. Sister Marie Agnes's supper was a bowl of consommé, a little poached fish with salad, and a jelly. During the meal, Sister Marie Agnes ate very little but Diana enjoyed her meal very much. They talked amiably about the estate mostly, but Diana finally asked her about her illness.

"I'm pain free most of the time, thanks to the wonderful staff here. I have liver cancer, with secondaries in several places. Since you came this afternoon, I realise that I have been waiting for you for a long time. Well, not you exactly, but for this to happen, shall we say. Perhaps, after all, it is God's will."

The maid came to remove their dishes. Sister Marie Agnes looked at her directly and took her hand. "My dear, now you must listen. You know now that my father was a complete patriot. You know that he also did the bravest thing that any man can do, he gave up his life for someone he loved. The taking of that life was murder. Those people who did it never knew they were murdering an innocent man. And they can't know now."

"WHAT?" exclaimed Diana. "But he was innocent! Don't you want his name cleared, don't you want his grave marked? By the way, I visit the clearing in the woods, you know, the lodge site, every single day. I just knew that something ghastly had happened. What possible reason could you have for keeping quiet? You are dying, no-one is going to come after you now, and I don't believe you'd care if they did. Would they put you on trial? What possible reason is there for you to want this?" she repeated. She was angry now, not angry with this woman strangely enough, but angry that an injustice would be left unrectified.

"Can't you see it?" said Sister Marie Agnes, grasping Diana's hands in an attempt to force understanding on her. "Diana, think! There are STILL people alive who did this. Do you think, after everything I have done, I can tear those lives apart now? Don't you think I would have come forward a long time ago to clear my dear Papa? Think, Diana. How could people whose families believe they were heroes be turned into common murderers? And they too were patriots, weren't they? They believe justice was served, that the man responsible for killing all those men paid with his own life. Those families cannot be told now that they did this to the wrong person."

Diana sat back, stunned. She hadn't thought it through. "But is he never to have his name cleared?"

"Of course. I have left documents with the lawyers. I have made a complete statement, but on condition that its contents are not to be revealed for another twenty years. That will leave a good safety margin. By then, anyone who was actively involved in killing my father will be dead. Their families may have to live with what they did, but by then it will be mostly grandchildren and great-grandchildren who will probably never care or even bother to inform themselves. The young don't care about the war, about patriotism or honour and duty. In any case, I can't think about them, I can only think of the people who were involved. Trying to protect them is only the least I can do. And in any case, when I made that arrangement, I had no idea that the truth would ever be uncovered. Believe me, my only concern is the protection of the community in the village, nothing else."

Sister Marie Agnes had beads of sweat breaking out on her face, and she winced in pain. Diana made a move to get

126

help, but Sister Marie Agnes took her hand and bade her sit down again.

"There is one major point you are missing, Diana. In my eyes my father was a hero of France – but when the truth comes out there will still be people who believe he was a traitor. You are forgetting that he shielded someone who really *was* a traitor."

Of course – she had missed the point, how obtuse could she be? This old lady really was a murderer herself. And her father knew it and protected her. *Of course* he would be condemned by many for doing it.

"Does anyone at all know any of this?"

"No-one. The lawyer doesn't know what my statement contains." She took a deep breath and her pain seemed to ease a little. There was a knock at the door and the nurse came in with a little tray of medication. Diana left the room whilst the nurse gave Sister Marie Agnes an injection and administered a little pot of tablets. She helped the old nun into bed and made her comfortable, before indicating to Diana that she could return to the room.

"Do you know this is God's work? The fact that *you* bought our house, the fact that *you* had faith in my father without knowing a thing about him and most significantly, that *you* found my little tin box and then finally, *you* found me."

"Actually," Diana realised the nun was tired but wanted to give her this final piece of information before leaving her to rest, "There is something else I've brought with me. Are you feeling strong enough to carry on talking or would you like me to leave it until the morning?"

"My dear, if God has brought you, who am I to say I'm too tired to talk to him? Do, please tell me everything now."

"I'll be two minutes; I just have to fetch something from my car." Diana left the room and went out to the car park.

She checked her phone for messages and saw that Simon had again texted. "Later," she thought.

She had been in two minds as to whether to put the photos and the little book in another bag, wondering if the sight of the German document boxes would upset Sophie, as Diana always thought of her. But in the end, she had left them as she found them. Presumably this was also as Sophie had last seen them.

She need not have worried; Sister Marie Agnes didn't seem to recognise the boxes for what they were. As Diana took her seat, she put the boxes on the bed-table and picked up the top one. As she opened it, Sister Marie Agnes saw the photos on the top and let out a little cry, and slowly again tears rolled down her cheeks.

"This is the first time I have seen anything at all from my family since that day I left the Chateau. The Germans came to the house while I was still waiting for someone to take me away and I was so unhappy and miserable, I barely noticed what was going on. But I do remember the Germans emptying all the drawers of Papa's desk, the drawers in the kitchen, the bedroom were cleared and I remember Aimée crying and trying to keep something in her hand which she didn't want to hand over. I think it was the framed photo from Papa's desk of my parents with me as a baby but I really can't recall." Sister Marie Agnes was flushed and her hands trembled as she held the little batch of photos.

"These two boxes were found when the developers were clearing the attics. They think the Germans were too busy in the end destroying their own documents to bother with these, but I don't suppose we'll ever know why they survived."

"Because God wanted you to bring them to me," Sister Marie Agnes smiled broadly. "You can't escape it, Diana, you have been His instrument in all this."

Diana squeezed her hand and gave a little laugh. "Well, I suppose I can accept that, after all. He's been very good to me so far."

Sister Marie Agnes reached into the box and looked at the receipts, clutching the photos to her chest with one hand. She held up one receipt. "Do you see this? This was a saddle my father had had made for me for my tenth birthday." She was holding up a yellowed piece of paper with a corner missing, but to her, this was a part of her life which she thought lost forever.

Diana said nothing whilst Sophie took each piece of paper from the box, inspected it and laid it on the bed table, little bits of her past which the Germans couldn't be bothered to destroy because they were so insignificant.

"I imagine that since Papa's body was found as it was, the Germans must have thought he was connected to the Resistance in some way or at least he had knowledge of who they were, that's why they came and took everything from the lodge. I don't suppose they found a single thing which would connect him to any Resistance activities but they took it all anyway. When I left Saint-Sulpice I had nothing at all, these things you have brought me are the only things I have seen for all these years."

Diana gave her a moment to look at her past. She then took the second box, a record book of payments to estate workers, an inventory of the belongings – paintings and other valuable items – they had been obliged to leave at the chateau when they moved to the lodge, presumably made by de Lusignac for future reference. Then she took out the little book which Diana believed contained bank information from the bank in London, concerning funds deposited with them.

Diana kept the little book back until Sister Marie Agnes had had time to look at this connection to her past. "Here is the payment list of the gardeners, isn't it strange to see these names now and wonder if some of them are still alive or if they have children or grandchildren? Look, here's Luc, always in trouble in the village - and his brother Jules. They used to get free firewood, which they were supposed to take home to their mother, but Luc used to go to the market and sell it. He was a real rascal. And Collette, she used to do the laundry and did the most exquisite needlework. She was an old woman even then."

Sophie's tears were unstoppable and Diana really began to wonder if this had after all, been such a good idea. Wasn't she just satisfying her own curiosity? Was she really part of some holy plan to bring this poor woman all these memories? She kept silent and allowed Sophie all the time she needed to reconnect with the names of her childhood, to capture something of the happier times they represented.

"There is one more thing. Did this belong to your father?" Diana held out the little book to Sister Marie Agnes, who took it with a shaking hand.

"This is Papa's writing; he always did a T with a curling down stroke!" She dropped her land into her lap and closed her eyes, tears spilling down her cheek.

Diana took a face cloth from the bathroom and dampened it with cold water. As she dabbed Sophie's face, the nun opened her eyes and looked at Diana, who sat beside her. Diana thought she saw pure happiness for a second in that face and she would never forget that moment. Equally, she knew she would never recount that revelation to anyone else, ever. But if happiness it was, it soon passed into sad nostalgia.

"Sister, do you know what this is?" Diana asked after a few minutes.

"I'm not sure that I do, it looks like another of his record books."

"Sister, I believe it is the record of sums of money he gave to the Resistance on behalf of the government in London. The British financed many undercover activities with the Resistance in France. They had some sort of system whereby money was paid into accounts in London, in return for local funds being used to finance some of these operations. I believe your father was one of those people who could raise loans and was repaid by placing funds in this account."

A flash of memory of that dreadful night came to her of her father handing over money to the men in the woods.

"I have contacted the bank, who would not confirm that an account in your father's name existed, but they did ask for any information I might be able to put their way. In my mind, that means there probably was an account but I have no idea if it still exists, what happened to the money or anything. That would have to come from you. I have here the letter they emailed to me, they sent the original in the mail."

"A bank account in London? Surely the lawyers would have known about it? What do you think I should do?" Sister Marie Agnes was looking carefully through the little book. "I suppose the Germans must have thought this was just another estate account book when they took all the papers from the lodge. It's all such a shock, I can't think what to do next."

"Well, the first thing would be to have the lawyers contact the bank to find if anything ever existed, and if so, what happened to it? You'll have to give them a written authority to act on your behalf, but you should be able to find out fairly quickly. I don't know how long bank accounts can lie dormant before they are closed. Of course, your father may have had other papers relating to this account but if so, they weren't in either of these two boxes."

Sister Marie Agnes looked searchingly at Diana for a moment. "I want *you* to do it." Sophie's face now dried of tears. "I want to find out about this, and if there is any money, I know exactly what I want to do with it."

"Me? Oh, Sister, I don't know. It's true, I feel as if I'm part of your story, but there are people who are good at this sort of thing, they'll find out everything."

"Please, Diana! I firmly believe you were sent to me. I really do. Please do this for me."

"Well, I suppose it won't do any harm just to contact the bank, and see what they say. The Pelling Hancock Bank is a very famous old merchant bank, mostly used by people with a lot of money, and these days by rich Arabs, Russians and Chinese. Alright, I'll talk to my husband and see what I can do." She gave the old woman's hand a small squeeze.

"I realise, of course, that you want to tell your husband all of this that you have discovered," said Sister Marie Agnes, "but I would ask you please, please keep this knowledge between yourself and anyone else you feel needs to know. I know it can't be long, but I'd like to think we could leave this buried at least for a while longer. Perhaps it's a vain hope. I have many times thought of bringing it all out into the open, but I cannot imagine the effect on those old people who are still alive. If you find any money, I'll leave instructions as to what is to happen to it. I just need to think about it a while longer. But please, Diana, this is important. I want to do whatever I can in any small way to make amends and protecting those left behind is perhaps the only thing I can do now."

Clearly the old woman was worn out, she still clutched the photos to her chest and lay back on the pillows. Diana realised that she was also very tired, so she decided to go for a stroll in the evening air and phone Simon before going to bed herself.

Diana softly collected the photos and other contents of the boxes and slowly replaced them, realising that Sophie was now fast asleep. The tin box containing Klaus's letters was beside her, Diana left it there so that it would be the first thing she saw when she awoke. She dimmed the light and crept out of the room. When she opened the door to go outside, she realised she didn't feel like talking to Simon right now. But obviously she must.

Deceit was alien to her; she had never kept secrets from Simon. Since they had first met, she couldn't remember a time when she had done anything like this. She was torn between keeping the lie going and telling him part of the truth, promising a full explanation later. Still undecided she reached for her phone. It went to the message recorder when the rings went unanswered, and Diana assumed Simon had gone for an early night. She left a message that she would be home tomorrow, leaving in the morning and she would call him when she got home. She was relieved that she wouldn't have to explain right now, not in this place with Sophie asleep in the building behind her. In fact, she wished she wouldn't have to explain at all, but realised that when she had agreed to go to London to the bank, Simon would have to know. But all the same, she wished he didn't.

****

Diana woke early, she hadn't slept well although the bed was comfortable and the building was quiet at night, the silence broken only occasionally by the ringing of a patient's bell and the sound of professional feet walking the corridors, going to respond and offer comfort. There was a knock on the door as she was finishing dressing.

"Come in."

"Good morning, Madame Lewis. Sister Marie Agnes would very much like you to spend a little time with her before you leave. Would you like to take your breakfast with her? She's been awake for some time and had her pain medication so she's feeling fairly well at the moment." The matron herself had been to deliver the message. "What time did you think of starting your trip home?"

"I thought I'd leave at about eleven, if that's alright. I am so grateful that you put me up last night, and I'd like to give you this donation. I've left the payee blank so you can put it to whatever use you think fit."

"That's most kind, thank you very much." The matron didn't open the envelope, but tucked it into a pocket.

Diana had written a generous cheque but felt that no amount of generosity could equal what these people did to comfort and ease the terminally ill. She packed her overnight bag and went downstairs. She checked her phone but Simon hadn't rung again.

Diana knocked lightly on the door and went in. Sister Marie Agnes was sitting in her chair by the window with the two boxes and her little tin box beside her on the table. She also held an envelope in her hand.

"Good morning, Diana. Please come and join me, coffee will be here in a minute. Are you well this morning, and how is your husband?"

"Good morning, Sister," Diana bent down to kiss the nun's cheek, not the two-cheek standard greeting kiss, but an affectionate gesture from one who feels an amity with another.

"I asked Matron to write a letter for me yesterday after you had left. I had a little sleep and awoke knowing that I had something to do. It is a letter of authority for you to act for me in dealings with the bank, and wherever it might lead. You may speak on my behalf and make decisions. Matron and another nurse witnessed my signature, there is another letter stating that in their opinion, I am not being coerced and I am not incapable of understanding. You need to sign the authority also in front of me, Matron and another witness, Matron would have been happier to have an attorney draw up a legal document, but I want you to leave today with the authority at least. In any case, I will ask a lawyer to instruct the bank and tell them what I have asked you to do. We'll try to make sure you have all the documentation you need. Matron looked the bank up on the computer last night, so before long they should have everything they need."

Diana was amazed at Sophie's apparent determination that no obstacle should stop her from obtaining any information she needed Then, she realised with sudden comprehension, that Sophie was not prepared to wait for all the legal documentation from a lawyer, in case she should die before anything could be formalised.

"You haven't told me what you would like me to do with the money, if there is any, if I can find it and if they will release it to me." Diana wanted this information before she left that day, for the same reason – if Sophie should die and there was a sum of money to be disposed of, what should Diana do if she had no instructions?

"Yes, I'll get to that. But there is something else I'm going to ask of you. I know you now own the large part of the estate including the lodge and the boat house. Could you bear to do something for me? It is generally accepted that my father's body was burned with the lodge. These photos and papers are all I have to make a memorial for him. Could you bear to find a corner somewhere and bury these and mark the spot with just a small cross or something? It's all I have left of my family; it would mean so much to me."

Again, her eyes filled with tears as Diana took the boxes from her. "But, please, if you would be good enough to get rid of the boxes themselves and put the things in something else."

"Of course I will. It would be a lovely thing to do and I'd be honoured to do it for you."

Then the old nun pushed the tin box towards her. "And I'm going to ask you to do the same thing for this. If you could put back under the boat house and leave it there. I don't know what you're going to do with the boat house, but if you are going to rebuild it, just leave this underneath. But I'd not like anyone else to read these letters, ever. So, would you?"

"Of course I will." Diana smiled.

"You see, my father believed I was too young to understand the true meaning of love. But I did. Klaus and his love for me has remained with me for all these years. During those times when I was first taken to the convent, my guilt nearly killed me, the only thing that stopped me from killing myself was the love that Klaus had for me. Oh, I knew I'd never see him again, but it kept me alive. Does it shock you that I once thought of committing that terrible sin? No? You cannot imagine what a sixteen-year-old mind can do when laden with guilt and shame."

Diana had never been a judgmental person and found it very difficult to condemn this woman for what she, as a bitterly hurt, naïve young girl had done. Diana hadn't condemned the girl's father when everyone seemed to think he was guilty. Simon had always told her that she was in for a rude awakening one day with her simplistic outlook on life, but even that she refused to believe.

She jumped when she realised Sister Marie Agnes was speaking again. "This time yesterday I could not imagine this would have happened, your coming here and giving me back something of what I have lost, part of my family, part of the man I loved. I cannot tell you how much this has meant to me. And it is because I feel you are very special in my life now, I am going to ask one more thing, you can probably guess what it is."

"Yes, I believe I can." Diana took the old woman's hand, it felt cold and small.

"Yes. I would like to be cremated and the ashes scattered on what I believe to be my father's grave. Would you do that for me? You cannot imagine the peace you have given me. I can never be forgiven by those people who died that day, but I think God has finally forgiven me. My heart feels lighter than it has since the last time I saw Klaus."

"Now, there remains the question of the money. Sister, I really must have your instructions. If there is any money, I really do need to know what you would like to do. Of course, you can always give it to the church. In fact, aren't you obliged to do that?"

"Of course, and I have always done that. All the money for the estate which the lawyers managed to get from the developer went to the church. Never in my life after I came to the convent have I ever owned anything. Nothing. This money, if it exists, belonged to my father, but also to those people in the Resistance who fought for France. I have been thinking a lot about what I should do. And then," Sophie smiled, "we may be counting many chickens before there are even any eggs. There may be nothing at all, not even enough to cover your expenses."

"Alright, that may be the case, in which case there is nothing to be done. And please don't worry about my expenses, they won't be great and I would do it with pleasure. But what if there is a substantial sum?"

"I want you to trace the families of those men who were shot, and the leader who was hanged, and give the money to their families."

Diana was silent. Eventually she answered the nun's quizzical look. "Sister, you can't. Those people will never take money from you. You can't give it to them under false pretences and you can't give it anonymously because even if they don't know it came from you, *you* know they wouldn't accept it if they did. No, I'm sorry, I can't be party to that. Please don't ask me." Diana was upset. This whole event had taken a different turn than she expected.

"Don't you think something good should come out of all this?" Clearly Sister Marie Agnes had no idea why Diana had raised the objection. "What do you suggest then, Diana? You don't think some restitution is due to those people?" Sister Marie Agnes looked surprised and hurt at Diana's reaction.

"I can't believe you could even think of that. Think, Sister, think." Diana felt a rising panic, trying hard to control her emotions and wanting to scream at the obtuseness of this woman.

"Diana, please don't upset yourself. We have had no time to make real plans or have any discussions, this was something that came to me as the just thing to do."

"Well, it isn't."

"No, I realise that. Please don't be angry with me. I'm not thinking well at the moment. Could you call the nurse for me, please, Diana?"

Diana's kind temperament replaced her anger and her concern for Sophie overcame her. She called the nurse, who came with medication and an injection. Diana went outside to call Simon and then changed her mind. She couldn't possibly discuss all of this now. Diana couldn't believe how complicated her life had suddenly become. She was keeping secrets from Simon, she had agreed to be a trustee of God knows how much money and she was emotional about a wartime traitor, a woman responsible for all those deaths.

Twenty minutes later, Diana went back into Sister Marie Agnes's room.

"Diana, would you agree to this? When you've been to the bank, if there *is* any money, would *you* give some thought as to how it should be spent? If I give it straight to the church without any conditions, without any safeguards, there will be no direct benefit to anyone, it will just be absorbed into the general coffers. I'm unable now to think of anything useful or helpful to you. I have given you all my faith and trust. It has all been such a shock, such memories I have revisited."

"Oh, Sister, I can't leave you like this. I've upset you and I haven't -"

"No, Diana, don't ever think that. You have brought me more happiness and comfort than I have had in years and years. Please don't ever regret this meeting. After all, God ordained it. Ask for his help and God will help you. God bless you, child."

****

Diana left the hospice with a feeling of total unreality. It seemed such a long time since she had come here. Her mind was totally absorbed with the task ahead of her and mostly, how to talk to Simon and admit that she constructed this charade. Somehow when she had been sitting with Sister Marie Agnes, everything had seemed so right. Now, away from Lourdes and the hospice, she was beginning to realise that she had never been prepared for complications. Her life had been tranquil, warm, safe, calm and happy. Now she felt unsettled, guilty and heavy-hearted. Firstly, there was Julian, turning her emotions into something she didn't recognise. Then her discovery that de Lusignac was not the traitor but an innocent man who had died a terrible death. Finally to discover that not only was he innocent, but had gone to his death in the knowledge that his own daughter had been the traitor, and this information had lain undiscovered for years until Diana insisted that they buy this house.

And she realised with shock that she really didn't want to tell any of this to Simon and had no idea why. "It's because I feel guilty," she thought. "I've never kept any secrets from him and now I don't know where to stop."

She was already having to plan what to tell Laurier. She had given her word to Sister Marie Agnes that she would try to treat it with enough confidentiality that the village in general would never hear of it until her statement was revealed. Even at this point, she was beginning to wonder if that was at all possible.

Clearly, Jean Claude wanted to know something because she'd told him of her need to find Sophie. She decided to keep it simple and say that the notebook contained details of Sophie's father's bank in London and she needed to talk to Sophie to let her know how to find the funds.

More secrets. More subterfuge. She wasn't equipped for it, she didn't like it and the thought crossed her mind that an act of betrayal had brought all this about. Out of betrayal comes more betrayal, she thought.

Diana arrived home at about five, having stopped just once for coffee and to fill up with petrol. She was barely aware of the drive, her mind was so full of the events of the recent past and with the now-distant past. The house was warm, the heating had been on and she decided that the evening would be spent in the kitchen. She didn't want to go and light a fire in the drawing room and she was sorry she'd asked Jean Claude to come now. She had practically promised Jean Claude the truth, and in all honesty, she really did want to share this with him. She wanted to share it with someone.

She took home-made lasagne out of the freezer, made a salad, took a Camembert out of the fridge to bake in the box, and put fresh fruit on the table. She then went up for a shower. Standing in the window of her dressing room, she saw lights in Julian's house, but didn't see any movement. She sat with her towel round her and rang Simon. He answered on the second ring.

"Hello, darling, I'm home." Diana found she was actually very pleased to talk to him. "We seem to have been missing each other's calls and messages for the last day or so. How are you, darling, are you definitely coming home this weekend?"

"Dee, darling, I'm so pleased. I have really missed you, was your trip successful? When did you get home?"

"Oh, about an hour ago. How's your research going? I do miss you so much, it would be wonderful if you came home this weekend."

"Yes, I had planned to. Are you alright? You sound a bit down? Everything alright with the house?"

"Oh, yes, I'm fine. Just a bit tired. By the way, Jean Claude is popping in this evening, something to do with the stuff in those boxes. I asked him to find something out for me."

"Are you still into that de Lusignac thing, Dee? I've actually had a bit of an idea about that, which I'll tell you when I get there. It's just a thought going round in my head, but it could be something. Talk you to later darling. I love you. 'Bye."

She still had the phone in her hand. "A bit of an idea about that?" What did that mean? Diana had no idea but she didn't like the frisson of doubt which crept across her tranquillity. If she was to be honest, she hadn't really felt anything like her usual calm since her discovery of the little tin box.

Jean Claude arrived at quarter to seven. Like most people now, he rang the bell at the kitchen entrance. She crossed the hall to let him in, and he bent down to kiss her on both cheeks. She felt a surge of tears, her throat was throbbing with the effort to keep control and it completely overtook her. She put her hands over her face and wept. Jean Claude simply took her in his arms and held her until she had gained some control. He let go of her and went into the cloakroom, he came out with a wet towel for her face and walked with her to the kitchen, with his arm across her shoulder.

She sat down at the table and he poured her a glass of wine and one for himself. He drew up a chair close to her, put his hand on her arm and waited for her to tell him the cause of her misery.

She missed out nothing. Despite her promise to Sister Marie Agnes, she told Jean Claude every detail. She cried through her words, her pain for the whole tragedy of it now taking over. And now of course, she felt she had betrayed a trust. "She thinks I've been sent by God, Jean Claude. I ask you, sent by God and here I am, betraying her trust with the first person I come across."

"No, you are not betraying anything. She asked for secrecy for the sake of those people who were involved, not for you to suffer. And they will not be betrayed. You and I are the only people who know. I presume you haven't yet told Simon."

This brought on another bout of tears. "I've never kept anything from Simon. Never. I even lied about where I was going, how is he ever going to forgive me that?"

"My ex-wife will tell you that there are some lies small enough to be forgiven, and others which are going to cost a lot of money. This, I think, falls into the first category."

Diana smiled for the first time and got up to put supper on the table.

****

Diana had hardly slept; it seemed an age since she had had a good night's sleep. At 4:30 she got up and showered, her mind ill at ease with now having to explain to Simon where she had been and why she had lied about it. For the life of her now, she couldn't imagine why she had done it. She knew he disapproved of her 'obsession' with the whole de Lusignac story and her visits to the clearing. She felt better after a cup of coffee and was just making toast when the doorbell rang; the postman was always incredibly early, so she was surprised to find Julian standing the other side of the glass door.

"Good heavens." Diana smiled at him but looked a little concerned as well. Early morning calls were not generally good news.

"Hello, I saw your lights on and then I saw through the door that you were already up and in the kitchen."

"Are you spying on me?" Diana was half joking but there was an element of surprise too.

He smiled "No. I've been most of the night with John Porton-Watts. His wife has gone into some sort of decline. She wouldn't come out of her room last night and he called me. We had to break her door down, I'm afraid. She was sitting in a chair just staring, a sort of catatonia I suppose.

She was very cold and we were worried that she'd taken something."

"Oh, God, the poor woman. Well, poor John too. How very sad, what's to be done in a case like that? Is there anything I can do?" Diana was genuinely unhappy to hear of such distress.

"Well, we called the doctor, who suggested taking her to hospital, but John thinks she's better off at home. She doesn't speak French and she wouldn't be able to cope. Not that's she's able to cope now. The doctor gave her an injection and when she fell asleep we carried her to bed, she was still sleeping when I left a little while ago. John thinks they'd be better off selling up and going home – the sooner the better in my opinion. The trouble is, they probably will have a bit of trouble selling their house in the current market, so I suggested that perhaps Jean Claude and Angus might buy it back from them. If not, I'll buy it myself. They need to get away."

Diana stared at him, amazed at his generosity and total kindness to someone in need of immediate help.

"God, Julian, can you afford to do that? It's a huge gesture."

His face wore a worried expression. "Honestly, Diana, I am very concerned that she's going to do something really rash. John is worried out of his mind. He agreed to go to bed to get a couple of hours sleep when I left, but he's talked all night. He's going to find it a bit of a wrench leaving here, though."

"Because he has a friend here." Diana handed Julian a cup of coffee and plate of toast when she said this.

"How did you know?" He couldn't hide his surprise.

"I saw them once. It was something about the way the two of them were together. Does Eleanor know?"

"He doesn't think anything reaches her now, but for what it's worth she apparently always knew and they found a way to live quite amicably. He was discreet and they actually really liked each other, but then the son let them down so badly. He really couldn't leave her much anymore, so his friendship was suffering. He decided then to go back to England, find a place to put her and take Gaston with him. Does that sound cruel and unfeeling?"

"I don't know them well, but if she's really that ill and not able to take much in, then it seems a sensible thing to do. What was that about the son?" Diana was sad for a couple that not long ago, had had rank, position and wealth.

"Ah. Well. That's part of the problem. The son is in prison, serving a sentence for fraud and theft. Something to do with embezzling money from funds he had access to in his job and forging cheques. Not sure about the details and quite honestly, I think it was probably the last straw for Eleanor's mental state. She used to be the most appalling snob; having a son in prison proved to be more than she could cope with in additional to the loss of their honour and money."

"You really are an incredibly kind man. You really care about those people and their dreadful situation."

"Yes, I care." He looked up from his coffee and Diana had to control her urge to put her arms around his neck and hold him.

"Anyway," he changed the subject. "How did you enjoy your visit with your friend?"

She paused. Why was she so reluctant to tell Simon everything that had happened, yet her urge to tell everything to Laurier and now Julian, was so strong? She trusted both men, but surely shouldn't she trust Simon more than either of them? Because neither Laurier nor Julian would ridicule her investigation and Simon would: or at least, he would disapprove. No, that wasn't it either. Anyway, it would sort itself out at the weekend and she'd tell Simon everything. In the meantime, she poured Julian another cup of coffee and went to fetch the two document boxes and the tin box.

As she walked back into the kitchen, her heart jumped at the sight of his lovely face, so contorted with worry for his neighbour. She stopped herself from giving him a hug. How strange, she thought, Jean Claude can hug me and I feel nothing but friendship and comfort, yet I daren't make physical contact with this man because I want it so much.

She put the boxes on the table and began to talk.

"Say something." Diana was trying to interpret the look on his face, and Julian hadn't said a word for a long time after she finished speaking. She was putting the documents back in the boxes when she said it.

"I agree with Sophie, Sister Marie Agnes is it? Sophie, anyway. You were sent here. What on earth made you think of asking Laurier if they'd found anything in the first place? Without that, you wouldn't have the little account book. What made you go to the boat house for those pine cones? It's all just too amazing a convergence of coincidences. And no, of course I will keep the trust. I think Sophie would quite understand that you need to talk to someone. Laurier's a good chap, he'll keep his word and so shall I. And she's given you quite a task, hasn't she?"

"It's the last thing I expected when I went there. I'm going to contact the bank after I've talked to Simon at the weekend. I still feel terribly guilty that I still haven't told him anything, but it's so hard over the phone. I feel his attention is only half on what I'm saying, he's so caught up in his work. Actually, I'm not sorry I followed my instincts to go and find Sophie, but I am sorry I lied to him as to where I was going. It's not something we ever do, lying. He'll be very surprised and disappointed, I think."

Julian said nothing and sipped his coffee.

"I'd ask you to dinner on Saturday," said Diana, "but Simon's not coming until Saturday morning, and I've a lot to tell him. But I'd like to return your invitation."

"We're not on that sort of footing, surely?" he said. "At least, I'd rather we weren't. After all, there aren't many people I'd call friends on whom I can arrive at six-thirty in the morning for breakfast," he laughed. "I must go. I had planned to go away at the weekend, but I'm reluctant to leave John, to be honest. Apart from Gaston, he doesn't really have anyone else to talk to."

"You really are a very nice man," she smiled. "Going to Paris again? Celeste tells me you have a lady friend up there." She really didn't want confirmation but couldn't help herself from asking the question.

"And she'd be right. I do. And she *is* a friend, not a lover or anything else. She's a friend we've known for years, she's Josh's godmother, a friend of Edwina's from school and a lovely woman. You'd like her very much. But Celeste would be terribly disappointed, so don't enlighten her." He smiled at her.

She went with him to the door and put her hand through his. If she hadn't been so tired and confused about her feelings, she would never have made such an intimate gesture. She was inviting a situation she had tried so hard to avoid.

"Sorry, I didn't mean that. I'm not sure what …why …" Diana put her hand to her forehead.

He looked into her eyes and her heart thumped in her chest. "Diana, I'm going to be very frank. No, don't say anything. I will do nothing whatsoever to put you in an intolerable position. I will settle for whatever you will let me have. If it's to be friendship, I will live forever with that in the knowledge that it's what you want. And if ever you need me, wherever you are, I will come. I am older than you, I see a woman who is just experiencing things which many of us have had to deal with much earlier in life. But the fact that you haven't has given you a wonderful outlook on life, belief in the goodness of others, concern for their welfare, determination that others' happiness is your prime reason for being on this earth. And it shows in your lovely character and your personality. I have never met anyone with your innate goodness and I love you."

She said nothing but it seemed so natural for her to move into his open arms. He made no attempt to kiss her on the mouth, her arms were around his neck and neither wanted to break free. Diana slowly dropped her arms and he let her go.

She went back into the kitchen and sat down. Apart from Simon, she had reached this age without seriously being attracted to another man, and yet she was sitting there with her heart beating faster and wanting Julian. She picked up the phone to call Simon, he was always up early when he was working, and it was now nearly eight o'clock, so he should be already dressed and starting his day.

"Good morning, darling," he said as he answered the call.

"Hi. How's everything going? I'm so looking forward to your coming down, I've so much to tell you." She felt that preparing him for something important was the right approach.

"Really? I'm curious now. Give me a hint."

"No, darling, honestly, it's not that important and I really need to show you something, without that the story doesn't make much sense. So be patient."

"I take it then it doesn't have to do with replacing that awful chandelier in our bedroom?"

"No." She was so relieved that the conversation had moved on. "Is your research going well? You haven't said much about it. Is it working out well with Chris, is he good at his job?"

"Oh, I can't fault the research. It's just that I was hoping the story would gel better with what I've found out. It's not quite coming together as I'd have hoped, although I haven't told Edwards yet."

"Perhaps you need a break away from it," said Diana. "Can't you stay longer than the weekend?"

"No, not really, we've a couple of appointments with someone at the *Departement* records office on Monday and we've tracked down someone who had a load of old photos, showing streets and buildings before all this development in Neuilly."

They chatted about inconsequential things for a while and then he rang off to start his day. He still made no suggestion that she join him and now that she had a task of her own to perform, she was quite glad.

She logged on to the bank's website and obtained the number and the background information. There were no obvious departments to call, just one number. She spent some time scanning the letters of authority, her passport, her *carte de séjour* and anything else she could think of which the bank might require. She was just in the middle of scanning when the thought came to her that she really ought to make a copy of everything, before she buried the contents of the boxes. If she was going to make copies, perhaps she ought to have notarised copies as being true to the originals. Sophie wanted them to be buried, but what if she changed her mind later? What if her pain and illness made her wish she'd kept them? The more Diana thought about it, the more she thought it would be a good idea.

Why she thought this, she had no idea, but the idea grew until she became sure that it was the right thing to do. She made two copies of everything, put them in a folder and made an appointment with a *notaire*. The *notaire* would keep one copy. The appointment was for 9am the following morning, Diana didn't want to leave the documents overnight with the *notaire* and would wait whilst they were notarised. Even to her, it seemed like an odd thing to think of doing, but nevertheless it was what she wanted. She was confused by nearly everything she was thinking and doing.

All day her thoughts were full of Sophie, Julian, Simon and the boxes. She thought she would never settle to anything until it was all resolved one way or another, she must tell Simon and she must visit the bank. She must come up with some idea as to the disposal of the funds, whatever they were or even if there *were* any.

And Julian. What about Julian? She couldn't pretend even to herself that his declaration was a surprise. She had always felt it, his love, his affection or whatever it was. With her arms around his neck, it had felt wonderful. The temptation to kiss him was so strong, she stopped herself with difficulty but knew that if he'd made a move to do it himself, she would have allowed it.

****

After Julian had left Diana, he returned home, exhausted from his night with John Porton-Watts. But even through his exhaustion, he felt the exhilaration of holding the woman he adored. He had carefully not made any move to threaten their fragile relationship, kissing her would have been a mistake but God knows, he wanted to.

He felt a certain pity for her. She had never known her world to be so convoluted. It must be hard for her to accept so many challenges at once. She knew that the old woman she had visited was a murderer. She obviously couldn't grasp the true meaning because she couldn't see that much evil in anyone; she searched constantly for mitigation in Sophie's favour.

And of course, there was a further challenge awaiting her of which she was totally ignorant. Her husband. And the distinct possibility that he was having an affair, or so Julian believed.

Julian was never, ever going to be the one to reveal what he thought was going on. He couldn't possibly be the cause of the hurt which he knew she would find intolerable. When it had happened to him, the pain and confusion was almost more than he could bear, and he had come through some very challenging times in his life. To his certain knowledge, Diana never had.

When Julian met Edwina, she was a beautiful and lively widow. Her children were well looked after, but not well loved. As he started courting her, the children became very fond of him. He found it easy to return the children's affection: with Josh it was so open and uncomplicated; admittedly, with Phoebe it was far harder but worth the effort.

Julian's great grandfather had started a small market garden, taking horse-drawn trailers of vegetables to markets and acquiring more land little by little. When Julian's father took over, mechanisation made the farming very profitable, he was one of the first to rip out hedges and make huge fields of growing areas. He also started selling bedding plants and young vegetables for planting out. In the post-war period when mortgages became available and people were no longer renters but home-owners, they became proud gardeners too.

His father realised that gardeners needed more than plants, they needed tools, fertilisers, fencing and other equipment. He opened the first proper garden centre in Somerset, followed by another shortly afterwards. By the time Julian was old enough to join him in the business, he owned eleven garden centres in eight counties. Julian enlarged the centres to incorporate restaurants: they became swimming pool installers and built gazebos and summer houses.

When Julian was fifty-seven, he was approached by a multi-national corporation with an offer to buy his business. The offer was very attractive and came at a time in their lives when change was brought on them.

On the surface, their life seems to have been blessed with nothing but good fortune. He had a thriving business, a beautiful wife and two children who adored him. Phoebe's problems became apparent at a very early age. Her tantrums and mood swings were unpredictable. Edwina refused to recognise that Phoebe needed professional help and employed nanny after nanny. Phoebe showed artistic talent but no inclination to engage with anyone. She became very remote and withdrawn; Edwina's response was to leave the child to her own devices.

Phoebe adored Julian but would even become hostile to him if he wasn't instantly available to her when she needed him to be. As she grew older, her volatility was having an effect on the whole family. Edwina wanted Josh to attend his father's old school as a boarder, and suggested sending Phoebe to some sort of institution. Edwina had always been what his mother would have called 'flighty' but he loved her. He had been overjoyed when she had accepted his proposal of marriage, he couldn't believe he was so lucky.

He had bought the apartment in Paris when he was just starting out in the business with his father. After he married Edwina, they would often spend time there whenever he could get away, she to shop in the Paris fashion houses and he to spend time in the Louvre, the Quai D'Orsay or simply to sit at an outside table of a café and just enjoy being there, smelling Gauloises cigarettes in the air and drinking strong, black coffee. When the children were young, they had shared a room but as they grew older it became impossible for all of them to stay there. He never sold his apartment, he loved it and would visit it alone when Edwina would go away for weekends with friends and the children were at school, but with the family they always stayed in a hotel. They all loved France, especially the southern areas, but Phoebe's increasingly bizarre behaviour and unpredictability made travelling difficult now. But on occasions, especially if business required it of him, he made trips to Paris and would stay in his lovely little apartment.

After several years, if his marriage had fallen short of his expectations, he wouldn't acknowledge it. His suggestion to Edwina that they have a child of their own was met with disdain. She wanted no more children. He accepted her decision and told himself it didn't matter, they had a good marriage and two lovely children. Phoebe was now spending time in a school which allowed her to board, but she could also come home at weekends or at other times: for example, birthdays and other family occasions. Julian wasn't altogether happy with the school, but Edwina was insistent that it was the right thing to do, the child needed specialist education.

They had a lovely house in Sussex. The garden had been created by Edwina with the help of a specialist firm of landscape gardeners; she had shown flair and an understanding of the changing seasons, requiring colour all year round. The end result had been a masterpiece of winding paths leading into yet another arbour or quiet nook. Julian was so proud of her achievement and he adored her.

Julian had gone to Nottingham to talk to a company which made ride-on mowers. The hotel was bleak, the food unexciting and the anticipation of an evening and night spent there was depressing. A few hours in his car and he would be in his own home and his own bed; the prospect was too enticing to ignore.

It was nearly midnight when he arrived home. The house was well-lit, which he thought strange: he would have thought Edwina would be in bed by now. There was a BMW parked in the driveway. Even from the outside he could hear faint music as he got out of his car. He opened the front door and heard the music. He was about to call out when he heard noises. Those noises were instantly recognisable: everyone has heard them, or made them. Noises of sex, moans of pleasure and urges in urgent voices. Edwina was lying on the rug, the rug they had chosen together, her legs were wrapped around a naked man whose movements were bringing Julian's wife to her moment of ecstasy. Her eyes were closed tight in that expression of expectation of what would burst through her body at any moment. Julian stood rigid and his pain was pounded into him by witnessing that very moment brought to his wife by another man. He felt no anger, just pain and more pain.

He reached for support, for the door handle which slipped away from his hand and the door slammed. The couple's eyes turned towards him. He had no wish to witness the uncoupling; he turned and walked out to the hallway. He had no idea how long he sat there before Edwina came through the door.

"I've let him out through the garden door. You don't have to see him."

Julian searched for something to say, he had words of anger, pain, humiliation and hatred on his tongue but could say none of it. All the words were in his head but to put them in any sort of order to make her understand what he was feeling was impossible.

He expected abject apologies, tears, begging for forgiveness, even lies. But she offered none of it. She simply walked past him and went upstairs. He heard the bathroom door close and heard the water start to run as she prepared a bath.

By the time he went upstairs, she was already in bed. "I suppose you want me to ask for forgiveness. I would of course, if I thought it would do any good. But you won't forgive me, will you, so what would be the point?"

Her callousness defeated him. "I can't talk to you right now; I'm sleeping in the guest room."

He didn't sleep, of course. He kept seeing the rising and falling of the pair on the floor in his home, on the rug where the children played, where he played with the children. Eventually he went downstairs to the kitchen, made tea and took it to his study. What did he want to do? He had no idea. Did he want a divorce? Did she? Was she in love with this man? The point was, did Julian still love her? Oh God, yes. Yes, he did. Could he still live with her now, could he make love to her after this? Yes, yes, yes of course he could. In fact, he wanted to. Now. Was it just an exercise to reassert his rights? He didn't know but he was filled with inexplicable lust – certainly not soft expectation of love-making, but pure lust.

He ran up the stairs and threw open the bedroom door, threw off his dressing gown and walked towards the bed. And she laughed. She laughed in triumph. She knew men only too well, and she knew Julian better than he knew himself. She knew all his weaknesses, his longings and mostly his need for her, physically and emotionally.

She stopped laughing when she saw the look on his face. "Julian, I -"

She got no further. He turned and walked out. A sheet of ice descended on his lust and his love. All the pain, humiliation and adoration was wrapped up into one package and frozen.

The following morning she came to breakfast as he was finishing his coffee. Before she could say a word, he said, "I'm collecting the children next week at the end of term and we're going to Paris. We'll stay at the Dorchester on Friday night and leave on Saturday. Here is what will happen. This house is our home, never again will you entertain anyone here, of either sex that is. For the sake of the children, you will live here during the school holidays and take care of the children." He took a sip of coffee and looked at her with a raised eyebrow, asking for confirmation. "That is, of course, until we've decided, both of us, what we do next."

"Yes, of course. Julian, listen, please-"

"Be quiet. At the moment, you can have nothing to say that I wish to listen to. I have never been an unkind man, but should you ever bring our family and our home into your sordid dealings again, you will wish you had never met me. Please don't make the mistake of not believing me."

He paused to drink more coffee. He looked at her once more: she was trembling and looked defeated.

"Julian, please let me speak. Please let me say this. I don't want a - it's all over, I promise, I can't explain what - I don't - I have no excuse or explanation to offer. I can't even ask for forgiveness, but please, please don't cut me out of your life." She burst into genuine tears.

His heart was not moved at her distress, the ball of ice refused to melt.

"Well, that's up to you. All trust has gone. You cannot make a hole in someone's life and expect to fill it with apologies. Do you want a divorce?"

"Oh God, no!" she exclaimed in genuine alarm. "No. No, I don't. Do you?"

"No," he replied. "At least, not yet. I haven't had time to sort out how I feel yet, except you can't hurt me any more than you did. I won't have the children harmed by divorce but it all rather depends on you. You need to think of them now, Phoebe especially. She's a frightened, confused little girl. A divorce right now would only mean I would have to fight you for custody and I won't do that to them. Now, from now until the end of term I shall stay in London, collect the children on Friday and go straight to Paris. You may join us, but there are conditions which are not negotiable. I will take a suite and you will have the guest bedroom. Tell the children that you are not sleeping well and you don't want to keep me awake. And you will look after the children as you should. No shopping trips unless it's for things for the children. Instead, take the children out and about. We will do things as a family, for their sake."

He finished his coffee and got up from the table. Edwina looked fragile and lost but it didn't touch him. He knew he'd been cruel. It wasn't that he didn't care, it just didn't move him. What one human being can do to another, he thought as he went out of the door. He looked back. "Deal with the household matters. Tell Mrs. Farmer that we'll be away from Friday and we'll be back in about two weeks. Unless, of course, you decide not to join us, in which case we'll have something else to decide."

Julian had gone to London and attempted to carry on with business meetings, but his thoughts were constantly on his situation. He felt, now that he was away from Edwina, that a divorce was inevitable. If they were able to prepare the children gently, perhaps things wouldn't be too bad for them. His concern was only for them. Edwina, he knew, wouldn't be alone for long. Was there such a thing as an amicable divorce? Would she agree to let him have the children? Clearly, she had never been the best of mothers, but that was far removed from letting someone else take her children.

How Edwina had spent the next few days, he had no idea. Presumably there would have had to be some contact with the lover, to put an end to whatever sordid relationship they had. Julian did not know if the man was the only one, nor did he want to. It made him feel ill to think he had almost made love to her that night. He hadn't been thinking clearly and she had always been able to create a need in him.

Edwina surprised him on the day before he was due to pick up the children. She had arrived in their suite whilst he was still at work and he had found her there on his return. As he opened the door, he saw her sitting in a chair by the window.

"Hello, Julian. I was feeling rather tired, so I thought I'd come up today instead of tomorrow morning. It would have been quite a long trip to come here and then go to fetch the children. I hope you don't mind."

"No, I don't mind. Are you well? You look rather done in. Do you want something, some tea or something?" His tone, whilst not friendly, had lost its cruel edge from the last time they spoke.

"No. As a matter of fact, I'm not really feeling at all well. I've had a sort of pain in my chest, rather like a tight band, for a day or two. I'm hoping it will pass so that I can come with you and the children, but to be honest, the way I feel at the moment, I think I'll be letting you go away with the children on your own. Please don't read anything into that, I've no other reason except I really don't feel well." Edwina had a sheen of perspiration on her face and her skin had a greyish look.

Julian was concerned, Edwina was never ill. Her hair looked a little unkempt and her appearance was less well-groomed than usual.

"I think we should call a doctor, Edwina. It's unusual for you to be ill, and you do look unwell." She seemed to have a little more trouble breathing. She looked pathetic and his compassion led him to take her hand. She nodded her agreement, but her breathing was taking all her time. He dropped her hand and walked over to the telephone; as he was calling reception he heard her fall to the floor.

"Reception, an ambulance quickly, my wife is having a heart attack." He dropped the phone and ran over to her side. "It's alright Edwina, don't worry, it's alright, help is coming. Just try to breathe a little more easily, help is coming."

"I'm - scared. Please, don't leave me."

"I'm here, I won't leave you, it's alright, I'm here." He could already hear a siren in the street below. "Help is here, Edwina, help is on its way right now."

It seemed forever, but in reality it was only a matter of minutes before the door flew open. Julian realised the housekeeper was with the paramedics and had let them in with her pass key. They kindly but firmly nudged him out of the way and got to work. They spoke on their radios, attached her to various cables and put a pill of some sort under her tongue. They gave her oxygen and spoke reassuring words to her. Her eyes were full of fear and searched for Julian. He answered the paramedics as best he could about her general health, any medication and the period immediately before the current crisis.

With a jolt he realised that she had been unwell almost as soon as he had left for London and she had spent a few days in Sussex on her own. Mrs. Farmer did not live in, so Edwina was alone with her illness through the night, which must have seemed interminably long. Her effort to get to him in London had been phenomenal.

The next few hours seemed like a dream to him, they had an unreal quality which left him confused and feeling a weight of guilt which was crushing. She had been stabilised in the cardiac intensive care unit and certain tests were now being ordered, including something which required her to be taken to an operating theatre but he didn't take in whether or not she would be given an anaesthetic. The doctor spoke to him of heart damage, valve trouble, by-pass operations and cardiograms.

Neither Julian nor Edwina had had any major surgery requiring hospital stays. The children had been into casualty once or twice, John with a broken wrist from climbing trees, and Phoebe to have her appendix out. But they had been a remarkably healthy and fit family. Julian seemed not to understand what was happening – she didn't smoke, she played tennis and went to the gym, drank moderately and kept herself in good shape. How could she have had a heart attack? The doctor explained that she had probably had a heart problem for a long time which was undiagnosed. "If they don't give any trouble, they can go undetected for years."

He sat for hours, it seemed. People came and went and he was vaguely aware of other ill people in the unit and weeping relatives, but the reality refused to imprint itself in his mind. He was sitting waiting for her to be brought back from wherever they had taken her, when he suddenly thought about the children. He was supposed to collect them tomorrow. Mrs. Farmer and her husband were always willing to help out when there were problems, such as staying with Josh when Phoebe had managed to run away from her school and Julian and Edwina had to go and collect her. The poor woman was shocked when he called and told her what had happened, and of course, she and Barry would go and pick up the children. Josh's school was twenty miles from Phoebe's but they would all be back in Sussex by late afternoon and Mr. Lawson could talk to the children before their supper.

Julian sat beside the empty bed-space waiting for Edwina to come back from whichever department they had taken her to; he wasn't even sure if he'd been told, so much had been discussed in an urgent and serious way. His thoughts and feelings were so confused, he would have found it impossible to voice his emotions right now.

The doctor finally came to him and told him that Edwina was now stable. Initial tests indicated that a by-pass would be required almost immediately, she was over 90% blocked, whatever that meant. Did he hear correctly; did he even ask? He was told that he could stay with Edwina for a few minutes when she returned but he should then go and get some rest. She would spend the following day having further tests and surgery was planned for Monday.

She looked a little better when she was wheeled back to her place. She had an oxygen mask on her face and was connected to some kind of monitor which showed an alarming number of graphs and flashing numbers. There were various other tubes and needles sticking into her hand but her breathing seemed easier.

Her eyes filled with tears when she saw him, and he sat beside her holding her fingers, avoiding the alarming-looking needle thing sticking out of her hand.

"Darling, I'm so pleased you're here."

"Of course I'm here, I'll be here for as long as you want me to be."

The tears poured down her face and her distress was hurting him, he was sure that she was supposed to be calm and quiet. "Edwina, darling, don't think about anything at all except getting better. Let's get this operation done and get you home. We all want you home. You have to be brave for a few days, this operation is quite routine now, so they tell me. I'll be as close as they'll let me."

"Julian, you will never know how sorry I am -"

"Don't. It's over. Don't, darling, please. Just get better and come home to me. Please just think about that and nothing else. I'm not."

He kissed her forehead and stroked her cheek. He knew it wasn't as easy as that but they were going to have to try. For the moment, the most important thing was to get her through this. Then, he made himself a promise that he would do everything he could – everything – to find a way to make their life together work, which would mean that he would have to make a supreme effort to damp down the dark thoughts when they came and the pictures in his mind of his wife reaching an orgasm with another man as he had walked through the door.

Of course, one of the driving forces of this determination to start again was his own guilt. Somewhere in his mind was the thought that infidelity was usually the fault of both parties. Didn't he bear some responsibility for not making her happy enough that she wouldn't have to seek love elsewhere? Was it love? What did she feel for this man? Were there others? Or was this just a momentary lapse? Was his anger with her partly responsible for bringing on this cardiac problem?

He was just too tired now to even try to find answers. On his own in London he had felt justified in his coldness to her the last time he had seen her. Now, he was digging deep to find the love he had had for her, and if he didn't quite find that, he found something else he thought he could live with. Acceptance. That would do for now.

****

160

Edwina tolerated surgery very well and within ten days was out of hospital. They returned to Sussex just before the children were due to go back to school. Josh had accepted fully the reason for not spending time with his parents, he was overjoyed to see them return home. Phoebe was silent at the start and sat at the kitchen table, painting with a ferocious determination. As the time to return to school arrived, she reverted to screaming about imaginary children in her house, voices in her head and colours changing in front of her. Julian would hold her until she quietened down, and talk to her about her painting. Even at an early age, her talent was exceptional.

There was a special needs school close to where they lived, which believed more in helping the children achieve a level of capability to live normally with their affliction and within the family, whilst still accumulating some of the knowledge which they needed to get by in the world. Phoebe was still a little young to be accepted but a generous donation from Julian ensured that they took her a year early. The change in the child was phenomenal. She still had the odd tantrum and nightmares were not unusual, but her personality was less fearful and aggressive and at times, loving and helpful. But her painting was her life and the school was only too happy to have a student with a recognisable talent which they were able to encourage.

Over the next few years, Edwina was apparently happy just to be at home with Julian and the children. She still occasionally went on shopping trips but would always ask Julian to go with her. He never did – his outward trust in her was a way of assuaging his guilt at having brought her illness to the fore, as he firmly believed he had.

If Julian had lost his all-consuming love for her, it was replaced by a sort of easy companionship. He knew she was no longer able to hurt him: he would never allow her – or anyone else – to reach those depths of his feelings again. He was safe from that kind of pain. They made love frequently and it was good. If it lacked the part where his heart expanded to enfold her, it was still good. She knew how to give him what he wanted and did so willingly.

Their decision to move to France followed the amazing offer to buy the business from Julian. He had not been thinking of selling, but suddenly it seemed as if fate had determined it. The children were grown, Josh had won a place at Harvard Business School and had obtained his MBA after which he fulfilled his ambition to work for his father. Phoebe had had enormous problems to overcome for a few years, but then a proper diagnosis of her problem meant that the treatment offered her a way to live as she wished but was protected at the same time.

A corporation with interests in the leisure industry made an offer for the Lawson Garden Centres and after obtaining a directorship for Josh, Julian had left the business one Thursday evening and never looked back.

When Edwina and Julian had first seen the estate of *La Chênaie*, *La Maison Neuve* was still under tarpaulins, scaffolding and ladders. Their own house was almost finished, but Julian wanted some changes made. Two of the other houses were also near completion and the others were finished. Edwina and Julian looked around *La Maison Neuve* one evening when the workmen had gone for the day and Edwina said, "It's very lovely, of course, but I don't think anyone could ever be happy here."

"That's an odd thing to say, Ed. What's wrong with the place? I think it's gorgeous, or will be. Look at the view." He wasn't sure at what point he'd stopped calling her 'darling' and started using her old nick-name again. He'd called her, 'Ed', when they'd first met and she'd hated it. Now she seemed not to mind.

"I really wouldn't want anything this big. I like the one we've chosen, it has a lovely-shaped garden, and I can start from scratch. I'm really looking forward to doing another garden, I can see it all in my mind. When do you think we can move in?"

They had been the first ones to move in, followed shortly afterwards by Hilary and Bob Findlay, who bought the first house on the left inside the gate. It had been a happy time: they took French lessons, planned the garden, drove miles looking at bushes and trees for sale, and made frequent trips back to the UK to see Phoebe and Josh.

The landscape gardeners they had employed to carry out the work were helpful and pleased with Edwina's design: she had spent a lot of time driving in the French countryside looking at what grew naturally, trees and bushes which looked at home in this climate and environment. But there were always corners and ledges which needed her special touch with bedding plants and perennials.

It was whilst she was planting her adored dahlia corms that she gave a small cry and pitched forward, dead before her face landed in the soft soil. Julian ran to her and turned her over. He brushed the soil lightly from her cheeks and from her hairline and looked down at her face. He gently picked her up in his arms and carried her into the house. He laid her on the bed and went to the telephone. As he waited for the doctor, he realised he felt no pain. She had wiped out all of his deep feelings that night on the rug: his pain then had been all but unbearable. He felt regret for her passing, she wasn't old and should have had years yet to enjoy her life. Regret. But that was all. The ball inside was still frozen.

All of that had changed the night he met Diana. If it could be said that someone's goodness shone out of them, it could be said of Diana. He watched her as she came into the room, all of his indifference disappeared in a few seconds of emotion. He stood observing, hoping that she would do or say something which would immediately cancel out this feeling he had. Since he had met her, she had consumed all his rational thinking. He wanted nothing more than to be with her, to look at her and to touch her. None of which was his right.

She looked wonderful, he wanted to tell her there and then. Her hair was loose around her shoulders, held back from her ears by two sparkly combs, the only jewellery she wore, apart from her modest engagement ring and wedding ring. There was no artifice with this woman. Hilary had described her as 'a bit mousey' but that was so far from the truth. To him she was one of the most natural women he had met, he almost resented the swirls of emotion he was feeling, recognising that she would now make him vulnerable to being hurt and suffering pain yet again. But then, he thought she was incapable of such cruelty.

When Margaret had come banging into his house, saying that Diana could be in trouble the night they had found her by the lake, his heart had squeezed with anxiety. When they found her, it was all he could do not to gather her in his arms and keep her there.

He had never understood what people meant by 'deeply' in love, 'madly' in love. How could there be degrees of love? You loved or you didn't love. Physical longing was part of it to be sure, but for him at least, it was the pure emotion of wanting that other person to be part of you and only feeling half complete when that other person is absent. He felt like that about Diana.

Before Julian had first met Simon, he had formed an idea of what he thought Diana's husband would be like. He was sure to be intelligent, kind, generous and thoughtful, she wouldn't live with less. The reality couldn't have been more different. Julian found an egotistical, vain and selfish man. He was good-looking enough and sure to appeal to women, but his whole air was of someone who felt entitled to adulation and attention. He watched Diana with him: she adored him, that much was evident but whether this was reciprocal, he doubted very much. And that was before his recent discovery.

Simon had accepted the offer of the flat in Paris for a few months to undertake his research. Out of curiosity, Julian had bought Simon's first book; it was interesting enough, the sort of thing one might pick up before going on a long journey, certainly not an intellectual giant of a book – but that was alright, he himself was fond of fairly easy-going but enticing novels at times. The story was solid enough but the characters were somewhat vapid. Anyway, it had been successful enough that the publisher was evidently happy for a sequel, even after so many years.

Simon had been installed in the Paris flat for a few weeks when a letter arrived at *La Chênaie* for Julian stating that some routine maintenance to the heating system in the Paris flat was to be carried out. Although each apartment had controls on the radiators, like many older buildings, the apartments did not have their own boilers, but a central boiler. This was due to be serviced and the apartments would be without heating and hot water for a whole day. Anyone having problems after the boiler was re-started should phone a particular number.

Julian thought this important enough to pass on to Simon and had called him on the landline at the apartment. A young-sounding woman had answered the phone. Julian was aware that Simon had a young researcher helping him, but he had gained the impression from Diana that it was a young man called Chris. Diana certainly thought it was.

Without thinking it through, Julian hung up the phone. He was on the point of redialling and thought better of it. A sort of premonition swept across his consciousness. It was a beautiful morning, it had rained heavily overnight and he could hear the water dripping off the leaves in the woods. He took his coffee outside and strolled around the garden whilst thinking what to do. He didn't want to jump to the obvious conclusion, but a suspicion had lodged in his mind and would not be pacified. Recently, Diana had been busy sorting out her house and shopping, he'd seen little of her and had not tried to overwhelm her with his presence, therefore he had no knowledge of any visitor Simon might

165

have, even with Diana's knowledge. He finished his coffee and felt a certainty of what he should do next.

A decision made, he went back inside and started the routine for leaving the house overnight, turning off his computer and leaving lights on a timer. His cleaner wasn't due the next day and he was sure to be back by tomorrow afternoon. At the station, he almost turned back. This really wasn't his business, and if his suspicions were confirmed, what did he intend to do about it? Was he really going to find Diana so grateful to be told of her husband's infidelity that she'd fall into his arms?

He'd worry about that later, but for now, he had to know. He couldn't bear the idea of Diana suffering the same kind of hurt and pain he had gone through and told himself it was to save her from all of that.

His train arrived in Paris just after six in the evening. He decided to stay overnight in a hotel but would call at the apartment first. His taxi dropped him outside and he had no way of knowing whether or not Simon was at home. He used the keypad to let himself into the foyer, went through the courtyard and into the main building. He took the cranky little lift to the second floor and stopped outside the door to the apartment. He rang the bell.

A pretty girl of about twenty-two or twenty-three answered the door. She wore a long shirt – probably Simon's, he thought – her legs and feet were bare. The bedroom was immediately on the right and through the glass door he could see that clearly, the bed had not been made that day.

"Hello, I'm Julian Lawson. Is Simon here?"

Simon came to the door of the drawing room, unkempt but at least he was dressed. He was not happy to see Julian.

"What on earth are you doing here? You should have let me know you were coming." He still didn't invite Julian into the room.

"I'm on my way to stay with friends, and I had this letter this morning. It will be a nuisance; they always leave maintenance until the weather turns colder for some reason. But I'm staying literally five minutes' walk from here, so I thought I'd let you know. If you have trouble with the heating after they've finished, you can ring me if you like and I'll deal with the engineers, unless you feel your French is up to it." he smiled and waited for Simon or the girl to offer some sort of explanation.

The girl had silently removed herself to the bedroom, closed the glass door and drawn down the blind; she returned wearing a pair of jeans now. She offered no explanation as to who she was and Julian looked at Simon for some response.

"Oh, thanks, but I'll manage, I can always get Diana to speak to them if I'm stuck." Julian looked enquiringly at the girl. "By the way, this is Chris, my researcher."

Julian smiled coldly in her direction but the girl looked very ill at ease and after a muttered, "hello," wandered off in the direction of the bathroom.

"Look, Julian," said Simon, taking him by the arm and turning him towards the door, "It's not what you think. I wish you hadn't caught us being this informal, but that's all it is – informality. It's difficult to work and live in a small apartment and not become - well, informal." He smiled at Julian, a sort of man-to-man demand for understanding.

"Well, that's a word for it I've never heard before. In any case, what makes you think you need to explain to me? Having done so, you make it sound less - shall we say, informal?" Julian's voice was brimming with anger.

"I suppose what I'm saying is that I know what it must look like, but please don't get the wrong idea. I'd hate Diana to be worried for nothing, because it *is* nothing, you know."

"It's difficult to get the wrong idea, Simon, when your clothes and hers are lying around in the same bedroom. In any case, I wouldn't dream of letting Diana think you are anything less than the man she believes you to be." He gave Simon a look of disgust.

"Then I can rely on you not to say anything? It would just cause a lot of trouble over nothing, you know."

Julian thought it strange that Simon used the word 'trouble' and not 'pain' or 'hurt', meaning trouble for himself, of course.

"No, I won't say anything but if I were you, I would terminate your – um - 'research' - as soon as possible and get back down to Saint-Sulpice. Diana misses you and she's all alone in that big house. And tell that girl to stop answering the phone, it could have been Diana who called."

"Are you telling me I can't stay here anymore? I still need to finish some work. In any case, Diana only has my mobile number, not this landline."

How typical of the man, thought Julian. He's totally unaware that his life – and Diana's – could come tumbling down but can't see past the point of his immediate needs.

"No, of course I'm not saying that. For one thing, you'd have to explain to Diana why you've been thrown out. But think about it, Simon, get back to her as soon as you can and put this - episode - behind you."

Simon saw him off with a false jollity and a back-slap, obviously convinced that they had reached an understanding that only can be made between two worldly men, leaving Julian very uncomfortable and disheartened at now being party to this infidelity. The best Julian could hope for now would be that Simon would give up this Chris, go back home to Diana and write his wretched book.

****

John Porton-Watts had watched Julian walk away after his sterling support through the night and then closed the door. He was exhausted and wanted nothing more than to sleep and find everything back to normal when he woke, but that would never happen. Not ever. When he had first found Eleanor in some sort of catatonic state yesterday, he really thought she had taken something, and God forgive him, he hoped she had.

Seeing her sitting in the chair, staring like a wild woman, her hair matted and tangled, he thought he'd finally be free; she'd quietly go to sleep and end this nightmare that their lives had become. He saw nothing of the beautiful young woman he'd married.

He'd gone to some ghastly ball with a friend, intent on grabbing a bottle or two and disappearing into the gardens with some handsome young chap: society seemed to be teeming with them. He was twenty-two and if the word beautiful could be applied to a man, it could be applied to him. Even now, some fifty years later, he had retained his good looks and slim figure. He had been popular and had had as many men friends as he had women friends. The Portons had married into the Watts years ago and the name carried through several generations.

He was already involved with a group of friends the night he really saw her for the first time. She'd been on the periphery of his social outings, having recently returned from Switzerland, but his sister Charlotte had included her in their group more recently.

The initial fortune of the Porton family had been made in trade. Over the generations, the estate had increased in size and gradually, the men of the family had no need to trade, they owned coal mines, timber yards and invested in tobacco in America. The Porton-Wattses starting producing a series of girls, who married 'society' men totally unprepared to run an estate for profit, let alone the necessity for the upkeep of houses like Porton Hall. As parts of the estate were sold off over the generations to keep young masters in horses and fine wines, the sum of the parts became too small for any profitable enterprise to support fine landed gentry families.

By the time John inherited the estate, it had been mortgaged twice and the returns from the estate were insufficient to meet repayments and to keep the sizeable house going.

But at the time when John met Eleanor, his parents were showing no sign of the debts they were accruing; they gave lavish house parties and launched their daughter with the best ball of the season. They kept a house in Eton Square and a string of hunters in the stables. The house was still fully staffed and there was no hint of the dip in the horizon.

Eleanor was the late and only child of a successful businessman. His lack of social niceties was something he ignored in himself but was determined that his girl would not start with that disadvantage.

At her finishing school in Switzerland she had acquired the polish and attitude of aristocratic families. Her mother had died when she was in her teens and she had adopted many of her mannerisms by watching the mothers of her friends, with whom she would spend her school holidays, in draughty country houses and weekend house parties with young people of wealth and position. She had met John in the season after she left the Swiss school. Eleanor had no illusions about her origins but was determined that her polish would net her a suitable husband with property and position.

She had set herself a goal that this season would be the first and last she would spend as a single girl. Some young man would receive her full attention and her beauty and arrogance would ensure that he was the right sort. She was very careful not to get a reputation for being flighty or easy, she was even gaining a reputation for being 'frigid'. But that was fine. Her choice was going to be the man to take her virginity. All of the girls in her set were happily giving themselves on tables in libraries, bouncing astride young men in leather chairs in studies and drawing rooms, or allowing grooms to mount them in stable lofts.

She was careful never to be left in a position which could be called compromising: she never went into dark conservatories with tipsy young men and always pushed them away when they danced too close and pushed themselves hard against her.

She was no-one's fool. The Pride-and-Prejudice world in which she lived was evident to her at a very early age. It was fine when she was very young, even later at finishing school where the differences in social status were hardly recognised. In the school holidays she was able to join friends at villas in the South of France, she joined skiing parties in Switzerland and her wardrobe was always up to date and of the finest quality. But clearly, money didn't buy breeding and although her friends' parents were good enough to include her, they admired her looks and her manners, she always felt apart and knew that her prospects would only be bettered by her own efforts. And this she was determined to do.

John Porton-Watts was perfect. He was beautiful. She had seen him at one ball but he'd left very quickly with a group of friends. Eleanor would inherit a sizeable sum, including a house in Connaught Square – a very suitable address, but it would never be enough for the Porton-Wattses. Everyone knew the Porton-Wattses were immensely wealthy: the daughter Charlotte had been launched with a brilliant ball, the gifts given to all the young guests had been superb. It had been rumoured that John's father wasn't terribly well and he would inherit Porton Hall quite soon. She would have to be clever but quick.

Eleanor's father had no country house handed down through the generations and therefore decided to give her dance at the Connaught Hotel. Eleanor herself was against such a thing, it seemed so common to have a dance anywhere other than a private house, but the house really was not big enough. She gave a lot of thought to her party. She didn't want the usual format. If she was going to be different enough to hold her party in a hotel, it was going to be totally different. She planned that the invitations would ask the ladies to wear pink. The girls then would blend one into another and no-one would stand out. She, of course, would be the only girl wearing a different colour – yet to be decided. Eleanor's beauty was unusual but she needed to be really singled out from everyone else for this to succeed. She had thought of asking the girls to wear white but thought they would look too bridal and defeat the object of her exercise.

There would also be entertainment. Something sophisticated but which would appeal to young people, it would need a lot of thought and planning. And she knew just who to ask for help. Charlotte Porton-Watts was not exactly a bosom friend, but a close enough acquaintance that she could ask her to lunch to talk over 'something I'd like your help with'. Unfortunately, the house in Connaught Square was being renovated and painted, was it possible to meet Charlotte somewhere else? Charlotte was kind enough to invite Eleanor for the weekend, her parents were having some people for dinner on Friday, but there would just be the family for the rest of the time. It was just what Eleanor had hoped, an opportunity to see John at home. But she'd have to work something out whilst she was there, nothing came immediately to mind.

Eleanor wasn't careless of her beauty, she knew she was very lovely, but in the circle in which she was moving, sons were expected to marry into the same social status; beauty wasn't going to be enough. She planned her weekend wardrobe with great care. The dinner would be held on the Friday evening, the guests would stay overnight and depart after breakfast the following morning. Charlotte had suggested that they start their planning for Eleanor's party on Saturday afternoon when John and a couple of his friends would be out riding, and her parents would be involved in their own social activities. Eleanor would return home to Connaught Square on Sunday after lunch. She would be accompanied by her maid Townsend and her father would send her with the chauffeur.

She realised this was the first time she had been to an adult weekend function alone since she left school. But still nothing occurred to her as to how to gain John's interest. But she was sure something would.

Charlotte seemed really pleased to see her when she arrived at tea-time on Friday. They had never spent any length of time alone, just the two of them, but they found each other's company entertaining and enjoyable. It seemed that Charlotte would probably announce her engagement within a couple of weeks and Eleanor would be invited to the party.

Eleanor's knowledge of sex was gleaned from Townsend, but she had a quick enough mind to engage the rest of the information. John was nowhere to be seen at tea and she wondered if he was even here; and of course, she couldn't ask; any slight indication that she might be interested in him would set alarms ringing in the family.

Charlotte's parents joined them for tea. They were pleasant but seemed inordinately interested in Eleanor's parents and their status. The Connaught Square address seemed fairly impressive but they quickly assumed the girl, despite her fortune, had unfortunate parentage and would therefore be of no importance in their search for a wife for John. Eleanor had other ideas and a plan started to form in her mind. She went to dress for dinner with the beginnings of a scheme.

Eleanor had kept her hair long when others wanted modern, short, bouncy, bobbed hairstyles. Her dress was a bold colour for a young, unmarried girl; a deep blue, with a full skirt and a stand-up wrap of fine tulle around her neck and shoulders which framed her face in blue froth. Her eyes were blue and she finished the whole effect with her mother's diamond and sapphire necklace with matching earrings. Her hair was swept up in a complicated, lightly plaited affair which Townsend did so well. She looked gorgeous.

From behind her door, she heard Charlotte on her way down, chatting amiably with her brother and then laughing at some joke he had made. She gave them a further ten minutes and went downstairs herself. As she went downstairs, John was talking to the butler in the front hall and stopped speaking when he saw her. She smiled and said, "Hello. I'm sorry, am I late?"

"No, of course not, we're having cocktails in the drawing room. Eleanor, you look lovely. Here, take my arm."

He spoke with the easy charm of a young man of society who was used to paying compliments and also accepting them. He gave her his arm and they went into the drawing room. The double doors were open and the evening breeze was fluttering the curtains. It had been a very hot day and the air smelled of freshly-cut grass and dew.

Eleanor had no doubt that even if John *was* interested in her, she was not marriageable material for him, his parents had made that perfectly plain. For her plan to work, she had to seem disinterested and distant. She made no eye contact with him during dinner, was charming to the older guests and complimented Charlotte on her dress and her family; she gave Charlotte's parents no cause to worry that this girl was out to ruin John's chances of making a really good marriage. John was used to the 'fast set', girls and young men who had the freedom and the money to run wild for a short time before settling down to a sensible marriage. He had been raised to believe that he was to marry well. And his parents intended him to.

Throughout dinner, she was aware that he kept watching her. She was graceful, elegant, beautifully dressed, spoke Italian, could ride and enjoyed a quick wit. She'd be such tremendous fun as a friend.

Eleanor's plan was as simple as it was old. She would seduce John in an attempt to claim ruined honour and pregnancy. She would seem to be unused to very much alcohol and he would have taken advantage of her slightly confused state. She would attempt to make things a little rough so that she would have a few bruises to show, perhaps some scratches from a bush - but first, she had to get John on his own outside. She would be tearful, gracious in blaming herself and not John, but nevertheless she would expect him to stand by her.

Tonight. It had to be tonight. She couldn't risk leaving it to the following day in case John went off with his male friends, who were never far away.

After dinner, the ladies withdrew to the drawing room, leaving the men to their port. Eleanor accepted a liqueur with coffee and watched for her opportunity: it surely must come soon, time was passing. When the men returned to the drawing room to join the ladies, John was not among them. To hide her disappointment, she fanned herself lightly and smiling at Charlotte, who was regaling a large-busted lady with news of her up-coming engagement, she walked out onto the terrace and walked slowly down the steps to the gardens. Where on earth was he? He wasn't joining his friends until the following day, so where had he gone?

From inside the house, with the lights on, it looked really dark outside but in fact, it was a lovely summer twilight outside, enough to see but not to be seen. Her father's ambition for her was to marry a young banker or businessman, but she wanted more. She wanted children with hundreds of years of aristocratic breeding behind them, she wanted portraits on the wall of ancestors who belonged to her sons.

The lights from the house lit most of the lawn up to the fountain, and she wandered towards the woods on the left. How beautiful it was with just the last threads of light passing through the tall branches. The path wandered into the woods like a silver rope in the rising moon, and she was so deep in her plans, she hadn't noticed that she had walked quite a distance. Her dress caught on a dead, fallen branch, which brought her dreaming to an abrupt end. She had better get back to the others.

She was just about to turn when she realised she couldn't quite remember which way she had come. She thought she could hear voices over to the right and walked towards them. At first in the gloom, she thought it was a large group of men, and then saw it was only three. One of them was John. And they were all naked. John was tied to a tree and the other two were being completely and utterly obscene, doings things to John and to each other. For a few minutes she stood, enthralled by what she was seeing, before revulsion took over. Should she run, make out she'd never seen anything? Then her answer came to her. In a flash, she believed her future was secure.

"Oh God, what's happening here?" She tried to sound panicked and hysterical. "John, what's happening, are you hurt?" Then she changed her tone. "John, whatever are you doing? Who are you all? Untie him, do it now." Her voice sounded shrill, panicked and almost hysterical. She seemed genuinely like a young, innocent girl who had happened upon a scene of depraved erotica.

Up to that point, no-one had said a word, all three were too shocked at her sudden appearance to even talk to her. The two naked men moved to untie John, who ran for his clothes, shouting for Eleanor to stay, please stay, he needed to talk to her.

The other two men picked up their clothes and melted into the woods, leaving John to calm this woman down and hopefully prevent her from making trouble.

Eleanor slowly walked the way she thought she had come and waited for John to catch her up. Actually, it could work out quite well, but she'd have to be careful. She had never seen a naked man and although she didn't see anything very clearly, she had listened to enough chatter from the girls at school to know what it should look like and what it is supposed to do. She also knew that there were boundaries, and men together with men was altogether so far outside those boundaries, as to be more than a disgrace, it was illegal and it would mean the end of honour and reputation for the whole family.

John was out of breath, his hair and clothes were unkempt. "God, Eleanor, I don't know where to start, except, please, please can you think about not telling anyone? Could you do that for me? I'd do anything in return, anything." His desperation was encouraging, but she would still need to be very careful.

She turned to look at him and managed to produce a shocked look, with tears lightly rolling down her cheeks. "Well, we'd better walk back together. It will look even more odd if we arrive separately, because by now every-one will assume we've been together anyway. What would they think of me? Why would I have gone alone into the woods with you if we didn't intent to...?" She seemed more collected than he imagined most women would be, having just seen a very erotic and intimate scene, with just an edge of fright in her voice.

"Yes, yes. Of course. But what about you, Eleanor? What must you be thinking? What must you think of me? Oh God, Eleanor, can you imagine if this got out? I don't know how much you know about these things, but you surely know it's illegal? Can you promise me you won't repeat what you've seen? I can't explain, if I could I'd tell you. I have always preferred men to women and now I'm expected to marry. I can't face the whole thing, I'm so miserable. Eleanor, PLEASE, slow down, talk to me." He was desperate to keep her talking and not let her go back into the house before he'd extracted some sort of promise from her.

"Are you in love with either of those men?" She was undecided whether to show outrage and disgust as a young, innocent girl might or to show understanding and kindness. She opted for understanding. She was overcome by a strange calm now. Everything would hinge on the next few minutes.

"Not in love, no. But they understand and enjoy the same things that I do."

"Who are they? Are they part of your group of friends?"

"God, no!" he exclaimed. "Actually, they're two of the servants, one works in the stables and the other is an under-gardener."

"Servants? Aren't you taking the most appalling chances? What if they talk about it?"

"We've been doing a version of the same thing since we were quite small children, their parents have always worked on the estate. We've just sort of grown into this more adventurous stuff."

They were nearly back at the house, and several people were on the terrace, smoking and enjoying the late evening air.

He took her hand to make it look as if the two of them had met each other by design.

"Marry me." She hadn't intended to come out with it quite like that, but it just had to be settled tonight. "Marry me and I'll let you have that certain part of your life to yourself. The only thing I'll ever ask is that you give me a child or two. In return, you'll have a wife who'll care for you and the estate. We'll be alright, you'll see. Oh God, we're nearly back at the house. You'll have to make it look to everyone as if you have just made love to me. We'll be alright together, you'll see. Your parents will overlook my lack of background if you convince them that we had to be together tonight, that we want to be together for always. And I have enough money to bring something to the arrangement. Quickly, John, we don't have much time."

She hadn't actually said she would keep quiet about what she had seen, but he was under no illusions that if he refused to marry her, some version of what she had seen would circulate and his family would be dishonoured. God! It would be a disaster, a total disaster.

He looked at her. Could she really be this calculating? What if he said no? It was a risk. Sex between men was illegal and the shame of being arrested with two servants was more than he could contemplate. His parents would be completely undone; his sister was shortly to be engaged to the son of Lord Henry Howen-Argeuse – the scandal would surely put paid to that.

They were going to be furious and disappointed if he married this banker's daughter. He wasn't even sure what her father did for a living, but he wasn't a gentleman, he knew that much.

"It's alright, John. It's alright, honestly. I shouldn't have said anything. I'm so embarrassed now. Please forgive me. I like you enormously, and I promise I won't say anything to anyone, ever. Please don't worry." She squeezed his hand to reassure him. She felt this was a master-stroke, she was being understanding but the unspoken threat would forever hang over him.

By now Charlotte was coming down the steps to meet them, John put his arm around her shoulders and said, "Eleanor and I are engaged."

****

Their marriage had actually been fairly successful. John's father had died two years after their wedding and John had assumed control of the estate. Eleanor had become the driving force behind him. When the extent of the debts run up by John's parents became known to her, she had enlisted the help of her father to produce a business plan for the estate. Many economies were made and staff let go, including the two servants Eleanor had found with John in the woods that night. She had waited for her moment to sack them, knowing now that any word they spoke of the affair would seem like disgruntled ex-employees and would leave themselves open to prosecution.

They both kept their sides of the bargain. He came to her room a couple of times a month until she was pregnant, and he was free to indulge his fantasies at a certain club in Town which catered for those tastes. When they were both at home, they had a surprisingly easy rapport with each other. Occasionally, John would have a male friend to stay for the weekend, but it was all done very discreetly and the guest always stayed in one of the guest rooms.

Eleanor became the complete lady of the manor, John had the perfect wife for entertaining. She was beautiful and thrifty and kept the household running on a much reduced budget. Under Eleanor's husbandry the estate, if not profitable, was at least out of debt. Her father's guiding hand, not to mention injections of funds from time to time, had ensured that their lifestyle, although not as lavish as in John's parents' day, was sociable and impressive.

As a child, their son David was much loved by both parents, was bright and intelligent and did well at school. He had an aptitude for figures and went on to university. After graduating, he worked for a brokerage firm where he learned the movement of money, the value of hedge funds and the fluctuations of the currency markets.

Townsend was still Eleanor's maid and kept her informed of the gossip in the kitchen; she was the only person who had knowledge of John's proclivities.

The business plan for the estate involved forming a company. John and Eleanor were both directors and when their son David was ready, the running of the estate was handed over to him. At the same time, he was a director of several businesses. Eleanor's father had been instrumental in coaching him and proposed his business studies courses. David was clever enough, he seemed to have a grasp of the rapidly changing financial world and it was a huge relief to John. David was a reliable, loving son and brought his future wife, Amelia, to meet both Eleanor and John very early in their relationship.

Eleanor's father died, leaving her the house in Connaught Square and some stocks and shares. There were also liquid assets amounting to about twelve million. All of this, Eleanor left to David to handle. The house was sold and the proceeds added to the funds.

Both John and Eleanor felt they had made a fairly good bargain. Outwardly they were a couple totally at ease with one another: privately John's early sexual adventures toned down into one or two fairly constant relationships as he grew older. Eleanor drew the line at entertaining his companions at Porton Hall after David was born, but her acceptance of his absences made life easy for both of them.

The first indication of any problems came when the cook reported that the household bills hadn't been paid for several months. Eleanor hadn't been well and the housekeeper hadn't raised the matter. Eleanor had periods of depression now, she explained to the doctor that there were blank periods when she had apparently been sitting for some time, without knowing that time was passing. She had no recollection of anything said to her during this period and realised that she was spending more and more time alone and introspective.

The household staff hadn't been paid and neither had any of the local storekeepers who delivered provisions to the house. David appeared less and less often at Porton Hall and eventually John was informed of the state of affairs.

Eleanor seemed incapable of understanding that the estate she had worked so hard for when she was younger, was now on the brink of bankruptcy. David had taken out two further mortgages on the property and the repayments had fallen behind. He had sold off some land and one of the larger farms, but there were still insufficient funds to meet all their debts. Staff were laid off and the gardens became untidy. Eleanor was seriously depressed and John spent more time now protecting her from bad news and keeping her safe.

The final blow came when news of David's arrest in London reached them. Neither Eleanor nor John understood the complicated financial dealings he had undertaken, but it would appear that most of it was fraudulent and clients had lost an enormous amount of money. David's trial took a year to come to court and his legal fees were beyond the immediate means of either Eleanor or John. The banks foreclosed on the mortgages on Porton Hall and it was put up for sale, together with most of the contents. The property sold fairly quickly, given the size of the estate, and when all debts and commitments were met, John and Eleanor had sufficient funds to enable the purchase of a modest house and with a sum invested, an income to allow a good standard of living without any extravagance.

They had both spent many holidays when David was young touring France as a family and the decision to move there seemed, to John, to be the answer. It would get Eleanor away from England and all its associations and hopefully, would bring her out of the state of permanent depression into which she had sunk. They had seen *La Chênaie* in a glossy magazine and decided to see the estate agent in Périgueux. John had made the decision to buy as soon as he had seen it. Eleanor seemed not to care. She had spoken very little since David was sent to jail to serve a five-year sentence. She had not visited him and wrote very rarely.

John found himself totally in charge of the family now, a role that Eleanor had always held when they were younger. Eleanor lived mostly in a quiet, uncommunicative world, rarely initiating conversation and never wanting to go out. She spent hours looking out onto the garden, sometimes with tears rolling down her cheeks and John felt helpless to comfort her. She had lost her status which had been bought at a high price: she had given up the opportunity to have a fulfilling marriage. David was the only child for her, John became incapable of making love to her afterwards. Even this she had appeared to accept since she had the position of mistress of the estate of Porton Hall and all the kudos that went with it. Now, betrayal of the worst kind had put an end to everything that ever mattered to her.

Betrayal by her own son. What mother could bear it?

When they first arrived in France, John had hoped that being removed from their painful situation would help her to recover, but plainly, it wasn't working. He found himself longing for the easy companionship they had once shared. He realised now that this would never be again.

He had met Gaston at the local language school. John had decided that he would learn French from a French-speaker, it would help him to get the most out of living in France now that he was more or less alone. Gaston was younger than John, but a slow friendship developed between the two men; genuine liking and affection soon became a soft and generous love. Neither man made demands on the other which were beyond their ability to give or against their wishes to do so. John felt happy. As happy as he could be, watching Eleanor's decline into a serious depression.

He had hoped that Hilary and Bob Findlay would be good friends and able to draw her out somewhat, but their own relationship was an extraordinary one. They were so totally devoted to each other that other people seemed to be an intrusion into their personal world. John envied them that, he had never really had that kind of involvement with another person. His relationship with Eleanor had developed into that of a good old friend, but he was losing that now. He had had one fairly long-lasting relationship with a man whose complicated family responsibilities had involved a certain amount of secrecy and it was that secrecy, in the end, which had doomed their love.

Gaston had appeared as a saviour from his total despair. John shared everything with him, his shame at his son's infamy and the inability to help Eleanor to recover. It was

Gaston who suggested a health resort in the Pyrenees, where he knew of a psychiatrist with a good success rate with chronic depression.

The trip had been fairly successful. Gaston had the grace not to accompany them on the trip but John thought that Eleanor was aware that there was someone in his life. Eleanor had recovered somewhat and had talked openly to the doctor. John had hopes that time would restore her and her disappointment in life would disappear. When they returned to *La Chênaie*, she seemed much brighter, enjoyed cooking and sitting in the garden.

Then Diana and Simon Lewis bought *La Maison Neuve*. When the big house was empty, Eleanor could almost blot it out. There was no possibility of their having been able to afford the house themselves, but for the period it was empty, she could make herself believe that it was just part of the landscape. And then that woman and her so-called writer of a husband had bought the place. Eleanor, now in a world of her own, who had been lady of the manor, mistress of Porton Hall, was now to be humiliated by the occupants of the big house, regarding their neighbours in their more modest homes with condescension.

John had met the woman and declared her to be a, "Sweet and a happy sort. Not in the least likely to be superior and condescending." Eleanor had no intention of meeting her. John seemed to think that because they were living in these houses that they were all of an equal status, and that the class system didn't operate here. How wrong he was. Eleanor above all knew about these things. Of course there was a class system, it didn't simply disappear because one changed country.

So Eleanor had withdrawn again, spending hours going over every detail of the last years of her glorious life at Porton, remembering dinners with the lord lieutenant, glorious balls for the daughters of friends and even

Charlotte's daughter, held of course, at Porton Hall. And steeping herself in her misery.

John had evidently found himself a new lover, and although she didn't actually disapprove, he might have chosen someone other than a French teacher, someone with a little more breeding. But what did it matter? No-one cared about her and her plight and she was alone. How could anyone understand the depth of her personal loss? Her money, her beloved papa, her home and position. All gone.

And these people on this estate? An ex-gardener with a little money; two most peculiar sisters; that awful woman at the end who never stopped talking; that fat woman with the French mother – something very odd about that daughter – and those people next door who developed property or something with the awful children. And now, the people who had bought the big house. If she stayed at the back of her house, with a view of the garden and woods, she could convince herself that there was nothing there. How cruel life was, how could it be borne? Her pain at David's situation was not something she could share with anyone, not even John. She kept everything in her heart, in her mind. There were times when she would look out of the window and want to scream at the injustice of it.

She wasn't sure how long she'd been sitting in the room, she vaguely remembered locking the door, wanting to sit with her grief alone, not wanting to see anyone. Was it the next day? Two days later? She did hear John calling and knocking but she couldn't face him; seeing him would make life real again, whilst she was enclosed in this room, nothing could carry on, everything came to a standstill, no more pain for a while.

Then suddenly, it was over. The door crashed open and John came in with that Lawson man. She was too tired to argue, she felt defeated and crushed. She felt herself being lifted and then there was another man, perhaps a doctor, talking to John. Then blissful forgetfulness. The doctor had given her something in her arm, and she floated away, happy for the first time in years.

****

Margaret watched Julian as he left through the kitchen door of *La Maison Neuve*; her spirits sank. She had never really thought she had the faintest chance of gaining Julian's interest, but nevertheless, it hurt to see him leaving Diana's house this early in the morning. Surely he hadn't spent the night? But then why else would he be leaving at this hour?

She turned away from the window and went to sit down at her dressing table. 'Well, honestly,' she thought. 'Just look at yourself.' Was it any wonder that he'd prefer Diana's simple loveliness to what she saw reflected back at her in the mirror? It hadn't always been like this, at one time she was considered to be attractive and after all, hadn't she been the one to capture Patrick's heart?

Patrick. How she had adored him. She picked up her hairbrush and her thoughts drifted away as she slowly pushed the bristles through her springy hair.

Her parents were one of the largest farm owners in that part of Somerset. The two sisters had gone to school in Wellington, her sister Jennifer had no ambition whatsoever and had cruised through her schooling, amiably doing the minimum necessary but somehow pleasing everyone with her almost child-like character. Margaret had worked hard and had left school with ambitions to go on to university. She had a gift for technical drawing and had thought of a career in architecture.

Then a farm accident had left her father with a severe back injury which meant he could only walk with crutches and needed a wheelchair to go into town. His wife had died two years before, a fact which most people felt contributed to the accident, since he had taken to drinking heavily. They had been a close and loving couple and her death from cancer had left him bereft and unable to cope. He had become careless around the farm and Margaret found herself taking on more and more of the responsibility. She employed a farm manager and between them, they made a hugely successful dairy business: they diversified into ice cream and specialist cheeses which they supplied to leading food stores in London and other major cities.

She had been approaching thirty when she met Patrick. The village had combined with another village to put on the annual harvest festival dance. Both of the sisters had attended these dances since they were in their teens, but now that they were older, they were the ones arranging the decorations and sitting chatting instead of dancing every dance with all the young farmers and farm labourers as they had done when they were younger.

Philip Dennison owned the adjoining farm and had long pursued Jennifer, who by this time was gaining a reputation for being rather easy, if not exactly promiscuous. Margaret had tried to talk her, trying to convince her that Philip would not wait forever while she wasted her time with any man who happened to take her fancy at the time. She was ruining herself and her chances of any long-term happiness, not to mention a family of her own. Margaret tried being brutal with Jennifer. She told her that sex with anyone and everyone was making Jennifer look old, not to mention how many times her heart could stand being broken while she imagined herself in love every time.

The problem with trying to tell Jennifer anything she didn't want to hear, wasn't so much that it fell on deaf ears but that her eternal childish optimism blinded her to the actual fact that Margaret was right.

On the night of the harvest dance, Margaret was going to the hall early. She had been there in the afternoon hanging up decorations, but she went home to shower and change before going back to take the tablecloths to set the tables for the buffet. A couple of helpers were already there and she spent an hour preparing the tables with cutlery and china which had been left there in boxes from two of the local pubs.

Her sister arrived with a man in tow, a man Margaret had never seen in the area before. He was slightly taller than Margaret, with floppy brown hair which he was constantly pushing to one side. He was well-built in the muscled sense, fairly tanned and with an easy manner. 'Another of Jennifer's men, I suppose,' thought Margaret. 'I wonder how long this one will last.' She wiped her hands on her apron and went over to speak to them.

"Oh, Maggs, this is Patrick, he's not been here long. He's working for the Wilkinsons over at Denham Farm." She turned towards Patrick. "And this is my darling sister, Margaret." Jennifer smiled up at him, while Margaret's heart sank. She could see that Jennifer was already seeing him as her next lover. Margaret could also see that this was going to end in heartbreak – again. Patrick was friendly but showed no extraordinary interest in Jennifer. It was clear to Margaret that Patrick was not the type to settle down, too much of the traveller about him, she thought.

People started to arrive bringing flans, fruit tarts, salads, piles of fresh bread rolls, whole hams, cold roasted chickens and an amazing collection of desserts, with pots of cream and custard. The music was provided by a local band. Cider, beer and wine were served in large quantities and the party started to get louder and livelier.

Margaret watched Jennifer clinging on to Patrick's arm, and whilst he appeared not to mind, he paid her no overt attention either. When the dancing started, Margaret decided to head off home. Her head was aching and she was feeling old. She had a meeting with Ben Milton, their farm manager, the following day and she wanted to check over some figures before she went to bed.

She made a cup of coffee and took it out to the large patio to the rear of the house. Her father had had it built after his accident. It was made of large flagstones with a pretty pond set into the middle and raised flower beds around the edge. There was a shaded area to the left, provided by a pergola covered in a grape vine which grew remarkably well in that sheltered spot. Margaret could still see her father sitting out there with a bottle of Laphroaig beside him, his favourite peaty malt whisky. His life had not been easy since the death of his wife; his injuries gave him a lot of pain and inconvenience and since Margaret had taken over the running of the farm, he had rather given up on making an effort. Margaret had loved her father and seeing him disconsolate and in pain worried her. It was a shock however, to find him one morning on that patio, glass smashed at his feet, dead of an apparent heart attack.

She sipped her coffee and thought of going back into her study to check over the papers for the morning but before she had moved, she heard a footstep coming around the side of the house. She could see a figure of a man by the light coming from the open kitchen door and window. "Who is it?" she called, not in the least alarmed, assuming it was a neighbour. As he came closer she could see it was Patrick.

"Hello, sorry to intrude but I've brought your sister home. I'm afraid she's a little the worse for wear. I've left her in the sitting room but I think she needs help to get to bed. Someone at the dance said they'd seen you leaving so I thought you'd probably come home, then I saw the lights." His voice was softer than she'd remembered from their fleeting introduction. "Would you like me to give you a hand to get her upstairs?"

"No, I'll probably just make her comfortable on the sofa. She has an amazing capacity for recovery, she never has a hangover when the rest of us would be flat out with misery. She'll wake on her own in a few hours and take herself off to bed." She picked up her mug and went towards the kitchen door. "Would you like a drink or a cup of coffee? It's very good of you to look after her like this, come on in." They went into the kitchen. Margaret put the kettle back on the Aga and went in to check on Jennifer. She was sleeping peacefully, with a little trail of dribble out of the corner of her mouth. Margaret dabbed Jennifer's mouth with a tissue and turned her slightly more on to her side, covered her with a throw and kissed her forehead.

"She's fine. Tea or coffee? Or would you prefer a drink?"

"Oh, coffee's fine, thank you. I do love this kitchen, it's what every farmhouse kitchen should look like." He gave her a warm smile.

She found him easy to talk to, he knew a lot about farming and especially dairy herds. His grandparents had owned a farm in Lincolnshire but had not kept up to date with modernisation and the farm had been sold some years before. He enjoyed working at Denham Farm, didn't mind hard work or irregular hours and thought he'd enjoy living here in Somerset

They talked on about horses, Margaret and Jennifer had three and they were Jennifer's passion. Jennifer would work for hours with the horses when she would do almost nothing else on the farm. Margaret had learned long ago that if the farm was to continue, she could not look to Jennifer for help. Talk turned to Jennifer. Margaret was certain that Patrick was now destined to be Jennifer's new love but couldn't see any obvious or deep interest from Patrick. Time would tell.

It was quite late when Patrick left and Margaret found that she had enjoyed his company, their talk was friendly and easy and she felt just a little stab of jealousy. Margaret had long ago given up the idea that she would find love, marry and have a family of her own, so she was disturbed to find herself attracted to Patrick. After he had left, she checked on Jennifer, turned out the lights and went up to bed.

While she was at her meeting in the farm office the following morning, she saw Jennifer through the window, dressed for riding, showing no signs of the blistering hangover she deserved. Margaret got up and opened the window. "How are you this morning, Jen?"

"Good morning, Maggs, you left early last night, didn't you enjoy it? What are we having for dinner tonight, I've asked Patrick to come over, is that alright? Do you want me to do anything?" Margaret smiled at the typical disjointed thoughts which made up Jennifer's conversation.

"Yes, of course he can come, I'll fix something or other. Where are you riding today?"

"I'm going in the manège with Blix, he's a bit too feisty at the moment, we're going to have to change his oats, I think, mix it with a bit more barley and he can have a couple of bran mashes this week." Jennifer could talk about her horses for hours when nothing else could hold her attention for more than a few minutes.

"OK, darling, I won't be much longer here and then I'll go and find something for dinner tonight." She smiled as she closed the window and turned back to the table, covered now with spread sheets and account books.

"So, everything's ready for the VAT inspector, is there anything else we need to discuss today, Bill?"

There were no other matters which needed her attention. They had decided to take on another farm labourer since their last herd expansion; building the new dairy to make exotic flavours of ice cream left them a little short-handed. The new ice cream machines would be installed in a few weeks and they would start interviewing almost immediately.

There were two upright freezers in the utility room, the right hand one for meat and home prepared dishes, the other for desserts which Jennifer would turn out periodically when she had the urge to cook; vegetables frozen in season, cakes and sauces made up the rest of the contents. Margaret stood looking at the list on the door – pheasant casserole? Steak and ale pie? Chicken curry? She decided on the steak and ale pie, baked potatoes and broad beans which she had spent hours shelling while watching the Wimbledon finals on television. She found some smoked trout pâté as a starter, and her mother's favourite recipe iced strawberry soufflé for dessert.

Dining room or kitchen? Mother's silverware or the everyday stainless steel? For heaven's sake, she thought, he's not coming for you, he's coming for Jennifer. As if reading her thoughts, Jennifer came through the kitchen door and said, "Oh Maggs, let's eat in the kitchen. We're going off to an engagement party later, so don't make a huge fuss."

"Whose engagement?"

"Oh, someone Patrick knows, some farming friend from somewhere near Bristol, I think. Anyway, we might stay over, so don't worry about us. If we do come back, we'll creep in so we don't wake you."

"We? Are you thinking of bringing him back here to sleep?" Margaret wasn't surprised that Jennifer would sleep with someone she hardly knew but she very rarely brought them home to the farm.

"We'll see how things work out. Oh, that looks lovely. Can we eat about seven-ish? Have you seen the martingale I left in the mud room? I wanted to try it on Phoenix tomorrow. Did you order the straw? By the way, the farrier can't come on Monday, he'll phone when his van is back. I'm going for a shower." She kissed Margaret on the cheek and was gone, patting dust from her sweater as she went. Margaret watched her leave with a fond look; so typical of Jen, she thought.

When Patrick arrived at six-thirty he brought a small ready-made posy of flowers, already in a little blue vase. Margaret now felt a little awkward with him, the prospect of having him sleep in the room across the hall from hers, making love to Jennifer, put their previous easy friendship now on a different footing.

She put the flowers on the table and gave him a drink – his choice was the same peaty Laphroaig which her father so loved. "I hear you're probably going on to a party." Margaret tried to sound normal and not let her disappointment show.

"Yes, it's a friend of mine who's just become engaged and I'm going to be his best man, so really I have to go. Jennifer thinks we could come back here, but I think I'd rather stay there."

Margaret breathed a sigh of relief, and her opinion of him improved a little.

Supper passed pleasantly, the food was tasty and he ate with a good appetite. Jennifer twittered in her usual manner all through dinner and then left to freshen up before they left to go to the party. Before she came back, Margaret used the opportunity to speak to Patrick about her sister. "Patrick, I hate to sound like a mother hen," she began, "but Jennifer is very vulnerable. You have probably guessed that she really doesn't think things through before she gets involved in relationships and she has paid a heavy price from time to time."

Patrick looked thoughtful. "Margaret, please don't worry. I'll take good care of her and if you'd prefer us to come back here, we will, or at least I'll drop her off, but it will be very late."

"Thank you – sorry I had to say something, her choices are not always as sensible!"

Margaret saw them off and returned to the kitchen to clear up – typically Jennifer just left the table and flitted off. She left a light on in the hall in case they returned and went to bed.

****

The following morning, Jennifer came down early for breakfast, alone. Patrick had dropped her off at four so it was a surprise that she was already up and dressed at six-thirty. Margaret looked at her, she seemed withdrawn and tired.

193

"Are you alright? How did the evening go?" She touched Jennifer's arm across the table. "Don't tell me you've got a hangover," she laughed.

"No, no hangover, I'm fine, just couldn't sleep. I think I'll give Phoenix her worming paste and give her a good grooming. It's raining slightly anyway, so it's a good day to get some stable jobs done."

"Why don't you just take a break today? You had a really late night and you really don't look well." It wasn't just that she looked unwell, she seemed to have changed overnight. Some of her child-like quality seemed to have been eroded, she seemed somehow more mature, but not naturally so.

"Has something happened? Is everything alright with Patrick? You seem very unhappy this morning?"

"Yes, I'm fine, but to be honest, I think it's you he's interested in. If he is, I wish you wouldn't encourage him. I don't think he's right for you, I really don't, so *please* do as I ask, *don't* encourage him."

Margaret frowned in surprise. "Darling, of course I won't. I don't think for one moment you're right, I wouldn't dream of taking him from you even if such a thing was remotely on the cards." She got up and went over to Jennifer. She put her arms around her and was now seriously worried.

"Did something happen? Darling, did he do something to hurt you?" She looked into her sister's eyes, looking for reassurance.

"No, honestly. I've just been rather silly and as usual, I'm paying for it. Don't worry, darling, I'm fine. I just need to spend a little time with my babies. But I'm not joking, Patrick is more interested in you, he never stopped talking about you, it was a bit creepy."

"Creepy?"

"Well, maybe not creepy, but just a bit - sort of, I don't know - obsessive, you know?"

"I'm sorry, if you like him that must be very unpleasant. I promise I've done nothing to encourage him."

"Oh, I know, Maggs. Maybe I'm wrong, and I *don't* like him. I don't like him at all."

Margaret was very taken aback at this revelation, normally Jennifer never took against anyone, it was usually the men who left her, heartbroken and puzzled at their departure. Margaret thought perhaps Patrick was not someone who enjoyed being with a woman who had a bit of a reputation. The more she thought about it, the more she was sure this was the reason. He's just a little old-fashioned, she thought.

Jennifer spent many hours with her horses – her babies, as she called them – and seemed to recover some of her earlier uncrushable optimism. Patrick's name wasn't mentioned and he didn't come to the farm for a couple of weeks.

Then one Sunday afternoon, he arrived unexpectedly. Jennifer spoke politely enough, greeted him as a casual acquaintance and excused herself. Margaret made tea and they sat together, talking about anything and everything. These meetings developed over the next few weeks into a comfortable habit and even Jennifer seemed to thaw towards him.

One day after he had been coming to the house for a couple of weeks, he asked Margaret out to dinner. It was the first proper meeting between the two of them. Jennifer seemed, if not exactly pleased, resigned to it, although she reiterated to her sister several times that she didn't think Patrick was a very nice person. She gave no details; it was just her feeling about him.

Margaret had never known such elation. She felt young, light and very, very happy. Patrick was considerate and helpful and he had been very restrained in his physical attentions. They had never actually made love yet, but Margaret was determined that it would be soon. Patrick didn't want her visiting him at Denham Farm. Having been cross with Jennifer at the prospect of her sleeping with Patrick at the farm, she now contemplated this for herself without any compunction. Her opportunity came when Jennifer decided to visit some friends in Yorkshire to go to a horse show.

Jennifer left early one Friday morning and wasn't due back until Sunday night. Margaret spent the whole of Friday cleaning and cooking, preparing the bedroom with fresh linen and flowers. She lit the fires in the drawing room and the bedroom, the flickering flames looked very romantic and she was so impatient to see Patrick. She had thought ahead to where this might be going and put thoughts of marriage firmly behind her. She was older than Patrick, not by much but in her mind that made marriage an unlikely outcome. But for now she was happy. She had had a couple of affairs, none of which had made her feel as she did now.

Patrick arrived at about four and while she was putting the kettle on, he came behind her and put his arms around her. She leaned back and enjoyed the feel of him. She took the kettle off the burner and turned towards him.

"It's our time now," he said. He led her upstairs and through the open door to her bedroom. In her mind, she had played this scene a hundred times and never quite believed it would happen. He was in turns gentle, demanding, teasing, urging her on and then calming her down until she was frantic with wanting. He tormented her and ultimately picked the moment when he brought her to her climax. Strangely, he didn't reach that point, and only afterwards did she even think about it. She regained her breath and reached out to run her hand over his chest and stomach. He was still aroused. He lay beside her for a short while and then rolled towards her to touch her once more, his fingers making her tremble. This time he was more urgent and less considerate, almost brutal in fact, but she felt his climax and was happy.

"What happened that time, didn't you feel anything?" he asked her.

"Of course I did, it was wonderful."

"I disappointed you."

"Of course you didn't, God I'm sore and exhausted, it was just perfect bliss Patrick."

"But it didn't happen for you that time."

He seemed suddenly insecure and anxious. She wasn't prepared for that, he'd always seemed so strong and self-assured. "Patrick, listen. Please don't think things which aren't true. I have never felt like that; it was absolutely wonderful. Let's go down and open some champagne, relax by the fire and let me just believe that this wonderful day has really happened."

The weekend followed a certain routine, Margaret still had responsibilities on the farm and of course, with Jennifer away, there were the horses to be cared for. Even though Eric, the stable hand, was there most of the time, there were still evening stables to do, making the horses comfortable for the night. Jennifer wouldn't have automatic water dispensers in the stables because she wouldn't know how much they were drinking. She'd lost one horse years ago to colic because he wouldn't drink enough, he was afraid of the water dispenser. So she'd had the dispensers disconnected and filled their hanging buckets with water every day and every evening.

Then on Sunday afternoon came Patrick's surprise. They had just finished lunch and Margaret was thinking ahead to Jennifer's return and Patrick's departure.

"Will you marry me?" Patrick had put his hands on her shoulders and looked at her with such an intensity of love, she had felt her heart pound. She had never even considered that this would be a possibility. She had thought, perhaps, she might ask him to move in but she was even wary of doing that.

"Well, will you? Please? I love you so much, I can't bear to be without you. I think we have every chance of being very happy together, and I'll do everything I can to make sure of it."

Still she hesitated, as if not quite believing that he was serious. She looked at him and said, "Yes. Yes, I will. Of course I will. I'd be over the moon to marry you." She still couldn't believe this had happened. "Patrick, you can't leave now just after proposing. I'm reeling, I'm so thrilled and a bit overwhelmed. I can't just let you pack you bag and leave. I want you with me, we've things to talk about and mostly, I love and adore you. You'd better stay on for a bit, what time are you due back at Denham?"

"Actually, I've left there, I'm staying with a friend in Stawbridge."

This was news to her, he hadn't mentioned a thing over the weekend, and now it seemed, he didn't have a job. She wasn't so much surprised that he'd left Denham, people tended not to stay there very long, the working conditions were not good, but nevertheless, for someone who had just asked her to marry him, she felt this was quite an important development in their lives.

"What did you have in mind then?" She knew the answer before he said it.

"Well, I'll come and help you run this farm. You won't want to move away from here anyway, will you?"

Actually, he was quite right. If she'd had time to think it through, that was the decision she would have come to herself. But still, she wished he'd said something at the beginning. When Jennifer arrived home, she was surprised to see champagne set out on the table with three glasses. She received the news of her sister's engagement with surprise, which she tried to turn into happy surprise for her sister's sake.

But before this went on for very long, she was going to have to have a talk with Margaret.

As things turned out, Jennifer never did talk to her sister about her worries. Margaret and Patrick were married in a quiet ceremony six weeks later. Patrick had moved straight into the farm when they got engaged, so apart from a weekend in Paris as a sort of honeymoon, the three of them settled to life together at the farm.

For the first year, everything seemed blissful for Margaret. She was very much in love with Patrick and apparently, he with her. His occasional bursts of possessiveness seemed to Margaret to be natural and rather wonderful. It made her feel cherished and told herself she'd been single for so long that some things which needed to be shared were hard to get used to. Margaret and Jennifer had always had a very close relationship, based on mutual recognition that Margaret was the strong and business-like one and Jennifer was the fun element, very loving and loyal.

Margaret had never thought of making Patrick a partner in the firm. He had seemed content originally to do whatever job he was equipped for but the business was firmly in Margaret's hands and those of the farm manager. After they had been married for a year, Margaret thought it was time they made a will. She had always had one but it needed updating, but Patrick had never made one. He agreed to go to Gilbert Franks with Margaret. Gil had been the family solicitor for years and knew the Grey family very well.

Margaret sat with Patrick while she outlined her requirements. The farm had been left in equal shares to the two daughters, so Jennifer was an equal partner in the farm and business. Their father had made provision that one daughter could buy out the other if they so chose, but neither of them could sell or leave their half outside the family while the other lived. It was a perfectly happy solution for both girls and neither had any intention of selling. But now there was Patrick. Margaret realised, but had never made mention of, the fact that Patrick seemed to own nothing. Having talked things over with Jennifer, Margaret was obliged to leave her half of the farm to Jennifer, but she could make financial provision for Patrick. She thought this would be the ideal solution. If Margaret died before Jennifer, Jennifer would inherit the whole but would also make some financial provision for Patrick. Patrick would therefore be financially secure but would no longer be able to live at the farm. Instead, he would have sufficient funds from a trust which the two women would set up to buy a house and to enable him to live quite well if he was prudent. Jennifer's willingness to agree to this was typical of her easy and amiable nature.

Both women were convinced that they had made good provision for Patrick, they would do the same if Jennifer got married and/or died before Margaret, so that neither husband could inherit the farm, but would be financially provided for.

Margaret had no idea how Patrick would leave anything he owned, but she assumed she would be the beneficiary. Gilbert explained the provisions to Patrick, who sat stony-faced throughout the meeting. The wills would be drawn up accordingly, the trust fund set up of which Gilbert and his firm would be the executors, and everything would be ready for signature in about two weeks.

On the drive home Patrick was silent and grim-faced. As they went into the kitchen, he slammed the door and rounded on Margaret.

"WHAT THE HELL DO YOU TWO THINK YOU ARE DOING?" His screaming voice shocked Margaret, she was speechless, incapable of response, her incredulity was total.

Without waiting for her to respond, he strode over to her and slapped her face, very hard. "How dare you both make a fool of me, how dare you treat me like shit on your shoe? I've had about as much as I can take of this, the pair of you make me sick. If you think I'm going to work myself into the ground in this place for you two for a bloody pittance, you can think again." He picked up the coffee mug from the draining board and threw it against the door, showering the flagstone floor with shards of pottery. He left the room, slamming the door behind him.

Margaret sat at the table, too stunned to cry, think or react in any way. She sat for over an hour, reality would still not sink in. Happily, Jennifer was out riding and would probably not come back into the house for another couple of hours; Margaret had no idea how she would tell her any of this, but she longed for the comfort of her sister's company.

Finally, Margaret took off her coat and went upstairs to their bedroom. She changed into jeans and a sweater, still unable to understand what had happened.

As she looked in the mirror, she saw a small trickle of blood by her ear where Patrick's hand had caught her earring, cutting into the side of her neck. How on earth had this happened? What could have possessed him? For a man who had nothing, to have his future protected and ensured would surely have been cause, if not for gratitude, at least an acknowledgement that they both cared enough about him to see that he would never be left without funds.

When Margaret and Patrick got married, Jennifer moved to the flat above the stables. She occasionally joined them for a meal, but for the most part she catered for herself. As it happened, Jennifer was to cook for them this evening in the farm house, and as Margaret came downstairs she heard the kitchen door close and Jennifer's bright, "Helloooooo. Hi Maggs, only me. God, Flax was a perfect pain today." All of Jennifer's horses had to have names ending in 'X', a small fetish of hers from childhood. "Do you know, he got the wind up his tail and the devil took over, he's going ... Good God, what's happened? Maggs, darling, come over here and sit down. Sweetheart, what on earth is wrong, you look awful. What's happened?" She put her arms around her sister and sat her down at the kitchen table.

Unable to contain her tears any longer, they rolled down Margaret's cheeks, her nose started to run and she cried. Jennifer waited for the gulps to stop. That her sister was upset to this degree was unusual in itself, but this was Maggs, always strong, never unhappy or unable to cope and always, always brave.

Jennifer had no doubt that Patrick was responsible. Slowly Margaret stopped crying and went over to the sink to bathe her eyes. "Just a bit of a tiff. It'll pass. I think he lost his confidence a bit in front of Gil, I think he felt a bit patronised."

"Patronised? I'd call it bloody lucky. Two women who have promised to make him financially independent? Patronised? Come on, Maggs, he can't surely have expected to inherit half the farm, could he? I think we've given him a generous future. We've done the very best we could for him. Just imagine if half of my male friends expected something from us, we'd have gone broke long ago."

Margaret gave her sister a hug and actually managed a laugh. "Jen, darling Jen. You're right of course. He is being unreasonable, but he'll understand."

"It was just a row, wasn't it? I mean, he didn't do anything - um, he didn't - well, hit you, did he?"

Margaret reacted without thinking. She flared, "Of course not! How could you think such a thing? Honestly Jen, you don't understand him at all. Why can't you just see it for what it was - just a row. I accept that he's not being in the least grateful, but I think most men would behave that way, something to do with their pride. But please, Jen, don't speak of him on those terms. I love him and he loves me." Tears threatened to spill over again and Margaret got up from the table to do something to escape her sister's scrutiny.

"Would you rather I didn't stay this evening? I can come over another time, perhaps you need this evening to make up."

"Perhaps that would be a good idea. Thank you, Jen, come here and give me a hug."

Jennifer hugged her sister, kissed her cheeks and left.

****

As she closed the kitchen door behind her, she knew for certain that Patrick had hit Margaret and she wished for the hundredth time she had talked to Margaret before the wedding. But how do you destroy someone's happiness? How do you tell someone the truth about a person they are so in love with, when they see only good? And in any case, would Margaret have believed her – believe that her beloved Patrick had hit Jennifer, raped her and totally humiliated her?

The fact is, Margaret would have defended him, told her she brought everything on herself with her promiscuous behaviour and it probably wasn't rape anyway, Jennifer was well-known for her easy sexual code.

But Jennifer now sorely wished she'd told Margaret everything.

And perhaps it *had* been a one-off. They'd been drinking, Jennifer had been teasing him and she would probably have let him have sex at any other time, but she was sure her period was about to start and she wasn't particularly comfortable. What he had done had been an appalling shock all the same.

At the engagement party, she wasn't feeling particularly well. Her lower stomach felt sore and bloated, her back ached, she didn't feel like dancing and was sorry she'd agreed to come. It was quite a long drive home and she hoped Patrick wouldn't mind if they left early. She had taken some pain-killers and, together with the wine she had drunk, she was starting to feel quite ill and very light-headed.

Patrick was not supposed to be drinking since he was driving, but he had had a couple of beers. He wasn't particularly upset when she asked him to drive her home and they left at about one am. They had been driving for about forty-five minutes when she asked him to stop, she felt really sick and thought she was about to vomit.

She had no idea where they were but she thought they were somewhere near Chard. There were hills around and woodland, but the dark was intense. Apart from the headlights, she could see nothing clearly. She got out of the car and went a very short way into the trees on the side of the road. She took some deep breaths and felt a little better. It was as she lowered her knickers to pee that she heard him come up to her. In the second it took her to realise he was there, he had pushed her forwards onto the ground. His weight held her down as he pulled off her knickers, which were around her ankles. She was face down and the force of his weight on her made her sick. As she vomited, she hoped he would let her go but he paid no attention. She screamed at him to stop, please, please let her go, but he paid no attention.

She could not have helped herself. He knocked her down when she was least prepared for it and he was much heavier than she. He seemed oblivious to her cries and pleadings, or if he did hear her, he paid no attention. After a few minutes, he knelt and roughly turned her over, forcing himself once more between her legs. At least in this position she could breathe more easily.

Then she felt something across her throat, a stick, branch, what? What was it? She lost any desire to fight, feeling ill and hoping that he would finish quickly. He was brutal and at the point where she thought he was going to finish, he withdrew from her and waited for a few minutes before continuing, all the time pinning her down with his weight and keeping whatever it was across her throat: lightly, but the pressure was there just the same. When he was ready to start again a few minutes later, he removed the thing from her throat, hit her across the face and drove himself into her. She had no idea how long he took. He kept stopping to recover a little, and then would start again.

Finally, it was over. He rolled off her, stood up and pulled up his trousers. He didn't help her up and she thought he was going to drive off and leave her there, but she didn't hear the engine start. She picked up her knickers, and wiped herself. She thought she was bleeding, she didn't care. She just wanted to get home. As she got into the car, he was behaving as if nothing had happened.

"Sorry it got a bit rough there, I got a bit carried away but then, you quite like something a bit different, don't you? Don't tell me you didn't enjoy that? I thought you'd planned it when you asked me to stop."

With disgust rising in her throat, she realised he was rationalising what had happened as a sort of game they had mutually agreed and quite honestly, with her reputation, who would believe that it was rape? God, how she hated him, but most of all she hated herself.

He started talking about Margaret, how wonderful she was, what a strong and capable business woman. How he admired her, did she have a special male friend? Jennifer was only half-aware of his chatter. She felt ill, bruised and totally humiliated. She just wanted to be at home, with her darling Maggs, with her horses and forget this evening had ever happened. She leaned back against the headrest and closed her eyes. She was just on the edge of sleep when he shook her awake. She jumped and screamed, thinking he was about to start something else.

"Jennifer, listen. Please. I can't explain what happened. It's not me, it really isn't. I think Harry spiked the drinks at the party because I've never in my life, never, done such a thing. Please believe me. I have never hurt a woman or done anything she didn't want me to do ever in my life. I believe women should be treated gently, I always have. I am still feeling a bit odd, a bit ill actually. I'm just going to have a breath of air, please don't be scared, don't look at me like that."

Jennifer couldn't believe the change in him, taking about Margaret at first and then this mea culpa, hurt-little-boy act. She was no longer afraid, but just felt really ill. She heard crying and realised it was Patrick. He was standing on the side of the road, weeping. She got out of the car and heard him saying over and over, "God, what have I done? God help me." She walked over to him and pulled his arm to get him back to the car.

"Can you ever, ever forgive me? I owe you both so much, I love you both so much, you are so special to me, I couldn't hurt you willingly."

The depth of his remorse was genuine, she was sure. She led him back to the car and said, "Patrick, let's both try and forget this. We'll never mention it again. We were hyped on alcohol, and heaven knows what was in the drinks. Never tell anyone, I don't think I could stand it, people would talk, you'd lose your job and you probably wouldn't be able to work around here ever again."

They had gone back to the farmhouse and he had dropped her off. She was determined that the whole sorry affair wouldn't be mentioned again, but by the same token, her forgiveness didn't extend as far as wishing to see him again.

Jennifer lay in the bath until the water went cold and then she stood in the shower for an age. It was dawn by then and she dressed and went down to breakfast.

And she had been true to her word, she had never mentioned the affair even to Margaret. She hadn't forgotten it but she never mentioned it. And then came the realisation that Patrick was seriously pursuing Margaret. Jennifer had never seen her so happy. What if it had been a drugged drink? Should she ruin Margaret's joy for something which she had probably contributed to? And Patrick did seem genuinely to love her, he was kind, thoughtful and Margaret was falling very much in love with him. She couldn't see Margaret's behaviour contributing to her own humiliation.

She had expected Patrick to move in, but marriage? She hadn't seen that coming. What to do? Say something? Not say something? She decided not to say anything. Margaret was sensible and had had enough lovers to know whether Patrick was really for her or not. Margaret had never been tempted to marry before, so Patrick was really lucky to have touched her heart in this way.

So, say nothing then.

After the wedding, Jennifer moved out of the main house into the lovely cosy flat above the stables. When her father was alive, they kept a husband and wife team to do housekeeping and horse management. The flat was bright, modern, two bedrooms both en-suite, and a big kitchen. The drawing room at the far end had windows on three sides, overlooking the paddocks, the woods and fields and the farmhouse. On the fourth wall was a fireplace inset with a wood-burning stove.

Jennifer loved it. She missed chatting with Margaret, but they still saw each other for dinner a couple of times a week. Patrick seemed besotted and totally devoted to Margaret's well-being. If Margaret had any disappointments in her joy, it was the fact that so far, she hadn't become pregnant.

One effect on Jennifer after the rape was that she became a social recluse. She had no doubt that her drive would return at some stage, but for the moment she was happy pottering about the farm, even helping Margaret in the farm office with the books and of course, working with her beloved horses. She felt strangely settled, she didn't go out because she actually preferred being at home. Yes, she was happy.

So it had been a shock to see Margaret in that state this afternoon. She felt sure that Margaret would not break down in that way over an ordinary row. Something more had bullied her into uncontrollable weeping. And Jennifer felt sure that some sort of violence was involved. If there was any way she could help her darling Maggs, she'd do it. But Margaret's reaction to her question of being hit made her withdraw what had been on the tip of her tongue to say. Now it was too late. She'd just have to leave Patrick and Margaret to sort things out between themselves.

The financial arrangements they'd made were very generous, he was guaranteed a settlement whichever sister died first so surely, it couldn't be that?

Poor Maggs. Hopefully, by the time they went to bed this evening, they would have made it up.

Over in the farmhouse, Margaret took the bags which Jennifer had brought over to the worktop. She thought she ought to start preparing dinner. Jennifer had been going to cook and the ingredients were in the bags on the table. Lamb chops – Patrick's favourite. Broccoli and potatoes. A Tupperware box contained one of Jennifer's apple and cinnamon pies; fresh cream.

Margaret felt worn out and hoped that when Patrick returned, they could either talk calmly about what had happened, or just simply make up. By nine o'clock Patrick still wasn't home. She resisted the temptation to go over to Jennifer's flat and sat in the chair by the Aga, absently flicking pages in a magazine. He came in at quarter to ten. She had no idea where he had been and she didn't ask. He came over to her, saying nothing: he put his arms around her. She got up from the chair to fully embrace him.

"I have no right to ask, but I do ask. I ask you to forgive me. I cannot tell you how sorry I am. It will never happen again and I can't imagine why you and Jennifer have been so generous. I promise, promise that I will never behave like that again. Darling, I love you so much, I am so, so sorry." His voice was trembling with emotion and anxiety.

Margaret was so relieved to see him, she hugged him, brushed his hair aside and kissed him. "It's alright darling, it's fine now. I'm just so happy to see you come home, I didn't know where you'd gone. Let's forget it, let's not dwell on this. It's the first time we've have an upset and if we keep talking about it, it becomes bigger than it really is. It's not a

208

threat to our marriage and I won't let it become one. I love you, that's enough."

They made sandwiches from the meat of the cooked lamb chops, long gone cold. They sat at the kitchen table and talked like people do when they have overcome a problem and are happy in the afterglow. It would all be alright now.

But it wasn't alright. Margaret was happily unaware that it was never going to be alright again.

****

Patrick had been so angry that morning at the solicitor's office. He'd felt like some sort of paid flunky. He'd chosen Margaret out of the two, she was much classier than her sister, smart, capable and very wealthy; moreover, she didn't have her sister's reputation of being an easy lay. She was older than her sister, not so pretty but the better bet in the long run. He was trying hard to stop them from prying too far into his background. He'd managed so far to keep the story going that he was from a once-well-to-do farming family, fallen on hard times, now working in a part of the country he loved and was just trying to work hard and make a life for himself.

In reality, he was a man who had spent most of his life living off women. Using his good looks and charm he'd managed holidays on the continent, months, sometimes years living in comfort, clothes bought for him, and the car, which was now fairly old and unreliable.

And his looks wouldn't last for ever. He needed a plan. By chance, the people he was working for at Denham had mentioned the harvest dance and he thought it would pass an evening and give him an idea of whether or not there were any opportunities with wealthy landowners. Those people always graced the things like harvest dances, giving the peasants a view of their betters, he thought bitterly.

He had met the woman, Jennifer, outside, who had latched on to him willingly enough. Fair enough, she was pretty, sexy and spoke with an expensively-educated accent. So far, so good. Flighty, though, he thought. But she'll do for now. Then he met the sister. Good looking in a more mature way and evidently – evidently – the one in charge. He'd ask around a bit this evening and get a bit of information about them.

Patrick was well practised around women, all sorts of women. From women much older than him to girls whom it was only just legal to shag. He could read women, their moods and mostly, their wants. Yes, he'd lived very well off women, he had no problem accepting their money and gifts.

Definitely, the older one was the better bet, but probably the wiser of the two as well. Different thinking required. He was trying to think it through to the end. Was he prepared to actually get married? He thought he could probably do it, then maybe after a few years, a few rows and a bit of, 'It's just not working for us, I love you but I need to go,' sort of thing and he could come out of it quite well.

Okay, first things first, find out how much work would be involved and how much they're worth. Village gossip being what it is, it didn't take him very long to get a picture of their situation. Yes, he was definitely going to work on this one.

He had worked well. The first conversation with Margaret was actually very pleasant. Perhaps this was going to be alright after all. His friendship with Jennifer seemed to get him closer into the family set-up and they were all fairly easy together.

Until that night. His old demon had revisited. Since he was quite a young man, sometimes he'd be having perfectly normal sex and just when he thought he be finishing, it wouldn't happen. Instead, he'd be overtaken by a feeling as if he had a tight band around his testicles, the pit of his stomach would cramp up and he'd have a strange feeling of tightness in his throat. He'd work harder until he was being really rough and still it wouldn't happen. He'd have to stop for a bit and then try to continue, he simply had to finish, the pain was almost unbearable. There were some women who liked it a little rough, but once a woman had actually screamed at him that he'd raped her. Afterwards he hated himself, hated what he had done but only a couple of times had women thrown him out.

But with Jennifer, it was the first time he'd actually had the feeling *before* starting to have sex. The feeling drove him on and he had actually raped her, there was no other word for it. And the self-detestation afterwards was almost more than he could bear.

He had been very careful with Margaret not to try to have sex with her until they'd been seeing each other for some time and in the end, it had been her suggestion that he come to stay for the weekend when Jennifer was away. He'd evidently pleased her, although on the first night he was very wary, hoping that his control would be absolute.

And so far, everything had worked well. In a whole year of marriage he had only had the feeling once, and he'd managed to keep everything under control. Perhaps he was finally overcoming whatever it was, this awful, awful sensation of part pain and part ecstasy that drove him mad.

Until that day. That awful meeting with that ponce of a solicitor. Somehow, the two sisters and their pet solicitor had had a meeting to draw up this plan, this scheme for paying him off, that's what it seemed like. Yes, fine, he was taken care of, but who then *would* be the final beneficiary of all this lot? Why not him? Because they were looking out for each other and to hell with everyone else, that's why.

He could just see the day when Margaret died and he'd have to creep out of the place like some servant who'd been given notice. And then what? Jennifer gets the lot? God, he'd been angry. And then when he'd hit Margaret, the feeling had started. He knew it would be the end of everything if he allowed these feelings to follow their natural course. He'd been sensible enough to walk out, he took the car and headed off to town. He knew where to find relief for these feelings, for any kind of feelings come to that.

When he'd arrived back, Margaret was really pleased to see him and he was sure her forgiveness was absolute.

Over the next few years, Patrick tried to accept his fortunate state, tried to enjoy the certain freedoms granted to him by being married to a wealthy woman and one with a position in the county. But when he accompanied her to functions he felt like the hired escort for the evening, a flunky in a dinner suit. At agricultural shows, she would disappear for hours with various land-owners, or cattle breeders, horse eventers and other country pursuit participants. She and Jennifer enjoyed these occasions and went from county to county, determined not to miss any one of them. To Patrick, they were all the same; animals, breeders and tractors. After the first couple of years, he stopped going and instead went to London.

If Margaret had any idea what Patrick got up to, she was never curious and exhibited a trust which Patrick betrayed at every opportunity. He still had friends with whom he could spend a few days at a time, going to places in which Margaret would never dream of setting foot, nightclubs on the fringe of legality where drugs and sex were readily available. Sometimes he would stay in an upmarket hotel and at other times he would find himself the next morning in some dingy flat with a woman, or sometimes a man, whose name he didn't know and would never see again. He had enough money to buy whatever he needed in these places to ensure his popularity and he was careful never to stay in places where he and Margaret had stayed together.

In these places, strange sexual behaviour was not unremarkable, his peculiar sex drive was not thought odd or dangerous and he enjoyed these visits for the freedom and lack of anxiety he felt.

He could then return to the staid life he led with Margaret, trying to make a place for himself on the farm and being a good and willing husband. It was true, they didn't make love very often now but that was perfectly normal, she thought.

Margaret had forgiven him on three further occasions when his anger and frustration had boiled over into vicious rows. On one occasion he had hit her again. Again she had forgiven him. On another occasion he had shaken her badly and given her a whiplash injury to her neck. She had eventually forgiven him but it had taken a long time and she tried to get him to agree to see someone who dealt with anger management. She didn't want him making love to her any more at that time, she was kind but firm. She just didn't want to, no other reason.

But on the final occasion, he knew something was going to boil over, he had been simmering on the edge of frustration for days. He couldn't think of anything in particular which had started it except finding Margaret and Jennifer talking farm business at the kitchen table, and neither acknowledged him when he walked in. He took a beer from the fridge and sat down, at which point the two women stopped talking. Jennifer got up to leave after a few minutes and Margaret started to set the table for supper. He felt they had been talking about him. They must have been. Why else would they fall silent?

Several small things happened. Margaret had been to see Gilbert Franks without telling him; he was sure it was to do with the financial arrangement they had made for him even though she assured him it had nothing to do with that. Then Margaret spent an evening with Jennifer and her latest fellow at a restaurant in the village and he wasn't included. Recently, he had tended to drink too much and became rather loud and bitter, but he blamed Margaret for that. Recently he had gone overdrawn at the bank and the bank had written a letter about charges for unauthorised overdrafts. Margaret had seen the letter, which he'd inadvertently left in his shirt

213

pocket when it went to the laundry. She took him to task severely for financial mismanagement, and in the heat of the row had told him that she was pleased she had never given him any responsibility for farm affairs.

It was all making him angry and he couldn't calm down. He tried, but every small thing seemed to wind him up. One morning, he'd risen early having been unable to sleep, he went out before breakfast, he stood against the railing of the paddock and the big horse, Blix, had come over to him, started to nuzzle his hand and then, without warning, had bitten him; Patrick's immediate reaction was to hit the horse with a closed fist on the top of his nose but Jennifer had seen him. The row that followed was horrible. Jennifer brought up his tendency to violence and he knew exactly what she was referring to.

His anger was boiling, his head was thumping with the blood pounding at the back of his eyes, Jennifer was standing in front of him, screaming at him as he turned and hurried back to the house. Margaret was in her dressing gown, talking on the phone: the boiler had broken down and there was no hot water so she was calling the heating engineer's twenty-four hour number. She ended the call when she looked at his face. For the first time ever, she was actually afraid of him. He caught hold of her by the hair and forced her up against the kitchen table. She cried out and tried to push him away, but his ferocious anger was now beyond anyone's control, let alone his.

His anger made him fearfully strong. He hit her hard across the temple and she fell to the floor. She vaguely felt him on top of her and then her senses returned when she felt the knife at her throat. She screamed and he pushed the point of the knife into her neck, telling her to shut up, just shut up. He had managed to undo his jeans but was having trouble penetrating her: he was blind with anger, frustration and hate. Margaret could feel the blood pouring down her neck onto the floor and her head was wet where it was lying in a pool.

She tried push him off, but he pushed her hand away and tightened his grip on the knife. Finally, he started to move inside her, but she could only think of the blood. He was screaming abuse at her all the time, but she could only feel the knife.

Margaret was sure that she was about to die. His cursing and screaming suddenly came to an abrupt stop and she felt his full weight slump on top of her.

Jennifer was standing over the two of them, holding a fire extinguisher. She had hit Patrick from behind with as much force as she could, hoping to halt this brutal attack on her sister. Patrick's voice had carried clear across the farm courtyard and Jennifer realised her sister was in danger. When she walked into the kitchen, shock made her incapable of seeing anything except the blood around Margaret's head. She reached for the fire extinguisher as the first thing which came to hand of any weight.

She reached down to roll Patrick to one side, and helped her sister to sit up. There was a tea towel over the back of the chair; she pulled it off and held it to Margaret's neck.

"Darling Maggs. Hold this tight against your neck, you'll be alright, it's not very deep and it's not a vein or anything, hold on, darling, I'll call for help." She reached into her pocket and pulled out her mobile.

Still holding on to Margaret, she dialled 999 and when asked which service, she asked for an ambulance. "My sister has been stabbed. Please hurry." The woman on the end of the phone was very calm and reassuring and asked if she could tell if the perpetrator was still on the premises. "Oh, yes, I've knocked him out, but please hurry, send the police, he might come round and start again." She was crying into the phone, trying to keep herself together to make sense.

It had not even occurred to her to check on Patrick, except that to note he was lying still and therefore not a threat to either of them.

215

The ambulance came after about twenty minutes and the police just a few minutes later. Margaret had been very, very lucky, the knife had gone through the flesh at the side of her neck, missing vital blood vessels and even though she had bled a lot, none of the major vessels had been ruptured.

Patrick, however, was dead.

The next few weeks were a strange mixture of anxiety, guilt and sorrow. The questioning of both women seemed to go on for ever. People came and went, hours were spent with the police and solicitors and then suddenly it was over. Jennifer was cleared, the two women buried Patrick and supported each other in their search for peace.

The decision to sell the farm and move away from the area came as naturally as if it had been pre-ordained. Neither of them could remember who had raised it first and it didn't matter.

The farm was bought by a large dairy concern, who kept Bill and the other farm workers on. The whole farmhouse had been cleaned and redecorated and Bill moved in with his wife.

The two women had taken a holiday in France with the intention of looking for a house with room for Jennifer's horses, now increased by two. They had found *La Chênaie* when they had stayed in Saint-Sulpice-sur-Lauzac. The hotel owner had been friendly and told them of *La Chênaie* when they mentioned they were looking to settle somewhere in the area.

They had really wanted a house with land, where they could run an equestrian centre, but at the time when they visited *La Chênaie*, they both knew it was the place where they wanted to live. The agent, Jean Claude Laurier, had also shown them a piece of land in the next village, with two small cottages, a hundred hectares of land (about two hundred acres) and plenty of woods for shade from the sun, for the horses. It all seemed perfect.

They had left Margaret's car in France after their visit and flew back to the UK to arrange shipment of their horses and personal effects. By mutual consent, they had left behind the furniture and only taken things which meant a lot to them.

As they were driving out of the farm for the last time, Jennifer stopped the car. She turned to her sister. "This is it, Maggs. New start. Well, almost. You'll always be there to mend my eternally broken heart when the next bastard lets me down, and I'll always be there to make sure no-one ever breaks yours again. What a partnership. I love you, darling."

They started the car and drove off down the lane to the main road.

****

Diana ran to pick up the phone as it was on its seventh ring. *"Allo, oui?"*

"Good morning, darling. How did you sleep?"

"Oh darling, I'm so happy, you'll be here tomorrow, we've so much to catch up on. I miss you, the house is so empty without you."

"Well, Dee, here's the thing. I can stay on here for another week and finish up, or I can come home this weekend, but then I'll have to come back for another two weeks."

"Oh Simon! You promised you'd come home this weekend. What can you do over the weekend anyway? All the offices are closed, you can't do much research over Saturday and Sunday." She hated the sound of whining in her voice, she sounded like a spoilt child but she was desperately disappointed. She was crushed.

"Well, it's really just a question of getting all this stuff into the right order to pack to bring home. I'd like to start writing fairly soon and it all needs putting in chronological

217

order. If I can stay and finish, I'll come home the weekend after and I'll be home to stay." He sounded so reasonable, Diana felt mean and selfish by asking him to come home. "And there's something else. I really need a car to bring all this stuff. I've a mountain of papers, so I thought I'd hire one from here on the Friday, then set off for home on the Saturday. It's only one more week, darling, then you'll be sick of the sight of me."

Diana had so hoped to tell Simon everything that had happened since she last saw him. She knew she couldn't possibly tell him everything on the phone, she wanted him by the fire with a glass of good wine, receptive and interested.

But it was one more week. That's all. Then she'd tell him Sophie's story. She'd leave him to start his writing and take a two-day trip to London, to the bank. She'd had an email introducing a David Hancock, Vice President, Pelling Hancock Investment Bank, who would be happy for her to make an appointment to come to the bank and bring with her the required forms of identity and authority. Diana really wanted to go, feeling the urgency of Sister Marie Agnes's declining health.

But one more week. She could manage that, she had plenty to do in the meantime. But she couldn't get on with what she wanted to do. She phoned the hospice to find out how the old nun was doing: there was no apparent change for the worse and Diana left a message that she'd probably come down again when she'd been to London.

In the meantime, there was the question of the burial of the two document boxes and the metal jigsaw tin. She really wanted Simon to be with her, she felt it was an important gesture, symbolic and frankly a little spiritual. She had no doubt that Simon would think it fanciful but for a writer, there were times when he showed very little imagination and understanding.

She poured herself another coffee and wandered out of the kitchen door to the front of the house. She saw Margaret's car on her driveway and on impulse, rang Margaret to see if she wanted to go on a shopping trip and have lunch out. Margaret was more than happy to go. She had stayed at home that day to go through some paperwork, something to do with the local property taxes, she explained, but she was more than ready to drop her plans and go with Diana for a break. Margaret wanted to call in at the stables first to see if Jennifer would be home that night at all, or if her love life had taken a turn for the better. They found Jennifer in the stables, saddling an adorable pony called Shrugs. He was named apparently because he was so willing to do everything, he used to almost shrug his shoulders as if to say, 'Why not?' Jennifer had lost Phoenix to colic in their first year in France, but Blix and Flax were still going strong, albeit retired and living a quiet and happy life.

Jennifer had no plans for the evening and would prepare supper for Diana and Margaret when they returned. Diana thought it was going to be an unexpectedly lovely day; they drove to Périgueux with the sun shining through the sun-roof and her disappointment in Simon's decision to stay in Paris receded with the distance as they drove from *La Chênaie*.

"The trouble is," said Margaret with a smile, "Every time Jennifer and Monsieur Whoever-it-happens-to-be-at-the-time fall out, we need a new stable manager! I have asked her to look elsewhere for her amours, but she never goes anywhere so the only ones she ever meets are ones at the stables!"

"We'll sign her up for one of those dating agency things." Diana was half-serious. "She'll have a bit of fun and you never know, she might find someone who is just right."

"Oh yes, I can see it now. 'Must Love Horses'! It's not a question of loving horses, it's being prepared to eat and sleep horses as well. No, she's a hopeless case, and I adore her."

"You two are very close, it's lovely to see because neither of you seems to overwhelm the other, you're so willing to let each other be separate people. I can't explain, but it's lovely, just the same."

"We've been through hell together. I'll tell you about it sometime. We're really rather protective of each other now. For a while, we were both in a sort of bubble, we wouldn't let anyone in, in case they came to destroy us. Sounds hysterical, but we had reason. But we've overcome most of it and we're fine now. No, don't be curious, I will tell you one day, this just isn't the time or the place."

"I'm hopeless at keeping secrets. It's not something that's ever been an issue in my family, and I suppose I haven't got the character for it. It's purgatory for me to know something and not be able to share it. Not necessarily bad things, but anything. Keeping something from those closest to me is really strange." Diana was aware that Margaret was giving her a searching look.

"No, Margaret, it has nothing to do with Julian!" Diana laughed at Margaret's obvious curiosity, "and I'm going to turn the tables on you, there is something to tell but it's not my secret, and this isn't the time or the place either."

They chattered amiably until they arrived at the car park in Périgueux. The rest of the morning passed pleasantly. Diana found a little boutique where she bought a pink silk blouse. They found the wonderful delicatessen which Simon and Diana had visited on their first trip here together. Margaret phoned Jennifer and told her not to cook anything for supper, they would go home loaded with pâté and cheese, olives and crusty bread. They bought pickled garlic cloves and chargrilled artichoke hearts, seafood salad and thick slices of ham.

Margaret and Diana wandered the little streets and picked a small Italian for lunch, both of the women professed a weakness for pasta. Tagliatelle with smoked salmon was a lovely light lunch. As they sat finishing coffee, Margaret asked about Julian. "Diana, can I ask you something? Tell me to mind my own business if you want, but I wanted to ask – are you having an affair with Julian?"

"No, Margaret, I am not!" Diana laughed, looking directly at Margaret and Margaret believed her.

"Only I saw Julian coming out of your house quite early one morning, too early for a neighbourly cup of coffee I thought."

"God, you really are a nosey old bat! And the answer is STILL NO! Margaret, tell me honestly, are you really hoping for Julian to come to you? If you are, is it really a lost cause?"

"Oh, I'm like one of those tragic heroines, worshipping from afar and grateful for any crumb he throws my way – not that he does, but I keep hoping that he might. But there's not much chance of that, is there? Tell me honestly, you do know he's in love with you, don't you?"

"Oh, Margaret, I don't know. He doesn't know me, if he is in love with me. He's a danger to everything that makes my life what it is. What can it be? Love at first sight? Does that really happen? I really do like him, and just because we're sitting here chatting like two very old best friends, I do find him very attractive. He's nothing like my first impression of him and I'd really love to have him as a friend, if he'll accept that."

"I can vouch for the fact that he makes a very good friend. Jennifer and I were both a bit of a mess when we got here. I was no longer married, I had changed my name back to my maiden name and tried to put the past well and truly behind me. He asked no questions, just set about being a chum, he and Edwina both. And when Edwina died, I'd like to think we were there for him, not overwhelming him but being around if he needed a chat or a companionable drink."

Diana looked at her friend for a moment before saying, "If you must know, the morning he came out of my house, he'd been up all night with John Porton-Watts. Apparently

221

Eleanor went into some kind of catatonic state and they had to break her door down. The doctor came and sedated her, giving John an opportunity to rest. Julian left at about six-ish and saw my kitchen lights on. He rang the bell on the off chance that there might be a cuppa and piece of toast on the go. Actually, it's rather nice, having friends who feel that they can call in like that."

Margaret, despite her acknowledgement that her feelings for Julian were not returned, nevertheless gladly felt her twinge of envy subside.

"That poor woman needs to be in a special place, with people who can cope with that sort of thing," said Margaret. "John is almost beyond being able to help her. And he needs a little happiness in his life, too." She looked at Diana. "You know, don't you?"

"How did you know that I know? Are you clairvoyant now?"

"No, it's just that your face gives everything away, you were just about to say something and then realised that I might not know. Honestly, Diana, you were right about not being able to keep secrets."

"Actually, no-one told me. I saw John and his friend together here in Périgueux one day. I'm glad that he does have a little happiness, but with Eleanor to look after, you have to wonder where it's all going to end."

"To be honest, I think he'd be happy to put her in an institution here, and then move his friend into the house. But they'll probably go back to the UK, if they can afford it. She doesn't speak French. I can't imagine being in that state and not being able to communicate. Nothing worse." Margaret sat thoughtful for a moment.

"Well, I don't think I'm breaking any confidences, but Julian said he would buy their house if they wanted to go and go quickly." Diana felt she could share that much with her friend.

"Oh, that's so typical of him! He can't bear to see someone in a plight; he'll always try to find a way to help. But I don't know if their finances would allow them to move back. Coming here was a kind of gesture to try to keep up some sort of grandeur, you know, being in the grounds of a private estate, locked away from the hoi-polloi and still trying to convince herself she's got a position to uphold. But of course, here in France, no-one gives a damn about all that, we're just an enclave of *étrangers* and all the more strange because we all live in one place together!"

"Well, I suppose we are a pretty odd bunch, if you think about it."

Margaret, true to form said, "Oh yes, a wide-boy property developer, a fallen aristocrat with a loony wife, two weird sisters, a lovelorn widower, a plump surgeon with a completely dotty wife, a very strange girl with an old Resistance fighter for a mother, and then there's you – the sugar-plum fairy, complete with perfect complexion, married to a third-rate writer."

Diana looked at Margaret, shocked and speechless.

"Oh, God Diana, I'm so sorry, that was a joke that went wrong, it wasn't supposed to sound like that, I really am sorry."

"No. No, I would have liked you to have thought more highly of him than that, but so be it. He's working on a new book which will be infinitely better than the last, you'll see. No, the thing that shocked me was the old Resistance fighter thing. What's that all about?"

"Oh, didn't you know? Our old Véronique was with the Resistance in the war, she was only about sixteen but she did her bit. Somewhere around here I think. Get her to tell you about it, it's quite a love story."

Diana so badly wanted to tell Margaret the whole Sophie and de Lusignac story, but really felt now that she had to tell Simon before taking anyone else into her confidence.

They drove back to *La Chênaie* and unloaded their shopping at Margaret's house. Diana went back to her own house to drop the car and check for emails and messages. Simon had written a very ebullient email, obviously pleased that Diana wasn't being difficult about his staying on, but apart from junk mail, there was nothing important. She closed off her computer and went to spend the evening with Jennifer and Margaret.

****

Margaret's chance remark had sent a shock wave through Diana. Véronique had never made any mention of having been in the Resistance, but then, why would she? Diana and Véronique had spent a little time together, had taken coffee together once or twice, but had never really had an in-depth conversation about anything, just pleasantries and easy conversation.

Diana wondered if she could broach the subject without having to say why she was interested.

As it happened, Diana was just driving to the village two days later to buy bread and the paper, when she saw Véronique and Francine walking down the drive towards *La Maison Neuve*.

"Oh, that's wonderful!" Véronique put her hand on Diana's shoulder through the open window of the car. "We were just coming to call to see if you would like to have lunch tomorrow, with Simon if he's here or on your own if he's not."

"Actually, he won't be here for another week or so, but I'd love to come if you don't mind having me on my own. Can I bring anything?"

"No, thank you, but Francine had found an excellent filet of beef and wants to do Beef Wellington. She does it very well, but timing is essential, so come at one and we'll eat at

224

one-thirty." She was just turning away when she looked back and said, "I go to Mass at ten, Francine doesn't go. Please say if you'd rather not, but would you like to come with me?"

"Actually, I would, I'm not Catholic but I should like to, thank you. How lovely, I'll look forward to it. Shall I pick you up, say nine-thirty?"

Véronique smiled and said, "Thank you, that would be kind."

Diana almost convinced herself that fate had intervened; she had been trying to find a reason to invite Véronique without making it look like an ulterior motive, and now this invitation had fallen into her lap. Perfect. And she had wanted to visit the church where de Lusignac had been taken and where Père Martin had taken charge of a distraught and bereaved young girl.

As she was driving out of the gate, Diana looked back through the mirror and saw the two figures just disappearing, still walking towards *La Maison Neuve* and it occurred to her that perhaps they used to walk in the woods before she and Simon bought the house. Perhaps she was being selfish, wanting to keep everyone out, what harm could it do for the few residents who wanted to, to avail themselves of a walk in the woods by the lake? She'd think about it.

She went on into the village to buy her bread, and in the *tabac* next to the café, she saw Julian buying his paper. He smiled, paid for his paper and waited for her outside. He kissed her on both cheeks in the normal way and invited her for a coffee.

The café was busy and the little tables were close to each other, but the general atmosphere was convivial and bright.

"A habit I can't break, even though it's a day old." Julian pointed to his Daily Telegraph.

"You do know you can get your paper on-line now?" Diana laughed.

"It's not the same. You can't stretch out in your favourite armchair with a computer on your lap. When you drop off to sleep, the paper slips silently to the floor, whereas the computer goes crashing to the ground, breaks the silence and costs a fortune to fix."

"Why, you sweet, old-fashioned thing, you."

"Isn't Simon supposed to be home today?"

"He rang yesterday, he thinks if he stays on this weekend, he can finish putting his research together and then the following weekend he'll be home for good. Actually, I was thinking of perhaps going up there myself, to arrange for the flat to be cleaned before we give it back to you. I can't imagine what it will be like after two men have lived there on their own all this time."

"No, don't do that!" Julian said it before thinking "No, actually what I meant was, the concierge has been cleaning for me for years, it's extra money for her and she knows where everything is and how it should be put back. No, please don't bother. Really. It's fine."

"Well, if you're sure. I am - well, we both are - so grateful that you have allowed Simon to use the flat all this time. I'm sure he wouldn't be ready to start writing now if he'd had to spend weeks looking for somewhere to live. You've been so incredibly kind and generous to us."

Julian noticed that Diana had said, 'two men'. He was right, she obviously thought Chris was a man. And she obviously had no suspicion whatsoever that Simon was having an affair. Julian had no intention of letting her find out: at least, not from him. He hoped that Simon would have taken to heart his advice to put an end to whatever it was that was going on and to return to Diana as soon as possible. He was surprised that Simon had chosen not to come home this weekend, but to give him the benefit of the doubt, he might truly have research to finish.

They drank their coffee and chatted comfortably. They had just ordered a second coffee when Diana said, "Did you know that Véronique had been working with the Resistance during the war?"

"Yes, I knew a little. To be honest, and I suppose I'm being unkind, but there were an awful lot of people *after* the war who claimed to be working with the Resistance. When I was told the story, it was just after Edwina died so I don't suppose I gave it too much thought. In fact, I only remembered the other day after you told me about Sophie's story. Why? You can't think she had any connection with the de Lusignacs, can you?"

"Actually, yes, I think she probably did. Margaret told me that she was in the Resistance somewhere around here."

"Well, that may or may not mean a connection to Saint-Sulpice. Anyway, what about it? No, don't tell me – you're going to ask her."

"Actually, yes, I am! I've been invited to lunch tomorrow. I'll be discreet, if she doesn't want to talk about it I won't push her, but can you imagine what an extraordinary coincidence it would be, if she actually knew something about it?"

"Diana," Julian leaned towards her across the little table. "Please be careful. Not everyone has memories they want to share. It can cause hurt and alarm."

"I'll be careful, and I won't press her if she doesn't want to tell me anything. It's so strange though. This story has just fallen into my lap, and I'm afraid I feel it's personal now."

"Well, just bear in mind what I said. It's tricky."

Julian paid for their coffee and slowly walked back to the little car park. He turned to her and said, "Will you have supper with me this evening?"

"Oh Julian, I don't think that's a very good idea, do you?"

"No, probably not, I suppose." He looked disappointed, but resigned.

"Julian, I don't want to hurt you, I really don't. But Simon has been my life for over twenty years, and still is. I'm very -"

"Please!" he laughed. "Please don't give me the I-am-very-fond-of-you-but speech or the can't-we-just-be-good-friends speech either." He put his arm around her shoulder in a companionable way, gave her a hug.

They reached the car park, he gave her a kiss on both cheeks in the French manner that everyone adopted when living there, and said, "Don't forget what I told you. Be careful."

They arrived back a *La Chênaie* at virtually the same time. Julian opened the gate remotely and they each drove to their own houses. As she approached *La Maison Neuve,* she felt suddenly lonely at the prospect of another week in that big house on her own and wished she had trusted herself – and Julian – enough to have accepted his invitation.

The weather was turning colder and wetter. Christmas was only a few weeks away. This would be the first Christmas in this house and the first she had spent away from her beloved house in London. And, it was the first Christmas in this house since the end of the war, when the Germans had left and the family had been destroyed.

They would have a party, she decided. A lunch party, not one of those stand-up-balancing-plates affairs, but a beautifully set table with a huge Christmas tree in the dining room, another in the drawing room and something in the reception hall. She had always adored Christmas, she wanted something in every room and had a passion for tiny glow-worm lights to illuminate all sorts of nooks and crannies. Her trees usually took her two days to put up and Simon had long ago given up offering to help. She liked her trees just so, and if he ever did help, she would go around after him and rearrange his efforts. It was one thing she insisted on having her way with, and in their marriage there had been so few.

On-line shopping was obviously in order. She would never have enough lights and other decorations for this house. The evening passed in a monumental shopping order from specialist Christmas shops, of which there were hundreds now. Apart from a short break for a sandwich and a glass of wine, she had spent five hours picking, choosing, changing her mind, choosing again and finally, buying. It was time for bed and she hadn't taken her usual late afternoon stroll.

She remembered the pile of pine cones. She made up her mind to go back to the little boat house after lunch on the following day. So she needed to add gold and silver spray paint and miles of green and red ribbon to her shopping list if she was to make the huge garland she now had in mind for the front hall.

This was the first happy occasion to be celebrated in this house since the war, she thought as she drifted off to sleep.

****

The following day was windy and wet. Diana wore an olive green raincoat with a matching rain hat and was amused to see Véronique wearing something similar.

"It just shows we both have the same sensible good taste," said Véronique.

They were able to park in the small car park next to the church. The church was about half full when they got there and Véronique took a pew halfway down. Diana followed Véronique in genuflecting, but refrained from making the sign of the cross, and followed her into the pew. They both knelt down in silent prayer for a few minutes and then they sat on the hard bench.

Diana seemed to Véronique to be lost either in thought or prayer and said nothing. In fact, Diana was trying to imagine in this very church, the coffin at the altar with the body of de Lusignac, the men coming in during the night and taking it away, Sophie sleeping in the building adjoining the vestry. It all seemed so personal to her. Normally, Simon would know everything she knew. But, she rationalised, it wasn't her fault that he wasn't there.

Diana found with amazement that she could follow the service. It was in French, not in Latin as she had expected. She knew nothing of Catholicism and just assumed that the Catholic Church had changed nothing for centuries. She found some of the words and rituals very odd, but then all religion to her was a mystery. She used to attend church with her mother when she was small, but religion was a very relaxed affair in their household. She admired people of faith but she never thought of herself as religious, although if pushed, she would have said that she firmly believed 'something' was responsible for making the world and everything in it. But if there was a god, he was personal to each being, he could be prayed to in whatever fashion anyone chose but she had a problem with the age-old question of why bad things happen to good people if 'he' was such a super being.

Véronique seemed to be known by everyone and after the service, it took a while to speak to a lot of the church-goers, exchange pleasantries and get back to the car.

"You seem to know a lot of people, you're quite a popular lady," said Diana with a smile.

"Ah, yes. Yes, I do know many people." She said nothing more, but Diana thought it might be a good way to introduce the conversation she wanted to have later.

Diana left her car at home and walked back to the Cookes' house. A delicious aroma greeted her as she walked into the front hall and she found she was very hungry. Francine was still a mystery to Diana. Véronique was outgoing, feminine, petite and had obviously been a great beauty at one time. Francine was the complete opposite. Diana was not a judgemental person and left room in her assessment of Francine for their relationship to improve. She was certainly an excellent cook; the lunch was delicious. There were no starters, which Diana always thought were a waste of time anyway. The pastry on the Beef Wellington was light and crumbly, the beef itself still pink in the middle and was melt-in-the-mouth tender. Francine served individual bowls of a vegetable selection to each person, which Diana thought was a lovely idea: all that handing around of hot bowls was avoided. The salad to follow was light and crispy, with a soft brie, a sheep's milk cheese and a wedge of Beaufort cheese. Dessert was a fluffy lemon soufflé. Diana complimented Francine with high praise and she was sincere, the meal really had been absolutely delicious.

Francine excused herself, refused an offer of help to clear up and settled Diana and Véronique in the drawing room with coffee and truffles. Diana seized the moment.

"Véronique, can I ask you something personal? But please, please tell me if I'm being rude or you don't want to talk about it."

"I can't imagine that I'll think you are being rude, and yes, of course if there is something you want to know, and if I can help you, I shall."

Diana thought for a moment. She was indeed going to have to be careful.

"Véronique, were you anywhere near here during the war?"

"Ah, I see. Yes, I see. Well, you obviously know part of it, in fact Henri told me he'd told you. Yes, it's a small village and nothing is secret for long, Diana!"

Diana smiled and put her hand on Véronique's. "I know the sad story of de Lusignac and his daughter. Would you tell me where you were?"

"I met my husband here."

"But I thought you were married to an Englishman, your surname?"

"Oh yes, he was English, he was part of a British air crew which was making its way down to Spain with an escape line. They were captured and he spent the rest of the war in a prison camp. But he came back for me."

Diana sat open-mouthed and waited for Véronique to start talking.

****

Véronique was sixteen when the Germans came to Saint-Sulpice-sur-Lauzac. She remembered the shock of seeing the first German uniform in the village, driving slowly through the village in large numbers. Soldiers sitting at the cafés, walking around the square, standing by the river indolently throwing stones into the water, all became common and unwelcome sights. Sights she thought she would never get used to.

Saint-Sulpice had been a quiet, almost too quiet, village. One of Véronique's childhood friends was Pierre Leclerc, whose family owned the inn by the river. It wasn't much of an inn, just a bar, a few rooms for the odd traveller, and a small restaurant which was open three days a week. Pierre always said that when he grew up and took over the bar, he was going to extend it and make a really good hotel of it. He had an older brother, François, who had no interest in the restaurant and was working for the railway, although he didn't like that much either.

Pierre had been training as a cook when the chef was taken to a labour camp in Germany, like so many other young men. So at eighteen, Pierre found himself in charge of the kitchen, as young as he was. The German officers still needed somewhere to go to drink and eat, thus the bar was left very much to its own devices.

Véronique's parents, Augustine and Serge Seignette, owned the village bakery. There was only the one bakery at that time and it supplied bread to two other tiny villages as well as Saint-Sulpice. The German soldiers had their own kitchen but bread was supplied by the Seignettes to the Chateau de Lusignac, for the officers.

The little school only took pupils up to the age of fourteen and in peacetime, children would normally have gone to the bigger school in Bergerac. The school still operated, but parents were reluctant to send their children on an unreliable trip with Germans all over the countryside. The buses were now irregular and often full to overflowing. Children of Véronique's age were then put to work with their parents on farms, or in shops.

Childhood stopped at fourteen in Saint-Sulpice. Where children used to play freely on the village streets and in the square, watched by old men sipping coffee and smoking rough cigarettes, their parents now kept them off the street, games were suspended and the atmosphere was a mixture of fear, resignation and suppressed anger.

Véronique rode everywhere on her bicycle with the big front basket and small trailer behind, delivering bread. Everyone was used to seeing her riding around the village and along the road to the next two villages, even the Germans stopped asking her for her papers on every journey. She would often deliver and collect letters, packages, traded vegetables and even medicines when other forms of delivery were unavailable. The local doctor trusted her to deliver medications to needy patients without delay and even the postmaster had used her to deliver packages when the van was short of petrol or out of action.

None of this was what either Véronique or her parents had planned for her, but everyone was learning to be pragmatic.

The first message she had delivered in secret was given to her by her father. She was to take a message hidden in a loaf of bread to the farmer known as Oleg Fournier. Fournier was the son of Russian immigrants, Olga and Alexei Petrov, who were millers. They had changed their name on arrival in France, thinking to give their family a better future. When they had settled in France, they bought the farm with an old mill on the river and produced the flour which the Seignettes used in their bakery. Their son married a local girl and took over the mill when his father died.

Véronique's task was simply to give over the loaf of bread and leave, there was no message to come back. So began her task as a courier. Far from wanting to leave his daughter out of these matters, Serge was so very anti-German, he viewed it as a duty and honour for her to be involved in working for her country.

When news came of the collapse of one of the escape lines, security became paramount in the minds of the Resistance workers. Many of the men and some of the women in the surrounding villages had been involved in escape lines, even before 1942 when the Germans arrived in this part of France. It was true that moving British and other people through this part of France had been much easier then, being in the *zone non occupée*; now it was extremely difficult, not to mention life-threateningly dangerous.

Pierre's brother, François, was avid in his hatred of the Nazis, and was one of the leaders of the local Resistance. Active resistance in the form of sabotage was carefully selected: the costs of retaliation were too high a price to pay for a couple of days of cut telephone lines, a small track of blown railway line or other small gestures of defiance. The escape lines were the speciality of the region and *La Cloche* had been very successful and was well known in London for the number of returned airmen.

François, with his ability to travel freely on the railway, had organised a line of safe houses and hiding places for the line to run down to Spain without problems. But at this stage of the war, there were more British air crew to move than ever, not to mention a few Jewish families trying to stay hidden and escape the fate of so many of their race. Numbers of air crew were beginning to stretch the resources of the escape lines, and the possibility of betrayal was ever present.

Véronique knew little of actual details and as she grew a little older, she was noticed more by German patrols at road blocks. Her parents became worried: her load had been searched several times, although hiding messages in loaves of bread was not a system used now. Véronique was given verbal messages, which she had always delivered accurately. Pressure on the groups was palpable, tension was almost tangible.

By the time the air crews from the collapsed escape line had arrived, Fournier's barn held twelve pilots, navigators and bombing crews. Another six men were expected in the next few days. It was impossible to arrange false documentation for all these men in the time available, and keeping them all together was also against all the rules they had worked out. Then there were the logistical problems of feeding all these extra people without being noticed. Finding extra supplies was difficult enough, but this needed careful and secret planning.

Véronique had played in the woods of the chateau as a child, sometimes with Sophie, but Sophie was always a strange child and preferred her own company. Véronique had always been adventurous and had played games by herself, and sometimes with Pierre and François, of seeing how far into the woods they could go and still find their way out without help. So she knew the woods very well.

Véronique would dress in dark clothes and take a big bag strapped to her back full of bread, sausage and any other supplies which could be spared. The curfew meant that she would have been in serious trouble and arrested if she had been caught, but there were never any patrols on the lane running alongside the river, because it came to a dead end at the bridge. She would take this lane, and at a point clear of the village, she crept up the bank, watched the road for a few minutes and then run across the road into the woods. Once in there, she knew the little paths and hiding places if she heard any activity.

She then stayed at the barn until daylight and would return along the main road, as if she had never stayed out all night and was simply out early.

It was during this time that she met Richard. Richard was part of an air crew which had been on the move down through France for weeks. He was about twenty-three, fair-haired and very good-natured. The confinement of living in safe houses and weeks of hiding took a heavy toll on some men, but Richard felt that every day they were out of the clutches of the Germans was to be celebrated. His good humour was impossible to ignore. The first time he saw Véronique, he felt such a thump in his heart, he was tearful with gratitude that this lovely girl would risk her life on a daily basis for him and his countrymen.

He had always ridiculed the notion of love at first sight. At twenty-three, and good looking, he had had his fair share of girlfriends but had never felt anything like the emotion when he looked at Véronique and her eyes met his. Sitting with her in this dirty barn, watching her hand out bread and sausage, helping to pass around water, he had never seen a lovelier woman. His French was school rudimentary French, but he had to talk to this girl.

He went over to her to help her with her loaded tray, and took it from her without speaking. They walked around the barn together and he knew he never wanted to be without her. Whatever happened, he would finish the war and come back for her, he knew that with absolute certainty. Now, all he had to do was to tell her.

When everyone had been fed, it was clear she was going to stay the night: probably too dangerous to leave with the curfew now several hours old. He resolved that by the time morning came, he would know everything about her.

The barn was huge, and although it would not have hidden the escapees from a major search, efforts had been made to hide them from a casual inspection. The upper level was piled high in front with old straw bales, the airmen climbed over them and slept behind them. He found a back corner and moved some more straw bales to make a small enclosed area. He took her hand and climbed over the bales into their own little space.

They lay so naturally with his arms around her and they talked. All night. She learned that his family owned a greengrocer's shop in a place called Westgate in Kent, it was by the sea and he loved it. He loved his family, his mother was the kindest person anyone could ever meet. His sister, Martha, was serving with the wrens, the women's part of the navy and she had just become engaged. He told her he had seen some terrible things in this war and the only reason he was anxious to get back to England was to carry on and do his part in bringing this war to an end as soon as possible.

They talked all night. Towards dawn he fell asleep with his lips touching her hair and Véronique had never felt happier. Crazy, she thought, we're in the middle of a war. I have fallen in love with a man who is going to leave in the next few days and whom I shall never see again, or worse – he'll be captured, or he'll make it back to England and then get shot down again, perhaps killed. But she had him for now and she loved him.

As soon as the sun came up, Véronique prepared to leave.

"I have to go; my parents will worry if I don't come back. I'll be back later with some more supplies. In the meantime, please tell all of your friends here how dangerous it is for them to be seen, even by other French people. We can't afford for anyone to know they are here. There are more arriving today and we are trying to arrange to get you all out, but you are going to be here for a few days. But, please – put yourself in charge of security here. The worst thing would be for everyone to decide things for themselves, someone needs to be in charge. You will have to sort out things like latrine arrangements, try only to go at night and cover up the holes with plenty of loose earth and leaves."

"Yes, don't worry" he said, stroking her cheek. "Oleg showed us where we could dig latrines." He felt no embarrassment talking to this girl about such things, her efficiency and concern for their safety left no room for such things.

It always took much longer to walk back by the road, but if she had come back through the woods and had been seen, it would have given the Germans another place to keep guard over.

Véronique realised that she was almost home and hadn't even remembered the walk; she had been completely preoccupied with thoughts of Richard and now, fears for his safety. He had travelled this far, through many dangers, but she didn't know him then. Now, he was hers. They hadn't as much as kissed but she knew that until she had word that he was safe, she would worry and he would never be out of her thoughts.

That night, her delivery was heavier than usual, there were five or six more air crew and there were a few extra supplies for the trip ahead of them, and no-one knew how long it would take. Money would be provided to buy some supplies on the way, but even that was fraught with danger. Fifteen men plus the leader, François, would be going with them. They were going through the woods to a point further down the river. Up to this point they would be in one group. Then they would split into two groups; one going over the hills and the other going on the river. Clothes had been found for all of them, but they each had determined that if they carried nothing else, they would wear their uniforms under their clothes. Nothing would persuade them otherwise. She felt a certain pride in this patriotism and she understood it completely.

When she arrived at the barn, she was pleased to see that there were no obviously signs of habitation – except one. The smell of a few men smoking. She would have to tell them to stop. It would be a complete give-away if any casual German patrol came around.

Richard jumped down as soon as she entered the barn, he had been watching for her through a cracked board up in the loft. They hugged and she told him of her worry about the cigarette smell. Since there were so many of them in the barn now, it was decided that they would eat up in the loft, it would be too dangerous to bring everyone down, even to stretch their legs for a while.

Véronique was anxious. She was always anxious until the escapees had left, but this was different. She let Richard and a couple of the other men take the supplies up to the loft and then climbed up after him.

"Listen, chaps. Véronique says she can smell cigarette smoke quite plainly outside, so I'm sorry – the fags will have to wait until you are well away from here."

There were several loud groans, and a couple of smart remarks. Tension was high and tempers were short.

"Please listen to me." Véronique stood in the middle of the disconsolate group. "A lot of people are putting everything – everything – at risk to help you. For the moment, nothing can be done to make you more comfortable, but you must understand, at this point, any risk *you* take doubles the risk of our people being caught. People like my family, people like Luc there, married with two children, and Oleg, all sorts of people you will never know are risking everything to help you, in order to help our country. We are all patriots and prepared to die for our country, but not to die for a stupid mistake which is avoidable. Now, put out your cigarettes and wait until you are well on your way before you take another."

Richard had never been so proud of anyone. There she was, petite, pretty and full of patriotic pride, telling these men a few homes truths. They ate their food quietly. There was no room to bring any wine, anything she could carry had to be made up of food for now and some for the trip. She had waited all day to be alone with Richard and they went to make their little corner once more.

This time, he told her all the things that young lovers say to each other. He thought about her all day, he couldn't wait until this evening to see her. He loved holding her in his arms and he was so very, very proud of her for what she was doing. This time, they kissed. She had never been kissed properly: she and Pierre had played at being grown-ups for a while, which meant a puckered peck on each other's lips. This was different, this was so tender, so deep and sent a thrill of strange passion through her. They spent the night holding, kissing, talking and just thrilling at being together. Neither of them had attempted anything more intimate, just being content with each other's lips and arms.

In the morning, before everyone stirred, he turned to her. "Véronique," he whispered, "I love you and when this is over, I'm coming back for you and I'm going to marry you." He looked at her with such intensity that she believed him absolutely.

"Richard, I love you too. We have so much that will come between us before the end of this war. You will be so far away, I will never know if you are alright, but if you promise me that you will come back for me, I will believe you."

They both knew that they might only have one more night such as this together and perhaps not even that, because although she wasn't sure of the arrangements – no-one was told more than they needed to know – she felt sure that they would be on the move tonight. She would know soon enough if she was told not to make any deliveries tonight.

She carried on with her chores during the day, helping in the bakery, hanging out clothes, trying anything to keep busy and wait until she was told to take supplies to the barn. When late afternoon came and no pack had been prepared for her, she knew that Richard would be gone as soon as night fell. She went down to the river and sat for a while, trying to stop the tears. She felt bereft. How could she love so deeply so quickly? She'd heard other girls talk of it being 'war fever' – it seemed to enhance any relationship because of the danger of the times. She was sure it wasn't like that between her and Richard.

The curfew sounded and she went back into the house. After supper with her parents, she went up to her room and cried herself to sleep. She was frightened awake by the sound of banging downstairs and the noise of boots on the cobbles outside. Her father came running upstairs and opened her door. "Get dressed quickly. Just get dressed and come down quickly now."

When she got downstairs, the outside door was open and there were German soldiers everywhere, rounding people up from their houses and marching them to the square. Véronique at first couldn't see what was going on, there were people everywhere and even more soldiers. They were pushed back against the walls until they were three deep. She pushed her way to the front and nearly passed out.

Lined up against the wall were the local village men of the escape line. Their hands were tied behind their backs and they were blindfolded. François was standing off to the left with a rope around his neck, the end of which had been thrown over the pole standing out from the market building from which used to fly the French flag. The end was then attached to the rear of a German staff car. Slowly silence descended on the crowd, terror went through them when they realised what was about to happen.

Then another vehicle drove into the square, an army lorry with the canvas covering removed. Standing in the back, in their uniforms and their hands tied to the ironwork, were the air crews. The lorry drew to a halt and the tailgate was let down. Kneeling were two German soldiers, with machine guns now pointed at the wall where the French prisoners were lined up.

The colonel walked into the square and spoke to the crowd. He spoke in German with a French interpreter, the local Milice leader.

"People of Saint-Sulpice. Your easy days are over. We, members of the German Army, have tried to treat you well and left you to carry on your lives peaceably. We had hoped that our attitude of live-and-let-live would have shown you that we are honourable. Instead, you plot your pathetic plots and try to make fools of us. See where this has got you. Twelve homes tonight will have bodies to bury tomorrow. Yes, we will allow you to bury your dead, so look at them while they are still living. We have taken no more retribution for this act of treachery against the German Army, we are only making the responsible ones pay. But hear this. The farm responsible for hiding these people will be burned to the ground. The leader will watch his so-called faithful compatriots die before he himself will die. The airmen for whom you have made this stupid gesture will watch these men die and live with it for the rest of their lives. The airmen themselves are leaving for Bordeaux, to be questioned and then imprisoned. There is no more active war for them. So what did all this loss achieve? For those of you thinking of taking up the reins that these men have dropped tonight – do not do so. I warn you. You will not find us so lenient in future. Each act of treachery will result in retribution that no-one will ever forget."

An air of disbelief fell over the crowd. Then one started screaming as she tried to push forward to get to her son, standing up against the wall waiting for the shooting to start. She was dragged away and the soldiers fired into the air to re-establish calm.

Véronique watched in horror. She looked for Pierre in the crowd, to see if he or his parents were watching poor François, but her eyes were so full of tears, she couldn't see through the crowds of people all pushed together. She then looked at the lorry containing the air-crews. Richard was searching the crowd for her, his face anxious and distressed. He couldn't see her anywhere, the lights of the vehicles were directed towards the men up against the wall, not into the crowd.

He had to see her face, just once, but he was unable to catch sight of her. Then suddenly, she had pushed herself to the front and stood immediately in front of and between two German soldiers who were facing the crowd, ready to quell any trouble. He saw her and read the message in her face. He kept his eyes on her and she did with him.

The sound of guns being prepared to fire rang out, the crowd started crying and wailing and a single shout of, 'Vive La France' rang out. Suddenly the night air was full of explosive sounds, smoke, stench of blood and screaming from the helpless crowd. All through, Richard kept his eyes on Véronique and she tried to do the same, but as her lifetime's friends and their families were being put to death, the tears overcame her and she was unable to stop her crying. Then it was over. The silence was horrible, the only thing heard was grief. Profound grief. Then the colonel shouted once more. The staff car started up and François was yanked off his feet. He had tried to say something as the rope tightened, which could have been, 'Vive La France', but no-one was absolutely sure. It was, however, put on his grave as his last words. The driver and aide got out of the car and tied off the rope to a pillar.

The villagers couldn't move. Shock, horror, fear and loathing swept through the assembled families. Screaming and crying started as the Germans pulled out, back to their barrack accommodation, the officers back to the chateau for self-congratulation. Pierre stepped out from the crowd, holding up his father, who was completely overwhelmed with grief. They walked slowly over to where François was gently swinging from the pole. Someone appeared with a ladder and Pierre climbed up to cut his brother down. Several men came forward to catch his body as Pierre cut the rope, they then laid him gently on the ground and stood back to allow his father to hold him and embrace him.

All around the square, the scenes of abject grief and unbearable sorrow were repeated. Véronique walked around seeing the dead faces of people she had known all of her short life. She had watched the lorry drive off with Richard still trying to look at her, she was the very last thing he saw as the lorry went around the corner and out of the village. For most of what remained of the night, people helped each other carry bodies into the church. The old women who normally took care of the dead to prepare them for burial were unable to cope, partly because of the numbers involved and partly because they, too, were affected by loss, one of them had lost a son and one a husband.

No-one could even think far enough past what had happened to ever see a time when the village would recover from this.

Clearly, none of the dead men had talked or tried to make a deal with the Germans, since the remaining members of the Resistance who were not going on the escape trip had not been rounded up. Obviously, the escape line was now too compromised to even think of starting up again.

But who had betrayed them? The answer became clear the following morning.

Enough coffins were brought from the woodcutter's yard in Bergerac for the bodies to be laid to rest. Philippe de Lusignac had appeared at the church in the morning, comforting families and talking to groups of men. He went off with one group and was never seen alive again.

The Germans left the village very much to their own devices for the next few days and when de Lusignac's body was found outside the gates to the chateau, they simply put it in a coffin and sent it to the church. They never made any enquiries as to how he had met his fate and it became obvious, even to his most loyal supporters, that he had either mistakenly or deliberately told the Germans of the escape. Some people believed that some threat was made against him by the Germans, perhaps to kill Sophie or something along those lines, since they were sure he wouldn't have willingly given away the group after all he had done for all that time to help them. Others believed that his relationship with the Germans at the chateau was too close and he was only serving the interest of himself and his daughter, whatever it cost.

But the end result was still the same: all the men were dead and the British had been taken to prison camp. And de Lusignac would forever be branded a traitor.

The village buried their dead, killed the person they believed to be the collaborator responsible and the war went on. Some form of reality and normality returned to the village and people tried to go about their business as they had before. The Germans themselves seemed more subdued after the event of that Easter.

****

The news of the invasion of the Allies reached Saint-Sulpice but it was received with quiet anticipation rather than joy. Their pain went too deep for any unreserved celebration. The war continued until one day, the Germans were gone. One night, many lorries and cars drove through the village, there was quick marching of many pairs of boots and they were gone.

An air of unreality spread across this part of the country. The Americans came, went through the chateau for any documentation, films or any other records but found nothing except piles of ash. They questioned anyone who might have had any useful information, made their records and in turn, they departed also. The village was left once again to find whatever passed for normality in their lives.

Véronique was as deeply affected as everyone. Never had anyone ever expected that young children, teenagers and old people would ever have to witness such barbarity. How do young people recover their youth after an experience like that? She had had no word about Richard, except for one message which had been passed through numerous messengers, to say that he was in a prison camp in Germany. She had no way of knowing where he was or even if the message was accurate. But he had promised to come back and she was sure he would.

A routine of sorts was re-established. Markets opened once again, fishermen went out in their boats without restraint and children were able to travel to school. Families visited other families in neighbouring villages without having to pass through roadblocks and patrols. The postal service slowly came back to full function. People went in search of news of lost relatives and slowly stories of the Resistance and the escape lines became known. The British and American governments honoured Saint-Sulpice and other towns and villages which had held true to their patriotism and had aided the Allies.

The village of Saint-Sulpice prepared for its first Christmas without the Germans. The longed-for peace and freedom did not bring with it the elation and euphoria which might have been expected: the wounds were too raw and the churchyard too full of patriotic French citizens.

Véronique continued helping her parents. By this time petrol was more easily available and her father had bought a little van to make deliveries. He taught her to drive around the roads and lanes which, for so long, had been patrolled by Germans. She enjoyed the solitude of driving around on her own, her spirits alternating between thrilling expectation at possible news from Richard and despair at receiving none.

On this particular day, she had returned from a two-hour round trip and was just passing the point in the road where she used to come up from the river bank and dash across the road into the woods. She saw a figure standing by the side of the road, waving. She stopped the car and stared in disbelief and shock. There was Richard, her Richard, running towards the van, coat flying open and his face pink with cold. He was laughing as he reached the van, he pulled open the door and taking her arms, pulled her towards him. They were laughing, crying, kissing and talking.

"Your father told me you'd probably be coming back this way, I don't know what I'd have done if you'd come back on the other side of the river! God, Véronique, I came back as soon as I could, I've been counting the miles to get down here."

"I can't believe you're here. I can't believe it. But I always knew you'd come back for me, I knew it. I have missed you every day and my thoughts have always been with you." She was laughing, crying and running all her words together.

They had so many things to say to each other but it was the trivial things which poured out: how did he get here? How had she been? How was her family? How had the village recovered?

They got into the van and drove back to the village. He turned to her and said, "Véronique, listen to me. Before we go in, there's something I need to say. I want to marry you, I'd like to marry you here, with your family and your friends around you. But the thing is, I'm not sure. I really don't know where …"

He was struggling to actually say what his heart was feeling. The air crews which had been captured that night were the reason that all those poor men were shot and François, poor François, was made to watch and then hanged. He imagined that the villagers would not be happy, and might even be angry, that one of the airmen had come back.

Her parents had always been aware of her feelings for Richard, she had told them after the first night she had spent in Fournier's barn. After the massacre, his name had not been mentioned but they were aware that Véronique spent the rest of the war and the newly-formed peace waiting for him.

He explained as best he could. Véronique understood his dilemma, although as far as she knew, the hatred after the massacre had been directed at the Germans, not against the young British airmen. But then, this was the first time one of them had come back.

They arrived back at the bakery. Véronique's parents lived in the house next door and the two properties were connected by a door. Véronique had moved into the little flat above the bakery: it was really just a bedroom with a sitting area, a tiny bathroom and an even tinier kitchen area. She took her meals with her parents, her relationship with them was close and loving and they were immensely proud of her for her unfailing work with the Resistance. Now she was going to ask them to make a sacrifice.

She had absolutely no doubt that her future was with Richard. She had loved him since that first night in the barn and had never stopped. Now she had a decision to make. She could go with Richard to England and marry him there, or she could take a risk that bad feeling would erupt in the village by marrying him in the village. But marry him she would.

They talked it over with her parents. As far as they knew, no-one at the moment knew Richard, who he was or what he was doing here, he was just another stranger in the town. People were drifting all over the country now looking for family, friends or just seeking work.

Her father took her in his arms, crying. "You have to make your life now, you have been loyal to France, to your family and to your friends. It is time for you to do what your heart tells you to do." He turned to Richard. "You will honour and cherish her, I am sure. You have shown that you love her by coming back for her. This place will have many bad memories for you but also happy ones. But it is time for you to go and make some new memories. It would be better for you to go, make your life together in England. Do not forget us, you will always be in our hearts."

There were many tears that day. A bottle of brandy appeared which Serge had been saving since before the war, intending to celebrate the end of the war, but somehow no-one had had the heart for it at the time.

It was decided that Richard and Véronique would leave as soon as possible, quietly and without letting anyone know that one of the airmen had come back.

"There's one thing I want to do before we go," said Richard. "I want to go and light a candle for those who didn't make it, not just those brave French men who died that night, but also for those men I was captured with, six of whom didn't make it either. I'm not a religious man, although I've called on God more than once over the past few years, but it's important to me, it's a promise I made to myself that I would do if I ever got out alive and could make it back here."

It was decided that they would leave in the morning, on the train to Bergerac and then make their way north. They went off to the church: being late afternoon they didn't meet anyone to speak to; a few curious glances but no-one stopped to enquire. Véronique went to the altar with Richard but sat in a pew whilst he spent some time alone with his thoughts and prayers. He lit his candle and came back to sit with her. The two of them sat there alone in the church, he took her hand and asked her, "Are you quite sure about this? Are you ready to leave here and leave your family?"

"I have never been more sure. I have waited for you knowing that you are the only person I ever want to spend my life with. I'm ready." She looked at him with such love and devotion, he had no doubt that they would be alright.

Père Martin stepped out of the vestry, he spoke to Véronique. "I've just seen your parents; they've told me what you are going to do. My children, would you kneel, both of you? I'll give you a blessing and we will pray together for a moment."

They knelt side by side at the altar. In their minds, their marriage was being celebrated right there and then.

It was a sombre meal with her parents that night. Véronique on the one hand wanted to share her happiness with her family and her friends, but ultimately believed it was for the best to leave and start her new life with Richard far from here. Richard slept on her old little bed in her parents' house and she went to her little flat to pack. She sat on her bed and thought about the step she was about to take. She was excited, but knew that part of her heart would always be here.

She didn't sleep much that night and at dawn she was ready to go. The first train was at six-thirty a.m and as they took their leave, her heart was breaking to see the tears running down her father's face. Her mother was trying to comfort her father and to remain brave but even she lost her composure as the two young people turned the corner towards the little station and out of sight.

****

The journey back to Kent took them four days. They stayed in little *auberges* on their way north, staying as the married couple that they considered themselves to be. On the way, they had a lot of time to find out about each other, telling each other everything. They spent hours on trains and in buses, but time meant nothing to them.

On arrival in England, Véronique felt suddenly terribly homesick. She spoke a little English but Richard's French had improved so much that he was practically fluent. In prison camp there were language classes given by fellow prisoners: it was possible to learn Italian, Portuguese, French, Russian and Polish. Mostly the classes were a way

250

of killing time, but Richard had worked hard because it had always been his intention to come back and marry Véronique.

Richard's parents were wonderful. His mother greeted Véronique as if she were a daughter, and his father treated her with great respect and affection. On the way to England, Richard had explained what his plans were for them and their future. His father owned two shops: a greengrocery and a hardware store in a little parade of shops. Both shops were doing well and Richard would be taking over the greengrocery. There was a flat above the shop and as soon as they were married, they would live there. In the meantime, Richard would live there on his own and Véronique would stay with his parents.

The house in Westgate faced the sea with only the road and a promenade between. It was a classic Victorian three-storey sea-front house, the rooms were large and airy and Véronique's bedroom seemed enormous to her. The wedding was set for three weeks' time and in the meantime, she and Richard spent some time making the flat comfortable and cosy.

Her homesickness came in waves but for the most of the time, she was happy. Richard's mother, Sarah Cooke, had a friend who loaned her a dress and veil for her wedding. Richard's best man, Nigel, was one of the air crew he had been in hiding with in the barn, and then later imprisoned with. Nigel had not coped very well with the arduous time on the escape line and by the time they arrived at Fournier's barn, he was close to breaking point and wanted to be left behind. It was Richard who looked after him, who stayed beside him and kept him going. They had remained friends and although Nigel's family lived in London, they still managed to see each other from time to time.

The wedding was a joyful occasion. Sarah gave Véronique a pearl necklace which had belonged to her mother, and Richard gave her a pair of pearl earrings. She looked lovely and Richard was so proud.

They went to a hotel in London for a couple of days; Nigel took them to meet his family and within days they were back in Westgate to start married life.

Richard proved to have great business acumen. The shop next to the hardware store fell vacant and Richard bought it and turned it into a fish and chip shop, he put in a married couple as managers. Two years later, he bought the house next door to his parents as a new home for his growing family – Véronique was pregnant. Over the next few years, he bought five other shops and another house in the same street to run as a bed and breakfast. People were starting to take day trips and even short holidays.

When their daughter Francine was born, Véronique thought she would like to take a trip home to visit her parents and take the baby. She had frequent news of the village and by now, of course, everyone knew she had married one of the airmen. They thought it was a good time to go.

Véronique wasn't prepared for the wave of emotion which hit her as she stepped off the train. She and Richard would speak both French and English at home, but here French was being spoken all around her. She was happy and excited as she saw her parents standing on the station forecourt waiting for them.

The four weeks passed so quickly. They visited all their old haunts, walked by the river, leaving the baby with her parents; and went to the church. In the village square which held such terrible memories for them, they sat at the café and inn.

Pierre had achieved his ambition and had extended the building to become an hotel with a restaurant and a terrace overlooking the river. He had married a local girl and had two sons, Henri and little Pierre.

For all the re-acquaintance they made with everyone, no-one talked of the terrible events of so recent a time. The war was over and people were moving on with their lives. However, little plaques appeared all over town, marking places where people had either been shot or where a hero of France had lived.

Someone asked Véronique if she could ever come back to live now that she was married to an Englishman. She had thought about it and said, "Yes, maybe. One day."

****

Diana had listened to Véronique's story without speaking. She felt tears on her cheeks. It was a happy story in the end, but what heartache do some people have to suffer before any kind of joy comes into their life?

"When did Richard die?" she asked.

"Five years ago. He sold all his business interests a couple of years before that. Francine was born a mathematician," she laughed, "but had no interest in any of the businesses. She went to university and went on to become a chartered accountant. Richard was always happy for her to do anything she wanted, a real Daddy's girl!"

"Did he tell you much of his imprisonment?"

"No, not really. When he came back for me, we had so much to say to each other, and then later, he just seemed to want to forget about it. I don't suppose any of them could forget, any more than we who were left in the village could forget. But time does soften the edges, doesn't it?"

"I know this will sound strange, but in a way, I don't understand how you can bear to live here. This place, the memories, this estate!"

"But don't forget, this village was my home. I suppose I always knew I'd come back one day. If it had been Richard who was put up against a wall and shot, perhaps I might feel differently. But to be honest, I love it here. Oh, to be sure, there are ghosts but when I go down the drive to the big house – sorry, your house – I don't see de Lusignac's treachery, I see a place which is loved once again, and it's peace I feel, not sorrow."

Diana's every instinct was to rush to de Lusignac's defence, but she could say nothing, especially now.

Diana looked over to where Francine had taken a seat. "And you, Francine, how do you feel here?"

"Honestly? I've tried to love the place, I've been coming here on and off for years with Mum and Papa, but I don't think I was cut out for country life. I was a partner in a busy city firm of accountants and I miss it. My personal life wasn't that great but I did have a job I loved. When Papa died, I thought my right arm had been cut off. He and I had some sort of understanding, I never had to explain how I felt, he never seemed angry with me, but more, much more, he was never disappointed in me."

"Disappointed? Why on earth should he be disappointed in you? Do you mean because you didn't take over any of the businesses?"

"Yes, there's that, but there's more than that. I've never been pretty, socially adept, witty or someone whose company was in demand. I've always been solitary and studious. Then I met someone and we had an affair. He was married, of course. It ended badly after a number of years and caused endless grief to his family, for which in the end he blamed me. But he didn't seem to notice that I had fallen apart too. Papa never criticised me, never judged me harshly." She glanced across at her mother and smiled. "And you were okay too, old bean."

Diana saw true affection between the two women. Francine had been more outgoing on this occasion than any other, and she came to the conclusion that her apparent reticence was actually shyness. How quick we are to judge people just because of their appearance, thought Diana.

Véronique was speaking again. "We went to the old barn to scatter Richard's ashes. Of course, it isn't an old barn any more, it was burned to the ground; it's a modern, very smart barn conversion, although it's less like a barn and more like a cathedral, with plate glass everywhere – must be murder to live in in the summer!"

"So, what did you do?"

Both Francine and Véronique smiled conspiratorially. "Actually, we trespassed in your woods! Mind you, they weren't your woods at the time, so technically we weren't trespassing. I took the path I used to take to go to the barn and spread Richard all along the way!" She laughed aloud and Francine laughed with her. "Don't be sad, Diana. Richard, Francine and I had the kind of life some families can only dream of. And bad memories fade, you know. At the time, you don't think they will ever let you live in peace. But they do. De Lusignac paid a terrible price for what he did, and no-one will ever know why he did it. But I like to think it was not a decision of his own making, which is why I can live on his beautiful estate and enjoy it every single day."

But Diana knew why he had done it.

****

When Diana left, it was already evening. She had stayed talking to the two women for much longer than she had thought. She felt she had reached a level of friendship with both women and that it was a good omen. When she reached home, Simon had left her several messages and so had Julian. She was still steeped in Véronique's story, frustrated at her inability to tell her the truth and she didn't really want to speak to anyone at that moment. She went up to run a bath as the phone rang again.

"Hello, Dee darling, did you have a good lunch? Must have been, you've been out for ages."

"Hello, darling. Yes, I have had a wonderful day, really interesting. What an amazing life some of these people have had. You know, my life has been so quiet and sheltered by comparison, I'm only just beginning to realise how very privileged I've always been. Anyway, I'll tell you more when I see you. How are things going? I did tell Julian I'd come up and clean the flat when you're ready to leave, but he insisted that I don't. Apparently it's the way the concierge earns a little extra money, I wouldn't want to step on anyone's toes."

"No, I've already spoken to Julian, I offered to get one of those companies in but he told me the same thing. She's been looking after his flat for years, so it's best left to her. No need for you to come. Listen, Dee, I've been working on an idea for another book."

"Oh, great! That's wonderful! How exciting. What's the story?"

"Well, I'd rather wait until I see you, but it's one you can help me with."

"That's wonderful! I'd love to! I can't wait to hear all about it. We've so much to catch up on, you've been gone so long."

"Well, that's the other thing, I thought I'd leave here on Thursday, come down and spend some time writing. Then, if this other thing works out, I can do some of the research while I'm down there, ready for when this book is finished. To tell the truth, this one isn't going all that well. I haven't done much writing yet, but it's not quite working out as I'd hoped."

Diana recognised the ground-work. He was getting ready to abandon this story in favour of this new one, whatever that was. She had seen it all before. When he'd been working on the book which was eventually published, he lost heart several times and started going off at tangents, but she and her mother encouraged him and nurtured him until he stuck to his original intention.

When he eventually came down, she would do everything she could to keep him focused and productive. It wasn't that they needed the money. Diana felt that he needed to achieve something. Looking back, his life had been made up of one discarded project after another. It is true his book had done quite well. It was never going to be a literary great but it was an easy read, enjoyable and light. He wasn't what she would call a gifted writer, but he was able to tell a story in an approachable way. But it had all been so long ago. He had started other stories, done some research and then gone on to something else.

So, Thursday it was. It would come around soon now. She had missed him, it was true, but she felt strangely different. She felt involved with the history of the place, as if she had somehow taken part. Simon wouldn't understand. But so much had happened since that first remark of Hilary's. She felt as if she had stepped out of her old life and taken on parts of everyone else's. She had relived Véronique's danger and heroism as it was being told, she had suffered with Sophie and as always, she had believed in de Lusignac.

Diana took her bath and her last thoughts before sleep were of the courage of a young girl, braving the dark woods to bring help to people of another country and who risked death every time she did it.

After Diana had left, Francine and Véronique had sat together, with a cup of hot chocolate. "I am a little worried about Diana."

Francine looked at her mother. "Whatever do you mean?"

"I can't quite put my finger on it. She seems so - I don't know - like someone with a secret. You know, someone who wants to share something?"

"Mum, honestly, is this your old sixth sense telling you that all is not right? Look at her, she's gorgeous, she's rich and she has a handsome husband. God, Mum, if she had any problems at all it's probably worrying over what colour her next car will be."

"Don't be cruel, Francine. She's not a superficial woman, she thinks and feels things deeply. Most people who weren't involved are not really interested in what happened back then, those terrible times. But she was. Curious. I think she probably has a story to tell herself."

"For heaven's sake, Mum," Francine laughed. "She's just a very uncomplicated woman who loves a good story. She paid you the compliment of letting you tell it to a willing audience."

"No. You're wrong, *cherie.* There's something there, I know it."

****

Diana spent the next couple of days preparing for Simon's arrival. She thought she would invite everyone for Sunday lunch. It would be a few days after Simon finally came home, but before he started writing in earnest. It would give Simon an opportunity to meet everyone and then he could be left in peace to get on with his book. Diana felt sure that once he was living at *La Maison Neuve*, whatever problems he was having with his book would be resolved. He just needed his own space with peace and quiet.

Diana dialled Simon's number, but it went to voice mail. She didn't want to leave a message but immediately she rang off, he called her back. "Sorry, couldn't get to the phone in time."

"Catch your breath, darling. Whatever are you doing? You sound quite exhausted."

"No, I'm fine. Hi. How are you? Everything alright?"

"Yes, fine. Better than fine actually. Listen, I thought, before you got busy, we'd have everyone to lunch on

Sunday. Some of them have been incredibly kind to me and I'd like you to meet them. Then we'll leave you alone. Promise. So, do you mind?"

"Of course not. No, it would be lovely. But please – promise me you won't serve lamb!" Simon hated lamb, he didn't even like the smell of it cooking.

"Promise! I do miss you, darling. I can't wait for Thursday; I'll have one of your favourites waiting for you when you get here. The weather for the week doesn't look too good, heavy rain so you'll have a pretty awful drive. Has Chris gone already or is he staying 'til the bitter end? Are you going to have to take him home or anything? Pity I didn't meet him; do you want to ask him to come down here for a while before he goes off?"

"No, darling, that's ok, it'll just be me on Thursday. I love you. Talk to you later."

She put the phone down and sat down at her little desk in the kitchen. There would be about eleven or twelve of them for lunch, ten if John didn't come. She doubted very much whether Eleanor would come anyway, but she'd make sure she was included in the invitation. Diana was a great list-maker; her mother's efficiency had taught her that much. 'Lists never lie, the memory does', – one of her mother's sayings.

Margaret and Jennifer said they'd be delighted, as did Francine and Véronique. Julian said he'd come with pleasure. Diana wasn't quite sure whether to phone the Porton-Wattses or whether to drop them a note. In the end, she thought she'd spare John the embarrassment of having to explain why they couldn't come over the phone and wrote a note instead. She also wrote one to the Findlays, since she couldn't remember ever having had their phone number. She pushed the note through the Porton-Wattses' letter box and walked on up the drive to the Findlays. As she was almost at the front door, the door opened and Hilary was standing there, in red trousers, blue sweater and the old multi-coloured scarf.

"Hello, come in. We were just talking about you. Come on in. Oh, yes, leave your shoes on, no - don't bother - oh alright, but there's no need. Bobby, Diana's here."

Diana was ushered into the drawing room. The house was identical to Julian's but without the magnificent conservatory. The only other time she had been in here had been the night of the drinks party. Empty of people, the room looked homely, slightly untidy and very cosy. A big dog was curled up on the sofa, evidently no threat to anyone. Two leather armchairs were very well used, two sofas covered in a nondescript colour were almost swamped by the number of brightly coloured cushions and, by the window stood a baby grand piano.

"Actually, I haven't come to stay, I've just brought you an invitation to lunch on Sunday. Simon is coming home on Thursday and we thought it would be nice for him to meet everyone before he starts work. Oh, hello, Bob." Bob had walked into the room, drying his hands on a tea towel, evidently doing something in the kitchen.

"Hello, Diana. Sorry but please don't shake hands. I've just been doing my daily soak in something Hilary found, some herbal thing to soak my hands in for an hour a day."

"And does it help at all?"

"Of course it does," he said nodding his head vigorously and winking in Hilary's direction. In other words, Diana thought, it makes no difference at all but he's doing it to please Hilary. Lovely man. She smiled her understanding.

Hilary went off to make coffee, giving Diana an opportunity to study Bob a little. She hadn't really had a chance to talk to him when she'd come for drinks, but she rather liked what she had seen. He was plump – not a word used very often now – the word conjuring up a vision of exactly what she saw in front of her, a congenial man, with kindness written all over his face. His devotion to Hilary was evident, and he was much easier to talk to on a one-to-one basis.

"We began to think the big house would never sell, but we're so glad you're here now."

"That's a lovely thing to say, thank you. We do feel very welcome. I love the house and walking in the woods. Do you by any chance know if there are fish in the lake?"

"Well, I believe Julian has seen trout rising but it's not a thing I know a great deal about. Julian's your man, he's an ace fisherman, or used to be."

"You knew his wife, Edwina, didn't you?"

"Yes, she was a very keen gardener. Always out there in all weathers, planting stuff and digging stuff up. The son's a lovely chap, too. Terrible shame about the daughter, so much talent, really incredibly talented. You should get Julian to show you some of her work."

"I've seen the two paintings in his front hall, are there others?"

At that point Hilary came back in with a tray on a little tea trolley. Diana hadn't seen one of those for years, her mother had one inherited from *her* mother. There followed the business of pouring tea, handing around sugar, little plates for cake, pulling out little tables and handing out napkins. All the while, Hilary was keeping up a nervous series of half-sentences and swallowed endings. When they were settled with their individual tables, she seemed to subside into calm, as if a huge worry had been lifted from her.

They talked for a while about Diana's house and her plans to rebuild the boat house in the spring. Hilary's chatter seemed to calm down and she spoke virtually normally.

Bob had been talking about the history of the area when Diana asked, "Hilary, you mentioned when we first met that you hoped the stories of this place wouldn't put us off. Did you mean the story of de Lusignac?"

"Yes. It's common knowledge that this traitor was responsible for the deaths of all those men in the village. Just think. He lived here! When we first came, we knew nothing until after we'd bought the place. Of course, no local French person would ever come and live here."

Diana had to choke back her immediate response that not only did a local French woman live here, but one who was directly involved.

How could this have become so complicated? Diana hated deceit, she loathed any kind of secrets and she was now a repository of so many. Trying to change the subject and change the atmosphere, she said, "I understand you were a surgeon, Bob?"

"Yes, it was all I ever wanted to do. But it's a lottery whether or not arthritis is going to pick your number. I did some tutoring for a while but I'm really a hands-on type of doctor. Poor choice of words though, wouldn't you say?" he smiled.

Diana had noticed some photos on the top of the piano, showing Hilary and Bob with some African children, obviously taken in Africa.

"Tell me about these children," she said.

"Hilary and I used to spend some time in Africa, working in a little hospital in Ngambwe, doing small operations like hare lips and other disfiguring features."

"I thought you were a vascular surgeon. I'm sure that's what someone told me."

"I was a general surgeon first and foremost; it was where I thought I could do most good. The vascular speciality came about by accident really. But general surgery remained my first love. And my old girl here was my second!" He stretched out his hand towards Hilary, who took it with a look of complete devotion.

"So you met at the hospital?" asked Diana.

"Hilary was just a student nurse when I first saw her and I had just qualified. We've been together ever since, haven't we, old girl?" He looked at his wife with pure adoration.

A ghastly smell started to seep around the room and Hilary jumped up and started to bluster again. "Oh, I'm so - Oh, Buster, how could - you terrible dog - come on, walkies. Diana, I'm so sorry. He's a bit of a windy - Buster come, walkies. So sorry, won't be a moment. Here, boy."

Clearly the dog was responsible and Hilary rushed off to fetch her coat to walk the dog, presumably. She went out of the patio door with the old dog and started to walk him around the garden. Diana looked out at her fondly, and smiled.

"You mustn't think Hil's a bit daft, you know." Bob said, smiling. "She's just a really good woman who's not very good in company. Don't get me wrong, she loves company, but she's not very confident and she then tends to waffle a bit."

"Oh, please, I don't think anything of the sort. I was only -"

"Yes, you did," he said but not unkindly or sharply. "Everyone does. She can't help it. She is the kindest and most generous person I have ever come across and I love her more than I ever thought possible for one person to love another."

"She's very fortunate, then. You are obviously so very happy together, a sort of complete unit. Did you say you used to go to Africa together?"

"Yes, about four years after we were married, we started taking our annual holiday to do some work for a charity. They had built a small hospital in the northern area of Ngambwe, a place called Umjali. The reason they chose that place is that there wasn't a doctor for hundreds of miles in any direction. They had raised money for this little clinic, about twelve beds in all, a small maternity ward and a staff bungalow. The bungalow sounds grand but really it was just

263

very plain, three double bedrooms and a sitting room. There was a veranda which was pleasant in the heat and the kitchen was about fifty yards from the bungalow. We felt we were doing something worthwhile, do you understand? It wasn't as if practising in England wasn't rewarding, but everyone here could get everything they needed. Over there, the word 'need' carried a whole different meaning. And we did this every year until ten years ago."

"Is that when your arthritis began to give you trouble?" said Diana.

"No," replied Bob, looking out at Hilary walking around the garden with Buster. "No, it was for an entirely different reason."

****

The Findlays had arrived in Umjali, the up-country clinic in Ngambwe, three days before and were once again settling into their routine. Hilary would scrub up to help Bob with his minor surgeries, many of which were carried out under local anaesthetic. Bob was qualified to carry out anaesthesia but he preferred to wait for another visiting doctor for the more serious cases, unless of course it was an emergency.

The little hospital area had grown since their last visit: there were three more staff huts, which housed trainee nursing staff and two more qualified nurses. There was also a small dispensary. For many reasons, the dispensary was heavily protected, with metal safes, and an armed guard was on duty twenty-four hours a day.

The kitchen hut had been enlarged and now employed three cooks. The little hospital was, as always, full.

The bathroom hut was now equipped with two baths, for which water was heated by a wood fire in a large boiler outside. The hot water then was piped through to both bathrooms, but only one could be filled at a time. The valve would then be switched to the other. The charity had dug two water wells some years before: the village of Umjali had clean water, but the advice was still to boil the water before drinking it.

The staff bungalow was more comfortable than the last time the Findlays had been there. A charity worker had collected rugs, cushions, lamps and a few pictures and had them shipped out. It took weeks and only half the shipment arrived, but it was still passable comfort.

There were no telephone connections, no television, and obviously no newspapers. There was the radio by which they could communicate with their head office in Kokomlemle, and they received news of world events this way.

There was a tiny airstrip, by which small aircraft could bring in aid workers and small amounts of supplies and it was through this route that the Findlays would arrive.

They quickly settled into life in Africa. In fact, they loved it. The work was intense and satisfying, and by the end of the evening meal at about eight pm, they were ready for bed. Whenever they arrived, they always overlapped by about a week with the outgoing volunteer doctor. On this occasion it was a middle-aged man they had known for several years. He was a Harley Street plastic surgeon, who tired every so often of wealthy ageing women who wanted to look younger than their years and had the money to buy their looks. He also worked for the NHS, repairing faces burned in domestic accidents or road accidents. But he felt most fulfilled when working in Africa.

On this occasion, the Findlays had been in Africa for about two weeks. The charity headquarters wanted Bob to accompany a couple of their officers to another location, where they were thinking of opening another hospital. Bob felt that any funds available should be spent on the present commitment, the hospital at Umjali, but he was outvoted and the visit to two prospective sites would take place the following week. The two men would arrive by the little plane and then they would go to Khidjadi by two air conditioned land cruisers which were being driven up by volunteers. They would spend two days at Khidjadi, sleeping in camps organised ahead of time by the advance party of six: two cooks, two armed guards and two drivers. The camp party vehicle was an old converted safari vehicle donated by one of the game reserves.

From Khidjadi, they would drive to Mandabo and spend two nights there. All this took a lot of organisation and the Findlays were not happy. It also required a third vehicle to follow them with supplies of fuel.

The Findlays felt that a fly-over would have given them as much information as they needed, the well-drillers could have done their surveys weeks before and all information collated and studied without this huge organisational headache. But the trip was to go ahead regardless.

Hilary realised that Bob would be gone for the best part of a week, driving up there, spending time and then driving back. It was going to be very strange without him. She wasn't nervous about being in the clinic on her own, the people were amazingly friendly and helpful. It was just being without him. She had often said that when they weren't together, she only felt half-complete. She missed him dreadfully.

Bob felt the same. He had been the envy of his fellow junior doctors. How this little, round, unexceptional fellow had managed to snare that young, jolly, bouncy, pretty girl was a mystery. They were inseparable from the first time he asked her out. Their marriage wasn't one of driving passion and heavy compromises. It was a marriage of total partners, exact halves one of the other, total understanding of each other's minds and hearts.

On the night before he left with the charity executives, they lay together, neither able to sleep, dreading the impending separation. They rose at dawn and took their breakfast together on the veranda and went to listen for the plane. The vehicles were ready and the camp party had left yesterday. They walked over to the airstrip without speaking, holding hands like young lovers and hoping, even now that the trip might be called off. It wasn't.

The two executives climbed out of the little plane and the pilot descended to give them a sack of mail, newspapers and magazines. If they were to make Khidjadi by night-time tomorrow, they needed to leave fairly quickly. Bob and Hilary walked back to the bungalow together to fetch his bag and his hat and stood hugging each other without saying a word. He kissed her quickly and was gone.

The first two days without Bob were busy but she felt his absence deeply. There was a breech birth which was complicated to deal with and a child who had been burned in a thatched hut fire. Dressings, medications, outpatients and dispensary took all of her time, but there was an air of sadness she couldn't dispel.

On the third day, she was dealing with the patients in the hospital when three men with rifles appeared in the doorway. The one in the middle introduced himself as Major Jeremiah Ndoboduma, he spoke incredibly good English and asked for the doctor.

The fact that these men were standing in the hospital with rifles didn't particularly worry her, it seemed all men out in the countryside bore arms of some kind, either pistols or rifles. And Jeremiah was polite, very well-spoken and clearly wanted the doctor. She explained that the doctor had gone up-country, there was only the nursing staff for the time being. Did they need some medical attention?

"You must come with me," Jeremiah said to Hilary. "Please."

"Come where? What is your problem? I can't just leave these people," she said, waving with her arm to indicate the patients in the beds.

"I said, you must come with me."

267

"Jeremiah. Major. Please. I cannot leave my patients. Can you not tell me your problem, then I will help, but I simply can't walk away and leave them."

Jeremiah turned to one of his men, who walked past her and took one of the nursing orderlies by the arm and forced her to her knees. "PLEASE STOP! PLEASE!" Hilary cried out. "Please, this will solve nothing, tell me what it is that's wrong and perhaps -"

"What's your name?" he asked Hilary.

Up until this point she hadn't felt fear. But she did now. "I'm Sister Findlay. My husband is the doctor and he has gone up-country. I am here alone with three other nurses and two nursing orderlies. The hospital is full as you see. I can't leave."

Again, he spoke to his henchman, who walked outside and return a few minutes later with Nurse Tamali and Jogo Nziri, one of the nursing orderlies. The screams of a woman in labour could be heard from behind the rattan screen.

"Sister, you are to come with me. Now. If you don't, there will be no patients here for your nursing staff to care for, and therefore no need for nursing staff. DO YOU UNDERSTAND?" He spoke again to his right-hand man, who walked behind the screen to the screaming woman. A shot rang out and the woman was silent. One of the major's own fellow officers stood wide-eyed at the shooting, which had just killed a woman and her unborn baby. He turned his head but was sensible enough to keep quiet. Clearly the major was not a man who would support his orders being questioned.

Hilary understood what she had failed to understand when this man had first walked in. She was to go with him or he would kill everyone. She had no doubt of that now.

"Please. If I go with you, will you leave everyone alone? Please, I beg you." She looked at him with fear clearly evident on her face as unbidden tears fell down to her chin.

"Where is your radio?"

"It's in the ward office, just over there. Please don't hurt anyone, please. I'll do whatever you say." She pointed to the little office at the end of the ward, and he spoke again to one of his men. The shots blew the radio to thousands of pieces. Hilary felt the hopelessness of her situation and had no doubt she would be killed along with everyone else if she failed to do as he asked. She had to try to get some word from him of agreement that no-one else would be hurt.

"Major, I'm going to come with you, but you need to tell me the problem so I can bring whatever I'm going to need with me. Do you need antibiotics, or what? I will help you, we all will, but please don't hurt anyone." Her voice was quivering with fear and apprehension for what lay ahead, but her main concern was the lives of the staff and patients.

"Bring saline, morphine, antibiotics, dressings, disinfectant, everything you think you might need."

"But I might need to treat *what*?" she persisted. He turned to look at her.

"Sister, you have ten minutes. My man will go with you, you will pack what you need and he will bring it back here. Ten minutes."

"May I leave a message for my husband? Please let me do that." She thought one of the others would tell Bob what had happened, but she wanted to leave him a word from her. She also had a dreadful feeling that the others might not be alive to talk to Bob.

"We'll leave word for him. Just pack your medicines."

They went over to the dispensary hut and she unlocked the safes. She loaded two laundry bags that the gunman handed to her with everything she could think of. It would leave the hospital short but they would be able to order more from Dagos.

As she was loading, she was trying to think of how to leave some sort of message for Bob, but the gunman was watching her closely. She could think of nothing to leave or any action to take which would give Bob any indication as to what had happened to her, or where she was being taken. "OK, I have what we need, I think." The gunman was too busy looking around the room, she thought he might be looking to see if there was anything he could steal without the major knowing about it.

She hadn't heard their vehicle draw up when they had arrived, but now she saw they had come in a Land Rover-type vehicle, she wasn't sure which. There were two more armed men in the vehicle who now got down to walk over and collect the drugs.

"Where are the keys to that vehicle?" Jeremiah said, pointing to the clinic's own Toyota land cruiser.

"In my bedroom."

"Go with him and bring them here."

The same gunman who had gone with her to the dispensary came behind her now to follow her to the bungalow. She stood in the middle of the room as if she couldn't remember where the keys were. She was desperately trying to find some way to let Bob know what had happened, a message or a clue of some kind. She then pointed to her bedroom and walked into the little corridor. The chest of drawers was against the far wall, and on top were her small amount of cosmetics. "Do you speak English?" she asked.

He just looked at her. Evidently not. She made gestures of wanting to change her clothes and open the drawers to take out a cardigan and a few others things. He understood and she looked around as if wanting to find something to put them in. He saw a hold-all on the chair in the corner and went to get it, but first he inspected the inside and the pockets.

She took the opportunity to grab a lipstick, she pushed her clothes to one side in the open drawer and wrote MAJOR NDOBODUMA. I AM CAPTIVE. She picked up a handful of underwear and knitwear and walked towards the guard, leaving the drawer open, so that he would not have to come back to the dresser. She dropped the clothes into the bag and walked quickly towards the door, remembering at the last minute to pick up the keys from the night table.

The major allowed the bag after he had inspected it and told her to get into the vehicle, a Toyota as she now saw. He climbed in together with her guard. There was also the other officer, who had looked so shocked at the shooting in the clinic, but so far he had not said a word. The major clapped him on the shoulder as they got into the vehicles. The remaining gunmen went back into the hospital and as they drove away from the hospital, the sound of rapid gunfire left her in no doubt that not one person would be left alive to give any information as to what had happened there. She cried out in desperation; she cried for the helplessness of it all, for the pointless and barbaric loss of all those lives, and for her wonderful Bob who, she was sure, she would never see again.

The drive seemed to take forever. It was dawn before they pulled off the dusty track into a natural bowl between two low hills. Despite the heat, the area was fairly green and trees were quite thick, affording shade and cover. There were about ten huts built in a circle, each one would sleep about ten people, she guessed. She was also surprised to see about twelve tents erected, obviously the contents of some of the boxes a famous charity in the UK put together for times of emergency. Each tent again could sleep ten people. She wondered how these tents had been purloined, but at this point, she really didn't care.

She quickly saw the reason for the greenery – it was a sort of oasis, the small stream from the side of the hill running into a large, dark pool, evidently quite deep.

On the drive, Major Ndoboduma had said little but had passed her a water bottle from time to time. He had allowed her a toilet stop when she had asked for one. She hadn't asked him why he was doing this, she imagined it would become evident before long. She was steeped in despair. Strangely, she didn't fear for her life as much as she feared for Bob. What would he do without her, how would he carry on?

At this point, she had relatively little hope that she would be left alive after she had done whatever the major needed her to do. She hadn't once pleaded for her life. The major thought that was admirable and to be honest, he hadn't thought that far ahead. But it would all depend on how the negotiations went. It was early days and no direct approaches had yet been made by the foreign government. He still had time to think about all that.

She got down from the Toyota and saw several other four-wheel drive vehicles parked under a large camouflage-netted area. One vehicle was extremely badly damaged and looked as if it had been on fire.

"Sister, listen to me. I have several prisoners here who need attention. These prisoners are extremely valuable to me and must be alive and well when the exchange takes place."

"Exchange? Oh, you mean hostages? Don't you? You mean hostages?" Even to her ears, her voice was shrill and almost hysterical.

"Listen, Sister. This will mean the difference of whether you live or die and -"

"Do you mean like those poor devils in the hospital?" She was almost shouting. "What did they ever do to you, what kind of threat did they pose to you and your - what are you? An army? A rebel group? Rebelling against what? What could possibly justify killing all those people?" Hysteria was threatening to overcome her sense of survival.

Two gunmen were running across to them, hearing her shouting, thinking that she was some sort of threat to their leader.

He waited for her to finish: somehow his silence more threatening than his brutality. "As I was saying, this *will* mean the difference between whether you live or whether you die. There are three people in that hut who need help. I will make sure you have whatever you need, if possible, but you must do your best for them." He smiled at her to try to calm her and gestured with his arm that she should follow him. "Sister, please."

He took her over to one of the thatched huts. It was dark inside, although there was a hole in one wall. An armed guard stood just inside the door. As her eyes grew accustomed to the light, she could see three people lying on the floor on rough straw mats. A man, a woman and a child of about ten or eleven.

"*Aidez-nous, s'il vous plait, aidez-nous.*" It was the man who spoke. She could see now that he had burns over his arms and neck, his eyebrows were singed and his ear was badly damaged. The woman appeared to have a small head wound and although her eyes were open, she didn't seem to focus. The child was delirious, his leg badly broken and burned.

The hut was filthy. She turned straight away and went out of the door, she called for the major where she stood. "MAJOR! MAJOR! I need you here, NOW!" He had been walking over to one of the tents and stopped, turned and walked back to her.

"Sister, I don't -"

"This is disgusting. I want them out of that hut IMMEDIATELY. Give me one of those tents, I can wash the canvas walls with disinfectant. Those straw thatches are alive with insects and bacteria. I want them moved. Give me the supplies I brought and let me have this tent here." She pointed to one on the edge of the settlement.

"That's MY tent," he said

"I DON'T CARE!" she shouted at him in fury. "If you want these people cared for, I want them as far away as possible from everyone else, I don't want them breathing that foul dung fire smoke and they'll need quiet. These people are gravely injured, what on earth have you done to them? Why are they in this state and who are they?"

"I'm sure they'll tell you themselves when they are able. In the meantime, what more can I do for you?" He smiled: again the unspoken threat was evident. He gave orders for his tent to be evacuated and for her supplies to be brought to her. "And, Sister, it is not wise to address me with scorn in front of my men. And don't *ever* give *me* orders again. I have told you I will give you whatever you need, if I can."

His smile disappeared and he said, "I am not responsible for the state they are in. We stopped them at a road block, their guard car following was stopped and they tried to escape in that." He pointed to the badly damaged vehicle. "We shot the tyres and they ran off the road into a ditch, the car turned over and caught fire. We had planned the whole thing to be easy and with as little force as possible. The stupid man tried to escape, even though we had them covered from all directions, but he still tried to make a run for it. And this is the result."

"Trying to save his family, no doubt." She felt nothing but hatred for this cold and callous man. "Please don't tell me that they brought this upon themselves, this is barbaric, look at the state of them."

"Families are important to all of us." His tone was harsh.

"And what about MY family?" she asked. "What about my wonderful husband who won't know what's happened to me? He'll be desperate." She was crying now. "You said you'd leave him a message, or were all those bodies the message you had in mind?" She decided it was futile to argue with this man, whatever reasons he had for doing this, he had proved to be ruthless and murderous when it suited him.

The same gunman who had joined them in the car for the journey here appeared now to be appointed as her personal helper. So far, he had not spoken a word.

"Do you have anyone who can speak English?" she called after the major as he strode away.

274

Jeremiah called over his shoulder and indicated the man standing close to her. "His English is perfect; he went to school in Wiltshire. We both did, he's my brother." He laughed as he walked away.

"Bastard," she said under her breath. She turned to him and said, "What's your name? I can't keep referring to you as 'gunman'."

"My name is Isaac. And I'm not a gunman. I'm a freedom fighter."

"Yes, well, at the moment I couldn't care less what you call yourself, but all I've seen from you people is murder and barbarity. There are some gravely ill people who need help. I need a bucket or a bowl and that plastic container of disinfectant I brought with me. And plenty of cloths, sheets if you have them."

"Come with me."

He took her over to the tent on the far side of the compound. Inside there were boxes of towels, sheets, paper bags, cases of bottled water, toilet rolls, tins of various foods, powdered milk, and tea. One corner was full of odds and ends, including buckets, packets of washing powder, and a large pile of clothes.

She loaded his arms with sheets and towels, she took two buckets and some toilet paper. In the buckets she put six bottles of water.

When they got back to the tent, the last of the major's things were just being removed. She went over to the pond and looked at the water. It looked clean enough, it was being replenished constantly by the spring coming out of the side of the hill. She wouldn't drink it but for mixing with disinfectant, it was probably alright. She didn't once ask Isaac for help. She mixed the disinfectant and threw buckets full over the outside of the tent. She mixed some more and washed down the walls of the interior and then threw two buckets over the canvas floor lining.

"Isaac, I need something for mattresses. Tell me what I can use and I'll go and get it." Without a word, he turned and walked away. He came back about twenty minutes later with six sleeping bags. "Will these do?" he asked.

"Perfect. Thank you." She smiled at him in genuine gratitude. She might achieve more if she treated Isaac a bit more kindly, she thought to herself. She made three rough beds with the sleeping bags and covered them with sheets. As far as she could see, the sheets were new, or if they had been used, they had been laundered before being put in the boxes. Probably stolen from some refugee relief charity, she thought.

"Isaac, one more thing. I'm going to need something to make drip-stands. You know, something to hold the saline bags above the ground."

Once more, without saying a word he turned and walked away. He came back with some wire coat hangers. He found one of the metal supports for the tent roof, made a very small hole in the canvas, big enough to pass the hook of the coat hanger through and looked at her. "Will that do?" Again she smiled at him. He didn't return her smile.

Satisfied that the tent was as clean and practical as she 00.could make it, she then told Isaac what she planned to do next.

"I'm going to give the father and son some morphine to dull their pain, so I can move them over here and clean their wounds. I can't tell until I examine her whether the mother is in any pain or not, but I don't want to give her morphine until I've seen her."

Isaac nodded his agreement and they went over to the hut. The father seemed to be in great pain.

"Can you speak English?" Hilary asked.

"Yes, my name is Jules Levallois. I am the French *chargé d'affaires* at the embassy. This is my wife and my son. Please, can you help us?"

"I'm going to do everything I can, trust me. For now, I need to have you moved to a clean area, and it's going to hurt. I'm going to give both you and your son a shot of morphine, just enough to dull the pain a little because it's important that you can talk to me. Is that alright?"

"Oh thank you, thank you. I don't know who you are but I'm so happy to see you."

She worked quickly, giving both father and son just enough morphine to help, but not to send them to sleep. She told Isaac they were ready to move and he called for help. They took the boy first: he whimpered but didn't cry out. Although the father tried not to show his discomfort, his pain was only too evident but he bore it well nonetheless. The mother remained silent and looked drugged as she was helped to her feet and walked with the help of two men.

Once she had seen them put onto the beds, she set about putting up drips of saline to counter the effects of dehydration. She put another small dose of morphine into each drip, and allowed the patients to settle for a few minutes. In the meantime, she told Isaac he was to keep a record of what doses she had given and at what time. He took the clipboard she held out to him.

It took her hours to clean the wounds. The father and son both had wounds full of maggots but she wasn't dismayed to see that. Maggots did a wonderful job of cleaning and debriding wounds, albeit horrible to look at. The burns were cleaned but needed to be left to the air to dry. She covered them with a light gauze dressing, just to keep dust and other insects from entering the open areas.

The boy's leg was a different matter. The break was clean but the bone was sticking out through the skin, it was going to be excruciating for the little boy to suffer the pain of putting the bone back together. Also, she was going to have to debride some of the skin around the wound in order for the bone to go back in.

277

She had some local anaesthetic, which she put around the wound to deal with the skin and to clean it generally. She didn't know how much more morphine she could give the boy. He seemed to be mostly unconscious, but he opened his eyes from time to time. She decided to act quickly.

"Isaac, I need to set his leg. I need something to make a splint but more importantly, you are going to have to hold him whilst I do it. It's better to give him the pain relief afterwards and let him rest whilst his leg heals. I've put as much local anaesthetic in there as I can, but I want you to hold him very still while I push and bind the leg with a splint."

Isaac went and came back with a slat of wood. He found a stone, put the slat across and stepped hard until it cracked. He pulled the two pieces apart and said, "Will this do?" She said nothing but smiled her thanks, and this time he smiled a little. He looked down at the boy and seemed to be sorrowful and even showing tenderness, Hilary thought.

She made up a spray bottle of disinfectant and sprayed the wooden slats which would form the splint.

"OK?" she asked. Isaac nodded.

She put one hand under the boy's small leg and pulled up as the other pushed down. The little boy screamed once and then whimpered quietly. As quickly as she could, Hilary dressed the leg with the splints and bandages, and gave the child another dose of pain-killer. She reckoned she could leave him to sleep now and absorb saline for about four hours. She had brought intravenous antibiotics with her and she gave both father and son a dose to go through the drips over the couple of hours.

Hilary turned to the mother. She had been sitting upright on her bed, her legs curled up to the side of her and she was holding on to her ankle. Hilary went over to her. She took her hand, which was ice-cold. "Hello, I'm Hilary. I'm a nursing sister and I'm here to help you." To her shock and surprise, the woman pulled back her arm and struck Hilary full across the face. Hilary, who had been kneeling, fell backwards.

"You pig. You work with these people, they have done this to my family and you work with them. You pig." She went to hit Hilary again.

"Madame," said Hilary, grabbing hold of the woman's hand "I am a captive like you. They came to my hospital, took me by force and killed everyone in the clinic. They did all that so that I could come and help you. My husband has no idea where I am and I am in as much danger as you, probably more since I am of no value to them, but you are."

The woman looked at her wildly, and started to cry. "I'm sorry. I'm sorry."

"Listen to me. I need to look at your head wound. Are you hurt anywhere else?"

The woman shook her head. "Are they going to die?"

"Not if I can help it. I am doing everything I can, but now I need to look at you. Will you let me do that? What is your name?"

The woman nodded and said, "Aurélie. My name is Aurélie."

The head wound wasn't too serious but it had bled a lot as head wounds generally do. She had a nasty lump near the temple which concerned Hilary. The woman's pupils were reacting normally and she didn't seem to have any other injuries, but she had a habit of staring without blinking, which was worrying. Hilary tried to question her more closely, but she was unresponsive and, feeling there was nothing more she could do, she gave the woman an injection. Within twenty minutes all three patients were sleeping.

Judging from the fading light in the tent, she realised it had taken all day to take care of the patients. She had thought of Bob so many times. It would be days before they even realised something was wrong. He wasn't due back for another three days, then what an appalling sight would greet them. She had no idea where she was, she had the impression they had driven north and then turned east, but she couldn't be sure. She hadn't noticed where the sun had gone down, but its rise in the morning would show her the east.

She was thirsty, tired and hungry and needed to go to the toilet. Isaac was sitting outside the tent talking to another man. "Alright?" he said.

"Where can I go to the toilet? And someone needs to sit with them while I do, but please, just at the opening, don't go in. Infection control is difficult enough in these circumstances, I don't want some unwashed lout going in there." She was beyond caring about causing offence. *She* was offended. She was offended by the whole thing. Hostages. What for? Money? How did two brothers whose family obviously had the means to send them abroad for an education get into this business?

Isaac took her over to towards the pond. "We use this for washing. The latrine area is over there." He pointed to an outcrop about a hundred yards away. "There's a spade at the side, we dig a new latrine every so often, but whenever we use it we throw a bit of that lime powder over the top."

She went over to the outcrop. Isaac stayed where he was. He could still see her head but even if she wanted to run, she couldn't now. She couldn't leave those poor people. As she squatted down, she smiled to see four toilet rolls sitting on a stone.

****

When she returned from the latrine, she stopped by the pool to wash and sat on the edge, disbelief still prevented her despair from completely taking over. Isaac patiently waited for her and she realised she was very tired, absolutely worn out in fact. When she got back to the tent, someone had left

280

another two sleeping bags, a plate with some sort of stewed meat and yams and another six bottles of water.

She ate quickly, finding the food spicy but really quite good. The meat was tender and the vegetables absorbed the flavour of the spiced gravy. After she had eaten, she set about examining the patients before settling them down for the night. The boy seemed quiet, whimpering slightly in his sleep. She changed his saline bag and hoped he would sleep for a while longer. The father, Jules, was sleepy but managed to answer her questions.

"Jules, have you been able to pass water yet? I'm worried about dehydration, how long were you without water?"

"I asked to be taken outside just before you arrived. I did manage something but not a lot. My son's trousers were wet, so I think he also managed to pass something, but my wife has not moved since we got here."

"Had she drunk any water?"

"No, she threw it away when the guard gave her some. He didn't offer her any more."

"I think if she doesn't drink, I'm going to have to put a drip up for her, but she doesn't seem very co-operative."

She changed the saline for Jules. "If you need some more pain relief, I will give you something to take by mouth. I don't want to use too much morphine for obvious reasons. It will make it harder for you in the long run and I'm not sure how long we'll be here, so my supply must be for emergencies now."

"I'll manage. I feel a bit better now, the pain is bearable and I'm still sleepy."

"Aurélie, wake up please. Aurélie, it's Hilary, I'm going to examine you. Aurélie, wake up." Hilary shook her. She woke up but very slowly and her words were slightly slurred. She had difficulty focusing. Hilary managed to give her a drink of about a third of a litre but it was a start. Hilary was concerned about the woman's lethargy. If she could only talk to Bob. "Oh Bobby, where are you?" She felt despair threatening to overwhelm her.

The boy slept for most of the night, never moving when Hilary changed the saline again. Jules was awake on and off through the night, but Aurélie seemed to sleep through.

The following morning, the three of them appeared to be asleep when Hilary went to the latrine. There was no sign of her guard but even if she knew where to run to, she could not now leave the three hostages: clearly the major knew that. She stopped by the pool. The temptation to get in completely was overwhelming, but it looked deep and she was always a little afraid of being out of her depth.

When she returned to the tent, she started to prepare to change dressings and wash the patients, Jules was awake, and so was the boy, she was pleased to see. He still whimpered a little but he was coherent and looked less pale. Aurélie was still apparently asleep.

"Jules, I need to get you all moving a little today. One of the problems is that even with two sleeping bags under you, the ground is hard and I don't want pressure sores developing. Apart from that, blood circulating is the best thing for healing. I won't put you through too much, but we all must move around a bit."

"What about Davide? Please don't make him do too much."

"No, I won't but we must turn him and rub his back. It's only to avoid even more problems, Jules."

"Yes, I understand, I'm so …" At this point he broke down and caught the sobs in his throat. "My poor family. God, what have I brought them to?"

"Where on earth were you going? I don't even know where we are."

"I believe we are in Minkoka National Park. On the east side there is a tourist station with a few cabins and a couple of rangers. We were heading over there for about a week before going back to France. But where we are exactly, I have no idea."

"Jules, I must tell you, I am very worried about Aurélie. For someone with just apparently superficial injuries, she's not responding very well."

"Well, she -" With that, the tent flap opened and Isaac put his head in.

"Don't come in here, I'm trying to prevent infection," she barked at him.

"The major wants to see you," and he left.

"Are you alright for a while?" She turned to Jules. "I'll be back soon, the saline will be fine for a while yet, but I think we can probably slow it down and get you back on fluids. That way, you can move around more easily. And I'm going now, I'll try to find out what's happening."

Jules smiled at her, and she stroked Davide's cheek. He responded with a wan smile. Two of the three were showing signs of improvement. It cheered her immensely.

Jeremiah was sitting at a table under a group of shade trees. "How odd," she thought. "Under any other circumstances, this place would be perfect paradise, but right now it's a hell."

"Good morning. Please sit down." He actually stood as she approached. This was getter stranger by the minute. It all seemed surreal and yet she had gone past the point of feeling threatened, even though danger was in every hand-held weapon which pointed in her direction.

"Good morning, major. What did you want to see me for?"

"How are the patients?"

"How explicit would you like me to be?"

"Just honest, that will do."

"Well, the boy I think will be alright if we can get him up for a little bit. Lying flat down is not good for too long. The father has severe burns which look clean enough, but I want him to move around, too. I want him to flex his arms a little so the skin doesn't grow taut. His ear will probably have to be remade by a plastic surgeon. But he's coping with the pain well enough. I haven't given any of them morphine this morning, I'm hoping we can stick to oral pain relief. But the mother - the mother is concerning me greatly. Major, can I possibly not speak to a doctor?"

"That won't be possible. You will have to manage. But she is vitally important. Has the husband told you who she is?"

"No, her name is Aurélie Lavallois but that's all I know, he's the French *chargé d'affaires,* who is leaving shortly for France. At least he was."

"Her maiden name is Aurélie Masson."

"It doesn't mean anything to me, she's - oh, God."

"Yes, she's the sister of the French President, Dominic Masson."

Hilary gasped. "What have you done? Are you mad? You know the French won't negotiate with terrorists. You're mad!"

"Of course they will. The French *always* negotiate, or don't you ever notice how many French hostages around the world are suddenly released? They *say* they don't negotiate, but they *always* do. And we're *not* terrorists, we're f -"

"Yes, I know, you're *freedom fighters,* whatever that means. And if Madame Lavallois has any value to you at all then you'd better get her to a hospital, because the French certainly won't want her back dead!"

"It can't be that serious, she was hardly hurt at all."

"I believe she *is* badly hurt. I believe she has a head injury which will lead to her death if left untreated. So much worth does she have now, major? You know the French won't leave it unpunished. And I for one hope they don't."

"She can't die."

"Major, listen to me! Listen to me! I CANNOT SAVE HER. You can threaten me all you like, but I can't save her. And you have very limited time in which to do something."

The major stood and clenched his fists, drawing deep breaths.

"Go back to the tent. Stay there until someone comes for you."

Hilary left feeling very frustrated. The man was mad. How could she possibly treat a head injury? Even if she could get the other two fit to travel, the situation for Aurélie was grave.

On impulse she turned back. "Major, let me take the woman out. I'll take her somewhere where she can be picked up and I'll come back. I promise, I'll come back. You still have the president's nephew and his brother-in-law. Any gesture from you right now will go better for you. Let me do that, please. You don't have much time. For the other two, I can get them onto oral fluids and pain killers and one of you will have to learn about dressings. We can do it. But PLEASE, think! She WILL die. What is it you want anyway, that's worth three lives, or four if you intend to kill me? What is it you want? Money? From a man whose father educated him in England, you probably have more in the bank than I do."

"Money? Of course it's not money."

"Then tell me, please. I can't see anything is worth this, so please, tell me." She sounded angry and bitter, her voice just below shouting, but so angry.

"I intend to get some people released from jail in France, that's all."

"That's all? That's all? I was right, you *are* mad. I suppose they're terrorists, just like you."

"Oh no, they're much better at it than me. They are experts." He smiled and enjoyed her total incomprehension.

"God, you are sick. Whatever is so wrong in our world that you had to kill all those people at the hospital? I can't imagine what my poor husband will think has happened to me, I can't bear to think of him suffering like that." She angrily wiped away the tears which had tumbled out of her eyes. "Oh, I understand. Poor little rich boy got bored and looked for some worthy cause. Is this it? Does this do it for you? Or have you got something nastier in mind?" She was shouting now. Isaac and a couple of the other guards look alarmed but Jeremiah waved them away.

"If I thought you'd understand I'd tell you. But you, with your simple do-good attitude, salving your conscience by working with the natives for a little while before you disappear back into your comfortable lives, you couldn't possibly begin to understand."

"Conscience? What the hell are you talking about? What absolute rubbish. Isn't that kind of garbage spouted by every would-be tin-pot dictator, because that's what this is really all about isn't it? With your private army, your hostage-taking, your middle-class accent − you couldn't even manage a proper kidnapping. Now, you are going to be hero to no-one. All you will do is bring trouble to this nation, ruin its chances of overseas help just so you can call yourself President Je - is that ridiculous name even your real name?"

By now, many of the soldiers had gathered around, ready to take down this mad-woman, screaming at the major and making him angry.

"You're pathetic. The world has seen so many like you. At this point, this very point in time, right now − this is what I've always called a finger-post moment. I don't know if you even know what the hell I'm talking about. A finger-post? Yes? No? A finger-post is one of the old sign-posts that used to have a shape like a pointing finger showing the different roads you can take. Right now you are at yours. You can forget this madness and help me get this woman to safety, or you will go to hell. Because they will come for you. And God knows, these things never end well. SHE IS GOING TO DIE. DON'T YOU UNDERSTAND THAT? Do any of these men know that death is on the horizon for them long, long before there is even the slightest chance of your crowning yourself king or whatever you have in mind for yourself."

"Get back to your tent. Go now!" he ordered her out of his sight, his fury plainly visible, his arms were shaking with the effort of keeping his clenched fists by his side. His desire to strike this woman to the ground was overwhelming, but he still needed her.

Hilary had never in her life, ever spoken to anyone like that. It was not in her nature. She was wild with fury. Not fear. She knew now that there was a strong possibility that she would not make it through this hellish situation in safety. Even if rescue was a possibility, the poor woman would die unless rescue came soon, and even so, if her head injury was as serious as Hilary suspected, the outcome was not looking good.

****

When she got back to the tent, Davide was half sitting, trying to shuffle his bottom up to raise himself up a little. She rolled her sleeping bag and put it behind him. "Can you drink something?" she asked him.

"*Oui, merci.*" His voice was croaky but he was looking brighter. She gave him a drink and asked if he could eat something. He nodded. She kissed his forehead. Jules was also more mobile and also said he would concentrate on taking in fluids for both himself and Davide. She could then remove the drip. Aurélie was still very lethargic. Her pupils were slightly more dilated than before and he colour was very pale.

"I'll go and find some food. Try to talk to Aurélie and see how responsive she is."

"Hilary."

"Yes?"

"I heard you with that man. Do you really believe what you said?"

"Oh God, Jules, I'm so sorry." She glanced at Davide. Jules shook his head.

"No, the conversation was too fast and angry for him to understand."

"Yes, I'm afraid I do. I have to be honest. We'll do what we can. Be brave. Stay positive for Davide. Move about a little if you can and flex your arms without breaking the skin. I'll be back soon."

She walked out of the tent towards where she thought the cook was working. As she passed behind one of the huts, she heard shouting. She realised Isaac and his brother were having a terrible row. Some of the soldiers were standing around looking uneasy. She had no idea what language they were speaking but it was clear, a major row was taking place. Somehow, she felt she had been the cause, and irrationally, it pleased her.

She found the cook and was amazed to find a young boy of about fourteen in charge of the steaming pots. She said, "Do you speak any English?"

He did, but not well. However, they were able to communicate. He gave her a big bowl of some sort of maize dish, similar to porridge. He also gave her three pieces of sugar cane, indicating that it should be sucked and chewed, and the fibrous strips could be used for teeth cleaning. Then he handed her a leaf wrapped around four fairly large pieces of barbecued meat, four spoons and another leaf with boiled rice. She smiled her thanks and told him he was kind. He seemed to understand and broke into a broad grin with the most amazing set of brilliant white, perfect teeth. What in

God's name was this child soldier doing in this hell-hole? Then she realised that she had seen many young boys of a similar age wandering around with weapons.

How could anyone recruit these children to kill? Apart from the men in the camp, the two surrounding hills were filled with men, a large army for a madman to be in charge of.

The row was still going on as she walked slowly, trying to balance the things the cook had given her. One of the guards came up and took the bowl of porridge from her and the sugar cane, leaving her to carry the leaves and the spoons. She smiled at him and his simple kindness brought tears to her eyes. As she tried to thank him, he smiled and shook his head.

Davide managed remarkably well. Hilary was so pleased to see the change in him and the bravery with which he bore his pain. Jules was also eager to eat, but Aurélie was still slipping deeper into unconsciousness. After they had eaten, Hilary got one of the guards to come and help her get Davide to his feet. He was so incredibly brave, his pain must have been unbearable for a little boy, but they got him outside to urinate, that alone made Hilary feel as if he was making progress. Jules wandered around a little, but found the latrine just too far. She helped him to a tree and dug a little hole. All in all, both patients had made huge physical and psychological strides.

Apart from a brief sighting of him in the morning, Hilary had seen nothing of Isaac; she had heard what she thought to be him rowing with his brother, but he had not come near the tent.

In the evening, Hilary went again to the cook tent, collected some food and took it back to the others. They were just starting to eat when Isaac burst in.

"Get out of the tent into the open. Get over to the latrine area if you can, away from the trees and out into the open."

"What's happening?" She was shrill with alarm, fear and desperation. Oh God, what now? "Isaac, tell me, what's happening, please tell me!"

"I have sent a radio message, giving our location to the authorities. I can't do this anymore. No more killings, no more. I can't take children hostage and no one will thank us if this woman dies, it will only make us hated everywhere. It was all - for nothing. All for - nothing."

"Does your brother know? Is he - has he agreed to this? Where is he?" Hilary was so confused. Isaac seemed to be having trouble breathing.

"He knows I've betrayed him. He's gone - with most of the soldiers who follow him everywhere. He found out what I'd done." And with that, Isaac fell forward on the floor and Hilary could see the wound in his back. He'd been shot. "Get clear - of the tent - when help comes they will start shooting - some soldiers still - stay here - it's better if - you can get out."

"Isaac, stay still. Let me help you."

"No, get out, get out. I told them - I said - four hostages - child - dying - woman. Please - forgive me - forgive me - forg ..." Isaac died in her arms and as his hand opened, the keys to the Toyota fell out of his dead hand.

Hilary could not even think of moving Aurélie. And Davide could not move on his own. Jules was in no state to help her. How to get to safety as Isaac said? And the soldiers who were left, would they turn on them? She needn't have worried, the only soldiers left were the cook and three or four other young boys, barely in their teens, who had put down their rifles and sat waiting for whatever fate awaited them; confused, afraid and betrayed, abandoned by Jeremiah.

Hilary had no idea how long it would be before help arrived. She went out of the tent to see what the soldiers would do. All the adult soldiers had gone, along with the major. These child soldiers were no older than twelve or thirteen. Without waiting to pick up their rifles, she ran to the car and reversed out from under the camouflage. She drove out of the cover of the trees into the open. Confident now that the danger had left with the major, she was only concerned that the rescuers would not arrive shooting. Perhaps if she signalled, they would recognise that the danger had gone, she realised that was what Isaac had been trying to tell her.

By now it was completely dark. She flashed S-O-S with the headlights for what seemed like two hours, but in fact it was less than an hour before she heard the thwacking sound of helicopters. She kept flashing S-O-S.

As the first helicopter landed, she ran toward it and shouted "Do you have a doctor?" With relief she saw a red cross painted on the helmet of the first man out. She grabbed his hand and ran back towards the tent. They were quickly followed by two more men with red crosses, whom she assumed were also medical staff. They set to work with Aurélie, as Hilary was trying to explain her condition.

They were firing questions at her as they were working. Two stretcher bearers arrived, gently lifted her on and were gone.

Davide looked bewildered as his mother disappeared out of the door, but Jules and Hilary reassured him as best they could. They heard the helicopter lift off. More medics appeared and loaded up Jules and Davide. Davide put out his hand for Hilary, fearful to let her out of his sight now. She took his hand and they left the tent together, he on the stretcher and she alongside. Jules was behind on another stretcher.

As they left, she saw the boy soldiers and the cook on their knees with their heads on the ground. "What will happen to them?" she called. "They didn't hurt us; they wouldn't leave us in the end."

The medic shrugged his shoulders.

****

Bob wiped a tear from his eye as he finished recounting the story to Diana. "Aurélie survived but her eyesight was damaged. She had suffered a haemorrhage. Jules left the diplomatic service to take care of her. They have a lovely house overlooking the Bay of Naples. We go to see them quite often. Aurélie is so fond of Hilary, it's heart-breaking when we leave. Davide has just qualified as a doctor and is going to join *Médecins Sans Frontières.* He adores Hilary, he's been here a few times."

Diana had listed to Hilary's story with astonishment, growing admiration and respect for the woman. "How on earth does anyone get over something like that? And it must have been horrendous for you, not knowing what had happened to her."

"Actually, by the time I heard anything at all, it was nearly all over. The charity's head office had been concerned that they couldn't make radio contact with the hospital. They sent the plane down and they found - well, you can imagine. Bodies everywhere and they'd been there for a couple of days. By the time we got the radio message and got back, the bodies had been taken away and they realised Hilary wasn't among the dead. I was nearly out of my mind. I found her message inside the drawer. It turned out the authorities knew of this Major Jeremiah; he'd been recruiting men around the region for a while."

"Who was it he wanted out of prison?"

"Some fellow looked upon as the arch terrorist and hero, actually a major gun-runner. He was in France raising funds and buying weapons to send back to Jeremiah and his crew, to try to overthrow the government when he was captured."

Diana was looking out of the window at Hilary, who was slowly walking around the garden chatting to her dog.

"What about the SOS message? That was rather clever, wasn't it?"

"Oh, it's the first thing you learn when you are out in the bush. You can do it with a torch, a car headlight, a car horn – almost anything."

"Was Hilary alright afterwards? Did she cope alright with all the shock?"

"Actually, she was a bloody nuisance to some people!" he chuckled.

"Nuisance? What on earth do you mean?"

"It was the boy soldiers and the cook. They had stayed behind with Isaac, you see. Hilary badgered everyone when she got back to find out what had happened to them. Eventually the charity located them at some prison and got the two boy soldiers into another charity's programme for rehabilitating these children who have been abducted from villages and have no parents to return to."

"The cook?"

"Hilary pounded the corridors of every government department until she found out where he was imprisoned. I think both governments would happily have shot her at the same time! She wrote letters, implored ministers and finally got him released. He now works at one of our charity's hospitals. This is him." He picked up a photograph of a man of about twenty-four, smiling broadly with his arm around two little children. He had married and kept in touch with the Findlays.

"You look puzzled, Diana?"

"No, not puzzled, just - I don't know, humbled, I suppose, would be the best word for it. I've never heard such a story of bravery and compassion. Yes, I just feel terribly humble."

Hilary came back as Diana was getting up to leave. "So, you'll come to lunch on Sunday?"

"Yes, we'd love to, thank you." Hilary walked Diana to the door. As she stepped out, Diana turned to Hilary and said, "You are truly an amazing woman."

"No, really - I didn't - really, I don't think -"

Diana put out her hand to rest on the other woman's arm, stopping Hilary's bluster. "Hilary, you *are* an amazing woman." The other woman just smiled an embarrassed smile and said, "Thank you, dear."

****

Diana walked home slowly. She needed to walk in her woods. In the space of a few short months she had discovered people of immense courage and integrity, people who had endured loss, betrayal and pain. It was true what she had said to Bob – she was feeling incredibly humble. Her life had been so easy, so free of trauma and anxiety, how unbelievably lucky she had been. She had never been tested, never had a moment's regret or complication. And yet here, in this small corner there were people of monumental bravery and character.

She walked for a couple of hours, absent-mindedly picking up more huge pine-cones to add to her store. Was the whole world made up of people doing remarkable things and she was just - what? She felt like a shadow next to these people. Inadequate and feeble.

She went back to the kitchen and phoned Simon.

"Hello, darling."

"Hello, Dee darling, how are you? You sound a bit down, are you alright?"

"Yes, just missing you, I think. I'll be so pleased when you are here, I've so much to tell you."

"Won't be long now, sweet, and I'm really excited by my new project. Can't wait to tell you, it's perfect and you'll be such a help. You wait, it's going to be great! And we'll be able to work together on it. You'll be vital."

"Really? I can't imagine why or how."

"Just wait and see. I'm nearly organised, only two more days now and I'll be down."

Diana sat down at her little desk in the kitchen, planning Sunday lunch. She played around with a few menus but couldn't really settle. She felt uneasy without knowing why, but put it down to her earlier feeling of inadequacy. She made some supper and found herself just mooching around the house. Nothing she wanted to plan seemed to gel. An air of disquiet had hung over her since talking to Simon. Perhaps it was just hearing his voice and missing him so much. She also worried that he was about to drop the project which had brought them here in favour of this new idea, whatever it was and however exciting it seems to be at the moment.

She took her book and decided on an early night. She had trouble falling asleep and then finally dropped off at about one am.

She had been asleep for about an hour when she suddenly shot up in bed. She was bewildered for a moment, and then put the light on. She breathed hard for a moment or two and then it hit her. "Oh my God, Simon's going to write de Lusignac's story!"

She got up and had no idea what she was doing or where she was going. She forced herself to sit for a moment. Simon, who knew so little of the whole history, was going to write the story! Then she knew what she had to do. She had a quick shower and went into her dressing room to dress. It was two thirty am, four or five hours' drive would get her to Lourdes, if she left at three she'd be there by eight-ish. Time to see Sophie and then get back on the same day. Oh, God, Simon, what have I started?

She dressed and ran downstairs. She thought she'd make coffee to drink on the way. She was just waiting for the kettle to boil when the phone rang. Fear gripped her. No-one rings in the middle of the night unless it's bad news.

"Hello?"

"Is everything alright? Your house is lit up like a beacon. Are you OK?"

"Oh Julian. Thank God. Are you up? Can you come over?"

Julian arrived in a matter of minutes, looking very worried. "Diana, what on earth is wrong?"

"I've just realised Simon is going to write de Lusignac's story. I need to go down to Lourdes to see Sophie. I must tell her. Simon doesn't yet know the other half of the story, about Sophie I mean, or the bank account or anything, but he's going to write this book and it's going to be so painful for some people. I have to go and tell her." She was breathless and tearful.

"Yes, OK, but slow down. Stop getting into a state, that won't help and I'm not sure that driving down there at three am is such a good idea."

"No, I have to go. Simon will be back in two days, I have to let her know, Julian. I have to tell him everything and when I do, it will - oh, God what a mess. This is just the very thing Sophie wanted to avoid."

"Do you want me to come with you? Actually, that's not a question, I *am* coming with you."

"Thank you Julian. Thank you so much, it would mean a lot. And it would be so good not to have to do that drive on my own. You are an angel."

"Yes, I know! Now, where are your flasks or travelling mugs?"

They set off at about three fifteen am. As they drove away, with Julian driving her car, there were no other lights on in any other house. 'Perhaps John Porton-Watts is finally having a decent night's sleep,' she thought.

They had been driving for about an hour when Diana said, "What on earth were you doing up at two in the morning anyway, to even notice that my lights were on?"

"I hadn't actually been to bed. I do this sometimes. I was writing emails to Phoebe and Josh. Then I started browsing the internet – fatal just before bed. Then I made some coffee and put on *The Jewel In The Crown*. One of the best pieces of television ever made, captured the era so well. Then I was just thinking of going up when I saw your house sending out beams in every direction."

"So, you haven't been to bed at all and you're driving my car? Very sensible. Are you sure you don't want me to drive?"

"And how much sleep have you had?"

"Well, not much, I must admit. It's probably anxiety over this Simon thing but I don't feel in the least tired."

They drove in companionable silence and stopped for petrol just outside Lourdes. Diana found the elusive road to the hospice but it was still early.

"They serve breakfast at eight am, so we'll leave it until that's been done before we arrive. If Sophie's well enough, they will get her up before breakfast, so she'll have it sitting in her chair."

At eight thirty, Diana pushed open the front door and breathed in the familiar smell of polish and disinfectant. A nurse came towards them and told them that Sophie was quite well and she was indeed sitting in her chair. They waited a moment while the nurse went to tell Sophie that she had visitors.

"Diana, how lovely and what a surprise, and is this your husband?"

"No, Sister, this is a kind friend of ours who drove me down here this morning." She introduced Julian who discreetly took a plastic visitors' chair to the back of the room.

"This morning? Why this morning? Is everything alright?" She looked anxious.

"No, we're fine, Sister, it's just I have something I need to tell you." Diana drew her chair up to the side of the old nun's chair.

"Sister, the last time I was here, we agreed that I would tell my husband everything. Well, he hasn't been home yet and he's coming on Thursday. I had planned to share everything with him. But - I, um - he's going to - I think he's …" Diana stopped and looked at the old nun.

"Diana, what is it, something is worrying you?"

"Oh, Sister. I think he's going to write the de Lusignac story. And he doesn't even know half of it yet. He doesn't know about you or the letters or anything. But he will. Even if he didn't, just writing the story will be awful. There are people in the village that you and I have agreed need to be left in peace now. I can't believe this has happened, I can't believe I didn't see it coming."

Sister Marie Agnes was silent for a few minutes. "Diana, I think you know I am not concerned about secrecy for my own sake. And I may be worrying unnecessarily about the others too, but it's something I wanted to avoid. But perhaps it's for the best, I don't know. Secrets never improve with keeping, do they?" She turned her head towards Julian.

"What do you think? Julian, is it?"

"Yes, Sister. Well, I think Diana is right, he does intend to write a book. Her husband is a novelist, not a biographer. So the story could be disguised to be another village with different people. But he won't do that, at least not to the extent that it would be unrecognisable. On the other hand, he MAY write a factual book, in which case, he'd leave nothing out. He knows nothing beyond what happened to de Lusignac. For him to learn the rest, Diana will have to tell him. Or on the other hand, Diana is now going to have to keep something from her husband for ever. For example, how would she explain going to the bank in London? And then if she is the trustee of any fund that may result, how would she explain that also? Keeping secrets is alien to Diana, but she's horrified at the prospect of Simon's book telling of people's tragic loss for entertainment."

The nun looked at Julian. "What would you recommend?"

"Tell Simon everything, in the hope that he has the good sense and judgement to write a different book, I suppose. Or even bring him to see you with the hope that his need to publish will be diminished by hearing your reasons for wanting it kept secret for another few years."

"Is that a possibility, Diana?"

"I honestly don't know. Simon gets enthusiastic very quickly, but does lose interest equally quickly if things are not going well. For example, the project he was working on is not coming together as he thought it might but he's fired up about this new project, which I believe is de Lusignac's story. What I really want to know, Sister, is what you think? There's no way we could stop him from publishing if he did do an investigative piece. And I'm not sure if appealing to his finer feelings would work. I'm just so sorry I started this."

"Why don't you two go and have some coffee? Matron will send some into the sitting room for you. Let me have a think for an hour and then we'll talk again."

Julian and Diana were shown into a lovely bright sitting room, with two bay windows overlooking the orchard, now bare of leaves but with sun filtering through the branches casting waving shadows. The room was warm, both Julian and Diana were now tired, and Diana closed her eyes for a few moments. She awoke to feel Julian's hand on her arm offering her a cup of coffee. Julian had been watching her dozing, wanting to leave her sleeping but knowing that they had to finish what they came for.

"Come on. Drink some coffee and then we'll see Sophie again. She's a remarkable woman in a way. I thought I'd probably hate her for being such a coward, but actually, the poison sort of leaches away, doesn't it, when you see an old, dying woman?"

"Julian, she was sixteen, for heaven's sake. She was a simple young girl, thwarted in her first love and reacting like any teenager by taking it out on grown-ups. Her rebellion just had more serious consequences than she imagined. What on earth are we going to do?"

"Firstly, see if Sophie comes up with something. If not, we'll talk about it on the way home."

They sat for about an hour then walked back to Sophie's room. She smiled at them when they came in. "Julian, bring your chair up her next to Diana, where I can see you."

They sat down and waited expectantly to see if Sophie herself was going to give Diana an idea of how to proceed. "Diana, I won't ask you to keep secrets from your husband, particularly when they are not secrets of your making. So, this is what I think. In the first place, we may all be misjudging him. He may be amenable to not writing a factual story if he knows that there are people still alive who were involved. Secondly, under no circumstances, if he writes any kind of book, is he to use the letters or the contents of my father's boxes. They were given to Diana for a specific purpose and one which I would hope now she would carry out before Simon arrives. They are very personal and private. I trust Diana. And I feel I can trust you, Julian. If he does decide to write a novel, it will still hurt some people. So, the best thing would be that he doesn't write anything at all, at least for another ten years. By then it probably wouldn't matter to anyone, who knows? But I don't think there's much chance of that from what you say." Sophie shifted slightly in her seat and closed her eyes for a moment. "Diana, I'm sorry. But I'm leaving it to you, just like everything else I'm afraid."

Diana put her hand on the woman's arm. "Please don't distress yourself, Sister. I'm sorry I had to come and tell you, but you are the most important one in all this. But, I will if I may, bring Simon to see you if it all works out as I think it will."

"There is something else you may not have thought about," Said Sophie.

"What's that?"

"Well, as I said, there are people still alive in the village who were directly involved in my father's death. They may *still* feel justified in killing him because he *did* shelter the true traitor. There will be others for whom this book is one truth too many and they may retaliate. Against you. Against all of you. Against the property. The village won't be divided again: if one acts against you, they all will. It's something you need to think about."

Diana and Julian stood up to take their leave. Diana promised to talk to Simon to find out what exactly he had in mind and bring him to visit Sophie in the near future.

The pair were silent for the first half hour of the journey home, sorting out in their own minds how to proceed. Sophie hadn't actually expressed a preference for any particular course of action and realised that it all might come out into the open now, regardless of consequences.

Diana turned to Julian and said, "Will you come with me tonight to deal with the boxes? Actually, I've had an idea which will both do as Sophie wants and also make sure no-one else will ever find them. What do you think if we burn the photos and stuff and scatter the ashes, the same with the love letters? That way, they'll never be found for sure? Do you think that would count as carrying out Sophie's wishes? I think it's more fitting somehow. She's already asked for her own ashes to be scattered there. What do you think?"

"I think it's the perfect solution. We'll do it. Then you can honestly tell Simon that Sophie wanted it that way."

"I asked her about the comb in the box, you know, the silver-backed comb?"

"Oh, yes?"

"Klaus gave it to her. It belonged to his mother and he stole it from her bedroom to take with him as a good-luck charm! Wasn't that sweet? And then he gave it to Sophie because he had nothing else to give her."

"Except his love."

The drove back chatting and falling into silence, then slowly the talk changed to being the casual conversation as if they were two old friends. Diana asked him if he knew of Hilary's exploits in Africa. He knew some of it, he remembered the case in the papers when the kidnap had occurred: after all, it was the sister of the French president. Diana was ashamed to say she didn't recall it, but was going to do some research. Now *there* would be an amazing story, but there was absolutely no chance that she was going to share that with Simon.

Julian also knew something of Véronique's history, in that she had lived in the village at the time of the massacre, but he hadn't known of her work with the Resistance escape line.

"Aren't people remarkably modest about their achievements? My God, if I had done half of what those two women have done, I'd write a wretched book myself. I'm staggered by the people I've met since we came here. I've done nothing with my life really, achieved nothing, my life has been incredibly simple."

"But it's that simplicity which is so appealing. You don't have violent opinions about people, you're not vitriolic, your inner calm and integrity shows through and that's what people love. It's part of what I love about you."

She didn't feel threatened by his love any more, he had shown himself to be honourable and kind, and a really good friend, which is what she needed more.

They arrived home at about five in the evening, it was already almost dark. They were going to go to the clearing at about nine, after they had both had a chance to shower and eat.

Diana phoned Simon, who seemed in ebullient mood and almost ready to come home. She sensed that he was really looking forward to it now, whereas before she had the distinct impression that he was putting off his return.

She was just boiling some pasta when the phone rang. It was Margaret.

"If you two keep driving in and out together at all hours of the day and night, someone is going to put four and five together. What have you been up to? If you tell me you've spent the day in a sleazy hotel making steamy love all day, I shan't come to lunch on Sunday. Or rather, I shall come but I shall be horrible and embarrassing!"

Diana laughed delightedly. The prospect of Margaret standing up in her breeches on Sunday informing the gathering of her suspicions amused her. "I'll tell you all about it soon, I promise, but it's not sex in the afternoon, nor in the morning nor the evening come to that! In fact, it's not anything of a personal nature at all, and you'll have to be content with that for now. Anyway, how did you know we were driving in and out at all hours?"

"The necessity to pee in the middle of the night, to be blunt. And there was your house using up all the resources on the planet, lights blazing, car doors slamming and furtive driving out of the gate. I demand to know what's going on."

"And you shall. BUT. NOT. YET."

"OK. But it had better be good, my imagination is working overtime."

"It will be unexpected, that's all I will say. And close your damned curtains."

"What? And miss all the excitement?"

After Margaret had hung up, Diana put some herbs in a small dish with some butter and heated it in the microwave. When the pasta was ready, she poured the herb butter over

303

the top and mixed it up. Some parmesan cheese sprinkled over the top and a good grinding of black pepper, and she was ready to eat; she was starving.

****

Julian knocked on the door at about a quarter to nine. Diana was dressed and ready to go. She had found a metal ash bucket and took a box of matches, some firelighters and a trowel. She had put the papers from the two German boxes in a bag and had burned the boxes on the drawing room fire. Somehow she felt that this was a fitting end to the last piece of German occupation of the property.

"What do we need a trowel for? Aren't we going to scatter the ashes?" asked Julian.

"Well, we can't very well burn the silver comb, so I thought we'd bury that in the little tin box."

It had been raining earlier but although it had stopped, the cloud covered the moon and they needed the light from their torches as they left through the kitchen door and crossed the lawn. They reached the clearing and went in to the middle. Diana put a firelighter in the bucket and put the papers and photographs on the top. Klaus's love letters they intended to burn at the boat house. As the flames caught, she fed the papers in little piles and watched the last of the de Lusignac family mementos curl and blacken. When there was nothing left except glowing embers in the bottom of the bucket, they spread the ash, letting it fall where it may.

Without a spoken decision, they both stood in silence for a few minutes, reflecting on what had happened here. Then he took her arm and led her out of the clearing and around the lake to the little boat house.

For Diana, this was the saddest little part of the whole thing. Klaus's words of love were sent soaring up into the air and then there was nothing left but crumbling pieces of burnt paper. His German lettering of French endearments were now gone.

Diana pulled out the trowel from her pocket and they went around to the side of the boat house where Sophie had originally found a hole to push the tin box into. There wasn't much left of the floor of the boathouse now so they picked a spot where they could dig a hole and conceal it afterwards. It was unlikely that anyone else would come around to this part of the lake, but they took great care nonetheless to cover up the little area with stones and mud.

Diana picked up the bucket and trowel and turned to leave. "Come and sit with me for a while." As Julian spoke, he pulled a plastic rubbish bag out of his pocket. "All the comforts of home, you won't get your bum wet. And …" with a theatrical flourish he pulled a bottle of champagne out of his large pocket in his Barbour coat and two glasses from the other. "Everyone deserves a wake," he said.

The cloud was clearing and the moon gave the most beautiful light on the lake, mist was rising and the whole evening was etched in her mind as being memorable and peaceful. "It's the nicest wake I've ever been to. I do feel that we've done the right thing, it's only a shame Sophie couldn't be here. Thank you for coming with me. It's a strange thing, but I don't think Simon would have understood why I wanted to do this or why Sophie wanted it."

"Do you love Simon very much?"

The question took her by surprise but she only hesitated for a moment before saying, "Of course I do, Julian. What a question. We've been married for twenty years."

"That's no guarantee of unending love."

"Didn't you love Edwina?"

"Yes, I did. I couldn't believe how she could have even looked at me when we were younger. But she was cruel and unfaithful. I never forgave her exactly but we found a way

305

to live with it. She changed after her heart operation and we made peace of a sort. I have missed her but I think I miss my idea of being married."

"I'm so sorry, Julian, really. I can't imagine that sort of pain. The one thing I am sure of is Simon's love for me."

Julian hoped that her faith would never be shattered as his had been. He hoped that this affair in Paris would turn out to be a momentary middle-aged-man thing and he would come down to *La Chênaie* and be what Diana believed him to be.

Diana loved looking at the lake, how perfectly still the water was in the moonlight, a few leaves gently breaking the surface calm from time to time. But the cold was beginning to seep through the plastic bag and they collected the bucket to walk back to the house.

It seemed perfectly natural and normal for her to slip her hand through his arm as they walked slowly back, the lights from the house warming the night colour of the lawn.

As they reached the kitchen door, he bent down to Diana but still didn't kiss her on the lips. They hugged and he kissed her on the cheek. "Thank you for doing this with me. I'll email the hospice now and they'll give Sophie a copy to tell her what we've done. She'll be happy, I think. She seemed worried that Simon might use her letters and photos. I'm sure he wouldn't, but it's going to give her peace of mind."

Julian's faith in Simon's honour and integrity was coloured differently to hers. He had no doubt that Simon would use anything which would be of benefit to Simon.

He turned to leave and Diana spoke again. "Julian, I'm sure you find it strange that I can't find it in me to condemn Sophie for what she did. Don't think for one minute I condone it, but I don't think she got off scot-free, I think she's paid a price."

"That's one of the things I love about you, Diana. You are not judgemental or even prepared to condemn. I have a motto for you which could have been written for you. 'Single Virtue is Proof Against Manifold Vice' – in other words someone -"

"- Is not totally bad if they have one redeeming feature or have one done redeeming deed." She finished the sentence for him.

"You see the good in everyone. It's a wonderful trait, don't ever let anyone rub it out."

With that, he left.

****

On Wednesday morning Diana rose early, she had a mountain of things to do before Simon's arrival the next day. She drove off to Périgueux, to the market and to visit the little shops specialising in cheese and other delicacies. She had decided to serve a cold buffet on Sunday, but a good one. The table would be beautifully set and the meal put on the sideboard. That would eliminate the awful business of passing vegetable dishes up and down the table and making sure everyone has had some of everything. Buffets were more friendly and less formal. Celeste was happy to earn some extra money by coming in to help carry dishes and clear plates.

The butcher in Périgueux specialised in beef. She chose a sirloin strip and then horrified the butcher by asking him to remove all the fat. Her method of roasting a piece of beef to serve hot or cold was to put it in the hottest of hot ovens after covering it in a thin film of oil and roast it for about forty-five minutes. This way, it was charred on the outside and red in the middle without drooling blood. She would also cook a ham on the bone and use her mother's lovely silver ham holder.

After she had bought the meat and the cheeses, she went back to the car to leave the weighty purchases and returned to spend more time browsing and looking for specialities. She found a fishmonger where she bought the huge gambas that brought back memories of holidays. She bought smoked halibut, something she had never seen before, and a selection of other smoked fish.

The morning had passed very quickly and she still had a few more things to buy, but she could buy those in Saint-Sulpice. It was only Wednesday but she planned to spend Friday cooking the meats while Simon was organising his stuff in his study. She would make a good old English trifle and a lemon soufflé.

When she arrived home, she saw there was a message on the phone from the hospice: the message had been left four hours ago. Diana called the hospice and the matron answered the phone. Matron told her that Sophie had taken a turn for the worse during the night and was very weak. She would probably not live much beyond the next few hours and she had told the matron that she was to tell Diana, "Thank you for everything. Put your faith in God and pray for my soul." It was a farewell.

No sooner had Diana put the phone down than it rang again. Again it was the hospice. Sophie had died.

Diana rang Julian to tell him. "I'm so sorry, Diana. Don't be sad, she was very ill, you know."

"Yes, I know. But I …"

"What?"

"I have these strange fancies. You'll think I'm really simple. But I can't help it."

"Tell me."

"Well, I just have this strange feeling that she wanted to be out of Simon's reach, which is why she was so determined that we disposed of the letters."

"It's not fanciful at all. You have developed a bond with her and her history and you don't want Simon to endanger that, which you fear he might."

"God, you think I don't trust Simon to do the right thing."

"Yes, that's exactly what I think. That's why you went to warn Sophie. If you really thought Simon would let well alone, you wouldn't have bothered."

"That makes me more sad than you can imagine."

"Knowing you, I believe it. I'm here if you want to talk, Diana. Don't let this get on top of you. I'm here."

As she put the phone down she wondered how on earth Edwina could have been so cruel and unfaithful to Julian. He seemed such a genuinely good person, kind and open-hearted. But maybe she just didn't find what she was looking for or needed in Julian.

The day passed very quickly. She had spoken to the hospice several times about Sophie's funeral arrangements. They were to be very simple. She was to be cremated, but the church in Lourdes, which was used by the patients, would say Mass for her. Diana planned to go down for the funeral once the day was set and then would pick up her ashes a week later.

Given her long day yesterday and her busy day today, she phoned Simon to tell him that she was going to have a bath and go to bed early. He told her he was planning to get an early start the following morning, no later than eight am. He would therefore be at *La Chênaie* by about four or five in the afternoon. He would return the car to Hertz in Bergerac on Friday if he felt like it, or on Saturday.

On Thursday morning, Diana left Celeste polishing and vacuuming, André was filling up log baskets in both the drawing room and dining room. Although the open fires were charming and comforting, Diana was a firm believer in wood-burning stoves. Modern stoves had huge glass fronts and gave the same warming effect as an open fire, but heated more efficiently. And she felt she could safely leave a room with a fire burning.

She went off to Saint-Sulpice to buy flowers and the rest of the things she needed for Sunday. Bakeries were open on Sunday morning so she would be able to buy really fresh bread. The wine shop still had a few bottles of Billecart-Salmon and she chose a Saint-Estèphe and a crisp Chablis. She bought the day-old *Daily Telegraph* and looked at the news consuming the world as she drank her coffee sitting inside the café, the outside days were few and far between now. The news of course was available twenty-four hours a day on television or the computer, but she tired of drab voices delivering bad news in morbid tones, or listening to hypocritical politicians delivering promises they had no intention of keeping. The newspaper could deliver the same news but in palatable format and without the news readers treating the listener as half-baked, ill-educated idiots.

Diana waved to Véronique and Francine as she drove down the left-hand side of the driveway, as the mother and daughter were walking up the right hand side.

As the time for Simon to arrive drew nearer, she felt unaccountably nervous and wished it were possible for Julian to be with her when she discussed all the recent events with Simon. She put the meatballs in Madeira gravy in the slow oven of the range cooker and put the mashed potato in the cool oven: she could put it into the hot oven later. There would be just the beans to cook and she had made a chocolate and salted caramel cheesecake. She wanted a clear hour before dinner to bring Simon up to date.

Diana heard the bottom door to the kitchen open as he called out, "Honey, I'm home."

She laughed "You fool. Come here, I've missed you so much." He hugged her and gave her a long kiss. "It's so good to have you home, I've so much to tell you."

They spent two hours bringing in all his boxes and bags and installing his things in the study. He put his two suitcases in the dressing room. "I love what you've done with this room. The room looks so cosy and comfortable; does Madame sit at this chair in the window answering her letters?"

She smiled, anxious now to get him downstairs and relaxed while she talked to him. "Come on down, darling, we'll have a drink before dinner and there's something I need to talk to you about."

"God, that sounds ominous. Is everything alright?"

"Oh, yes, it's nothing sinister, it's just things which I've found out and things which - oh, just come on down and I'll tell you everything."

She poured each of them a glass of Chateau Talbot which she had found in Périgueux and sat in the armchair at the side of the fire. Simon sat on the sofa and stretched out his legs with a big sigh. "This really is a fabulous house, you know. It really feels like home. And I'm just so fired up about this new project, I can't wait to tell you about it, but you go first, you look as if you're about to burst!"

She laughed and sat a bit further forward in the chair as she started to talk. She told him everything. She told him about finding the boxes, about the little book leading to a bank account in London. She talked about finding Sophie, finding the tin box. The only thing she didn't tell him was that she and Julian had returned to see Sophie to discuss their suspicions about Simon's project. She also didn't tell him of their little cremation ceremony.

When she had finished, he sat looking at her almost open-mouthed. He seemed stunned and lost for words. She was just starting to think she had misjudged him and began to feel guilty when he said, "Oh, Dee. It's perfect. Absolutely bloody perfect. I can't believe it. You have no idea what this means, because, you see - I'm going to do de Lusignac's story"

311

Her stomach clenched.

He started to speak again. "I had thought originally to do a factual book, you know like those stories of wartime treachery, heroism, murder – that kind of thing. Then it seemed better to write it as a novel, there really wasn't much there for a really gripping exposé or anything. Now this is just perfect! With all this information, it's great. I can write the factual book after all." He stood up and was pacing around as his voice grew loud with excitement. "I can't believe this has just fallen into my lap like this. I always wanted to be a writer of a serious piece but this is beyond anything. Where are the documents? And I must, absolutely must see Sophie. Sophie, for heaven's sake! I can't believe everyone got it so wrong for so long. Sophie!" He hadn't really stopped to look at her or even draw breath. "Can I see the papers? Why on earth didn't you tell me what you were up to? God, you clever old thing, who'd have thought it? There was me working away on something in Paris which looks like a dead end and in a few weeks you've done all this, you're amazing. It's going to be a fantastic story."

His hand was rubbing his forehead as if he couldn't quite believe what he'd heard and he was trying to rub in some understanding. He looked over at her and stopped pacing. "What's the matter?"

"Simon, you can't. You really can't."

"Ho! Wait a minute, what do you mean, *can't*?"

"Simon, there are still people alive in the village who were directly involved, their sons and daughters live here. *We* have to live here; you can't do it. I know you think it's a good idea, but if you write the story, you'll have to write it as a novel and write it about another area entirely. You can't link it with Saint-Sulpice or the people who live here. But even so, the people who live here will *know* that it's about them."

"That little traitor, all the time living in hiding. It's a huge story, of course I'm going to write it."

"SIMON, STOP!" Diana raised her voice. "She wasn't living in hiding. Listen to me, sit down, be quiet and listen to me." He started to talk again and she shouted, "SHUT UP, JUST SHUT UP!"

He was stunned.

"Listen to me, Simon. If you wrote the story at all, it would have to be unrecognisable as de Lusignac or St Sulpice and that would be almost impossible to do. The people who were involved, some of whom are still here, believed they had murdered a traitor. Instead of which, he was a desperate father who made a terrible sacrifice to save his young, naïve, heartbroken daughter. There will also be some of those who were involved who will believe they did the right thing *because* he protected her. This place took years to heal. Years. Take a walk around and look at the plaques on the walls, the bullet holes in the walls which have never been repaired, the damned flagpole from which Henri's uncle was hanged."

"Dee, how long have I wanted to be taken seriously as a writer? This wretched novel I've been working on hasn't come together as I hoped -"

"But you haven't even started writing yet. How can you tell?"

"Because I can't see where the story is going. And I can't see where it would end. I want to do *this* story. These people can't expect to bury this story for ever."

"They haven't *hidden* it. They didn't *know* it. And it was a terrible time. You can't possibly know, but I've spoken to someone who *was* there and it *was* the most dreadful time for the whole village, even those who didn't lose a loved one knew everyone who was shot. Simon, don't do this story. Please, don't do it."

He ignored her plea. "You've spoken to someone who was there? Who? Who was it?"

"I'm not telling you. That's not the important thing."

"Let me see the documents."

"No."

"Why ever not? Don't be so bloody stupid."

"Don't speak to me like that! The reason I won't let you see them is because Sophie didn't want anyone to see them. They became *my* property when she signed over everything to me. And I say no."

"I actually held those damned boxes in my hands – where are they now?"

"Alright, I'll tell you. They were burned and the ashes scattered on de Lusignac's grave, or what we believe to be his grave. The same with Sophie's letters from Klaus."

He looked at her as if she were mad. In fact, he believed she had committed the act of a mad woman.

"How could you? Did it never occur to you that I might want to see them? When you went off on this stupid little fantasy of yours, did you never think of me? Come to think of it, you've become rather an accomplished little liar haven't you? Or at least, a grand keeper of secrets, which you've always detested. God, you're such a hypocrite. You selfish, selfish bitch!" He was red in the face and shouting, his words bit into her heart. They had never, ever had an exchange like this. Never in their married life had he ever used such language to her, she had never given him reason. And now he was looking at her as if he hated her.

"You had the opportunity to help me achieve something special and you've arbitrarily decided against me."

Diana was really angry now. "Don't be so melodramatic and think of other people for a change. Think for a minute. You are being ridiculous, and very cruel. Never in our life together have I ever done anything against you. But this is not yours to do. It's not your story, it's not our history, it belongs to the people who lived it. And Sophie died yesterday. I'm sure you'll think she did it to spite you. When I saw her on Tuesday she -"

"You saw her on Tuesday? You went to see her on Tuesday? What for?"

"To warn her about you."

"Warn her? Warn her about me? Dee, I don't even know you at the moment. Here you are, sneaking around the countryside without telling me, plotting against me. You really are an underhanded, conniving, spiteful bitch!" He fell silent but was seething, his anger boiling in his head. Diana stood up and held a hand forward as if to stop the flow of spite.

"Stop this, Simon. Stop it now. We are in danger of not recovering from this if this continues. You talk of not recognising me? Well, I can't believe the man saying all these dreadful things is the man I have loved for over twenty years. Where on earth did all this come from? Or is it what you've been thinking all along?"

"Don't be so bloody stupid. Of course not. We wouldn't have stayed married if that's what I thought. It's just that what you've done is so underhand and deceitful. Dee, I want this story, I know it would be the making of me. I can do it without the papers, you know. I'll talk to people, people would love to be in a book, they love a bit of fame, regardless of what you think. This is misplaced fear, you know. I'll get old photos from the families, take photos of the plaques in the village. You're wrong, you know. People will want this to come out." Diana stared at him in disbelief.

"*You're* the one who's wrong. I told you, I've talked to someone who WAS here. People just want to move beyond that history and have done so remarkably well. You won't find the kind of welcome you think you will."

"Who IS this someone? I want to meet him."

"No."

"I'm going to write this story, Dee and no-one can stop me. It's a huge story, I'm sorry the old girl has died before I could expose the truth but - when is her funeral?"

315

"Simon, this is not going to happen. I want you to spend the weekend thinking things over. We can talk about it calmly and rationally without your calling me horrible names and you'll know that we're right."

"We? Who's we? Are you all in it together then? And you can forget it. I'm writing the story. And I'm coming with you to London to find out what's in that bank."

Diana put her glass down and walked out of the room. She closed the drawing room door behind her and walked towards the staircase leading down to the kitchen, her refuge. She stood at the top of the stairs and put her face in her hands. She was beyond weeping. Simon's venomous attack had been so unexpectedly vile but then so had her response. She hadn't weakened and broken down in the face of his verbal abuse, she had become angry.

But for all that, she knew that nothing would change his mind. She went down to the kitchen and opened another bottle of wine. She took the meal out of the oven and put it on the draining board. There was absolutely no way she was going to sit and eat a companionable meal with Simon now. She wondered what had gone so horribly wrong. Perhaps he would calm down and everything would be alright in the morning. She made a sandwich and sat at the table, feeling shocked and miserable.

Simon didn't come down to the kitchen that evening and when she went up to bed, he'd already gone up himself. He wasn't in the bedroom but there was a light on in the guest bedroom. She didn't knock or go in but went to her dressing room and as she closed the curtains, she saw Julian standing in his upstairs window. Her guardian angel. She actually lifted her hand and waved but had no idea if he had even seen the gesture.

For the very first time in their marriage, they spent the night apart because of a row.

****

316

Diana woke before it was light and got out of bed. She walked over the hall to her bathroom and dressing room and on impulse, went to the door of the guest bedroom. She was in two minds whether to knock and go in, or just go in without knocking; she didn't know how to act in this strange situation. She was just about to knock when she heard his voice murmuring, obviously speaking on the phone. Who on earth could he be talking to at this hour?

Finally she knocked and entered without waiting for a reply. He was indeed talking on the phone but he was still in bed, the room was dark except for the strange luminous glow from the phone. He rang off without a word.

"Hello. Simon, I can't bear this. This isn't how we are together."

"I know, darling. Come here. I didn't sleep last night. I nearly came over a dozen times."

"Who were you talking to?"

"Oh, Chris had some papers I need. They've just turned up and I suppose I need them so urgently that it needs a phone call at six in the morning!" he laughed.

"I'll make some coffee. Are you getting up now or do you want it up here?"

"Come here." She sat down on the bed again and he put his arms around her. Pulling her backwards onto the bed, he put his hand under her nightdress and began to make love to her. He was a good lover, he knew her tender spots and knew how to do what she enjoyed. He took his time and it was good for both of them.

At breakfast, Diana said, "Simon, we still have to clear the air over this. Have you thought at all about it?"

"Look, Dee, the story is out there. If I don't write it someone else will, you know it can't stay secret for ever. It's a wonder it's stayed hidden for so long. It is a wonderful opportunity for me. How often does anyone get the chance to write something like this and have such a mine of information still around? You'll see, it'll be fine. After all, the two villains are both dead, aren't they?"

"Is that how you see them? You can't see any mitigating circumstances for either of them? We haven't had children, but don't you think a father would do anything for his child? He had been a hero in the Resistance until then, and would have continued to be so. His daughter was a sad little thing, totally bereft of friends, and apart from her father, any family. She lived with an old servant and she was just ripe for the first sign of affection that she met with. And Klaus was just the same. Young, inexperienced, frightened and a bit of a mummy's boy."

"Who is this person you have spoken to, who was here at the time? Someone in the village, of course, you must have met loads of people by now."

"Simon, I can't help you. I can't stop you but I have this terrible feeling that it's going to be a barrier between us. I really don't want you to do this. Really. But I can't keep fighting. If you won't do as I ask because it's me who's asking, then I have nothing more I can use. But think of this. Sophie mentioned something which, at the time, I thought was ridiculous, but I'm not so sure. She said that this might have repercussions on us. Our lives here might be made very difficult."

"What nonsense. Dee, that's absolute rubbish. What? She thinks the Resistance is alive and well and living in Saint-Sulpice?" He laughed aloud and poured some more coffee.

"You need to think of others, Simon, this might well affect all of us here at *La Chênaie*."

"You mean people like that dotty old woman who came here that first day?"

"She's not, and don't say things like that. She is probably one of the bravest women I know. You have no idea what she's done, she is an amazing, heroic woman."

"By God, Dee, you've changed your tune. Don't tell me that old nun's given you religion!"

"Please, Simon. Just think about it for a while before you start something you can't retract. Please. I'm asking you to just think."

Diana stood up to clear away the breakfast things. She had planned a happy day, cooking and making desserts. She wished now she hadn't invited everyone, she felt fretful and a little panicky. She wanted to talk to Julian, he'd know what to do and what to say. As if reading her thoughts, Simon said he'd take the car to Bergerac, and he'd catch the train to come back. He wanted a bit of a breather and he'd walk back from the station.

Diana watched him drive out of the gate and felt a sense of relief mixed with anxiety – what was he going to get up to? There wasn't anything he could do today, was there? He couldn't start investigating today? She dialled Julian's number. She was about to hang up when he answered.

"Julian, can I come over for a few minutes?" She tried not to sound desperate.

"Of course. Are you alright? Where has Simon gone, I just saw him drive off?"

"He's gone to take the car back to Hertz. He'll be gone for a couple of hours, but I really need to talk to you."

"Come on over then."

Julian let Diana in, he was waiting at the front door. They went through to the kitchen and he had already started some coffee.

"Thank you," she said as he handed her a cup. "I need this today. I'm afraid I overdid the wine last night. Simon and I have had a horrible time. Unexpectedly horrible, he was absolutely vile. He's just determined to write this story. When I tried to talk him out of it, he turned so nasty, I've never heard him call me names or shout at me like that. He was totally lost in his own needs, he wouldn't listen to me and nothing will stop him from writing this story. To be honest, he slept in the guest room last night and I was pleased he did. I was so angry when I went to bed but worse than that, I didn't think we could recover from what was going on. He was cruel and spiteful. I can't stand it and I don't think the situation warranted it. He was like a spoilt child who has been thwarted." She drank some coffee and felt a little less queasy. "Oh, Julian, what are we going to do?" She put her face in her hands, totally defeated.

"Simon isn't um - violent, is he? I mean, he doesn't hit you or anything?"

"God, no. He's never done anything like that. But then, on the other hand, he's never called me a bitch either. It was horrible. Then this morning, he was so sweet I really thought he'd changed his mind, but it was all a ploy to try and get me on side. Julian, he's actually going to do it. He's going to talk to people in the village, talk to local records keepers and everything. And he's threatening to come to the bank in London. What on earth have I started?"

Julian didn't want to know what 'so sweet' meant: he could well imagine. The thought of Diana and Simon spending last night together was a torment to him, so he was thrilled when Diana said they'd spent the night apart. Clearly Simon had made up for it this morning. What on earth was Diana doing with a jerk like that?

"Does he know that we went to see Sophie on Tuesday?"

"I let it slip that I'd been, but I stopped myself from saying we'd gone together. I'm just not good at keeping secrets. Have you by any chance got an Alka-Seltzer?"

Julian smiled and went upstairs, coming down a few minutes later with the little foil packet. Waiting for the fizz to stop, he leaned down and kissed Diana on the top of the head. "Poor girl, you've had a horrible time. But here's the thing. If he decided to go ahead with this book, what are you going to do? Will you stay with him or will you go? Isn't that the choice before you now? Or don't you think this is a make or break situation? This is what you have to decide now."

"Do you know, there was one point last night when I thought I hated him. I have never, never felt like that in all the time I've known him. What a mess. Perhaps I should do what I've told him to do, and take a few days to think things over and see how it's going to develop. You've been such a help, I know really I'm the one who has to decide what to do, but I can't. If our marriage is to survive this, it's going to mean compromise, but I can't see where his side of the compromise will come from, and I can't - I can't compromise on a promise I made to Sophie. Anyway, see you on Sunday?"

As he saw her to the door, he said, "Diana, if things get a bit sticky and you want to find a quiet place, come through your woods, where the fence line runs from the right of your house. There's a gate into my back garden, that's how I used to slip into the woods for a walk. If I'm not here, there's a key to the kitchen door, guess where? Yup, under the plant pot just outside!"

"Thank you, Julian, you're such a good friend." She gave him a hug and left.

She went for a walk down to what she now regarded as de Lusignac's grave and sat for a while. She knew that this was the first time she had felt real, heart-wrenching unhappiness. Can a marriage fail over the span of a couple of hours of heated conversation? Was this how marriages came to an end? She had seen a side to Simon she had never known existed: nasty, spiteful, hurtful. Was love enough to forgive all these things? But for the time being, she knew what she would do.

And what about this book? There really was nothing she could do to stop him; she knew that now.

****

321

Simon came home much later than she expected. He seemed distant and quiet. "Are you alright? You seem a bit exhausted."

"No, I'm fine. Look, I've been thinking. I really want to write this book and I've spoken to Edwards about it. He thinks it would be great for my career and let's face it, the story is out there now."

"No, it isn't, Simon. But if either of us are to have any life at all, we can't keep fighting over it. So, I've decided something myself. On Monday I'm phoning the agent in London and telling them not to re-let the house in April when the present lease is up. If you are determined to do this, you need to be here but I don't. In the meantime, I'll take a service apartment and then move back to Holland Park when the house is empty."

She said all this in an unemotional and quiet manner, even surprising herself. She hadn't actually thought of this until a couple of hours ago, but it seemed so obviously the answer.

"What is this, Dee? Blackmail? I do what you want, otherwise you're leaving me?"

"I didn't say I was leaving you. I'll be in London, that's all. How we carry on after that is rather up to you, but I don't want to be here and be party to what you're doing. We each, it seems, have to do what we think is best."

"I don't recognise you, Dee, this isn't like you at all."

"No, it's not, is it? Anyway, this is what I suggest. We have everyone coming for lunch on Sunday and I have quite a lot to do. If we can possibly put all this aside until after the weekend, each take time to reflect on our present positions, it would benefit us both. We've given each other a battering emotionally over the last few hours and I'm quite sure that what I suggest is the best way. If you are going ahead with the book, you'll need me out of the way, and I *want* to be, it's as simple as that. Whether we can ever live here together again as our home after you've written this book, I can't say at the moment."

Simon did look tired, but he smiled and agreed. Diana could tell his mind was already working on his research for this new, exciting project, one that would mark him as a serious writer.

Diana was busy for the rest of the day and Simon spent most of it upstairs in his study. Supper was a slightly strained affair, with both of them consciously avoiding the subject of the book. They agreed to go to the village together the following morning for Diana to buy flowers and they would have lunch at Henri's.

They slept in the same bed that night, but he made no move to make love and neither did she.

On Saturday morning it was windy and wet, the wind coming from the east. Simon came down first and put on the coffee, but he wasn't really acquainted with the art of getting wood-burning stoves working. In the drawing room, the embers from the day before were still glowing but needed riddling and for the new logs to take fire, the vents needed to be opened. After several smoky attempts he decided to wait for Diana to come down and went back to the kitchen.

He sat down at her desk and decided to check his emails, using her computer. Waiting for the computer to warm up, he idly opened the drawer of her little desk and saw a folder marked 'François Lartigue – Notaire'. Thinking it to be something to do with the house purchase, he put the file on the desk and opened it. For a moment, he wasn't sure what he was looking at. It seemed to be notarised true copies of old documents and photos, mostly old receipts. There were also copies of pages of a small book, with notations and figures.

With a shock, he realised he was looking at copies of Sophie's papers, the ones which Diana had burned. And the little book must be the book she was taking to the London bank. And there they were! Klaus's love letters. He was furious, anger choking his throat. She had lied to him. The papers in the original may have been burned but the bloody woman had had copies made before her little cremation ceremony. God, how she had changed. At one time she would NEVER have kept anything from him. Since they arrived here she was like a different person, full of secrets, demands and tantrums.

"Put that back. It won't help you and you are not having them." She sounded cold and angry.

"What a devious creature you've become." He closed the file and stood up.

"I had copies made because … to be honest, I don't know why I did, I suppose I was afraid of having only the originals around. I don't know, I just thought it was a good idea at the time. It all feels so personal to me, I suppose, selfishly, I also thought I wanted to keep a part of the history if Sophie had wanted to keep the originals. But she didn't. And the reason she didn't is that she didn't want other eyes to see them. So you must honour that and put them back. Now that you've seen them, I'll destroy those too. I should have done it at the same time as doing the others. Frankly, it just didn't cross my mind, I'd almost forgotten that I had them. I should have destroyed those too."

He closed the drawer.

"And the bank won't talk to anyone else but me, so there is no point in your coming. I wouldn't allow it in any case."

"Wouldn't allow it? *Wouldn't allow it*? My God, Diana. What's happening here?"

He walked past her and went up the stairs. He wasn't sure how to conduct himself any more. Her opposition to his writing the book was spilling over into all areas of their marriage right now. It was obscene, this obsession she had with this place, this history. It was as if she was living in the past, as part of the family.

Simon and Diana had managed to avoid each other for most of Saturday. Needless to say, their planned trip to the village finished with Diana going on her own and Simon taking refuge in his study.

In the evening Diana prepared fresh cod for supper with a salad and dauphinoise potatoes. She went upstairs to his study to call Simon and found him slumped in the armchair, an almost-empty bottle of scotch beside him. She had only ever seen him drunk once, when his book had been accepted for publication. Then though, he had been a happy drunk. Right now he looked careworn and unhappy. She roused him by shaking him gently, although she felt anything but gentle. He opened his eyes with the confused look that most drunks have, as if not knowing where he was or why he felt so terrible.

"Do you want some supper? If you do, it's ready in five minutes."

"God, what time is it?"

"Seven-thirty. I did supper early because I have quite a lot to do for tomorrow. Why not go and have a shower and I'll hold supper for you for half an hour?"

"Okay. I'm not sure if I can eat though."

"You must eat something. If you don't want fish, I'll wait 'til you come down and fix something else for you." She turned to leave and he called out to her.

"Dee, please don't leave me. Please."

"Go and shower. I'll see you downstairs."

He came down dressed in clean chinos and a clean shirt. His hair was wet and he had a bewildered and confused look about him. "I'll just have some toast and some coffee."

"Sit down and I'll do it for you."

While she was moving around the kitchen, making space between piles of plates and napkins, glasses and serving bowls, he looked at her and wondered how they would resolve their impasse. "Dee, are you really set on going to London? I mean, if I don't write the book, will you still go?"

"Why? Are you thinking of abandoning the idea? Honestly?"

"No. But I'm hoping we can reach a compromise. I don't want you to go."

"Simon." She placed his toast and the butter dish in front of him. "Coffee won't be a moment; do you want some jam?" Without waiting for his answer, she put two pots of jam on the table in front of him. "Simon, I think it would be for the best at the moment, at least. Something has changed with us and I'm not sure that even if you had said you would give it up, it would make any difference now." She spoke quietly and sadly. "You know, I've spent my whole life never understanding how people can get themselves into this situation. Does it all boil down to differences in priorities? Because something is important to you and quite the opposite is important to me, does that mean the end of us? What's happened to us in such a short span of time? You spoke to me as if you hated me. I can't live like that. Perhaps it's not entirely your fault that I have lived a charmed life and I'm just not prepared for that kind of vitriol. But I can't live with something like what happened bubbling along just under the surface. I never thought the day would come, ever, when I'd be happier living somewhere without you. I do love you. You are the only man I have ever loved, you know that. Ever since we met in Paris, you have been the other half of me. But I realise now that I have given up more than you during the entire length of our marriage. I've done it willingly because I love you. I have never put a price on anything you've asked of me. Now I'm asking you to give this up. And you won't. I won't leave immediately. I still need time to consider that what I'm going to do is right. I'm asking that while I'm still here you can forget this project and let me live in peace for a few days, or weeks, whatever it will turn out to be." She looked at him, trying to find the

326

slightest sign in him that he had even understood her dilemma, her torn loyalties.

"Well. You certainly have changed and I don't think it's because I called you a few names, for which, incidentally, I am truly sorry. No, I think something else is going on with you. It's true that you've enabled me to bathe in your sunshine, and I admit I've been terribly lucky. But can you honestly say that you've given up something that was so important to you that it's left a permanent mark? Financially, you've carried me when things haven't been going so well, but you've never shown any sign of having had a problem with it." He looked as if his anger was still hovering just underneath a veneer of civility.

She took a moment and finally said, "I haven't. Never. But think back. All the asking has been one way and I'm not talking about money. That woman producer on the television programme? You can never imagine – never – how that felt. The hurt was a physical pain, bad, bad pain. Not the fact that everyone else but me knew, it was how sure you both were that I was too stupid or loving or devoted to even believe it. When you asked me to forgive you, and all the promises you made, I believed you and I forgave you. Really I did. And I have never mentioned it since and that was fifteen years ago. I had even made myself believe that it had never happened anyway. So don't tell me that you have made any comparable compromises. Nothing compared to that. My willingness must have given you such confidence. I have never gone against you in anything. Except this."

Simon hadn't touched his toast and was looking rather ill. He got up from the table and rushed to the toilet in the hall. He was clearly being very sick. When he came back into the kitchen, Diana had prepared an Alka-Seltzer and a large glass of iced water. He sat down at the table. "I don't want to live here on my own. Please don't go."

"You won't be on your own. Celeste comes in every morning now from Monday to Friday and André comes three times a week. He'll bring in logs and generally keep the place tidy outside. He's doing some work for me on the boat house which I want him to finish. He is also a whiz with the central heating system, the valves and dials need some understanding."

"I can't believe you're talking like this. It's as if you've already decided and are preparing to go."

"Well, the only thing which would stop me … Well, I don't need to repeat it, you know what it is."

"Diana, I can't. Edwards is very keen and it's become very important to me."

"Well, then. Let's have lunch with our friends tomorrow, never forgetting of course, that you may be bringing about the end of their peace and tranquillity too. Then we'll make our individual preparations. In the meantime, I have lots to do. If you want some more food, let me know. You really should eat something, you know, you'll feel better. I'll bring you something up to the drawing room in about an hour or so, you'll feel more like it by then." She smiled at him and started clearing away his plate and busying herself with bowls and dishes for the lunch the following day.

He looked at her in confusion. Here she was, planning to wreck their marriage and she was talking about a lunch party tomorrow. He went upstairs, but not to the drawing room. He went into the guest bedroom and closed the door.

****

Sunday was cold and frosty, but absolutely gorgeous. The sun sparkled on the frost and the grass looked like a carpet of diamonds. Diana had not gone in to Simon this morning but had left him sleeping. He came downstairs looking haggard and grubby.

"I'm going away for a few days," he said, running his hand through his hair. "I'll stay for lunch and then I'll go. If you are still determined to go to London on your own, then you will probably be gone when I get back, so we'll keep in touch by phone and see what we decide."

"Where will you go? You can't go back to Julian's flat."

"No. I've some friends in Limoges, I'll go there."

She didn't even ask which friends, Simon had always had friends in odd places and she never questioned him about them. He turned and went back upstairs to shower and change. Diana thought how bizarre it was, that the two of them were contemplating the end of their marriage, and she felt so calm, so completely sure that she would survive any of the pain that separation would bring.

Diana had prepared the sideboard with everything except the food, which Celeste and she would bring up later. The food looked amazing. The table was set with her mother's pure white linen place mats and napkins, starched to almost cardboard. Diana had made cockscomb napkins, something she had learned from an old *Mrs. Beeton's* belonging to her mother.

By twelve o'clock the first guest arrived – Julian. He kissed her on the cheek and looked at her quizzically. "Later," she breathed in his ear as he kissed the other cheek.

Véronique and Francine came at the same time as John Porton-Watts. When Hilary and Bob arrived, she gave Diana a big hug and squeezed her hand. Margaret had phoned to say she and Jennifer would be half an hour late, the vet was coming to see about a horse which had gone lame, "Thanks to that bloody useless farrier!"

Champagne was served and the sun put everyone in a good chatty mood. Margaret and Jennifer finally arrived, had one glass of champagne and they all went in to lunch. The dining room looked very impressive and the sun on the terrace outside warmed the room comfortably. The sideboard looked like an advertisement for a restaurant and everyone seemed to be appreciative. The nice thing about a buffet, she thought, was that its very informality meant that people would get up and have some more beef, or seafood or anything. No-one stood on ceremony and it was very convivial. Of the guests, Simon had only met Hilary and Julian before so was not quite as at ease as Diana with her neighbours, but the wines helped.

After dessert, Diana stood and said, "I think we'll have coffee in the drawing room. The loo is in the front hall and there's another in the downstairs hall."

It took about half an hour for people to go to the toilet and freshen up, then they all milled into the drawing room. Celeste had brought all the cups and accoutrements, and there was a selection of Armagnac, cognac, Drambuie, Cointreau and something Diana thought was disgusting, Benedictine. A platter of Henri's petits fours accompanied the coffee.

When everyone was settled in the warm sunshine, Diana stood up. "Listen, everyone. I have something to tell you all. The reason I am going to tell you is that it might affect us all."

"DIANA! DON'T!"

Everyone looked aghast at Simon who had shouted across the room to his wife. "But it's true, Simon. It could have consequences for all of us. You should know that. I tried to tell you."

Julian was the only one who didn't look surprised or curious.

"Don't, Diana. Please. It's not the right time. Leave it alone!"

"Actually, it's the perfect time. And it's my decision. You have made yours."

Simon got up and left the room without a word to anyone. Diana showed not the slightest inclination to follow him.

"I have something to tell you all which is in turn, a history lesson, a love story, a tragedy, a murder and an

330

exposé. I hope, when I've finished you will all forgive me for setting something in train which is now beyond my control and which does indeed carry the possibility of unpleasant consequences, although let's hope not."

Diana had their rapt attention as she began. She hadn't thought of doing anything like this until her conversation with Simon this morning. He would rather risk everything than give up this project. So be it. She had to handle it the best way she judged.

She left nothing out. From her first feeling about de Lusignac on hearing it told by Henri, to the meeting with Sophie. Then came what was, for her, the worst part. Simon's determination to write, not a novel, but a factual account of the entire history which, thanks to her, he now had in full detail. Clearly the impact of what she had just recounted was still sinking in.

"Here's the thing," she continued. "When Simon starts asking questions around the village, many people will resent it. It's not a story anyone wants brought up again. So for this reason I say it may have consequences. We may find that we are not welcome in the village. People may not want to serve us in the shops, and we could find ourselves ostracised and perhaps even threatened. Simon doesn't seem to realise the ramifications of the path he is set on. I started this whole thing with the intention of righting a wrong. But it's not as simple as that, because it may not have been the one wrong but another. In fact, I didn't actually have any intention at all, it wasn't a plan or anything pre-conceived. Like many things which turn out wrongly, it started very differently. Véronique, for you this is particularly hard. I have not told Simon of your involvement here with the Resistance, but it can only be a matter of time. I am so sorry. If I tell you that I have tried everything to stop this book, I mean everything, I am serious. I have told Simon that I am leaving. I'm not sure that it helps all of you, but it's what I have to do. It probably won't help you at all, in fact, but it isn't going to stop Simon."

Julian looked stricken. He had to talk to her alone, and soon. She carried on talking. "Sophie has made me her executrix and I have yet to visit the bank in London. I have no idea what I will find, if anything, but what she wanted to do was give the money to the bereaved families. My opinion at the time was that they wouldn't want to accept the money, but I'm open to suggestions if anyone can think of a good purpose. Is there anything anyone would like to say?"

John Porton-Watts put his brandy bowl down and stood up. "I don't know you very well, but I think you have shown an unbelievable amount of integrity. As someone would wouldn't walk out on a bad marriage, I think to be prepared to walk out on a good marriage for a principle shows great courage. I feel very sorry for you; you are obviously feeling this very deeply. I'm just sorry that I can't think of anything to help you. You see, I'm leaving too. My sister has found a good place for my wife, not far from where she lives. She is letting me rent a small cottage on her husband's estate. I'm changing my name, of course. Couldn't have the father of a jailbird living with his boyfriend on the estate as part of the family. But I'm terribly grateful to her and her husband, they have really been wonderful these last few years. I've tried to manage financially and every other way, but it's been hard." He looked around the room and smiled gently. "But for what it's worth, I think your place is here, in this house you love and with your friends around you. But I do think you are an incredibly decent person and I'm so happy to have known you at all."

Diana was completely taken aback. She felt tears roll down her cheeks and brushed them away with the back of her hand.

Margaret got up and came over to give her a hug. "I always said you were a daft old bat, *now* what kind of trouble have you landed us in? If I have to buy my bread in bloody Bergerac, so be it. But I will heap horse-crap on your head for a month if my oats suppliers refuse to meet my orders because of this!"

Diana smiled and hugged her friend back. Véronique had been very quiet and Diana looked at her. "Dear Véronique, I can't say how sorry I am. All this must be very painful for you."

"Actually my dear, you can't escape the past. Do you honestly think if your husband scribbles a few pages of what happened, it's going to be any worse than actually being there and hearing the shots? I'm so sorry I didn't know Sophie was still alive. It never dawned on me to ask. I just assumed she'd been spirited away and locked up in some nunnery, which I suppose she was. I always imagined she'd died years ago." There was a pause before she said, "Do you think I could come to the funeral with you?"

Diana looked at her in surprise. "Of course, I'd be very pleased to take you. Bob and Hilary, what do you think? Are you worried now that I've told you all this?"

"If there *are* any problems, which I doubt, then they will be short-lived," said Hilary. "If the book is ever written it's not going to be a blockbuster, is it? Does anyone ever read those 'True Accounts' or do they just put them on a bookshelf looking erudite? A few people in the village may become hostile, but we've been through worse, haven't we, Bobby?" She said all of that without a single stammer or bluster. Diana came to the conclusion that when something was important, she was focused and determined. When it was social and inconsequential, she stammered.

"We certainly have, old thing." He gave his wife an adoring look. "We certainly have."

Julian stood up too and said, "Before I go, and thank you for a fabulous lunch, it looks to me as if you have been worrying about the wrong thing. It seems that there will be people in the village who don't want this story to be resurrected. They might even be hostile, but it looks as if we'll all cope. You need to worry about your marriage. I think running away is the worst thing you can do." He looked at her directly and took her by the shoulder. "If anyone here has shown compassion and understanding for the whole unhappy and tragic event, it's you. I understand perhaps more than anyone because we've seen it through together. Sophie was very concerned that none of the living participants would have to hear of this and even more adamant that none of her love letters or family documents should be used. Well, we've taken care of that, we've -"

"Julian, I have a terrible confession to make. I have no idea why I did it but I had notarised copies made. I thought at the time, even before I knew Sophie was still alive, that these documents might be important. I don't know, I thought perhaps I'd need to keep part of that history. I have one copy here and the notary has the other. I honestly had forgotten all about them, I can't believe I did it, but I did. I can destroy the copy I have here, that's no problem and the notary won't let the papers go to anyone else."

"Well, no-one can use those papers unless you give permission, which clearly you won't."

Bob and Hilary stood up and made to go. They both thanked Diana for a wonderful lunch and told her that under no circumstances was she to worry about the rest of them. "We're all in this together now, dear. We'll cope. But John is right. You belong here." They both hugged her. Everyone else also made leaving gestures and left.

Diana went upstairs, expecting to see Simon in his study. He wasn't there. He wasn't in the guest bedroom or in the master bedroom. His bags were gone and she realised that he had left. They hadn't heard his car leaving because they were all in the drawing room, which overlooked the back garden. His Range Rover was gone.

She went down to the kitchen in a dream-like state, disbelief prohibiting the enormity of the situation to become reality. Celeste had cleared all the dishes and left the kitchen neat and tidy, with just foil covers on left-over food. She sat down at her desk to call Simon's phone when she pulled open the drawer. She saw immediately that the photocopies had gone.

She sat rigid with shock that he would do such a thing. She dialled his number which went straight to voicemail. "Simon, this is no way to act. You must return those documents, you must. I can't believe you would do such an underhanded thing. Is this now what we've come to? Please call me. Please."

It was dark outside now and she missed her walk. She felt disconnected and disjointed. She was more pleased than she could say about everyone's reaction to everything she had told them. She didn't feel that anyone was anything else but supportive. On the other hand, nothing had happened yet.

Diana's world had changed in a heartbeat, it seemed to her. The situation with Simon was unthinkable such a short time ago, and now? Was she really considering leaving him permanently?

She put the kettle on and absent-mindedly put a tea-bag in a mug and went to the fridge to get the milk. Her phone gave off the text signal. It must be Simon, she thought, he can't just leave like this. She put the kettle down and picked up her phone. The text read: DARLING, *WILL BE THERE IN 2 HOURS.*

OPEN THE WINE AND WARM THE BED

Diana looked at it puzzled. Where could he be that he was two hours away, could he have got that far? Given the way he left, it was a strange way to try to make up the continuous row they'd been having.

Then it hit her.

How could she have been so stupid? The message wasn't meant for her!

Her phone started to ring instantly. It was Simon. "Diana, that text message I -" She disconnected the call. How stupid she had been. Like a brain-storm, the truth finally became clear. 'The student', 'the researcher', 'Chris'.

God, how could she have been so blind? How careful and clever he'd been never to say the word, 'she'. Had he planned this all along? Had her stand against him just made it easy for him to do this? Was this all her fault? And was this really what all those secretive phone calls have been about? Wasn't the trip to Limoges planned all along? She didn't have any more answers but many more questions.

She felt stunned, unable to think. Yet of all the emotions she was feeling, the least of them was surprise. That he'd been capable of infidelity was not in question, he'd done it before, even if she had convinced herself over the years that it hadn't been true infidelity. But at this time of their lives, with the plans they had, the blow was hard and painful. She felt completely defeated by him. He had left her with nothing now. Anger and hurt were looking for equal places in her heart.

Without really thinking what she was doing, she put on her jacket and went out of the kitchen door. She just wanted air, outside air. The day had turned cold and windy, the wind coming from the east bringing the first real hint of winter. It was pouring with rain: insistent, major rain drops, the kind that can soak someone with very few drops. Without any plan or even being really aware of where she was or what she was doing, she walked. The pain was just beginning as realisation set in. How it hurt. It really hurt. Her small deceit had been as nothing compared to the life Simon had been leading. The injustice and spite cut her deeply. The tears were rolling freely down her face, mingling with the cold rain.

She had no real intention of finding the gate into Julian's back garden, she didn't even want to see him really. Or did she? She didn't want to see anyone. But she stopped as she reached the gate, a gate she had never noticed before, since most of her walks went in the other direction, towards the clearing and boat house. She opened the gate and went in.

His garden was in darkness. Her eyes were adjusted to the dark now and the lights from inside the house cast enough brightness onto the terrace for her to see the pool. There was a bench against a raised rock garden where she now sat, feeling drained and forlorn, hurt and helpless. She had no idea how long she sat there, crying quietly. She felt an arm raise her up and walk her to the house.

Without stopping anywhere, Julian took her upstairs and into the bathroom. He sat her on the wicker chair in the corner and ran a hot bath; he still hadn't spoken but carried on preparing the bath. When he judged it ready, he stood her up, took off her coat, carried her bodily, fully-clothed to the bath and laid her in it.

She sat in the fragrant hot water with her arms around her drawn-up knees and wept. Julian took off his shoes and she felt him climb into the bath behind her, also fully clothed. He held her in his arms and between his knees, he just held her until her weeping stopped. She leaned back into his chest and his chin rested on the top of her head. Still not a word had been spoken by either of them. It had been one of the most intimate and kindest gesture anyone had ever made to her.

After a while, he got out of the bath and reached for some towels. He wrapped a couple of towels around his waist and shoulders, and then reached for another pile of large, thick towels. "Here, you need to get out of those clothes. I'll find you something to put on. When you're done, come downstairs and we'll talk." He kissed the top of her head and she smiled at him.

She pulled the plug on the bath and stood up to take off her clothes. When the water had run out, she left her clothes in the bath and stepped out to go to the shower cubicle. She let the hot water run over her head and used Julian's shampoo, which smelled of some sort of spice. As she dried herself, she heard him coming back across the landing. He knocked on the door, and, holding the towel around her, she told him to come in. He handed her a pair of track suit bottoms, and a white T-shirt. "Both of these belong to Josh, he'd be pleased to lend them to an orphan of the storm."

"Is that what I am now? An orphan of the storm? It sounds so much more elegant than an abandoned and cheated wife."

"Are you abandoned? Come down when you're ready and tell me what happened." She came into the kitchen a few minutes later.

"During our never-ending row, he told me he was going to spend a few days in Limoges and he expected me to be gone when he got back, or words to that effect. I'm not sure if that meant he *wanted* me to be gone, but I'd actually left him in no doubt as to what I'd do. I assumed he'd be leaving the next day but after you'd all gone, I found he'd packed a few things, taken his car and left."

"Did he say when he'd be back?"

"Ah. Well. You see, that's when the text message came in."

"Text message?"

"Yes. Let me see, I want to get it right." She'd left her phone in the kitchen when she'd gone out into the garden. "It said 'Darling, will be there in two hours. Open the wine and warm the bed.' I don't think there's much doubt about that, do you? And two seconds later the phone rang. He must have seen that he'd sent it to the wrong person, but I didn't give him a chance to explain. I can't face it tonight. I don't even want to talk to him tomorrow. But I must. You see, he's also taken the file of copies of the letters and documents."

"What? God, are there no depths to which he won't sink? Honestly, Diana, he's a total and utter bastard. I told him in Paris to finish it. I knew he'd -"

"You knew? You knew what was going on? God, Julian, what on earth were you thinking by not telling me?"

"Think about it, Diana. Would you ever be the one to tell someone a thing like that? I told him to finish it. He said he would, or he led me to believe he would. And I wanted to spare you this very thing. Even though he didn't deserve any consideration, I didn't want to tell you because I knew what pain it would cause you."

"Actually, I was in that very situation with a friend once. Her husband was cheating on her and I didn't tell her. When she found out, I justified the fact that I hadn't told her for that very reason. I honestly didn't want to hurt her. Doesn't work though, does it? The hurt is the same whether it's now or whether the affair has gone on even longer because no-one has said anything. I don't know, I'm worn out. I can't think straight. How am I going to get those papers back?"

"Get yourself a lawyer. The French take theft very seriously. The papers are yours, you can prove that, can't you?"

"Yes, because I left a set with the notaire who made the certified copies. He's holding them for me in my name. And of course, I have now a copy of Sophie's will and her letters of authorisation. Do you know, I hate the thought of him and his - what is she? Is she really his researcher? I don't know. Anyway, I hate the thought of the two of them pouring over Klaus's letters. God, Julian, I'm so tired, I really can't think any more. Can I stay here? I don't want to go home."

"Of course you can. But first a light bite and a hot drink."

He made scrambled eggs on toast and tea. She was fatigued beyond being able to cry. He led her upstairs and without even asking, he led her to the master bedroom and opened the duvet for her to get in. He turned out the light on her side and went around to the other side. He took off his trousers and shirt and got in beside her in his underwear. He held out his arm and she snuggled into his shoulder. He made no move to make love to her or even kiss her. Despite her shattered belief in her marriage and her husband, she fell into an exhausted sleep.

Julian lay beside her with her head on his shoulder. He was thinking about how natural it felt to have this woman he adored in his room, in his bed. But her vulnerability was all too obvious and he would not endanger their relationship by trying to move it on to another level. Eventually he slept.

At six o'clock the next morning the telephone rang. "Julian. It's Simon. I can't get hold of Diana. Please don't get involved in this, but I need to know she's alright. She's not answering her mobile or the house phone. I did a really silly thing, I know she'll not forgive me, it's not about that. I just need to know she's alright. We need to talk, you see, and I'm worried."

"She's here."

"What? With you? God, you don't waste any time or was this going on while -"

"STOP RIGHT THERE! Don't even think about saying what you were going to say. Not everyone in this world behaves according to your standards, so don't you dare judge me by your own moral code. I found her outside last night in the storm, soaking wet and heartbroken."

"Oh. Right. Well, tell her to call me."

"No, I'll *ask* her to call you. And don't ring here again."

Julian's anger was barely controlled. Diana had woken during the exchange and reality came flooding back to her. She lay back on the pillow, unwilling to start the day and all the problems that would come with it. "Julian, I can't thank you enough for last night. I don't know what I would have done without you. It means a lot to me. I suppose I'd better go home and start dealing with it all. Would you come over later? About eleven-ish? Give me time to shower and put some ideas in my head as to what I'm going to do."

He saw her to the door and would have let her go with a kiss on the cheek, but she put her arms around his neck and kissed him gently on the mouth. He pulled her to him gently as their first kiss left them both breathless and aroused.

He disentangled her arms gently. "Diana. You're upset and emotional, fragile and exhausted. We should -"

"Yes, I know. You're quite right. Silly thing to do, I suppose." She looked up at him and smiled. "But it was nice, wasn't it?"

"Go home." He slapped her behind and pushed her out of the door.

****

Now she was totally confused. Kissing Julian had definitely not been planned but when it happened, it seemed the most natural thing in the world. But back to reality. All the lights were still on in the house from where she'd just fled the night before. Celeste would be here in an hour and Diana wanted to talk to Simon before she got here. If there was to be a row, she didn't want Celeste to overhear, even if she couldn't understand the words.

Diana went up to her dressing room with her mobile in her hand. She put it on the charger whilst she had a shower and changed. Then she sat in her favourite spot, the chair by the window, and dialled Simon's number.

"Hello, Dee? Thank God, I've been worried"

"Never mind that now. I want you to listen to me for a few minutes. Firstly, *I'm* not leaving – *you* are. I am staying in the house, so you and Miss whatever her name is – is it really Chris? I don't care, I don't really want to know. You and Chris will have to go somewhere else. I'd prefer you weren't in the village but if you're still set on writing this book, I suppose it's inevitable that I will see you around somewhere. But you are not welcome here. I hope that's understood. I know we have a community property agreement, but I'm talking to a lawyer today to see how that's going to work. I paid for the house and you have made no contributions which have been recognisable as such. So

341

I'm going to fight to have any rights you may think you have to part of the property annulled. Secondly, the papers, letters and photographs. I want them returned today by courier, with any copies you may have made. If you do not, I will seek to have an order taken out against you for the return of my property. Theft, I believe it's called. If you are in any doubt that I can prove that they are my property, the notaire who certified the copies has a second set in his keeping, in my name alone. I also have Sophie's will. Do what I ask and you won't hear anything more about it. Fail to return those papers and I will take action against you. The only thing remaining now is where to send all your things."

"Dee, for heaven's sake! When I left I was only going for a few days, I haven't had time to make any plans. I don't even know -"

"Yes. I know. You were going off for a couple of days to frighten me into submission and have whatever-her-name-is for company. Then come back, hoping that I'd give in yet again to what you want to do. Well, you couldn't have got it more wrong if you'd planned it. That text was not only your misfortune, it was the end of your reputation around here. So come back to the village, write your book and see what kind of reception you're going to get. But in the meantime, I am phoning the removal people in about two hours, which is all the time you have to tell me where you want it to go. If you do not tell me in that time, it will go into storage and will be no longer my responsibility. Do you understand?"

There was silence on the end of the phone. "Simon? Are you there?"

"Yes. Yes, I'm here. I can't believe this; this is -"

"Oh, stop! Just stop that! I'm not even going to ask how many times this has gone on in our marriage. I don't care. I just don't care anymore. I take it you're still intent on writing that book? No, don't tell me, I don't care."

"Look, Dee, please give me a few days to sort things out. I'll keep in touch and let you know - um - you know - about where I'll be and what we're going - um - where we go from here."

"This time yesterday Simon, I had a marriage to a man I loved. On the same day, you nearly destroyed me. I don't hate you. I just don't like you and I don't want anything more to do with you. You have nothing more to say about me, my property or how I live my life. You have two hours to tell me where to send your stuff. And I expect those papers here within twenty-four hours or the writ will be issued."

She was trembling from every muscle as she put the phone down. Where on earth had this courage and efficiency come from? It was true, she didn't hate him – but she wanted to hurt him. Hell hath no fury and all that. But by the same token, she felt proud of herself. She got through all of that without quivering or crying. Simon would only have heard strength and determination. Now, of course, she really did have to put some plans into action.

She arranged an appointment with a lawyer for the following morning and she just picked the largest removal company in the book. They would come on Thursday to pack up all of Simon's things. They had storage facilities in Bergerac and she was sure that's where everything would go. Unless Simon was a wonder at organisation, it wouldn't be possible for him to find a place to live in the meantime – but on the other hand, maybe Miss Whatsit had somewhere. She really didn't care.

Diana could hear Celeste clattering about in the kitchen. She'd be furious that Diana hadn't put any of the leftover food in the fridge and that it would all have to be thrown away. She decided to take the most direct approach.

"*Bonjour, Celeste. Comment ça va?*" Celeste gave her a look of frustration.

"*Madame, je -*"

"Celeste, my husband has left me." Diana started the conversation before Celeste could say anything further. Her bombshell left Celeste speechless and open-mouthed. "I am

343

now sorting out the house to have his things ready for Thursday, when the men will come to take them away. Would you help me with that? I'll give you his suitcase to pack his clothes and I will go around the house with stickers to mark the things he may take."

Celeste looked at Diana as if she had just spoken in Chinese. Her tears welled up and she rushed over to Diana and pulled her into a hug. "Oh, Madame, I cannot believe it. Such a wonderful couple - oh, Madame …" This would have continued for some time, but Diana's new-found determination took over.

"I'm fine, Celeste. Really. I'm fine, I just need some help this next week because things are going to be busy. Now, first things first, a big coffee and a chat. That's how we always start the day and that's how we'll continue. *Café, vite!*" She smiled at Celeste, who shook her head and started to make coffee. They sat and talked for half an hour, Celeste all the time looking pityingly at Diana.

Diana gave Celeste a shortened version of everything which had led up to this point, but not missing out anything important. "I have tried to stop him from digging all this up, Celeste, but I have to say, it's partly my fault. I found the papers and I started to investigate. But never did I want to cause any trouble for anyone. I can't believe this has happened. I'm afraid my husband is determined. It can only be a matter of time now before everyone in the village knows what has happened. What do you think?"

"I think people will not be happy. No-one talks about that time any more. Every year on May the eighth, liberation day, we have a little ceremony in the square, at the memorial. But although everyone goes, no-one ever stands around telling stories of that time. Imagine, though! It really wasn't de Lusignac? It wasn't him? Really? The daughter? It's all so sad and unexpected. I've grown up with that history and I know a lot of people will be very shocked. Am I allowed to tell people?"

"Yes, of course. It's no secret now. I'll let everyone know what, if anything, I find at the bank. There will be no stopping this book, I think, although I have tried. I have tried very hard, believe me."

"Believe you? Believe you? You have just sacrificed everything to stop it. Who could *not* believe you? Madame, oh Madame ..." Celeste dissolved into tears and hugged Diana once more. This time, Diana's tears flowed freely and she began the first day of her life independent of anyone else.

****

Simon's absence from the house felt less strange than she had imagined because he had spent so little time there, but nevertheless, once Celeste had left for the day, Diana was totally alone for the first time. Her conversation with Simon played on her mind. She had no idea where all that had come from, she hadn't planned it nor rehearsed it. She realised she was totally unreasonable when it came to giving him two hours to give her an address to send his things. But it made her feel good. And of course, she *would* send everything to storage if he didn't contact her.

Looking back over her life with Simon, she realised that she hadn't been just a willing wife, she'd absorbed his desires and wishes to such a degree that she had become a shadow of him, doing what he wanted when he wanted, agreeing with all his decisions and allowing him total autonomy for the last twenty years. She would have got to the end of *her* life realising that she'd been living *his* life.

She wasn't blaming him for her own failings. Was she just afraid of what he would have said or done if she had exerted her will? Or was she just someone who preferred the easy option? At this point she really didn't know. Probably a bit of both. Had she really been lacking in character all these years? But what had Julian seen in her that first time they met? She sensed even then that his interest in her was more

345

than just social, it was an attraction of more than a physical nature, he had seen something of her basic nature which he liked.

Well, there was no point in even conjecture now. Simon had gone and there would be no forgiveness this time. In truth, she had probably been blind to more than just the one affair, she realised that now. But was she really? Hadn't she had odd suspicions from time to time, if truth were told? Again, she had taken the easy option.

Whatever the future held, it started right here. Now.

She had put the suitcases for Simon's clothes in the master bedroom and Celeste had emptied the drawers of his underwear and sweaters; his shoes took up one whole suitcase. His suits were still hanging in the wardrobes and absently Diana ran her hand across the line of jackets and coats. He was a smart dresser and liked clothes. It was strange to think that some other woman would soon be looking after these same clothes, some of these they had chosen together: his dinner jacket had been made especially for him by the same tailor her father had used.

Well, it was all over now. Everything was finished. Even his chances of writing his book. By allowing the story to circulate, Diana had forewarned the village and ensured that no co-operation would be forthcoming for Simon in his endeavours. Celeste would have been hugging herself with delight at the news which had come her way. She would be the centre of attention in the village, being able to bring the shocking revelations to everyone. The information would be disseminated in a flash. No-one would talk to Simon now, whichever side they had been on. He wouldn't even be able to stay in the village. Notwithstanding his abandonment of her he was on a hiding to nothing. He couldn't possibly understand the close community who have been through such traumatic and life-changing events, events which affected generations through stories handed down. Even now, there were brothers and sisters who didn't speak to each other because of old feuds developed during the war, either between themselves, or between parents and uncles, aunts or even just neighbours.

The phone rang and as she picked it up, she knew it would be Simon.

"Hello."

"Hello, Dee. Can we talk?"

"Yes, of course."

"Look, I'm sorry I didn't get back to you this morning. You actually threw me for six. I can't even now give you a definitive answer about an address because -"

"That's alright. I was a bit impractical. In any case, the movers can move your stuff on Thursday into storage, I'll email you the details and then it'll be up to you to get in touch with them thereafter. You'll just have to trust me to send the things which I should send. Please let's not argue about who gets what. If there's anything you particularly want, let me know and I'll give it some thought. "

"God, Dee, you're in such a hurry. I really was hoping I could come down and see to things myself. Would you not at least let me come for a day or two to talk about everything?"

"I can't believe you would ask to come here. Actually, Simon, I don't want to talk to you about anything. I'm sure we can bring about this breakup without having to go through agonising meetings. I have a lawyer now; I'll email you his address. If you get a lawyer and tell him we don't want an acrimonious divorce, lay down the law a bit, we'll manage this without too much trouble for either of us."

Silence was all she heard and wondered if he was still on the line. Eventually he said, "Dee, I know I'm at fault, I know I've been stupid but - um -"

"Don't! Just don't! I don't want to hear it. I want it over as soon as possible. All of it. But now, here's the thing. Now listen to me because this doesn't have anything to do with

347

us, I mean our break-up. Your intention to write this book is now all over the village."

"Yes, thanks to you! You shouldn't -"

"Simon, shut up and listen. It's for your own good. No-one here will talk to you. No-one will tell you their stories and you can't stay in the village because no-one will have you. As far as our neighbours are concerned you have shown yourself to be a liar and a cheating husband. Betrayal is ugly in whichever form it comes, and the effects are long lasting: these people know all about that. Simon, finish the book you had started, leave these people in peace and go and live your life. I assume you'll want some sort of settlement. I'm not selling either house to pay you off so make sure your demands aren't excessive. I don't want a long legal battle. Are the Sophie papers on their way back?"

"Yes." He sounded deflated and sad. "They'll be with you tomorrow by DHL. Do you want me to let you know where I'll be?"

"No."

"Well - um - the - I suppose - well, goodbye then."

"Well," she thought, "I can still hold it together. There's absolutely no reason now why I can't go to London. I'll wait until after Sophie's funeral and then I'll go."

****

Sophie's funeral was set for Friday afternoon. There would be a Mass at the church in Lourdes, followed by a cremation. The service was to be held at two- thirty in the afternoon and the cremation was set for four o'clock. Early in the morning of the day before, Diana was just finishing marking things for the packers who were due any minute, when the doorbell rang. It wouldn't be Celeste, she had a key. She went down to answer the door, thinking it would be the uniformed men standing outside with packing cartons, but was surprised and pleased to see Henri.

"Henri! Please, come in. How lovely to see you, it's been a little while. I meant to come and see you but I've have so much to deal with."

"Yes, I heard. I'm so sorry. I cannot believe he is gone." Henri gave her a hug. "Tell me, Diana," he pronounced it 'Dee-ana', "tell me everything. I have heard part of the story, Celeste told Jean Luc, Jean Luc told Leila, Leila told her mother who told her sister etc. etc."

Diana took him down to the kitchen and made some coffee. She told him how desperate she was to get Simon to drop the idea of the book, how she felt so guilty for having uncovered the truth, but also understanding how important it was for the matter to be left alone. The last thing she intended was to cause distress in the village she had come to love and looked upon as home. She finished with the truth about Simon's departure.

"Yes, it's true he's been very unhappy with me because I wouldn't help him. I wouldn't let him have access to any of the documents and letters I found and I caused the problem between us. But at the same time, he was having an affair with another woman and had been living with her whilst he was in Paris. Please, tell everyone, Henri, that I believe I have finally convinced him that there is nothing for him here as far as the story is concerned. I can't be sure, but he's not a stupid man."

"Yes, he is. He has left you."

"He was so sure that he'd found a project that would enable him to be taken as a serious writer. It's hard for him to give it up. I don't think secrets are ever a good thing in the long run, it's not as if anything can be gained now and much to lose by opening old wounds."

"Can I ask you, please, could I come to the funeral with you? It's like laying the past to rest. It's a good thing to do."

"Henri, I'd be thrilled. The thing is, we'll probably have to stay overnight, it'll be too late to make the trip back. I'll book us into the Ibis in Lourdes, we don't need anything more grand than that, do we? I'll pick you up at eight-thirty, we'll have time to stop for a drink and lunch on the way down. Véronique and Francine are coming and, of course, so is Julian. Margaret said she'd like to come but she wasn't sure if she could get away, so we'll probably take my car and Julian's."

Simon had sent back the documents as requested and Diana intended to burn them as with the others. Diana was strangely touched when Bob and Hilary, John Porton-Watts and the two Grey sisters also wanted to go to the funeral. It was almost as if it was a gesture of solidarity, at the same time as laying to rest the sad history of the end of the de Lusignacs.

As the last of the removal men locked the van on Simon's boxes, Diana closed the terrace door and watched them leave. She texted him to tell him that his contract would be sent to the temporary address he had given her in Limoges and his things would be in storage in Bergerac. From there on, it was up to him.

To think that this time last week, she was excited at the prospect of Simon's return home. Now he was gone and she was looking at a final separation from everything that had been her life for the last twenty years. Simon obviously hadn't had time yet to decide how much he wanted out of this separation financially, but she was quite sure she'd find out soon.

****

The following morning, the little convoy prepared to leave. Bob and Hilary were taking the Grey sisters, Julian was taking John Porton-Watts and Diana would pick up Henri after collecting Véronique and Francine. They were all on the road by eight-forty; the journey was unrushed and pleasant. A weak sunshine had chased away early morning drizzle and cloud, but it was cold. A stop for coffee and a toilet break at the half-way point and they were on their way again.

On the drive down, Henri told her that the gossip and discussion hadn't stopped since Celeste brought her famous news. Simon would indeed have had a very difficult time; the old tensions between families and old scores were set aside and everyone was joined in solidarity against *l'anglais* who wanted to drag all their long-held personal secrets into the open to make a lot of money for himself and leave them all open to criticism and derision.

Strangely enough, Diana, who had been responsible for uncovering the entire story, was held in great esteem. Her apparent heroic deed of giving up her marriage rather than let her husband destroy good reputations had turned her into some sort of heroine. The village would have been devastated if she had left and they were all prepared to help her with anything she thought she might need.

Diana felt uncomfortable. She certainly didn't belong on a pedestal and all she wanted now was a quiet life. But hopefully, with Simon out of the way, things would settle down to a peaceful routine and all of this would be forgotten in time.

Lourdes in the winter was a strange place. Nearly every shop in the streets leading down to the famous grotto sold religious trinkets; rosaries, bottles for Lourdes water in the shape of the Virgin Mary – incongruously with the crown on her head, which unscrewed to open the bottle in order to fill it with Lourdes water. But more strange was that nearly every shop was closed for the season. Only one or two were open and Diana found the marriage between religion and commercialism in this place to be a bizarre, if not unhappy, union.

The church where the funeral Mass was to be said was in the middle of town. The car park was not far and at this time of year they had no difficulty finding a place. They had taken longer than intended at their coffee stop so there was no time for lunch. The matron from the hospice met them at the door. After Diana had made the introductions, the matron told them that it was not necessary for them to go to the crematorium. The service there would simply be a blessing since the official funeral would be here in the church. Also, it wasn't possible to tie up a time for the mass with a time at the crematorium. Diana wasn't really sorry. She disliked the whole crematorium scenario, the opening of the doors and the coffin sliding away and all that. Grim. No, a lovely church service and time to reflect, that was far more dignified.

The church itself had the most amazing stained glass windows in all shades of blue. They were modern and totally untraditional, but absolutely exquisite. The organ was playing soft, gentle music, nothing funereal, just a reflective background, a tuneful movement of air: she thought she recognised *In Paradisum*, a wonderfully evocative piece.

"Would anyone like to say a few words?" asked the matron.

"Yes. I would." It was Henri who had spoken. Diana turned to look at him, surprised but pleased. It had never occurred to her that there would be a eulogy of any kind.

"Then the priest will give you the signal." Matron smiled at him.

"Matron, could I ask. What is your name? I keep calling you Matron, but you've been so good to Sophie, I mean of course Sister Marie Agnes, I feel as if we're friends. Do you mind?"

"Of course I don't mind; my name is Juliette. Juliette Costeau. And you are Diana. Sister Marie Agnes spoke of you so much in those days since she met you. You brought her joy, you know."

Diana smiled as they started to file into the church. They had been seated for perhaps fifteen minutes when the hearse arrived. Diana was so pleased to see the coffin being carried on the shoulders of the pall-bearers. She hated the gurney/trolley thing which so many funeral directors seemed to use these days. Her father had been carried shoulder-high and it seemed such a beautifully dignified way to leave this world. Diana was lost in her own thoughts for the most part of the service. Then Henri stood up to speak.

"Good morning. I am here from the people of Saint-Sulpice-de-Lauzac to bid farewell to Sophie de Lusignac. A child of our village and like so many, one who bore the scars of war. Daughter of one of the bravest men, the last and truest son of the de Lusignacs. What father do any of us know who would do as much for a beloved daughter? As we lay his daughter to rest, we ask his forgiveness as we now let her take her leave with *our* forgiveness." He made the sign of the cross with tears rolling down his cheeks. He turned and said, "Diana, will you say a word?"

Diana stood up. "I have a quotation from Longfellow. I'm afraid I can't translate it into French, the words at least. I can translate the meaning, but Henri has already expressed it so movingly. The quote is this:

For 'tis sweet to stammer one letter
Of the Eternal's language – on earth it is called
Forgiveness.

It comes from *The Children of the Lord's Supper*. Sophie would be enormously grateful and sublimely happy to have heard the sentiments expressed today. Whatever black guilt I have felt for my part in opening this wound has today been laid to rest with Sophie. One more quote, one of my father's favourites by Young from Night Thoughts, seems appropriate now:

Hope, of all passions

Most befriends us here.

Diana sat down and reached into her bag for a tissues. Julian squeezed her arm. The Mass concluded and they stood as the coffin was borne back to the hearse.

As they gathered outside, they were deciding whether to go to the hotel immediately or to wander around town for a while. The main shopping street, away from the streets with the religious shops, was bustling with late afternoon shoppers. Everything was there, the greengrocer, butcher, shoe shop, chocolaterie, pâtisserie and even a shop selling lace. Everyone seemed rather subdued but restless. Finally Véronique said, "Listen everyone. I don't know about you, but if anyone else is game to just get in the car and drive home, I wouldn't object. This is a dreary town, not to put too fine a point on it. I'm sorry but there it is. If we go home, we'll spend a few hours in the car and we'll be sleeping in our own beds. Does anyone else think this is a good idea?"

The chorus of approval was unanimous. The mood cheered considerably on the walk back to the cars. They set off in much higher spirits, looking forward to getting back to their warm houses and the comforts of home.

On the way back, Henri asked Diana what she intended to do now. "Well, I'm not leaving, if that's what you mean. Henri, I love this place. France has always been a second home to me and I adore the house. I don't feel any of its sad past, I just feel a warm, loving home and I'd hate to leave. What the future holds I have no idea. I imagine I have a bit of a battle with my husband coming up, but so far he's given me no indication of what he intends to do. At the moment, guilt is stopping him from demanding too much, but that will change. I've seen it with other friends. But I'll just take each day as it comes."

"Good. I'm glad."

"For the immediate future, I'll go to London sometime next week and visit the bank. I'll probably try to meet my husband somewhere to start discussions about our divorce. Strange, that's the first time I've used the word." She fell silent for a moment and Henri said nothing. "Then I'll pop back here and pick up Sophie's ashes and scatter them in the clearing where we think her father's ashes are. Then I'll start a new phase of my life. Alone."

Véronique had looked to be asleep but she now piped up, "Oh, I don't think you'll be alone for too long." She chuckled.

It was just after midnight when she dropped Henri off at his hotel. He leaned across and kissed Diana on both cheeks. "You know, healing is a wonderful thing and I do believe it started today. Thank you." Not knowing what to say, Diana just smiled.

She dropped Véronique and Francine off at their house, saying, "You know, one of the best ideas I have ever heard was to come home this evening. You're brilliant!"

She wasn't surprised to see Julian standing at the glass kitchen door when she pulled up. "You'll have the neighbours talking. Here I am, a recently abandoned woman, receiving gentlemen callers after midnight. I'm shameless."

"Don't get your hopes up girl! I was just checking that you're alright before going to my bed. Why is it that everything with you has to be the middle of the night? Go on, I'll see you in, you can give me a quick drink, then I'm off."

They sat in the kitchen over an Irish coffee for an hour, until she felt so tired that she thought she could sleep well and long. At the door, he again took her in his arms and she didn't resist. They kissed as long-term lovers kiss, with deep emotion and familiarity. She loved the feel of his arms around her. At that point, she had no doubt that one day soon, they would make love. But not yet. She didn't feel as if she were free – not from the legal point of view, that didn't matter at all any more, but from her own spiritual and moral sense. But that would change soon.

Over the next few days, Diana and Simon talked several times. Simon had considered more than once asking if he could come back to her, remorse had set in and the finality of their situation was more than could bear at times. Chris wasn't the person he would have left Diana for: it wasn't meant to happen like that. Diana was, well, Diana was his rock. That was it. She was his rock. In every way.

Chris had been a clever, funny, sexy companion. If she was less sophisticated and well-mannered than Diana, it didn't really matter. It was a fling. She had helped him enormously with the boring search of records offices and libraries, a job he had always detested, which was why his first book wasn't as good as it could have been. She had been incredible in bed, adventurous and exhausting but the quiet, reflective, tender after-sex wasn't there. It was all slightly hyper and superficial. And now he had been so incredibly stupid and careless and it was going to cost him dear.

Diana had been dreadfully hurt and shocked at his behaviour. He couldn't believe it himself. At times, over the years, he'd wanted to scream at her for her ready compliance with everything, absolutely everything. His friends thought it would be wonderful never to have slanging matches and fights over things which would be brought up again and again like re-used ammunition year after year. But occasionally Simon wanted a bit of spark. A bit of fencing, something to show a bit of - well, life. She never argued, never demanded.

His friends were especially envious of her non-suspicious nature. The trips away with his friends that were, in reality, opportunities to have unbelievably good sex with women who had no intention of becoming seriously involved – well, with the odd exception, and then things got tricky – and he'd return to Diana's loving arms with the satisfaction of knowing that other women *did* have a spark and *did* make demands, of the sexual kind of course.

Actually, he'd been bored for years. After his book was published, the critics were not kind. The book had sold quite well but he'd never received the acclaim that writers of best-sellers get. Recognition. Admiration of fellow authors. Being taken seriously as a literary figure. And then this unbelievable opportunity had dropped into his lap and it was all Diana's doing. She had uncovered a story so absolutely incredible and it would have been the opportunity of a lifetime. Well, that was all over now. And Diana had seen to that as well.

His immediate problem was to decide what to do in the immediate future. Trying to get back with Diana was really a non-starter if he was honest with himself. He'd vaguely tested the waters but she had accepted that he'd gone and she had moved on quickly. Very quickly. Amazingly quickly. So, decisions. And he couldn't make any. He was aware that he was floundering, but it was early days yet. First thing was to have a meeting with her. Chris was over the moon, she thought now that Simon and she were going to live somewhere together, make a life together.

But in reality, Chris didn't feature in any of his plans, and he'd have to tell her very quickly before she became too entrenched in his life and work. For the moment, her little flat in Limoges was a base from which he could plan – but he'd have to be quick. In January, Chris was going back to the UK to university to carry on with her post-graduate work, he was never quite sure what she was doing, he'd never asked for details. Frankly, he wasn't particularly interested in her ambitions for her career.

Diana had said she was going to London on Thursday. He'd fly over and meet her, she'd let him know where. Obviously, staying in the same hotel would be a good idea but he wasn't even sure if he should do that. He didn't want to put a foot wrong in these next few weeks. Financially, she was going to have to make some settlement on him. The London house was hers outright and he was sure she wouldn't give it to him. Actually, even if she did, he wasn't sure that he could afford a Holland Park Avenue house and its upkeep. The house in France was also hers but she had put his name on some sort of community property deal, so he supposed she could buy him out of that.

Ideally, he'd have liked to go back to the village. But of course, by now, everyone there knew he'd left her. And there was bloody Julian, filling her with stories of finding him in Paris with Chris. Damn him. Such a short time ago, Simon was leaving Paris to go home to Diana. And it had all gone so horribly wrong. He had lost his temper and said unforgivable things. But, God, she was stubborn over this thing. His literary agent had been very excited at the outline he'd given him, promised he'd find a good advance when he'd seen a few outlines and the full publicity works to follow when the book was completed. Diana hadn't any idea how crushed he was, how unbelievably desperate he was for this story. If she did, she didn't care.

Now he had nothing except the outline of the original book he had started and didn't like. He'd have to make something of it now, but the thought of the opportunity missed made him boil with envy and anger. By now of course, even the whole village will have been warned. She'd made his position impossible and that was what she intended, of course.

Simon had given serious thought to writing the story as a novel, but even that was impossible; he needed much more of the facts from the people involved, at least people in the village with knowledge of what had gone on. Of course, all of that was now impossible too.

If truth were told, many authors would have been able to write a novel with the information he already had. Simon's imagination had its limits.

But if he had the choice, would he rather go back to Diana and face all the others than look at the future without her? They'd been happy enough, even if he had found it all rather tedious at times. They'd certainly never had the problems that some of their friends had had. Diana had worked at that little translation company, thinking she was doing something incredibly valuable – manuals, for heavens' sake, or technical papers which no-one except a few professors would ever read. What a waste.

Their respective wealth positions were in no way equal though. She had inherited a lot of money. He had inherited his parents' little house in Weybridge, a rich enough area but their pre-war bungalow wasn't quite in the location of the large, detached houses with two-acre gardens. He had made quite a lot of money selling it to a builder who pulled it down and built a one and a half million pound property in its place, as he had with the adjoining three properties.

Simon always felt that whatever he aspired to, he was never quite there. Almost, but not quite. And then the very thing which would lift him from being a mediocre writer to the realms of serious authors was stopped in its tracks. Thanks to Diana. Why couldn't she have just followed her characteristic formula of agreeing with and supporting his plans? Where had this fight and determination come from? And the way she handled his leaving had been totally out of character.

The threat to leave for a few days was to scare her into thinking she had seriously upset him. And of course, she had. If things had followed their usual course, she would have phoned him a few hours later and apologised, and he would have returned home having her agreement to whatever it was he was planning this time.

And then he had screwed up the business of the text message. He'd been driving and scrolled through his contacts to find 'Ingram' which was how Chris was filed, it was her surname. Unfortunately, he'd pressed ICE just above, ICE being his contact in his phone for Diana, his 'In Case of Emergency' number. He'd always been so careful before with anyone else that he double-checked the contact before pressing the 'Send' button. But he'd been driving, he was angry and he'd been careless. His heart thumped hard in his chest when he'd realised what he'd done and phoned Diana immediately to try to - what? Explain? Even he didn't know what he was going to say but somehow he'd have talked himself out of it. But she'd understood only too clearly and had hung up the phone.

The rest, as they say, is history, he thought. And now he was history. The next time he saw Diana would be to start talking about divorce. In such a short time Diana had found balls, he'd give her that. Such cold, calculating instructions coming down the phone from Diana, the woman whose middle name could have been 'Compliant'. He'd prodded a sleeping tiger, evidently.

Well, he'd have to have a plan in mind by Thursday. If he wanted to come out of this with anything like enough money to last for a while, he'd have to meet her as a contrite wrong-doer but already on the road to redemption. For a start, he'd have to get rid of Chris. Quickly. He had about a hundred thousand in the bank, but it wouldn't last long if he had to go back to the UK and find somewhere in London to live. So, he'd leave Chris and go to Brittany. It was winter, no tourists, he should be able to find somewhere to rent which wasn't too expensive. London was out of the question at the moment. His money wouldn't go very far and divorce might take a while.

Or he could go back to the UK and move to somewhere like Devon. Again: winter, no tourists, and outside London, rental property should be cheaper. The UK would be the better option in a way, there would be enough distance from Chris in case she started to make a fuss, and he wouldn't have a language problem. His French was passable and he'd always had Diana around, but living on his own there was a different matter.

Right. Decision made. Return to the UK. Tomorrow. He'd find a place to rent and get his stuff out of storage. Diana had put everything in boxes, including all the wretched notes and research papers for this damned original book he'd better write. When he'd proposed the sequel to Edwards he'd been sure he could probably get it published, since the first one sold quite well. But this new idea Simon had presented to him was brilliant. He'd been furious when Simon had explained why he couldn't now write it.

Chris wasn't going to take it well. In fact, Simon imagined she'd make a great deal of trouble. So another plan was needed. Confrontation with her wasn't pleasant. She had the violence in her that the young all seemed to have these days. Rows blew up very easily over mundane things and ended with silences, pouts and sulks, something he definitely wasn't used to. His plan was really mean and selfish, he knew that. But it was for the best.

"Chris, darling, I need you to do something for me. It's going to mean another trip to Paris, I'm afraid, but I can't go. I've got to see a lawyer about this meeting with Diana at the end of the week. Jerome had found someone for us to interview, an old nurse who was at the American Hospital at the end of the war. She'll see you tomorrow. Can you be an angel and cover it for me? I've really so much on my mind, my head's all over the place at the moment. I've got to carry on with the original book now, I've no choice. Would you do that for me?"

"Yes, but does it have to be tomorrow? She's not going anywhere, is she, this nurse?"

"God, Chris, I don't know! That's what he told me and that's what I agreed to. If you don't want to go, just say so. But it would help me enormously if you would, and if you would do it in good grace."

"Oh, alright. But I can't get back the same day. I'll have to stay in a hotel since we can't use Julian's flat any more."

"That's fine. Stay at the Holiday Inn, it's quite close."

"I'll catch a train at about eight in the morning then."

"Thank you, darling. It's a great help, you have no idea."

"This meeting with Diana. Is it going to be a divorce meeting or are you hoping for a reconciliation?" Her tone was getting strident.

"Reconciliation? There's no chance of that. Would you, in her shoes?"

"Does that mean you wish she would?" Again, strident and spoiling for a fight, which he wanted to avoid at all costs in case she refused to go tomorrow.

"Chris, it's over. I keep telling you. Now let me do some stuff and we'll go out for dinner tonight. I'm just popping out for a newspaper."

He went down the stairs to the main street. The flat was a pleasant enough little one-bedroomed place above a florist's shop, it was light and had a balcony overlooking the main street. Busy and noisy, but the young didn't seem to mind that sort of thing. He missed the elegance and quiet of Julian's flat and the beautiful home that Diana had created at *La Chênaie*. It was important that he speak to Jerome, a private investigator that Simon used from time to time to seek out people who were living in the area during the period when his book was set.

"*Allo, oui?*"

"Jerome, it's Simon."

"*Bonjour, Simon, comment ça va?*"

"Fine, Jerome thanks, just fine. Listen. I have a huge favour to ask you. Huge. I'm in a really difficult spot. I need to explain why I'm going to ask this favour of you. I'd really, really appreciate your help with this. The thing is, my marriage is threatened and it's all my fault. I've been stupid with -"

"Ah, with the little researcher, *n'est-ce pas*? I could see that coming."

362

"Jerome, you've done a lot to help, finding people and documents for us. And I intend to go on using your company. I hope to be working on something even bigger. But I have a problem. I need Chris out of the way tomorrow while I organise something and I'm sending her to Paris. Can you find someone for her to interview? I know it's asking a lot but I'm really doing what I can to rectify a stupid mistake."

"Well, it's short notice and we've found nearly everyone who could possibly have been any use to you, but I'll work on something. Tell her to come to the office and we'll work something out."

"I can't thank you enough. You've been a real friend. I'll email an address where you can send the bill."

"*De rien.* Good luck, my friend."

Hugely relieved, Simon went back to the flat. "Where's the paper?" Chris asked the moment he walked in the door.

"Oh, it was two days old, I decided not to buy it. I've heard the news on television anyway."

"Strange. I thought you could get newspapers just a day old in Paris now. Are you alright? You seem very edgy. Don't worry about this thing with Diana, people get divorced all the time." She walked off to the bedroom.

This thing? This thing? Whatever goes on in the minds of young people? Twenty years of marriage down the drain and she called it 'this thing'? But he *was* on edge. Plans once made should go into action immediately. Now that he'd prepared to leave tomorrow he wanted it over and done with. But he had to be careful, Chris was no-one's fool and if she at all suspected that she was being set up, he'd have real trouble on his hands. He'd take her to the station and put her on the train. He'd be the poor wretch trying to do the best by her but beset with problems at the moment which he was trying to sort out.

Chris wanted to make love in the evening before going out to eat. In his own mind, he thought he'd be noble and not

363

expect her to have sex, considering he was planning on leaving her in the morning. But she wanted to. Refusing might have caused more questions. So they had sex, really good sex.

They ate at their favourite little Italian restaurant, about a ten-minute walk from the flat. Simon knew he was withdrawn and unresponsive, but couldn't help it. God, he wanted to get rid of her now. Her childish and selfish behaviour was getting on his nerves and he was holding it together with difficulty. This time tomorrow he'd be in the UK and could breathe without her questioning everything.

When they arrived back at the flat, he took his book and went to the sofa, but Chris had other ideas. She sat beside him and stroked his hair. "What's wrong? You've been odd all evening."

"Chris, has it ever occurred to you that breaking up a twenty-year marriage comes with a few problems? It's the problems I'm trying to sort out in my head before I see that lawyer. Now, please, go to bed and I'll be in shortly – I just need to unwind a bit."

"Then come with me, I know just how to get you to unwind!"

"Chris! Please! Don't!" He pushed her hand away from his groin. She got up and left the room angrily, slamming the door to the bedroom. He had to make up with her, he couldn't afford now to have her change her mind about going to Paris.

His nerves were getting the better of him. He took a deep breath to calm himself and went after her. He cajoled, apologised, stroked, kissed and touched her. Normally, touching her for a few minutes would leave him ready to have sex, he was virile enough and could last long enough to satisfy a young girl who loved sex. But right now, he had to let his fingers stroke and probe her. At that point she was beyond caring whether or not he was fully involved, she writhed and arched as he continued to help her to finish.

He slept badly and rose at five am. He wanted to be sure that she'd catch the seven-forty-five train. He showered noisily and made coffee. At six am he went to the bakery on the corner and bought fresh croissants which he brought to her in bed, with steaming black coffee.

They left the house in plenty of time, and he held her hand as they walked down the platform to the waiting train. Relief at never having to see her again made him expansive and loving. As the train left the station, he positively ran to the taxi stand. He hadn't brought his car for fear of losing his parking place. He wanted to literally load up and get gone very quickly. Most of his clothes had gone into the Bergerac storage facility, so he needed to get them out as soon as possible, but first things first. Get out of here.

He was ready in an hour. Then he sat down to write the letter which he hoped would settle things once and for all. Leave her some money? He supposed he should. After all, he'd been living with her, so he owed her something. She had a little money from her parents, but he'd helped with household bills. Of course, at Julian's they'd just had to pay for food and drinks.

He'd been thinking about the letter all night. It all had to be his fault, he had to appeal to whatever it was she loved about him. But apart from sex and convenience, he really didn't know. Fine. Talk about how much he loved his wife, how he really wanted to try to make a go of it with her again, how he was so hoping that they could keep their love alive, too much in love to let this chance go by, etc., etc., etc.

He was quite proud of it in the end. He even felt tears running down his cheeks as he was imagining Chris's heartbroken little face, her big eyes spilling over with tears. In the end he left her a cheque for £2,500 which he thought was quite generous, but was smart enough not to mention it in the letter.

He felt positively light-hearted as he got into his car. He'd spend a few days in London. Diana would be staying at the Savoy, so he thought he'd treat himself and with a bit of luck, Diana would foot the bill. After all, what could be more natural than two people with so much to talk about staying in the same hotel. He'd sort out where he was going to live later. But for now, he put the car in gear and drove towards the north.

****

Diana took a taxi from the airport. It was wet and windy, a really grey day. She looked out at the dismal scene and felt oddly out of place. This town where she had lived for most of her life now seemed alien. So much had happened since she was here last. Everything seemed disjointed, and her previous life felt as if it had belonged to someone else. She was a different person, a different woman, a different wife.

There was a message for her at the hotel. Simon was already here and would like her to phone him in his room: he'd wait for her call. She wasn't sure if she wanted to do this today, this evening. She'd thought she might just have a bath and order room service. She had an appointment with the bank in the morning and really wanted to go back to France over the weekend. But thinking it over, she thought at least the first meeting ought to be today.

She asked to be put through to his room. He answered the phone very quickly, as if he knew she'd just arrived. "Hello?"

"Hello, Simon, it's Diana. Do you want to come up for a cup of tea? I don't really want to talk in the lounge or bar." She didn't want to go to his room either, she wanted the advantage of being on 'home' territory. All of this was still so new to her, having to be strong, determined and straight-talking.

"Fine, I'll come up." She gave him the room number and went over to the window. Rain was still streaking down the windows and she hated the outlook. France had been basking in winter sun, glinting on early morning frost when she had left. The airport in Bergerac smelled of coffee and other lovely French food smells. Heathrow just smelled of aviation fuel and burger fat.

She heard his knock and walked to the door. To avoid any suggestion that she might accept a kiss, she walked back into the room, leaving Simon to close the door.

"Hello, Dee."

"Hello. Have a seat. I'll order tea. Do you want anything else? I've just arrived so I'm longing for a cup of tea. But you can have what you want."

"No. Tea is fine, thank you."

"Well, I'm finding this rather strange, so we'll probably do well if we avoid any personal remarks and such, we need stick to the things we need to talk about. So, shall I go first and we'll take it from there? I'd like it very much if we don't talk about how we got here and who did what to whom. Just let's be practical. So, do you have a lawyer?"

"Actually, not yet. I arrived in the UK yesterday and I'm not going back. I haven't decided where to go, but probably Devon. I'll rent somewhere to stay while I write the book – the original book, that is. That's as far as I got. I thought we might use the same lawyer, I don't know how practical that is, but I don't think we're going to find too many things to argue about. I'm totally at fault. I'm just hoping that we -"

"Please! Don't say that you hope we can stay friends. I'm not vindictive, Simon, but we need to settle matters so we can go our own ways. What it's going to come down to is this – how much do you want?"

"What? God, Diana, stop this! I know I've done a really stupid thing, I'm not making any excuses or asking for forgiveness, but is this what we've come to? I *know* I can't write the book now, OK? But I can't bear this - this - this awful atmosphere between us."

"If it's not about money, Simon, then what are we meeting for? If you don't want any money, then we'll set the divorce in motion and sign the papers. At least be honest with me now, if you couldn't be before. So, do you want any money? If you do, how much?"

"How much? Dee, I'm not - oh God, I can't talk to you like this. What's happened to you? Surely things are not going to end like this? I don't blame you for being angry but have you come to hate me so quickly?"

"Things will be easier all round if you just name a figure. I don't want to go over what has brought us here, your affair, or any others too. Or anything else. If we're not going to talk about this, then we'll have to deal through lawyers. What did you imagine, we'd sit down and chat like old friends about how to bring about an end to this? So, I ask you again, how much do you want? I'll have the lawyer draw up the papers and we're done."

Simon looked at her. She looked wonderful. She was wearing pale grey trousers, a grey silk shirt and a cashmere long cardigan. She had a pink silk scarf around her neck, which softened the grey and gave her face a slight pink tinge. He noticed she had taken off her engagement ring and her wedding ring. She wore her mother's heavy gold bracelet, a gold necklace and gold shell earrings. But it was her self-assuredness which gave her the arresting look of a woman totally in charge of her destiny.

"Would you give me the London house? I only mention it as a starting point. It's not a hard and fast demand."

"Good. Because the answer is no."

"Dee, I can't talk to you like this. I hate to even say this but can you make a suggestion?"

"Yes. My suggestion would be that you behave well and walk away. With nothing. My disappointment is heightened by my certainty that you wouldn't do that. It's less of a woman scorned, Simon, it's a woman bitterly hurt and broken-hearted. So, if I sound cruel, then you just have to deal with it, it certainly didn't come from anything anyone *else* has done to me. So, clearly you expect something. I won't spend hours quibbling and haggling. I am prepared to give you £500,000 to divorce and with no come-backs. We each keep our counsel about how we got here. Yes, or no?"

"Well, the two houses are worth -"

"Yes or no? If it's no, you leave this room now and wait for my lawyer to contact you – or your lawyer if you let me know who it will be." Diana got up to open the door for the tea trolley. She poured tea and put a cup on the table beside him. She didn't offer the sandwiches or cake.

Simon sat dumbfounded and silent. Tears welled up and his throat started to throb. He tried to do quick calculations, was this her final offer? Could he get her to raise her offer? One try. "Well, Dee, if you could ra -"

"Then the answer is no? Fine. You know who my solicitor is. Let him know where you'll be or who you'll be using."

"Fine! Fine! OK! Fine! Could you just stop talking to me like this, Dee? I know I've hurt you. But this is dreadful. I didn't stop loving you even though I've done something stupid. But you sound as if you hate me."

"The lawyer will send you a cheque as soon as you give him an address. And I don't hate you. I don't have it in me to hate anyone. I thought you knew me better than that. Evidently not. I just want to be free of you. I don't like you. I don't like what you've made of our lives."

"Dee, please don't send me away like this. Are we ever going to see each other again? I keep saying, I know I've been stupid. It didn't *mean* anything. It really didn't."

"It did to me. It meant the end of my marriage. How can you do something like this and say it doesn't mean anything? Why is it that men think they can say it didn't mean anything and expect everything to be fine?"

"Don't tell me that all the happy times are wiped away for one stupid error. We've had an incredible marriage."

"Yes, it's true. You have made me very happy. But isn't that what married people are supposed to do? Trust, loyalty, fidelity and love. All those things I gave you willingly. How many of those did you give me? Trust? Because you knew you could trust me, you didn't have to earn it, I gave it to you. Loyalty? Just after your book was published, you went off for days on end on book signing trips. One trip wasn't, though, was it? You went and had a vasectomy without even talking to me." He stared at her absolutely aghast.

"Dee, please -"

"You never even asked me if I wanted children. I found the bill from the clinic. You even filed it in the family medical file, so sure were you that even if I knew, I wouldn't ever question you about it. And you were right. Then. I was so determined that my marriage was going to be based on all the old values, which actually meant that most of the time, you had absolutely no idea what I wanted, what I thought or what I felt. Fidelity? Well, there's nothing much to say about that is there? Love? Yes, I think you did love me. I think you probably still do, but without the rest, it's not worth a thing, I know that now."

He was crying openly now and Diana felt tears on her face too. But however much he felt humiliated and hurt, it didn't touch her any more.

"You think I'm being cruel and spiteful. It's your wages, Simon. It's the harvest of your betrayal. You've earned it. And I'm the pay-master – in more ways than one."

She felt spent. She had no more feelings of anything at the moment. She just wanted this to be over. She stood up, went over to Simon and kissed the top of his head. "Goodbye, Simon. Go and do something useful and constructive. Don't waste the future being angry over the past. I shan't." She went over to the door and opened it. He got up slowly from the chair and went past her to the door.

He turned to speak one more time, but the door was already slowly closing.

****

Diana leaned against the closed door. She was shaking and tears were streaming now, her nose was running and she felt sobs wanting to burst out of her. She had not believed how fortunate she was when they first met and he seemed so devoted. She wasn't glamorous, in fact she felt she was a little old-fashioned. But there he was. Handsome, witty and funny – and in love with her. It had felt so right, as if they were born to meet. He used to tell her she was the only woman in the world he ever wanted to be with, and she had believed him utterly.

What he had done to her unleashed her strong sense of injustice, apart from having shattered her love for him. What power one human had over the happiness of another. But that same power could bring about another's downfall. The night she had seen that wretched text message, it was if all the pieces of her life didn't quite meet, everything was off kilter with everything else. Sharp, jagged edges. And pain. A lot of pain. And knowing that nothing would ever be the same.

She realised that he lost respect for her when she took him back the first time. Perhaps respect was the wrong word. She had actually given him a licence for liberty – liberty to regard his marriage vows as elastic. She was under no illusions now, though. She didn't even want to try to think of how many times he had put their marriage on the line.

She ran a bath and while it was running, she telephoned the Pelling Hancock Bank. She was told that she was expected at ten in the morning and she would be met by Mr. Cooper and Mr. Bradley. She was not given any job titles, but assumed they were fairly senior members of the bank.

She sank into the bath and felt the strain slipping away. It was over now. All over. And now she had to do what she had advised Simon to do. She had to do something constructive and useful. A part of her was excited, but she still had a long way to go before the divorce was final and Simon was out of her system for good.

She rang room service and ordered a club sandwich, salad and a bottle of her favourite Saint-Estèphe. She was just drying her hair when the phone rang.

"Hello?" she was half expecting it to be Simon. She had hoped he would leave tomorrow, but she had no idea if he'd be around the hotel or not.

"Diana. Hello. How are you doing?"

"Julian. How lovely. I'm really pleased you rang. I was going to ring you earlier, but I'm sure you've had enough of my crying on your shoulder."

"Nonsense. You do it so well."

"Brute!"

"Yes, I know. Now tell me."

"It was pretty grim. I was determined not to do one of those awful scenes, reliving every minute of it. But I think you'd have been proud of me. Perhaps proud is the wrong word: I don't know that I'm proud of myself. I was very hard and cruel."

"Good."

"No. Really. I wasn't very nice. He's very upset."

"Good."

"Have you no heart?" she asked, laughing.

"Yes, I do. And unlike Simon, mine's in the right place."

"Can we not talk about him anymore?"

"Fine. When are you coming back? I'll come to the airport to pick you up."

"That would be lovely. I miss being there so much. London is grey, wet and horrid and I can't imagine that I

372

used to be so happy here. I'm going to the bank tomorrow morning. Then I'm seeing my lawyer in the afternoon. I may stay on here on Saturday to do some shopping and then come home on Sunday."

"Forget the shopping and come home."

"Do you know, I think I just might. Alright, let's plan for Saturday. I'll get the mid-morning flight to Bergerac. Actually, that's a brilliant idea. I don't want to be here anymore."

"Lovely. I'll meet you. One piece of news. Jim Wilson and Amanda are not coming back. Apparently their daughters didn't settle well at all at boarding school. The youngest one is only seven, poor little thing hates it. So, they'll probably put their house up for sale and you'll have new next-door neighbours."

"Well, so far I couldn't be luckier with my neighbours, so let's hope my luck lasts!"

****

The following morning Diana woke early: she hadn't slept very well but didn't feel exhausted. As she washed her hair in the shower, she wondered if she should treat herself to a haircut. She hadn't had short hair in years because Simon had liked it long. If the hairdresser could take her early, she might have time before the bank meeting. The bank was fifteen minutes' walk away, which was why she'd chosen this particular hotel. But they couldn't take her, so her decision was made for her, long hair it was.

After she had eaten a room-service breakfast, she dressed in a camel cashmere sweater, with a matching skirt. She wore brown knee-length riding boots and put her favourite gold and royal blue Hermes scarf around her neck. With her hair up in a chignon, she added small drop earrings, and her gold pebble necklace. As she looked in the mirror, she felt frumpy. Anyone looking at her would see elegance and good grooming, but she felt old-fashioned and matronly. Well, it would have to do. She took her camel coat and went out.

On her way through the lobby, she saw Simon at the desk, checking out. If he saw her at all, he didn't acknowledge her and she went through the main door out into the Strand.

When she arrived at the bank's address, apart from a brass plaque outside, there was little to indicate that behind the huge doors, there was a bank in full operation. Clearly it wasn't a bank where one took cheques to be cashed to buy the week's groceries, none of the usual trappings were evident. She rang the bell and the door was opened almost immediately by a very well-turned out woman of the late fifties. Iron-grey hair was as neatly pinned up as her own, and the navy dress fitted her petite figure perfectly. "Good morning, Mrs. Lewis. I'm Patricia Noble, I'll take you up."

The lobby where they waited for the lift had no natural light, but was cleverly lit by up-lighters giving a soft peach, warm look to the surprisingly small area. Two pieces of art work were on the wall opposite the lift doors, absolutely exquisite stylised Arabic calligraphy in gold ink, the most beautiful she had seen. When the lift doors opened, the reception area was again lit softly, but there was panelling of some light wood all around, and a matching reception desk, manned by another, older woman dressed like Mrs. Noble. The walls were also furnished with examples of the wonderful calligraphy she had seen downstairs and she couldn't resist taking a closer look. Two men were walking down the carpeted and panelled corridor to meet her.

"Mrs. Lewis. Good morning, I'm Bartholomew Cooper and this is Timothy Bradley." They both extended their hands, which she shook in turn.

"Good morning. How do you do? Diana Lewis. May I just say, I have never seen such beautiful artwork. It's arrestingly beautiful."

"Thank you. Our chairman commissioned a calendar some years ago of Arabic art and it was so popular, we've had them on the walls ever since. It doesn't matter how many times one looks at them, they never pall. Rather like our early monastic illuminated scripts. Shall we?" He invited her to go ahead of him through a door of the same panelling.

She found herself in a conference room, again well-lit but no natural light. The table could seat about fourteen people, but at the moment, there were three other men, who stood as she entered. Timothy Bradley introduced them as Winston Fletcher, the chairman, Samuel Sixsmith, managing director and David Hancock, vice president and investment services director. "Are you a member of the Hancock family of the bank's name?" she asked.

"Yes, there's actually never been a time when there hasn't been a Hancock on the board. The Hancocks always believed in large families, just to be sure."

Although they laughed and tried to put her at her ease, she felt a little overwhelmed at the presence of five men. "If you'll pardon me for saying so, I'm feeling just a little intimidated by such an august gathering." She smiled, but meant what she said.

Winston Fletcher, a man in his late fifties or early sixties, assumed the role of spokesman; Diana noticed that all the men deferred to him without saying a word. Good chain of command, she thought.

"Mrs Lewis, I think, before we begin, if you would be so good as to give David your letters of authority and your copy of the solicitor's letters, we can just establish your bona fides. Of course, we require some identification also."

"Yes, of course." Diana handed over an envelope containing all the relevant documents and a copy of her passport, together with the original. David disappeared for just a few moments and returned with her passport. "We're having copies made of the other documents, and will return the originals to you at the end of this meeting." He smiled and took his seat once more.

"Mrs. Lewis -"

"Please, would you address me as Diana? I'd be so much more comfortable and feel less as if I'm in the headmaster's office."

He laughed. "Of course. I'm sorry to make you uncomfortable. And please, call me Winston."

"How would you like to handle this, Winston? Do you need some information from me?"

"Diana, what I would like, or rather, what *we* would like is to hear the story from you from beginning to end. Would you do that? We have our own pieces to add but it would be better to start with you."

Diana looked at the men in turn. "Very well. It is a strange and very sad story and one which will divide your emotions and judgements. I ask you not to make any decisions about what you feel until you have heard it all." Diana felt the men's interest sharpen as she began her story. She told it well. She perhaps engaged Sophie's side more than an impartial reviewer would do, but they were able to make their own judgements at the end.

As she reached the end of the story, she realised that not one of the men had taken their eyes off her, nor asked a single question. "And I should tell you, gentlemen, that Sophie did not survive to find out what arrangements her father had made with you. We held her funeral last week." She was annoyed with herself to feel tears once more welling up in her eyes.

The first to speak was again Winston Fletcher. "Diana. May we offer you something? Coffee or a drink, perhaps? I'm hoping you will join us for lunch."

Diana realised she had talked for an hour. "A glass of fizzy water would be lovely, thank you. And yes, lunch would be delightful."

"Sophie's main concern was for the survivors and those still alive who have participated in her father's killing, their families and the village as a whole, if I understand you correctly?"

"Yes. There are two ways of looking at it. Firstly, that the honest men who believed they were killing a traitor will be mortified to find they killed a loyal partisan and a patriot. Perhaps there are others who will feel justified because he *concealed* a traitor. Either way, Sophie felt she could not be responsible for raising the issue and perhaps causing dissent in the village between those men and their families. The village was dreadfully affected by what happened and it took years for them to move on with their lives. Believe me when I say her concern was *not* for herself. I knew her. She lived with this every day of her life."

Winston spoke again. "I think perhaps we should now talk about our part in Baron de Lusignac's arrangements." He handed her a glass with ice and lemon and a bottle of Pellegrino. "Baron de Lusignac's father opened an account with us in 1894.

"The de Lusignacs were very modest people but extremely rich. Anyway, he opened an account and made his son the sole beneficiary. The wife had her own money and her own banking arrangements. The father, Charles, and later the son, Philippe, used to make trips to the bank from time to time, and we also had an arrangement with a code word which would recognise messages as having come from either of them. The father was quick to see war coming in 1914 and the son equally so in 1939. We have received and paid in sums and accepted letters and such from time to time, when so instructed. Since receiving notification from you that you had traced de Lusignac's heir, we opened a document which had been left with us, to be opened when someone came forward to make a claim on the account. It names Sophie as his heir and gave her full title to the account. I assume he thought she would survive to come and claim it herself in person. Since Sophie's death, her will and documentation makes you a trustee with full powers of access." He drank from his glass of orange juice.

The door opened and a woman dressed in black and white announced that lunch would be served in half an hour.

"I think, before we go any further, you would perhaps like to see what it is you are now entrusted with." He pulled a folded piece of paper out of his pocket and handed it to her across the table. She opened it and nearly fainted.

"£126 million? £126 million? Are you sure? There must be some mistake? Sophie can't have known. Why didn't she know? Why didn't you tell her, because I know she didn't know? Why didn't you find her? It wasn't that hard, I managed it." Diana felt the room closing in on her. She put her head in her hands and tried to breathe normally.

"Diana, we are not heir hunters. We had no knowledge of Sophie's existence until a few weeks ago, when you started your search and we heard from her solicitor. The instructions we received were extremely specific. We were to hold the account on Sophie's father's instructions for a hundred years from his accession to it. We were to invest and re-invest, remove our expenses and keep accounts, of course. All those, we do have for you, both paper accounts and everything on disc. De Lusignac himself stated that he would make arrangements for the account to be claimed. Don't forget, Diana, he didn't know how the war would end and I imagine he didn't ever want his daughter held to ransom by the Gestapo for her funds. If no-one had claimed the account at the end of the one hundred-year period, the trust was to be re-designated for the benefit of the people of Saint-Sulpice-sur-Lauzac. We had several similar instructions from other clients determined to keep their family's wealth from falling into German hands. Then we received an instruction that funds would be paid in by a certain department of the British Government. We have a branch of the bank in Switzerland and de Lusignac was managing to draw funds from his account there, presumably smuggled over the border and then used for the Resistance. In return, the British Government repaid his loans in sterling into this bank."

"After I informed you of Sophie's existence, did you contact her at all to inform her of the amount of money involved? It might have changed her decisions about many things."

"Our legal department contacted her, but her only response came from her solicitor, who informed us to refer all matters to you."

"I can't help thinking that her life choices might have been different if she had known of this money. I can't ever be sure, but don't think she was as happy as a nun as she might have been if she'd had alternatives."

Winston went on, "Please remember, our duty was to de Lusignac as the account holder. Sophie was not known to us. We didn't open his letter, as instructed, until someone – you – came forward to claim the account. In any case, we didn't hear about his death until a long time after, by which time Sophie was already a nun. But it wouldn't have made the slightest difference to our handling of the matter. We were commanded by instructions left by Baron de Lusignac himself."

The gong went for lunch. Diana thought it was a quaint old custom and they rose to go to their respective bathrooms to wash. A woman had appeared to escort Diana, and waited outside for her to take her to the dining room. The room itself was almost a copy of the conference room, pale wood panelling with a long table which could seat about sixteen. The table was set with white place mats and crisp white linen napkins. The lunch was a delicate salmon mousse with melba toast, perfect roast lamb still pink in the middle and smelling of rosemary and lemon, tiny boiled potatoes, broccoli with equal-length stems and dripping with butter, and a choice between raspberry pavlova and apple pie as dessert.

"Thank you, that was a superb lunch. Now, I really need to tie up business with you, I have a meeting with my solicitor in two hours."

"Diana, you should have brought him, he should be hearing what we've discussed this morning."

"I don't think so. He's a divorce lawyer. My husband - well, it's not important. But I do need to see him, I'm going back to France tomorrow."

"Well, then. I shall hand you over to David Hancock. I've given you the moral justification for our actions. You may agree or disagree, but our lawyers were content. Now, there's one more thing to give you. It's a letter to Sophie which her father sent here by one means or another, which arrived after his death. No-one connected this letter with any heir or daughter, there is nothing to suggest that we should have endeavoured to trace anyone. There were instructions to keep it until it was claimed. Our instructions were that it was vital to keep it here, under no circumstances was it to be sent to France. That's you now, the heir, that is."

"Didn't it dawn on anyone that Sophie could have been a daughter, that she might have been entitled to know of this account? When this letter arrived to be kept for her, didn't anyone think she might be traced?" Diana was becoming irritated by the constant defensive attitude of these men, as if the bank were on trial because of some shortcoming.

"Diana, I can't answer for what happened back then, but when a client gives a bank an instruction, that instruction is followed to the letter. To do otherwise would be pure folly and a bank's reputation wouldn't last long in those circumstances. We were given no authority to act any differently."

"Winston and Gentlemen, may I say something? I don't know whether or not *legally* Sophie should have been told about all of this, but it's all water under the bridge. Clearly, de Lusignac was trying to protect the account and leave it intact and profitable. But Sophie had really no choice, did she? She was spirited away after her father's death and I suppose she felt she had nothing left and nowhere to go except to go into a convent. Strictly speaking, and had she known about this money, she might have given the church an income with the interest, but my impression from her was that she'd given the church everything she had and enough was enough. So, there's really nothing more to say on that score. I realise I now have a huge responsibility and it's going to take some time to come to many decisions as to where the money is to go, or what the interest should be used for. I'll take your advice a lot of the time and I'll get independent advice also. But for now, I shall take the letter. I have a feeling he didn't intend for it to be general knowledge, but if it does contain pertinent information, I shall let you have it. I can't read it now, in front of all of you. I need to be on my own." She collected her bag and gloves and held out her hand for the letter. "Now if you'll excuse me, I'll take a day or two and then make another appointment to come over and meet you. Perhaps you'd let me have the accounts also, you said there was a CD with everything on it?"

"Diana, whatever you believe *should* have been our course of action, a bank's instructions from a client are sacrosanct. Absolutely. I am more sorry than I can say that Sophie never knew any of this. We are all here at your disposal, should you need us. In the meantime, we wish you the best of luck in your endeavours with this matter."

They all stood up and watched her as she shook hands with each of them. If they were disappointed not to have been told the contents of the letter, they were sophisticated enough not to show it.

Despite the elegance of the bank's premises, Diana was pleased to be out in the open air with natural light. David Hancock had given her a large envelope with the de

Lusignac accounts in it, and the letter for Sophie from her father was now in her bag.

****

Diana hailed a taxi and gave him the city address of the solicitor; someone she'd remembered from her friend Susanna's divorce. Diana had used his firm for the legal issues concerning the rental of the Holland Park Avenue house and various other matters that had arisen from time to time, but in all her dreams she had never seen herself walking into the divorce department.

Oscar Moody was a rather fussy man but a stickler with detail. She found his questions quick and to the point. The divorce would be fairly rapid if she had already agreed a financial settlement with her husband, and Moody would serve papers on him as soon as he returned an address or a firm of solicitors. Perhaps she could press him on that point if they were still in contact with each other. Diana told him she would arrange a deposit of funds into the firm's account from her bank and this would be used to pay the fees and to pay Simon the agreed sum.

As she stood on the pavement less than an hour later, she thought how strange that a twenty-year marriage could contain so little that it took only an hour to arrange to terminate it.

When she returned to the hotel, on impulse she checked if there was a flight later that evening; there was one at seven-forty to Bordeaux, she wouldn't be able to make the last Bergerac flight. Bordeaux was two hours' drive from Saint-Sulpice, whereas Bergerac was thirty minutes away. But she just wanted to be on her way back so she booked it and started to fling her belongings into her bag. She felt such an urge to return to France and put this place and its associations behind her.

From the airport, she called Julian. "Hello. Do you fancy a drive to Bordeaux?"

"Well, actually, I've been there before. But thanks anyway."

"You really *are* a brute! Get in your car and come and meet me, I can't stand this place another minute, and I'm dashing to get to the airport."

"Well, then, stop gassing and get on with it."

"Are you coming or not?"

"Yes, woman, yes! Now go."

As she walked out into the concourse on arrival, she went so naturally into his arms, it was really like coming home.

****

They drove back to *La Chênaie*, chatting amiably and laughing easily with each other. On the way she told him of the financial status of the account and he nearly choked when he heard the amount. She recounted her half-argument with the directors over the interpretation of the terms of de Lusignac's instructions. "By the way, did you know he was a baron?"

"Oh, God. Does that mean you're living in a baronial hall and are going to behave like royalty?"

"Only if it means you'll treat me like a princess."

He put his hand across her knees. "I'll treat you very well, if that will do."

She felt warm and suddenly light-hearted after the anxious few days she had endured. Diana felt incredibly happy to be back and the lights from the houses as they went down the driveway seemed to welcome her home.

Julian lifted the bag out of the car and followed her into the hall. "Do you feel like talking?" he asked.

"Yes, for a while. I want to read Sophie's letter. Will you forgive me if I read it first, then I'll share it with you? Put the kettle on, let's have tea."

She sat at the table with the letter in her hand, uncertain now that she wanted to do this. Julian reached into the drawer and handed her a knife. She smiled at him and picked it up, put the tip under the flap and cut open the top.

The paper was heavy cream paper, and with a jolt she thought it was probably from the same pile of paper as the fateful note Sophie had thrown through the window. She opened it slowly.

My darling Sophie,

If you are reading this, my darling, your papa will be gone. Never for one moment doubt that you are the most precious thing in my life. I love you and will love you until the last breath leaves my body. I loved you from the moment your wonderful mother placed your little body in my arms.

Do not spend your life in regrets, sorrow or guilt. You have your life in which you can do so much good. Courage my darling, for the dark days which are upon us.

If you survive this awful war, think only of the good that I have tried to do and which I ask you now to continue. Help others, help people that need helping, whether they are good or bad. I will leave you the means to do that.

If I regret one thing, it is that I deprived you of an education which would make you suited to face the world and make your mark through your own efforts. If you can, ensure that others are not similarly deprived.

Do good, my darling, and through that will come the peace you seek. Never doubt that you are loved and cherished. We have no need to forgive those we love; it is more natural than breathing.

All I have loved more than your mother and you, is my country, and I have done all in my power to ensure that

France will live free one day. I die France's most humble servant and most loyal patriot.

Vive la France.

Your loving Papa

Tiredness and sorrow overwhelmed her. Wordlessly she handed the letter to Julian. "She never saw it," she cried. "She never knew how much he loved her and forgave her."

"Of *course* she did. She *knew* he had died for her. The greatest proof anyone could ever have."

"Oh Julian. It's so very sad. His last words were really words of forgiveness. How peaceful she would have been if she'd known this. I suppose de Lusignac was worried the Germans might get this, but there's really nothing in here which would have endangered her."

"There is, you know. His promise to leave her the means. The Gestapo would have willingly taken it off her since her father was murdered. Don't forget, the Germans *knew* he wasn't one of theirs. Therefore, he had to have been one of the others. He almost admits it, enough for the Germans anyway."

"Dear Julian, you can always see straight when I'm always looking for the bend in the road."

"In any case, he's given you instructions as to what to do with the money."

"What?"

"The money. He's shown you the way. It's something you can do which will benefit the village."

"How?"

"Education. You can set up a bursary or endow a university place. For example, for the children of the village."

She stared at him with her mouth open. How could he always see everything so clearly? "That's a brilliant idea. But you know, I told Sophie that people here wouldn't want their money. Don't you think there might be opposition if they knew where the money came from?"

"Well, why don't you ask them? Have a meeting with the village leaders. Ask them, that way you'll know. Simple."

"You *are* brilliant. You really are. No wonder I like you."

"Well, that's a start. But it'll take some organising. I imagine, for a substantial fee, Pelling Hancock will set it up and administer it. You can be a sage trustee, everyone bowing to you when you walk the corridors in your honorary cap and gown."

"You really are a fool! But I still like you." She went to kiss him on the cheek but he took hold of her, pulled her to him and kissed her. She felt a rush of desire, and she murmured through his wonderful kisses, "Will you stay tonight?"

"Yes, but I'm not wearing a dog collar and lead. I've heard about what you powerful women get up to in the bedroom."

"Oh, shut up and get upstairs."

****

The meeting in the village had been a strange affair. By now, of course, everyone had heard the story. As anticipated, there were people who felt it has been a righteous execution and others who felt his act of unbelievable heroism to protect his daughter exonerated them both. No-one was ever pointed out as being one of those concerned, or even their family members, but the feeling that some of them were there was palpable, particularly two old men who were mostly silent, but to whom everyone seemed to direct their glances when it was talked about.

The meeting was in Henri's hotel, and a buffet was provided, with drinks. At the end of the discussion, Henri had asked for a vote on the proposal that an education programme with funded university places be set up. It was overwhelmingly accepted. The programme would include the total funding of accommodation, books and tutoring. The university places would also include overseas universities such as in America or the United Kingdom. It would be known as The de Lusignac Scholarship, Diana insisted on that.

The year that followed was a busy time for Diana. There were trips to London for meetings with the bank, papers to be drawn up, access accounts to be set up and fees agreed for the bank's part in the administration of the programme. The rules for the scholarship were outlined and worked in detail with the education authorities.

The lease for the tenancy of the Holland Park House was now up and Diana didn't renew it with the clients. She had seriously thought of selling it but still couldn't bring herself to do it. She and Julian would stay in the house on their trips to London and still it didn't feel the same any more. She always pined to be back in France.

Then, at the end of that year-long process, suddenly it was over. It was up and running, there were only annual trustees' meetings and there was now no longer any need to go to London frequently. So the decision to sell came more easily. The house sold quickly and they returned to supervise the packing. Most of the furniture she had bought for the tenants was given to a charity and in fact, there was little for them to do. With the new owner's permission, she had taken cuttings of a rose which her mother had planted to commemorate her father.

In all this time, there had been no word from Simon, the solicitor had tied up the conditions pretty well and after he had cashed his cheque he had disappeared to Italy or Spain or somewhere. She had heard recently that he had written another book but in the main, she didn't think about him at all. Their divorce had gone through without any problems at all, and he made no further demands on her. She lost contact with all their old friends, needing only Julian and her neighbours at *La Chênaie*.

****

On the day they left London, it was another grey, humid and miserable day. They were planning to take the late afternoon overnight ferry to Caen and spend a few days driving back to Saint-Sulpice. Julian and Diana had moved into their relationship as easily and naturally as if it had been pre-ordained. Julian had kept his house for his son and grandchildren to use as a holiday home. Diana was enchanted every day with their love for each other. The neighbours had accepted their situation as if it had all been achieved without the heartache and anguish.

Now, the last of the packers had gone, the cleaners had finished and it no longer seemed like her childhood home. The heavy door closed behind her with a rich, familiar, solid click. For as long as she could remember that sound had meant home, family, love and security. Excitement for the future couldn't dispel some of the regrets for the events which had led up to this point. She ran down the steps and reached for the gate for the last time. It clanged shut behind her and the metal railings were still vibrating as she got into the car.

Julian reached across and took her hand. "Alright?"

"Yes. Yes, I am. I didn't think I would be, but I am. You know, it's odd. I spent my whole life until the last couple of years dreading change, and trying to keep the bubble going. I must have been very naïve. Nothing stays the same, does it? Would we even want it to? If you'd asked me back then, I would have decried the value of change. It was unthinkable to me. But without all that change, we wouldn't be here, would we? You and me, I mean. And I love you so very dearly."

He leaned across and kissed her cheek. "Shall we go?"

"Yes. Yes, let's go."

The windscreen wipers swished back and forth, keeping slow time with Diana's thoughts as she turned the key to the house in her hand. All of the other keys had been given to the estate agent, but she couldn't bear to part with this one. It was the key she had been given as a child, her way into the safety and warmth of a loving family; it still had her old teddy bear key-ring on it.

As they drove through the afternoon London traffic Julian switched on the radio. "I haven't heard what's happening anywhere in the world for days, it seems. Let's get the news."

The time signal for four o'clock was due and they were just in time to catch the closing words of the previous programme. The programme was a popular broadcast looking at new books and articles.

"... *so you're not going to divulge the name of the person who gave you the title and who is the subject of the dedication of your book?*" The interviewer was just having the last word with the interviewee.

"*No, I'm afraid I'm not. The person will know from the title, and will know that I am forever grateful. I learned a hard lesson and like to think I'm a better person for it. I hope that person will be proud of what I have done.*"

"*Well, that was the author Simon Lewis, whose new book is published today. Please join us again tomorrow for another edition of* The Page Turner. *Thank you for being with us. Goodbye.*"

Traffic was heavy and neither Diana nor Julian had said a word about the radio broadcast. The afternoon news headlines came on and Diana seemed lost in thought. They came to a halt at a major junction traffic light, with a big bookstore on their side of the road.

A large cardboard cut-out figure was in the huge window-front. The figure showed Simon, leaning back against a wall with a yellow sweater draped around his shoulders, holding a copy of his book, a handsome hardback with a deep red shiny cover. On the front of the cover was a gold swastika broken in two, on top of a crumpled Italian flag. The notice read:

BOOK SIGNING HERE TOMORROW
BEST SELLING AUTHOR
SIMON LEWIS
WITH HIS ACCLAIMED
NEW BOOK
A NOVEL OF LOVE AND BETRAYAL
IN WARTIME ITALY
"THE HARVEST OF BETRAYAL"